UNDERDOGS

STEPHEN LEATHER

UNDERDOGS

MACMILLAN

First published 2026 by Macmillan
an imprint of Pan Macmillan
The Smithson, 6 Briset Street, London EC1M 5NR
EU representative: Macmillan Publishers Ireland Ltd, 1st Floor,
The Liffey Trust Centre, 117–126 Sheriff Street Upper,
Dublin 1 D01 YC43
Associated companies throughout the world

ISBN 978-1-0350-8330-5 HB
ISBN 978-1-0350-8333-6 TPB

Copyright © Stephen Leather 2026

The right of Stephen Leather to be identified as the
author of this work has been asserted in accordance
with the Copyright, Designs and Patents Act 1988.

All rights reserved. No part of this publication may be reproduced,
stored in a retrieval system, or transmitted, in any form, or by any means
(including, without limitation, electronic, mechanical, photocopying,
recording or otherwise) without the prior written permission of the publisher.

Pan Macmillan does not have any control over, or any responsibility for,
any author or third-party websites (including, without limitation, URLs,
emails and QR codes) referred to in or on this book.

1 3 5 7 9 8 6 4 2

A CIP catalogue record for this book is available from the British Library.

Typeset by Palimpsest Book Production Limited, Falkirk, Stirlingshire
Printed and bound in the UK using 100% Renewable Electricity by CPI Group (UK) Ltd

This book is sold subject to the condition that it shall not, by way of
trade or otherwise, be lent, hired out, or otherwise circulated without
the publisher's prior consent in any form of binding or cover other than
that in which it is published and without a similar condition including
this condition being imposed on the subsequent purchaser. The publisher does not
authorize the use or reproduction of any part of this book in any manner
for the purpose of training artificial intelligence technologies or systems. The publisher
expressly reserves this book from the Text and Data Mining exception in accordance with
Article 4(3) of the European Union Digital Single Market Directive 2019/790.

Visit **www.panmacmillan.com** to read more
about all our books and to buy them.

UNDERDOGS

CHAPTER 1

Andy Bird hated helicopters. He always had done, even though he appreciated their advantages over planes and cars when it came to reaching out-of-the-way places. He hated the noise and the discomfort, but more than anything he hated the fact that if something went wrong, they tended to plummet to the ground and burst into flames. The helicopter he was sitting in was an RAF Chinook with two counter-rotating rotors, but that didn't make it feel any safer.

Even through the noise-cancelling headset he was wearing, the roar of the Chinook's twin turbine engines and the rattle of the gearboxes were deafening. Bird looked down at Tyson, who was sitting between his legs, and smiled. The dog always looked ridiculous wearing his bright yellow noise-cancelling headset. It had been specially made for him, and was rumoured to have cost the best part of two thousand pounds, but functionality had clearly taken precedence over fashion.

Tyson was a mahogany-brown Belgian Malinois and his hearing was one of his canine superpowers – along with his sense of smell and ability to jump through flaming hoops – so his ears had to be protected whenever they were exposed to loud noises. And the Chinook was noisy, no question, one of the noisiest machines to take to the skies. Close to the ramp at the rear of the helicopter, the noise could reach 115 decibels. Unprotected exposure to that level of noise could result in permanent hearing damage within just a few minutes. The cargo area where they were sitting was a few decibels quieter, but not much, and the noise-cancelling headsets were mandatory. Bird had gone even further and pushed foam earplugs into his own ears before slipping on the headset. The headset was connected to the Chinook's communication system, so he could hear the crew talking among themselves and to the air traffic controller who was monitoring their progress.

Bird patted Tyson on the back. In addition to the headset, Tyson was wearing his personalized jacket system. It was made of Kevlar to offer protection against gunfire and shrapnel and was equipped with a speaker, a microphone, a GPS tracker and two video cameras, regular and night vision. Bird had no idea how much the vest had cost, but it was certainly also in the thousands.

There were seven other SAS men strapped in the cargo hold, plus an RAF crew chief and the Chinook's weapons system operator.

In charge of the mission was Sergeant Ben Warren, known as 'Sarge' by his men and 'Bunny' by his fellow sergeants. Warren was in his early thirties and had been in the SAS for almost a decade. He took no nonsense from his men or from the officers, but was always open to suggestions as how best to proceed, on exercises or in the field. He was cradling his carbine and had a Glock pistol strapped to his thigh.

To Warren's left was Peter 'Tweedy' Harris, one of the longest serving members of the SAS, with more than twenty years' service under his belt. He was on his third marriage and often joked that he only stayed in the Regiment because he had so much alimony to pay. The real reason was that – like most SAS long-timers – he was addicted to the adrenaline rush that came from putting his life on the line. He was the team's comms specialist, though they were all equipped with radios and earpieces to keep in touch with each other.

To Warren's right was Jordan 'Lurch' Brown, a demolition specialist who had worked in a quarry before joining the Paras and transferring to the SAS. Brown was a Geordie with ginger hair and a cheery face sprinkled with freckles. He had acquired his nickname on Selection in the Brecon Beacons because of his ungainly way of running with a full Bergen on his back.

Sitting next to Brown was Al 'Shotgun' Gatrell, holding his weapon of choice – a Remington 870 pump-action.

On Bird's left was Kieran 'Queenie' King, a Cornishman who was the team's medic and a skydiving specialist, a man who enjoyed the feeling of falling through the air so much that he spent most of his spare time jumping out of planes, the higher the better. His hair had started thinning as a teenager and he had begun shaving his head when he got to his twenties.

Ryan 'Tommo' Thompson was sitting on Bird's right. The lanky Welshman was the team's sniper, armed with a Gepárd GM6 Lynx rifle. Manufactured in Hungary and costing just under ten thousand pounds, the weapon was so powerful its .50-calibre rounds could blast through armour-plated vehicles and had been known to knock helicopters out of the sky. Thompson could empty the rifle's five-round magazine in under three seconds and hit a bull's-eye at a range of more than a mile.

The final member of the team was Yorkshireman Jake 'Gordon' Bennett, who was sitting next to the crew chief, reading on his Kindle. Bennett was a fan of military thrillers and was always reading the likes of Andy McNab, Chris Ryan and Mark 'Billy' Billingham, though he seemed to enjoy picking fault with the stories and 'that would never fucking happen in a month of Sundays' was a common refrain uttered as he read. Bennett had served almost as long as Harris, distinguishing himself in Iraq, Afghanistan and several African countries.

Bird had been on missions with them all at some time or other and knew that he could trust them with his life. Warren grinned and nodded at him. 'How's the land shark?' Warren mouthed.

'Raring to go,' Bird mouthed back. He reached down and patted Tyson's flank again. Tyson looked up, panting. His fur was reddish-brown but like most Belgian Malinois dogs he had a black mask, covering his mouth, nose, eye rims and ears.

The Chinook had flown out of Incirlik Air Base in Turkey, a facility used mainly by the Turkish and the United States Air Forces. The Americans had more than five thousand personnel on the base, and used it to store tactical nuclear weapons and fly missions into Syria and Iraq.

The SAS team had arrived on an RAF Airbus and within an hour of landing were being briefed in a windowless Portakabin by an MI6 officer who had introduced herself as Emma, though no one believed that that was her real name. She was in her early thirties with dark brown hair pulled back in a ponytail and oversized glasses perched on a snub nose. She was wearing desert camouflage fatigues with the sleeves rolled up and had tucked her trousers into what appeared to be brand new Timberland boots. Bird hadn't been able to suppress a grin when he had first seen her. Combat chic, made all the more ridiculous by the fact that she clearly had no intention of setting a booted foot off the base.

The SAS team had been given the bones of the mission back at Stirling Lines by the major who headed their squadron. Major Hawkins had told them that three charity workers had been taken hostage in Syria, and that MI6 had tracked them down to a disused factory in a small town called Albab, in the north of the country. The kidnappers were ISIS – the Islamic State of Iraq and Syria – and they had already approached the British Embassy in Beirut with a demand for thirty million dollars. The Foreign Office had refused to even negotiate with the hostage-takers, so the clock was ticking.

It was only when Emma began her briefing that the SAS team realized why all the stops had been pulled out – one of the aid workers was actually an MI6 officer. The MI6 officer had been using the name Edward Paterson and had been working for Oxfam. He had been in a truck with two Oxfam workers, Julie Munro and Denis Ferguson. Emma had stuck photographs of all three on a whiteboard. The kidnappers had killed the driver, a Syrian, presumably to show that they were serious.

A large satellite photograph of the factory was on another whiteboard, along with half a dozen photographs taken from outside the wire fence that encircled the building. Emma explained that the factory used to produce canned lentils for export, but had been abandoned more than a decade earlier. In one of the photographs a pick-up truck with a heavy machine gun in the back was being driven through a gate guarded by two bearded men carrying Kalashnikovs.

Emma had stressed that the mission was to rescue all three of the hostages, but that Paterson had to be the priority. If the kidnappers found out that he was an MI6 officer, they would probably torture him and extract what information he had about agents in the country.

There were four blueprints on a third whiteboard, each showing one of the floors of the factory. The SAS team gathered around it. It was the first time they had seen the internal layout of the building and it was crucial intel.

Emma had started to outline how she thought the SAS team could rescue the hostages, but Warren had cut her short, telling her that he would prefer to handle operational matters, but that he was quite happy for her to listen in. The MI6 officer had seemed quite relieved to have the responsibility taken from her and she perched on a stool by the door as Warren went over to the satellite photographs.

The SAS team had already spent an hour at RAF Brize Norton considering their options. The main entrance faced the gate, where there was a concrete guardhouse. The surveillance photographs showed two armed guards at the gate but there was no way of telling how many were inside the guardhouse. A frontal assault was clearly out of the equation. The fence was a good fifty feet from the building and was surrounded by bare earth with no hiding places, so attacking through there was also problematic.

It had been King who had suggested the parachute option, and all the men had groaned. No matter the operation, King would always suggest parachuting at some point. It was his thing. But in this case, as they studied the more detailed satellite photograph Emma had provided, it soon became clear that it was the best – possibly the only – option.

Now, on the Chinook, the crew chief stood up and held up his right hand, fingers splayed. Five minutes. The team began to prepare themselves, checking their weapons and harnesses. Tyson wagged his tail. His eyes were sparkling, he knew exactly what was happening and was clearly looking forward to it. Bird stroked the back of Tyson's neck. 'Good lad,' he said. He unhooked his harness and pushed the straps out of the way, then patted his lap. 'Up,' he said.

Tyson jumped up onto Bird's lap. There were two D rings fixed to each side of Tyson's Kevlar vest and Bird attached the two nearest to his own and pulled the straps tight. Tyson's tail was wagging faster now.

They were jumping from ten thousand feet, so they didn't need supplemental oxygen. Tyson had done jumps as high as twenty thousand feet during his training, and for those both he and Bird had worn oxygen masks. Ten thousand feet was a walk in the park for Tyson, though the fact that it was still dark added an extra wrinkle. Bird grunted as he stood up, slipping his arms under Tyson's chest and backside to take some of his weight.

All the men were up on their feet now. They removed their headsets, stored them under their seats, and pulled on Kevlar helmets, then checked each other's chutes and straps, fastened their weapons out of the way and adjusted their goggles and helmets. The crew chief pressed a button on the fuselage and the rear ramp began to descend with a grinding vibration that Bird felt through the soles of his boots. A strip of blackness appeared at the top of the ramp, and as it widened he started to see the stars in the clear night sky. King and Gatrell moved towards the crew chief. They would be the first to go. Followed by Sergeant Warren and Brown.

Bird would be the last to jump, so that the rest of the team would be there to help if there was a landing problem. Landing with a dog strapped to your chest was difficult at the best of times, and doing so on a factory roof was going to be a first for them both.

The ramp was fully down now and Bird could see the moon high overhead. A full moon, with the craters clearly visible. Without the noise-cancelling headset, the engine roar was deafening.

The crew chief raised his right arm, then brought it down and pointed at the end of the ramp. King and Gatrell took two steps and threw themselves out. The Sarge and Brown followed immediately. The Chinook was slowing, probably down to fifty knots or so, but that didn't mean they had time to hang about.

Bennett and Thompson went next. Bird looked over at Harris and grinned. 'Age before beauty,' he shouted above the roar of the turbines. Harris gave him a thumbs up, jogged down the ramp and jumped, arms and legs out in the starfish position.

Bird took the headphones off Tyson and handed them to the crew chief. Then he patted Tyson, took a deep breath, and headed down the ramp. He threw himself head first into the abyss, letting go of Tyson and throwing his arms out to the side. The air rushed by his ears and the engine sound immediately disappeared. Far below he could see Harris, but the rest of the team were lost in the darkness.

Bird's arms and legs were buffeted by the slipstream and he bent his arms and kept his fingers spread to give himself more control over his descent. He was mentally counting off the seconds. *A thousand and one. A thousand and two.*

After one second, he had fallen just sixteen feet. After two seconds he had fallen more than sixty feet. After three seconds, he was almost a hundred and fifty feet below the Chinook and still accelerating.

He began to rotate to the left, so he corrected his position. He could still just about see Harris below him.

He reached terminal velocity – 121 mph – after twelve seconds, by which time he and Tyson were falling two hundred feet every second. He could go faster if he pulled in his arms and legs and went down head first. That would increase his speed to closer to 200 mph, but this drop wasn't about speed, it was about accuracy. He started rotating to the right, so he pushed his right hand out to stop the turn.

He looked down at Tyson. The dog's eyes were half closed against the wind but he seemed happy enough.

Bird's mental count continued. *A thousand and fourteen. A thousand and fifteen.* His chute would open automatically at a height of three thousand feet, after freefalling for about twenty seconds.

One thousand and sixteen. One thousand and seventeen.

His chute came with a ripcord that he could pull if the automatic system failed. Bird had never heard of the system failing but they had always claimed that the *Titanic* was unsinkable, so his right hand was poised to grab the ripcord if necessary.

One thousand and eighteen.

He saw Harris's chute open far below. A second later he heard the ripping sound of his own chute opening and felt the harness yank at his shoulders. He immediately dropped his hands to hold Tyson, even though he knew the D rings were more than capable of taking the strain.

The chute snapped open and Bird reached up to grab the toggles on the lines that he would use to steer it. He took a quick look up to check that his chute was fully open and that none of his lines were tangled. He smiled. *Good to go.*

He switched his attention to the team below him. Harris had turned slightly to the right. Ahead of him and several hundred feet below him were two more chutes – Bennett and Thompson, but Bird couldn't tell which was which.

King was doing most of the work and the rest of the team just had to play follow my leader. Bird could just about make out King's chute, about half a mile away from the landing site. The factory was hard to miss – at four stories high it was twice as tall as any of the other buildings in the vicinity, most of which were square concrete cubes with flat roofs. To the east was farmland, to the west was a suburb of small houses interspersed with mosques. The SAS men were still over the farmland. King was flying parallel to the factory, waiting to make his final turn. Bird spotted Gatrell, a couple of hundred feet behind King.

Harris turned again to the right. Bird waited a few seconds and then followed.

The Chinook's turbines had faded away and now there was just the whistle of the air passing over the lines and the ripple of the chute overhead. And Tyson's panting. Tyson's eyes were wide open now and his tongue was lolling out of the side of his mouth. He was wagging his tail enthusiastically. He really seemed to enjoy parachuting, even though it was obviously a totally alien experience for a dog. Tyson had never shown any reluctance to jump and was always keen to climb on board whatever plane or heli they were jumping from.

Down below, King went into a slow left turn. Gatrell followed. Bird's eyes had become accustomed to the gloom and now he could make out the chutes of the Sarge and Brown, about four hundred feet behind Gatrell. They were flying in parallel but as he watched, the Sarge turned to the left and performed a slow circle to allow Brown to get ahead of him.

About three miles away on Bird's left was a walled compound with rows of brick buildings next to a car park filled with pick-up trucks, saloons and military vehicles. On the other side of the car park were dozens of small houses. Emma from MI6 had indicated the compound on her map, explaining that it was a base for the People's Defence Units, a branch of the Syrian Democratic Forces, drawing its manpower mainly from the Kurdish community but with Arab and foreign volunteers serving alongside them. Emma had been insistent that they give the compound a wide berth.

Harris was turning to the left. Bird gave it a few seconds before doing the same. He was probably two thousand feet above the ground.

He could clearly see the factory now. King was about two hundred feet away from it and had aligned himself perfectly. There were two concrete structures at either end of the building, which housed the lift equipment, and lines of air-conditioning units running around the perimeter. King was heading for the side of the building furthest away from the militia compound. From Bird's vantage point, the landing area looked like a tiny strip of bare concrete but he knew that it was about thirty feet wide and a hundred feet long, more than enough.

As Bird watched, King guided his chute down the centre of the strip, then flared and came to a halt. Within seconds he had gathered up the chute and was running to the nearest concrete structure. As he reached it, Gatrell's chute flared and he landed, at almost exactly the same spot where King had touched down.

King had cleared the landing area, and Warren was on his final approach. Warren flared his chute and performed a running landing, gathering up his chute as he ran. Bird smiled to himself. 'Show off,' he muttered. Running landings always looked good but on rough terrain they risked a sprained ankle or worse.

Brown's landing was more traditional, his flare brought him to a complete standstill, but he was dangerously close to the edge of the building. He rolled up his chute and ran over to the concrete structure.

Bennett was only a few seconds behind and he almost collided with Brown.

Harris was correcting his approach again, this time turning to the left. Bird followed his example. He looked ahead and could see that he was bang on target. The wind was ruffling Tyson's fur and his eyes were watering, but his tail was still wagging.

The sixth jumper – Thompson – landed, and was also dangerously close to the edge of the building. The wind must have been picking up.

Harris was already correcting his approach and Bird did the same. Harris flared and landed, and quickly began gathering up his chute. Two of the team left the concrete structure and passed either side of Harris, preparing to offer Bird assistance if required. Bird was a proficient skydiver but landing was a whole different experience when you had a seventy-pound dog strapped to your chest.

The roof of the building was rushing towards him now and then a gust of wind forced him to the right and he pulled hard on the left toggle to keep on the track. He was still pulling on the toggle when he flared and the chute swung to the left. He pulled hard on both toggles but it was an ungainly flare at best – his left foot touched the ground before his right and he felt himself pitching to the side.

Strong hands gripped his left arm. 'Got you,' said Warren.

King was already gathering up the chute.

'I had it under control,' said Bird.

'Course you did,' said King with a grin.

Bird knelt down and unfastened Tyson's harness from his own. Tyson stood up and shook himself.

'Looks like he wants to go again,' said King, handing the chute to Bird.

'He loves it,' said Bird.

They jogged over to the concrete structure, with Tyson following close behind. Bird stripped off his harness and dumped the chute next to the rest. He unfastened his Colt UCIW – Ultra Compact Individual Weapon. With its stock fully collapsed, the carbine was just twenty-two inches long. It was Bird's weapon of choice when he jumped with Tyson as its small size meant there was less chance of it smacking into the dog.

Warren and King went over to the concrete structure. There was a wooden door with a sign in Arabic. 'What does that say, Birdman?' asked Warren.

'Emergency exit, keep clear,' said Bird. Arabic was one of the five languages he spoke, near fluently.

Warren tried pulling at the door but it was locked.

Gatrell had his shotgun on a sling and he held it across his chest as he studied the door.

Warren put a hand on Gatrell's shoulder. 'Let's try prying it open before we start making loud noises.'

Gatrell nodded. 'Got you, Sarge.'

Warren waved Harris over. Harris was a breach specialist and a skilled lockpicker. Once they had decided they were going in through the roof, he had added a crowbar to his equipment list. He pulled it from his backpack and examined the edges of the door. He chose his insertion point, just above the lock, forced in the tip of the crowbar and grunted as he threw his full weight against it. There was the sound of wood tearing and the door opened half an inch. He forced the tip in further and grunted again. This time the door sprang open. 'Easy peasy,' said Harris. He slid the crowbar back into his backpack.

Warren eased the door open and peered inside. It opened onto a stairwell with bare concrete steps and a rusting handrail. He listened for a few seconds, then nodded and headed inside. Bird followed with Tyson at his heels. They headed down the steps, guns at the ready. The rest of the team followed. Harris brought up the rear. He used one of the chutes to jam the door open.

Warren reached the door that led to the third floor. He held up his hand in a fist and the men behind him came to a halt. The sergeant pushed the door to check that it wasn't locked, then he looked over at Bird. 'Is the Maligator ready to go?' he asked.

Maligator – a combination of Malinois and alligator – was one of the many nicknames the SAS had for its dogs. The Maligator was apt because Tyson's jaws were incredibly strong and almost impossible to pry off once he was in biting mode.

Bird knelt down beside Tyson and switched on the vest's microphone and flicked out and activated the two cameras. He took his tablet out of his backpack. It was encased in tough rubber and he flipped it open and booted it up. The screen was filled with a view from the regular camera of Warren's crotch.

'Is he looking at my balls?' said the sergeant.

'He's looking at the door behind you,' said Bird. He tapped on the screen to get the night vision view. Then he checked the GPS screen which showed Tyson's location on Google Maps. 'Good to go,' he said.

'Let's do it,' said Warren.

Bird leant over to Tyson. 'Search,' he said. He opened the door and Tyson slipped through. Bird stood up and studied the tablet. The night vision display was green, showing the corridor with doors leading off to both sides. Most of the doors were closed. Tyson moved steadily down the corridor, looking left and right. At the far end was another emergency door. According to Emma, the top floor had been used as accommodation for the factory workers. All the furniture and fittings had been stripped out years earlier when the factory had been abandoned.

Tyson reached the emergency door, turned and padded back along the corridor. Bird held the door open for him. 'Good lad,' he said, and patted him on the head. He slipped his left hand into the pouch on his belt that contained dog treats and held a few out. Tyson wolfed them down, then prodded the pouch with his nose. 'Work first, treats later,' said Bird.

The team headed down the stairs to the second floor. According to Emma, it had been used as offices before the factory was abandoned. Warren opened the door and again Bird gave Tyson the 'search' command. Tyson headed down the corridor and Bird and Warren followed his progress on the tablet. Most of the doors were open and they could see that the offices had been stripped of anything of value. Tyson moved down the corridor, looking left and right. There was movement to the left and Bird tensed, then he realized it was a rat, running down the corridor next to the wall. Tyson looked at it but didn't give chase.

Tyson reached the end of the corridor, turned and retraced his steps. He got back to the stairwell and Bird gave him some treats.

The team moved slowly down the stairs to the first floor, which Emma had said was originally used as a warehouse for the lentils after they were canned on the ground floor. Warren eased open the door and listened. He tensed when he heard music, the tinny sound of a small radio. He eased the door closed.

'Okay, no need to send the land shark in,' he whispered. 'Sounds like they're towards the middle of the building. And they're sure to be on the ground floor as well. The big question is, where are they keeping the hostages?'

'Makes sense they keep them on this floor,' said Brown. 'The higher, the better.' The rest of the team nodded in agreement.

'We're going to need to hit the ground floor the same time as this one,' said Warren.

'Plus, there's the guards outside,' said Harris. 'Once the shooting starts they'll be in like Flynn.'

'We hit both floors simultaneously,' said Warren. 'Me and Birdman will stay here. Tommo and Shotgun go back up to the second floor and over to the far side of the building. Gordon and Queenie go with them and then make your way down to the ground floor. Tweedy, Lurch – take the ground floor on this side. Let me know when you're in position. The moment we have the hostages secure, we call the heli for extraction. Hopefully it'll be here within ten minutes. As soon as the heli arrives we all go up to the roof. All good?'

The four troopers nodded and headed up the stairs. Harris and Brown went down to the ground floor, their guns at the ready.

The seconds ticked by. Bird could feel his heart racing, as it always did before combat. He was breathing slowly and evenly, but his heart continued to pound. He looked down at Tyson. The dog was panting, his ears up. He knew that they were getting ready to attack and was clearly up for it. 'Good lad,' said Bird.

'In position,' said Thompson over the radio.

A few seconds later, King reported in.

'Tweedy, are you good to go?' asked Warren.

'Affirmative,' said Harris.

'On three,' said Warren. 'One, two, three.' He pushed open the door and lifted his carbine to his shoulder. Bird followed, with Tyson at his heels. They saw Thompson and Gatrell emerging through the door at the far end of the corridor, guns at the ready.

The music was coming from a room on Bird's left, ahead of them. There were doors either side, both open. Warren went left and Bird right. Tyson went ahead of Bird, padding into the centre of the room. Both rooms were empty, and the two men moved back into the corridor. Tyson followed.

Thompson and Gatrell checked the rooms either side of their end of the corridor.

The music got louder as Warren and Bird moved down the corridor.

They were approaching a second set of doors when they heard rapid automatic fire below them, followed by the *crack-crack-crack* of a Kalashnikov. There was more automatic fire followed by King's voice over the radio, calm but talking quickly. 'Contact, contact, contact!' said King.

There was more gunfire, followed by silence. 'Six hostiles, all dead,' said King over the radio.

Before Warren could reply, a bearded man carrying a Kalashnikov emerged from the door to the left. His eyes widened but before he could raise his weapon Warren shot him in the chest, twice. As the man staggered back, blood pouring from his wounds, Bird moved forwards in a crouch, swinging his carbine to the left. He saw movement and his finger was on the trigger but he waited a fraction of a second until he was certain it was a valid target – a young man in a grey tunic and baggy trousers, holding a Kalashnikov across his chest. Bird fired twice, the first shot missed and buried itself in the wall, the second took the top off the man's head. Blood and brain splattered across the window behind him. He was still crumpling to the floor as Bird moved into the room. His eyes swept to the right. Warren went to the left, and Tyson was in between them.

There were two men and a woman sitting with their backs to the wall on Bird's right. They all had their knees up against their chests and their hands were bound. Duct tape had been wound around their mouths. Chains ran from around their necks up to a sturdy metal pipe in the ceiling. Bird recognized them from the whiteboard in the Portakabin. Standing over them was a young man who was probably in his teens, wearing a black T-shirt and blue jeans that were frayed at the knees. He was clean shaven, maybe too young to be growing a beard, but despite his youth the machete he was holding was a clear threat, so Bird had no hesitation in shooting him twice in the chest and planting a third round in his face. As the man fell to the floor, Bird realized there was another fighter behind him, this one older and aiming a Kalashnikov. Bird tried to bring his gun to bear on the man but he knew he was too slow, then there was a brown and black blur to his left and Tyson threw himself through the air, jaws agape. The jaws bit down on the man's left forearm and Tyson's weight pulled the gun down. The man's finger twitched on the trigger and the Kalashnikov went off. A round ricocheted off the wooden floor.

Bird heard Warren's gun firing and 'contact, contact, contact' through his earpiece but he stayed focused on Tyson and the man with the Kalashnikov. Tyson was shaking his head from side to side, keeping the man off balance. The Kalashnikov fired again but Tyson was relentless. Bird took two quick steps towards the man, stuck the barrel of his Colt under the man's bearded chin and pulled the trigger. Bird stepped back, but Tyson kept his grip on the man's arm as he fell to the floor.

Bird looked to his left. 'Four hostiles,' said Warren. 'All dead.'

UNDERDOGS

There were two dead fighters on the floor by the window, both young men in their early twenties.

Thompson and Gatrell appeared in the doorway.

'Tyson, leave,' said Bird and Tyson immediately released his grip on the dead jihadist's arm.

'Heel,' said Bird. Tyson immediately hurried over to Bird and stood by his right leg, his nose pressed against Bird's knee. Bird took some treats from his pouch and gave them to the dog.

'Hey, Sarge, why don't you toss us treats when we do a good job?' asked Gatrell.

Before Warren could reply they heard shouts from outside, a mixture of Kalashnikovs and small arms fire. 'Contact, contact, contact!' said King over the radio.

Warren nodded at Gatrell. 'Shotgun, you get the hostages sorted and up to the roof.' He turned to Thompson. 'Tommo, give us covering fire from the window until the heli is here.'

Tommo went over to the window with his rifle. There were more shots from outside and the sound of Heckler & Kochs returning fire.

'Come on, Birdman,' said Warren, and he jogged out into the corridor. Bird and Tyson followed him along to the stairs. As they headed down, the sound of gunfire got louder.

'Sitrep, Queenie,' said Warren over the radio.

'We're taking fire from hostiles in the guardhouse,' said King. 'And they're getting ready to use one of the pick-ups.'

Warren reached the ground floor and pushed open the door. It was mainly open-plan and most of the equipment and machinery had been stripped out, though there were half a dozen metal chairs and a few metal tables dotted around the room with the remains of a meal on them.

There were metal bars across the windows and most of the glass had been smashed. There were six dead bodies strewn across the floor. Their Kalashnikovs had been kicked to the side.

Harris, Brown, King and Bennett were lined up by the windows.

They had all flipped up their night vision gear – there was enough moonlight to illuminate the opposition. The firing outside was sporadic. Most of the shots were coming from the guardhouse.

The SAS troopers were choosing their targets carefully and firing single shots. 'Got one,' said Brown.

'How many?' asked Warren, bending low and jogging over to a window. He knelt down and took a quick look over the windowsill. Bird crouched down next to Warren. Tyson lay at his side, his head on his paws.

'I'd say eight,' said Harris. 'Seven now.'

'Tweedy, call the heli in. Tell them we're taking fire but we should have it under control by the time they get here.'

'How are the hostages?' asked King.

'Alive and well,' said Warren. 'Shotgun is taking them up to the roof. You see the guy in the black pick-up?'

'I see him but can't get a clear shot,' said Brown.

'What's he up to? If he starts using that HMG we're in big trouble.' There was a Russian-made Kord 12.7 mm heavy machine gun mounted on the back of the pick-up truck. Its barrel was more than three feet long and the weapon was capable of delivering up to 650 rounds a minute at a range of just over a mile. It wasn't the most accurate of weapons but at close range it would do a lot of damage.

'Tommo, do you have eyes on the pick-up truck?' asked Warren over the radio.

'The truck, yes, but I can't see the driver. He's keeping his head down.'

'Keep an eye on it. Slot anyone who goes near the HMG.'

'Roger that,' said Thompson.

'Heli is en route,' said Harris. 'ETA ten minutes.'

More rounds raked the ceiling. There were three small windows at the rear of the guardhouse, and most of the shots seemed to be coming from there. There were another two men on the roof but they were keeping their heads down and only firing occasionally.

Another of the fighters had taken position behind a rusting red pick-up truck.

Bird took a quick look over the sill. He could see the feet of the man behind the pick-up truck, but he was over a hundred feet away so it would be a difficult shot even if he wasn't under fire. He shouldered his Colt and sighted on the feet but then a hail of bullets made him duck back.

'There's a bad guy heading for the black pick-up,' said Thompson over the radio.

'Take him out, Tommo,' said Warren.

'I can't, Sarge, he's down low. I can't get a clear shot.'

Bird took another quick look. He could see the black pick-up but couldn't see the man heading towards it. He switched his attention to the red pick-up and again sighted on the feet of the man behind it. He pulled the trigger and saw a puff of sand to the left of the man's sandals. He corrected his aim and fired again, and this time saw the man's left ankle explode in a mass of red.

'Nice one, whoever did that,' said Thompson over the radio.

'That was me,' said Bird.

'The old ankle under the vehicle shot,' said Thompson. 'Good to see. I'll just put him out of his misery.' They heard a single rifle shot. 'Job done,' said Thompson. 'The bad news is that the other tango has just climbed onto the back of the black pick-up. He's crouched behind the shield so I can't get a clear shot. It's going to get hairy when he starts firing.'

Bird looked over at the black pick-up. The barrel of the heavy machine gun emerged from a square of armoured steel, behind which the gunner was taking cover. Black smoke belched from the exhaust; the driver had started the engine. That made no sense. The truck was already well within range; moving it any closer merely risked exposing the gunner to Thompson's sniper fire.

The HMG burst into life and rounds smacked into the concrete above the window, sending down a cloud of dust. All the SAS men ducked.

'Well, this isn't good,' said Warren.

They heard the engine of the pick-up roar. Bird took a quick look over the windowsill. The driver was nowhere to be seen, keeping his head below the dashboard. The pick-up edged forwards jerkily and the gunner began firing again. Bird ducked down as rounds whizzed through the glassless window and buried themselves into the wall by the door.

'Heli is six minutes away,' said Harris.

'Tell them we're taking HMG fire – if it's still going on when they arrive they're going to have to take care of it for us.'

'Roger that,' said Harris.

The HMG gunner continued to rake the factory with rounds and the SAS men kept their heads down. The firing came to a sudden end. Bird figured the gunner was having to change belts so he risked a look-see. The barrel was pointing skywards and the pick-up was continuing to crawl towards the factory. Bird sighted on the armoured shield but he couldn't see the gunner. He switched his attention to the windscreen but there was no sign of the driver. Bird fired two shots at the windscreen and it shattered. He smiled to himself. If nothing else, he'd covered the driver with broken glass.

The barrel of the HMG swung down and as it did, Bird caught a glimpse of a skullcap over a shock of unruly black hair. He swung his carbine around but before he could pull the trigger the skullcap exploded in a mass of red.

'Got you, you bastard,' said Thompson.

The gunner pitched over the side of the pick-up truck and fell to the ground.

'Nice one, Tommo,' said Warren over the radio.

'All part of the service,' said the sniper.

The pick-up truck continued to jerk forwards. It was about fifty feet from the factory, but without the HMG it was no threat. The fighters in the guardhouse continued to take pot shots but their hearts didn't seem to be in it.

Bird switched his attention to the radiator of the pick-up. He fired half a dozen shots and was eventually rewarded with a cloud of grey steam pouring from under the bonnet. A few seconds later the pick-up shuddered to a halt.

Bird fired two more shots through the broken windscreen, then the driver's door crashed open. A man appeared wearing a brown tunic and baggy trousers. He was screaming in Arabic as he ran towards the factory. He didn't seem to be holding a weapon but then Bird saw that he had something in his right hand.

'Grenade!' shouted Bird.

He aimed his Colt at the man's chest just as the man pulled his arm back and threw the grenade. Bird pulled the trigger twice and the man staggered back, red blossoms of blood spreading across his chest.

The grenade span through the air and for a second Bird thought it was going to bounce off the concrete wall but then it hit one of the window bars and crashed onto the floor behind him.

Bird whirled around. Time seemed to have stopped. He recognized the type immediately. It was a Soviet F-1, nicknamed the Little Lemon because of its shape and yellow-green colour. It weighed about six hundred grams, of which sixty grams was TNT. The steel exterior was notched, to prevent it slipping on sweaty skin, and to assist with fragmentation when it detonated. The fuse usually lasted between three and a half and four seconds. Bird knew that even though time had slowed to a crawl, he had less than two seconds to make his call. Once the TNT exploded, anything up to three hundred sharp-edged splinters each weighing about one gram would be sent spinning through the air at more than two thousand feet per second. The deadly shrapnel would kill at up to six metres and wound at up to fifteen metres, possibly more. Bird was well within the kill zone and everybody in the room would be maimed at best.

If only Bird had been quicker, if only he'd shot the man before he'd thrown the grenade, if only the grenade had hit the wall and not gone through the window. So many ifs, so many what-might-have-beens. Now there was only the present. A deadly grenade only a second away from detonating. And only one way to save the team.

Running wasn't an option. There wasn't enough time. The rule book said you threw yourself to the floor with your feet facing the grenade and hoped for the best, but when you were inside the kill zone, all bets were off.

There was only one option that made any kind of sense.

He grabbed at the metal table to his right and pushed it over on its side, the legs parallel to the floor. Plates and cutlery clattered onto the concrete. He dropped down to his knees behind the table, then pushed it forwards so that it dropped down onto the grenade. From the corner of his eye he saw that Tyson was still on the floor, his head resting on his paws.

Sergeant Warren was screaming at everyone to get down but Bird knew that if they hadn't already hit the floor then it was too late. He threw himself forwards to add his weight to the table pressing down on the grenade. He felt the explosion rather than heard it, and everything went black.

CHAPTER 2

Bird's eyes opened and he gasped for breath. He was lying on his back and looking up at grey clouds, high overhead in the night sky. His heart was racing and his face was bathed in sweat. He felt movement to his right and Tyson appeared, his ears up. 'Sorry, lad, did I wake you?' said Bird. He reached over and patted Tyson's neck. 'It's just the heebie-jeebies,' he said. 'It'll pass.'

The heebie-jeebies was how Bird always described it, but the few doctors he'd spoken to over the past year or so had called it PTSD – Post-Traumatic Stress Disorder. The last doctor who had examined Bird had been a lovely lady from an ex-servicemen's charity who had shown him a printed sheet which listed all the symptoms of PTSD, asking him to tick off those that applied. Bird could still remember the list.

Being easily startled or frightened.

Always being on guard for danger.

Self-destructive behaviour, such as drinking too much or driving too fast.

Trouble sleeping.

Trouble concentrating.

Irritability, angry outbursts or aggressive behaviour.

Overwhelming guilt or shame.

It had been a full house for Bird, even though at heart he knew that he had nothing to feel guilty about. Doing what he did had saved the other members of his team, and Tyson. Two collapsed lungs and two blown eardrums was a small price to pay. But shame, yes, in spades. Shame that he was no longer a warrior, just a civilian, and a civilian who was deaf with crippling PTSD to boot.

He looked at his watch and sighed. It wasn't even midnight, he'd barely slept for an hour. He pushed himself up so that his back was against the wall. He was in an alley off Camden High Street, one of his half a dozen regular haunts. The alley was quiet and he was tucked in between two industrial skips where the shops dumped their rubbish. Further down the alley was another skip used by Marks & Spencer and often, after closing, they would dump food that was past its sell-by date. The expired microwave ready meals were wasted on him – he didn't exactly have a kitchen – but that evening he had grabbed a couple of stale croissants, some sausages for Tyson and a carton of oat milk that was out of date but which hadn't turned.

Bird was sitting on several sheets of cardboard, which provided some insulation from the cold, and the skips shielded him from any wind. There was no shelter from the rain but the clouds weren't threatening a downpour so he was happy where he was for now. He was wearing a heavy-duty green parka with a fur-lined hood, a black wool polo neck sweater, brown wool trousers and black Altberg boots. The boots were one of the few things he had taken with him when he had left the SAS.

Tyson lay down next to him and put his head on Bird's knee. Bird stroked him behind the ears. 'Never mind, pal,' he said. 'This time next year we'll be millionaires.'

Tyson woofed softly and wagged his tail.

Bird reached over and grabbed his Bergen. He pulled it towards him, took out a bottle of water and drank. Tyson's plastic bowl was on the ground by the side of the cardboard and Bird poured some water into it.

The Bergen contained all Bird's belongings, pretty much. There were a couple of boxes of clothes and books in the attic of his ex-wife's house. He had no intention of ever going back, not that Sarah would even open the door if he did. She had a new man, now, one who didn't jump at shadows or wake up screaming most nights.

A man appeared at the entrance to the alley. He was young, late teens maybe, with a close-cropped beard and oblong wire-framed spectacles. He was wearing a North Face jacket zipped up, a red scarf wrapped around his neck, and sand-coloured cargo pants. He had a backpack over one shoulder and was peering down the alley. 'He'd better not be from the council, because I'm not moving,' Bird said to Tyson.

Tyson looked around and stared at the man. Bird stroked Tyson's neck.

The man started walking towards them. Tyson didn't growl, but he tensed and his ears were up. As the man got closer, Tyson got to his feet and stood staring at him.

The man stopped and smiled. 'What's your name, mate?' he asked.

'Why do you want to know my name?'

The man shrugged. 'Just being friendly.'

'I've got all the friends I need.'

'Well, that's good to know,' said the man. 'Anyway, my name's Joel. I work with a homeless charity.'

'Hopefully it'll get a home one day.'

Joel frowned. 'What?'

'Your charity. It must be difficult not having a home. Where do you keep your office supplies?'

Joel's frown deepened, then he realized what Bird meant. 'Oh, right. I get it. No, the charity works with the homeless. People like you. We help get you off the streets.'

Tyson continued to stare at Joel, his ears up. Joel said something else but he was looking at Tyson so Bird couldn't read his lips. He waved to get the man's attention. 'Joel, I have to see your lips when you talk.'

Joel turned to face him, frowning. 'Are you deaf?'

Bird nodded. 'Yeah.' He pushed the hood of his parka down.

'Sorry, I didn't realize. But you don't sound deaf.'

'Yeah, well you know that deafness involves the ears, not the mouth, right?'

Joel laughed. 'I mean most deaf people I've met sound deaf. They have trouble forming words.'

'I only went deaf a couple of years ago, so talking isn't a problem.'

'Can you sign?'

'I don't have any deaf friends, so signing isn't a thing for me. I'm pretty good at lip-reading, as long as I can see your face.'

'How did you lose your hearing, if you don't mind me asking?'

Bird shrugged. 'It was an industrial accident. What did you say before?'

'I was asking what sort of dog he was.' Joel had turned to look at Tyson again but when Bird didn't reply he realized his mistake. He turned back and repeated the question again.

'A Belgian Malinois,' said Bird. 'Belgian Shepherds, they're sometimes called.'

'What's his name?'

'Tyson.'

'After the boxer?'

'Yeah. He used to be called Scooby, but then he ripped a guy's ear off and nicknames stick.' He shrugged.

'He ripped off a guy's ear?'

'It's a long story.'

'But he's friendly, right?'

'He is with me.'

'Can I pat him?'

Bird nodded. 'Put your hand out slowly, back of your fist towards him. Let him smell you. But don't make any sudden moves. He doesn't like that. Let him approach you.'

Joel held his hand out hesitantly. Tyson moved his head forwards and sniffed, then looked at Bird. 'Friendly,' said Bird.

Tyson licked Joel's hand, then took a step towards him. Joel hesitantly put his hand on Tyson's head and stroked it. 'Good dog,' he said.

Tyson pushed his head against Joel's hand. 'There you go, he likes you,' said Bird.

'He's a lovely dog. So good-natured.'

'He has his moments.'

'So, can you tell me your name? Now that me and Tyson are mates.'

Bird smiled despite himself. Joel was a nice enough guy but Bird knew where the conversation was headed. 'Andy,' he said.

Joel offered his hand. 'Pleased to meet you, Andy.'

Bird shook. Joel's heart was clearly in the right place. Some of the charity and council workers who reached out to the homeless were patronizing or officious, but Joel seemed genuine.

'So, I can offer you a bed for the night, Andy, if you want.'

'So your parents are okay with me crashing at your place?'

'No, I meant there's a shelter . . .' He smiled thinly when he realized that Bird was teasing him. He wagged a finger at Bird. 'I fell for that, didn't I?'

Tyson's ears were up and he growled softly.

'Best not to point at me like that, Joel,' said Bird quietly. 'Tyson might take it as a threat.'

'Seriously?'

'Just lower your hand slowly. Tyson's accepted you as a friendly but it'll be a while before he trusts you.'

Joel slowly lowered his hand and Tyson stopped growling. 'That's amazing,' said Joel. 'He's very protective.'

'It works both ways,' said Bird.

Joel looked at Tyson for several seconds, then smiled at Bird. 'So, as I said, there's a bed for you in a shelter not far away. I can drive you there and book you in.'

'What about Tyson?'

Joel smiled uncomfortably. 'I'm afraid pets aren't allowed. Health and safety.'

'So what does Tyson do? Wait outside?' Bird shook his head. 'We're a team. Where I go, he goes. And vice versa.'

Joel sat down next to Bird with his back to the wall and stretched out his legs. He was wearing almost new Timberland boots. Bird flashed-back to the boots that MI6 Emma had been wearing on the day his whole life had turned to shit. He wondered where Emma was, and what she was doing to keep the country safe. Joel spoke again and Bird missed the first bit. Something about being former military.

'I missed that Joel, Sorry.'

'No problem. I was just asking if you used to be in the military.'

'Why do you ask?'

Joel nodded at the Bergen. 'Neatness like this comes from a spell in prison, or the armed forces, and you don't look like an ex-con.' He gestured at Bird's footwear. 'And they look like Army boots. You can always tell someone who is actually homeless. The daytime beggars and scammers wear flash trainers, the serious homeless go for comfort and durability.'

'Serious homeless?'

'It's a term I made up for those that have no choice other than to be on the streets. You'd be amazed at the number of street beggars that get picked up by minivans when their shift is over,' said Joel. 'For them it's a job. For you, well, I guess you're not here by choice. So, you didn't answer my question.'

'Army,' said Bird.

'Afghanistan?'

Bird shrugged. 'All over.'

'Must have been rough.'

'It had its moments,' said Bird. 'But I'm not complaining.'

'That's where you lost your hearing?'

Bird nodded. 'Yeah.'

'And how did you end up on the street?'

Bird shrugged. 'Difficult to say,' he said.

'Have you heard of the eight Ds?'

'The eighties?'

Joel shook his head and enunciated more slowly this time. 'The eight Ds. The letter D. Eight of them.'

'I've heard of the six Ps.'

Joel frowned. 'The six Ps?' he repeated.

Bird grinned. 'Perfect Preparation Prevents Piss-Poor Performance.'

Joel chuckled. 'That makes sense,' he said. 'But the eight Ds are the issues that can lead to homelessness – drink, debt, drugs, divorce, depression, domestic violence, dependency culture, and digs, meaning accommodation. Any one of those can lead to homelessness, but more often than not it's a combination of factors.'

'And you want to know which apply to me?'

'I'm just curious.'

Tyson lay down next to Bird again and put his head on his thigh. Bird reached over and rubbed the dog's neck. 'Drink – not really. Drugs – definitely not an issue. Debt and divorce sort of go together, at least when your ex-wife has a Rottweiler for a lawyer.'

'Domestic violence?'

Bird shook his head. 'I never raised a hand to my wife,' he said. 'Or to any woman. But I was impossible to live with. I ended up sleeping in the box room, but that didn't help.'

'What was the problem?'

'Nightmares,' said Bird. 'Rude awakenings. Scared the hell out of her a few times. Hence the move to the spare room. Anyway, how does dependency culture work?'

'A lot of guys in the Army get to depend on it,' said Joel. 'They house you, they feed you, they tell you where to be and what to do. It can be hard to move from that sort of environment into the civilian world.'

Bird grimaced. Life in the SAS was very different from life in the regular Army, but he wasn't about to explain that to Joel.

'Where were you before you started sleeping rough?' asked Joel.

'A pal of mine let me and Tyson camp out in his garden shed,' said Bird. 'But then the neighbours complained and the council turfed me out.'

'How long ago was that?'

'A few weeks.'

'Winter's not far off, Andy. You don't want to be sleeping on the streets then.'

Bird smiled. He and Tyson once spent a week in an observation post in the Syrian desert where temperatures had dropped to three or four degrees below zero at night. Compared to that, sleeping rough in London was a breeze. 'We'll manage,' he said.

'You hungry?'

'I'm okay.'

'You sure? I've got a sandwich you can have.' Joel unzipped his backpack and peered into it. 'Cheese and pickle, ham and cheese, or tuna?'

'Tuna would be great,' said Bird.

Joel gave him a plastic-wrapped sandwich. 'Coffee?'

'Are you serious?'

Joel grinned and took out a Thermos flask. 'All the comforts of home.' He twisted off the cup and poured in steaming coffee before handing it to Bird.

Bird took a sip, nodded his approval, then put it down on the ground. He unwrapped the sandwich and held half of it out for Tyson. Tyson bolted it down as if he was scared that Bird would change his mind.

'You're not local, are you?' asked Joel.

'Why do you say that?'

'Your accent. I'm pretty good with accents and I'd say you were from Manchester.'

'Close enough. Sheffield.'

Joel laughed. 'Not close at all,' he said. 'Lancashire and Yorkshire, chalk and cheese. But you've moved around a bit?'

'A bit. What about you?' Tyson looked longingly at Bird's half of the sandwich. Bird shook his head and took a bite.

Joel grinned. 'I'm a Scouser. Yeah, Liverpool born and bred.'

'Came to the Big Smoke in search of fame and fortune?'

'I wish,' said Joel. 'No, my parents moved here five years ago. Dad's a headteacher and they wanted him to run a big comprehensive in Tower Hamlets. Dad's always loved a challenge so we upped sticks and moved.'

'So you live with your parents?'

'I'm still a student, so yes, it helps keep costs down.'

'And in your spare time, you hassle the homeless?' Bird finished the sandwich and picked up his coffee. He took a sip, then a gulp.

Joel chuckled. 'I hope I'm doing more than hassling. I started doing it in my final year of school, just to get it on my CV, but I actually enjoy it. Believe it or not, I have helped quite a few people.'

Bird forced a smile. 'I'm sure you have, mate.' He held up the coffee cup. 'And I'm grateful for this. It's good coffee.'

'Made it myself on the Nespresso machine,' said Joel. He reached into his windbreaker and pulled out a business card. 'If you do ever need help, that's got my mobile number on it. Have you got a phone?'

'I have, but I'm not sure if I've got credit on it. But thanks.'

Joel pushed himself up. 'Well. I'll love you and leave you,' he said. 'I've got my rounds to do.'

Bird drained the cup and gave it to Joel, who shook the last remaining drops from it and put it into his backpack. 'Stay safe, Andy. You too, Tyson.' He flashed them a thumbs up and then headed down the alley.

Bird smiled at Tyson. 'He means well,' he said.

Tyson woofed as if he agreed.

Bird yawned. 'Time for bed,' he said. 'I just hope it doesn't rain.'

CHAPTER 3

The grenade span through the air and clattered on the floor. Time stopped as Bird stared at it. It almost defied belief that something so small could do so much damage. Bird pushed the table onto its side, the plates and cutlery crashing to the floor. Warren was shouting for everyone to get down. Rounds were smashing into the outside wall. Tyson's ears were up but his head was down on his paws. Did he realize what was happening? He had trained with flashbangs in the SAS's Killing House, but did he know the damage that a grenade could do?

Bird threw himself onto the table and pushed it down onto the grenade. Would it hurt? Would he feel anything? Or would it be just like turning off a light? Such a waste. If only he'd pulled the trigger sooner. If only . . .

Bird's eyes opened. He was gasping for breath and his heart was pounding. His mouth was dry and he rolled over and grabbed for his water bottle. Tyson was awake, watching him with his ears up. 'I'm okay,' said Bird. He sat up, crossed his legs and drank from the bottle before pouring some into Tyson's bowl.

He shifted his position so that he could sit with his back to the wall. He could always hear perfectly in his dreams. The *crack-crack-crack* of the Kalashnikovs. The thwack of the rounds hitting the factory. The clink of the hand grenade grazing the window bar. The thud as it landed on the floor. The crash of the plates and cutlery as they fell from the table. Warren, screaming at his men to get down. Every sound, as clear as a bell. But in the real world, there was nothing. Not even a ringing or a humming. Just silence. Permanent silence.

He'd been lucky, of course. Not many people threw themselves on a live hand grenade and survived. And those that did usually suffered crippling injuries and loss of limbs. Bird had got off lightly, but it had been touch and go. Both his lungs had collapsed as a result of the explosion, and if it hadn't been for King thrusting two surgical needles into his chest he would have died long before he'd reached the medical facility at Incirlik Air Base.

The doctors were amazed that he had survived the blast. The metal table had deflected most of the shrapnel across the room towards the door, away from where the SAS team were. Tyson too had escaped unscathed, though he had been unsteady on his feet for a few hours afterwards.

Once at Incirlik they had stabilized Bird before flying him and Tyson back to the UK, where he had spent two weeks having his lungs repaired. His ears weren't fixable, though. The doctors had been apologetic. The deafness he would have to live with.

Bird saw movement to his left. He turned and saw a man running down the alley, his long black coat flapping behind him like a demented bird. Tyson got to his feet, his ears up, all his attention focused on the man. The guy was in his thirties, overweight with thinning hair and jowls that wobbled with every step. He looked over his shoulder, tripped, and went sprawling, face first. He pushed himself up onto his knees and then awkwardly got to his feet. Another man rushed up behind him and grabbed him by the collar of his coat. The second guy was big, well over six feet tall with a square jaw and slicked-back hair. He wore a heavy overcoat that strained against his massive shoulders.

Bird stood up, still holding his water bottle. He wasn't sure what he was seeing. It could be an attempted mugging, a guy doing a runner from a restaurant, or a lover's tiff. He was reluctant to get involved – in his experience, getting involved in other people's problems never worked out well.

The guy who had fallen tried to twist around but the other man held him tight.

Tyson shuffled over to stand next to Bird, his ears up and his hackles raised. The skip to their left shielded them from view and Bird held that position. London back alleys could be dangerous places at the best of times.

Another man ran up, as big and heavy as the second one. He was also wearing a heavy overcoat that reached almost to his ankles. Both men wore highly polished black shoes and black leather gloves.

The second giant said something to the first one. They were too far away for Bird to read their lips, but the looks on their faces suggested that they weren't offering to take their prisoner for a slap-up meal.

The first assailant wrestled their prisoner to his knees.

The second reached inside his coat and pulled out a gun.

Tyson growled softly and took two steps forwards, but Bird reached down and patted him on the neck. This wasn't their fight.

The gun didn't have a suppressor attached and Bird doubted that anyone would be so stupid as to fire a gun so close to a main thoroughfare, but then the man on the ground pitched forwards and blood sprayed across the tarmac. Bird hadn't heard the shot but Tyson had and he yelped.

The first assailant looked around and pointed at the skips. Bird bent down and patted Tyson. 'Silent,' he whispered.

Tyson stood stock still, his jaws clamped together.

Bird stared ahead, hoping that the men wouldn't see him, but he caught a glimpse of boots and then the man with the gun appeared from around the skip. He had a broad jaw with a dimple in the chin and close-set eyes either side of a thin nose that had been broken several times. The man raised the gun. Bird threw the water bottle with all his strength and it hit the man in the face. Blood spurted down over the man's lips and he took a step back. Bird sprang forwards, grabbed the gun with his left hand and thrust his right hand under the man's chin, snapping his head back. Under normal circumstances it would have been an incapacitating blow, but the gunman was big and his neck was well muscled. Bird smashed his elbow into the man's chin and felt a satisfying crack, then he swivelled and brought the side of his fist into the man's groin. The man grunted and bent forwards, finally releasing his grip on the gun. Bird pulled the gun away and stepped back. It was a Glock 42, the smallest handgun they made, with just six .380 ACP rounds in the magazine. It was under six inches long, less than an inch wide, and weighed fourteen ounces unloaded. It was the perfect gun to carry inside a jacket, and would even fit into a pocket. The .380 ACP round was subsonic, much slower than a 9 mm round, which meant that there was less recoil when fired, in turn making the gun more accurate. In Bird's experience, accuracy was more about the gun than it was about the shooter. Though when you were shooting someone in the chest from three feet away, accuracy really wasn't an issue.

The man straightened up and said something but Bird didn't recognize the words. He was fluent in five languages but struggled to lip-read anything other than English.

'Put your hands up,' Bird snarled, waving the gun for emphasis.

The other man was bent over the body of the victim, rifling through his pockets. Bird pointed the gun at him. 'Stand up!' he shouted. The man did as he was told. He was a little shorter than his colleague but just as broad. His overcoat was longer and he had rings on all the fingers of his right hand, a makeshift knuckleduster. 'Hands in the air.'

The men looked at each other. The shorter one spoke and again Bird couldn't make out the words. Then both men looked down the alley. They had obviously heard something. Sirens, maybe. So, the cavalry was on the way.

'Stay where you are!' shouted Bird, but the two men ignored him and ran down the alley, back the way they'd come. Bird pointed the gun at them. His finger was on the Glock's trigger but he knew he couldn't pull it. Shooting someone in the back wasn't something he could do, not in a London street. In combat, perhaps, in the heat of battle where it was kill or be killed, but they were running away and no longer a threat, so he lowered the gun and rushed over to the victim. He rolled him over onto his back. The man's shirt was already soaked in blood. Bird put the Glock on the ground and pressed his fingers against the man's neck. He felt a faint pulse. 'Stay with me, guy,' hissed Bird.

The man's mouth was working soundlessly with bloody froth trickling down his chin. He reached up and grabbed Bird's parka. His eyes were wide and fearful. 'Eighty,' he said. Or at least that's what the lip movement looked like, though it was hard to tell because there was so much froth coming from the man's mouth.

'Easy, guy, don't try to talk. Save your energy.'

'Eighty,' the man gasped again, then his eyes closed.

Bird took off his scarf and folded it several times, then pressed it onto the wound.

The man's hands moved down Bird's parka, the fingers scratching on the material.

Tyson was looking towards the other end of the alley, his ears up and tail out straight. Bird looked over his shoulder. Two policemen were walking towards him. They were the reason the two attackers had run off. 'Help!' he shouted. 'There's a man here needs an ambulance!'

The officer on the left was a middle-aged woman, her colleague an overweight bearded man whose thighs were wobbling as he walked towards Bird. The woman was talking into her radio.

The injured man's eyes were closed now but the froth continued to bubble between his lips. Bird kept the pressure on the scarf, which was already soaked in blood. 'Come on, hurry!' he shouted.

The man's eyes fluttered open again. He stared up at Bird with unseeing eyes and his mouth began to move.

'Stay with me,' hissed Bird. 'There's an ambulance on the way.'

A hand gripped Bird's shoulder. It was the male officer. 'I have to keep pressure on the wound,' said Bird, shaking him off.

The hand gripped tighter. If the man was saying anything, Bird couldn't hear him. 'Get a fucking ambulance, this man is dying!' Bird shouted, as he continued to press the scarf against the injured man's chest.

Bird was yanked to his feet. The blood-soaked scarf stayed in his hand. He whirled around to face the cop and held the scarf up. 'I'm trying to save this guy's life!' he shouted.

'Gun!' shouted the female officer, pointing to the Glock on the ground. 'Gun!' she repeated, her face contorted with fear.

The male officer pulled a set of rigid handcuffs from his belt. 'Turn around please, sir,' he said.

'This man is dying,' said Bird. 'He has major chest trauma.'

'We'll attend to him once the cuffs are on,' said the officer.

The female officer pulled a yellow Taser from its holster. She fumbled with it as if she wasn't used to having it in her hands.

'You've got to be kidding me,' said Bird.

'Get on the ground now, or you will be Tasered!' she shouted as she brought the Taser to bear on his chest.

Bird pointed at the injured man. 'You need to get an ambulance here ASAP,' he said.

'An ambulance has been called, now get down on your knees or I will Taser you.' She screamed as Tyson leapt at her, his jaws open. She tried to point the Taser at him but she was too slow and Tyson bit down on her wrist. The Taser fell from her hand and clattered onto the ground.

Her colleague dropped the handcuffs and pulled his extendable baton from the pouch on his belt, flicking it out. He raised the baton and took a step towards Tyson.

'Oy!' shouted Bird.

The cop ignored Bird and lashed out with the baton, catching Tyson on the back of the neck. Tyson had been trained to regard the gun as the primary threat and couldn't distinguish between a Taser and a semi-automatic so he ignored the blow and kept his jaws fastened on the woman's wrist.

The cop cursed and raised the baton again. Bird stepped forwards and kicked the cop's left leg from under him. He fell back, arms flailing. Bird grabbed the baton from the man's grasp and held onto it as he crashed to the ground. The impact knocked the air from the cop's lungs and he lay on his back, gasping for breath. Bird smashed the baton against his knee, then raised it as a warning. 'Stay down, or I'll belt you,' he said.

The cop nodded, breathing heavily, splaying his fingers out in front of his face.

Bird turned to look at the female cop. He realized she was still screaming as she tried to pull away from Tyson. Bird kicked her Taser over to the skips. 'Release!' he shouted.

Tyson immediately opened his jaws and the woman fell back. She landed on her backside and glared up at Bird as she rubbed her injured wrist.

'I didn't hurt the guy,' he said. He pointed at the Glock. 'They shot him with that.'

'You were the only one in the alley, and we got here right after the shot,' she said.

'They ran off.'

'Of course they did.' The woman reached for the radio on the shoulder of her stab vest and pressed the transmit button. 'Officers down, officers down,' she said. 'Alley behind Curry's in the High Street. Attacker is an IC1 male wearing a green parka and dark trousers. Attacker is armed.'

'I'm not armed!' shouted Bird, then he realized he was still holding the baton. He tossed it to the ground.

'Attacker is armed and dangerous and accompanied by a vicious dog,' said the woman. She sneered and took her finger off the transmit button. 'You're in big trouble now, you tosser.'

Bird snarled at her. He bent down and picked up his Bergen, then looked at Tyson. 'Heel,' he said. He slung the Bergen over his shoulders and started running. Tyson raced alongside him, his ears back, sticking to his side. London police weren't generally quick to respond to emergency calls, but they tended to try harder when one of their own was involved.

They reached the end of the alley and stopped. Bird looked left and right. Traffic was moving normally, and no one appeared to be paying him any attention. He looked down at Tyson, who was standing by Bird's right leg. His ears were up but here was no indication that he could hear sirens. If there were any in the distance, Tyson's ears would be swivelling to get a read on the noise.

A young couple walked by, arm in arm, deep in conversation. The woman, a blonde in her twenties, saw Bird and she pulled her companion away to give him a wide berth. It was an all-too-common reaction, and one that Bird understood. He hadn't shaved for a couple of days and while he tried to grab a shower or at least a wash every day, he knew that his clothes probably smelt less than fresh.

North was to his left, south to his right. Hampstead Heath was less than two miles to the north, going right meant heading into the city. They had his description and a man with a Bergen and a dog would be hard to miss. He needed to stay off the main roads, and the Heath was probably the best place to lie low. He spotted a break in the traffic and jogged across the road with Tyson at his heels. The Bergen banged against his shoulders. He'd be able to move faster without it but it contained everything important he owned and there was gear in there that he'd need.

They reached the far side of the road and he looked both ways. No flashing lights, and no one seemed to be looking around, so probably no sirens. So far so good.

He walked quickly to a side road, Tyson sticking to his heels, Bird knowing that running or even a slow jog would draw attention.

The side road joined another main road and he turned left. Tyson stuck to him like glue.

The Heath was less than half an hour away at a fast walk. The Bergen was an inconvenience, nothing more. In the final endurance phase of SAS selection, Bird had completed the Long Drag, a forty-mile hike across the Brecon Beacons carrying a fifty-five pound fully loaded Bergen, plus a rifle, food and water. That had been challenging, especially as it had been pouring with rain all night. But the cops hadn't been after him on the Brecon Beacons, and failure wouldn't have meant spending ten years behind bars.

A blue light flashed on a shop window to his left and he whirled around. It was an ambulance. He couldn't tell if the siren was on or not. It raced past, heading north. Tyson looked up at Bird. 'All good,' said Bird, bending down to pat him on the neck.

They walked past a pub, black paint and leaded windows. Half a dozen smokers were gathered outside, huddled together as they inhaled their nicotine fixes. A woman with dyed-green hair and piercings in her ears, nose, eyebrows and lips made a clicking noise at Tyson. Tyson ignored her. The pub would be a decent place to hide, for a while at least, but Bird had no idea how quickly the police would get access to CCTV so it made more sense to keep moving. The more distance they put between themselves and what must now be a dead body in the alley, the better.

Bird increased the pace. One and a half miles. Thirty minutes. Then at least he could go to ground.

Tyson's ears swivelled and he looked over his shoulder. 'What is it, boy?' asked Bird. 'Sirens? Best we keep to the side streets. Come on.'

He waited for a gap in the traffic then jogged across. Tyson stuck to his heels. A black cab flashed its lights and Bird raised his hand in apology, even though the cab was going way too fast. They reached the pavement. Bird looked to the right and frowned. There was a police patrol car heading towards them. It wasn't speeding and its lights weren't flashing so Bird carried on walking. He watched the car from the corner of his eye, breathing slowly and evenly. He reached a shop window. If he turned left he'd be turning his back on the police car but if he went right he'd be going in the wrong direction. He decided it would be better to face the vehicle, so went right. The car began to brake and he caught a glimpse of the occupants – a grey-haired older man was driving, the passenger in the front seat was younger and wearing glasses. The car went by and for a few seconds Bird thought he was in the clear but then the car pulled a tight U-turn, though its lights still weren't flashing. Bird looked down at Tyson. He wasn't reacting to sirens, but the car had turned for a reason. If the cops were reacting to a call they'd accelerate and maybe hit the blues and twos. But they hadn't, they'd slowed, and that suggested that it was Bird they were interested in. Should he run, or bluff it out? He couldn't afford to make the wrong call because the moment he started to run, they'd definitely be after him.

'Attacker is an IC1 male wearing a green parka and dark trousers,' the cop had said over the radio. Armed and accompanied by a dangerous dog. The description was pretty much bang on, though he wasn't armed. But if they had heard the radio call, the cops in the patrol car would have no trouble recognizing him. Bird took a quick look over his shoulder. The driver was staring right at him, saying something to his colleague.

Bird looked down at Tyson. 'Run,' he said. He turned and headed down an alley that ran between a second-hand furniture shop and a bookmaker's. Tyson stuck to his heels, his ears up and mouth open.

CHAPTER 4

Bird chanced another quick look over his shoulder just in time to see the patrol car turn into the alley. The driver flicked on the full beams and Bird was temporarily blinded. He turned his face away from the lights, blinking to try to clear his vision. He slowed and Tyson kept pace with him.

The patrol car stopped but the headlights stayed on. Bird wondered why they weren't pursuing him but a second later his question was answered when an armed response vehicle screeched to a halt ahead of him, blocking the alley.

It was a white BMW SUV with blue and yellow squares on the side, but it was the yellow circular stickers displayed on the windows that identified it as a Trojan vehicle, one of several dozen that were constantly patrolling the streets of London. Bird had trained with members of the Met's Specialist Firearms Command – known as SCO19 – and with better-qualified Counter-Terrorist Specialist Firearms Officers, putting them through their paces at the SAS's training camp in Hereford. The Met's firearms officers were technically proficient, but most would go through their entire career without firing their weapon. Their orders were always to only fire as a last resort, if lives were in danger. The response cops in the patrol car would follow procedure and stay put, so long as there was a risk of guns being fired.

The Trojan officers carried carbines but they were locked in a gun safe at the back of the armed response vehicle. It would take time for them to get the weapons out, but with police ahead of him and behind him, Bird knew that his options were limited. He stopped, breathing heavily. Tyson sat down, his ears up and his tongue out. The front passenger door of the ARV opened and an officer climbed out, dressed in black with a Kevlar jacket and a black baseball cap, both labelled POLICE. The officer in the rear of the vehicle was bent over the gun safe.

'I'm not armed,' said Bird, raising his hands in the air.

'Yeah, well forgive us if we don't take your word for that,' said the officer. 'You left a gun in the alley but that doesn't mean you're not still carrying. Now get down on your knees and put your hands behind your head.'

Bird spread his fingers wide. 'I'm not armed, I'm not a threat,' he said.

'No one said you were, mate,' said the officer. 'Just get down on your knees so that we can pat you down.'

The driver's door opened. A grey-haired sergeant climbed out. The rear door opened and the cop in the back passed out a carbine. The sergeant took it and walked around the front of the vehicle.

'Listen, guys, I haven't hurt anybody, and I'm not armed. I'm happy to answer your questions but there's no need to get heavy with me.'

The sergeant held his carbine across his chest. It was a Sig Sauer MCX, a nice enough weapon but Bird had always preferred HKs when it came to carbines. 'Looks to me like there's blood on your jacket,' he said. 'Do you want to explain that?'

'A guy was shot, I tried to help,' said Bird. 'Look, you can pat me down like this. I'm not going to resist.'

The sergeant gestured with the carbine again. 'On your knees. Now.'

The officer in the baseball cap took a set of handcuffs from a pouch on his belt.

'I'm not going to tell you again!' shouted the sergeant.

The officer took a step towards Bird but stopped when Tyson growled. Tyson took two small steps forwards. His ears were back and his tail was down.

'If you make me kneel down, Tyson will think you're a threat,' said Bird.

The officer frowned. 'Tyson?'

'The dog.'

The firearms officer's hand moved towards the pistol on his thigh. Bird shook his head. 'Don't even think about reaching for your gun,' he said.

The man frowned. 'Why not?'

'Tyson has a thing about bearded men with guns.'

Tyson growled softly as if agreeing with him.

'So your dog's racist, is that it?'

'No mate. But if you start waving a gun around he's going to see you as a threat.'

'And then what?'

'Then it'll probably end badly for you. Don't raise your voice to me and don't make any sudden movements and everything will be fine.'

'You need to shut your mouth and get down on your knees,' shouted the sergeant. 'Or you'll be the one who it ends badly for.'

Bird slowly went down on his knees, grunting under the weight of the Bergen. Tyson's ears pricked up and he stared at the sergeant.

'Friendly,' said Bird. Tyson glanced at Bird and then continued to stare at the officer.

'What did you say?' said the sergeant.

'I'm just telling him that you're a friendly,' said Bird. 'But he doesn't always take my advice.'

'Well, if your dog wants to take on me and my MCX then he's welcome to try.' He took a step closer to Bird and raised the carbine for emphasis.

'Be careful what you wish for,' said Bird. The sergeant was now close enough for Bird to see the selector switch on the side of the carbine. It had three settings – safe, semi and auto. The sergeant's weapon was still set to safe, which meant he didn't see Bird and Tyson as a serious threat. Bird smiled thinly. Big mistake.

'What are you grinning at?' asked the sergeant.

'It doesn't matter,' said Bird. 'Let's just get this over with.'

'Pat him down, Amit,' said the sergeant.

'I'm not armed,' said Bird. 'There's no need for this.'

'Word is that you shot a guy five minutes ago,' said the sergeant. 'So we're going to check for ourselves.'

Amit took a step towards Bird. Immediately, Tyson growled and bared his teeth. Amit grabbed at his Glock.

'Don't!' shouted Bird, but he was too late. Amit pulled out the gun. Tyson became a blur. He sprang forwards, then launched himself through the air. Amit's eyes widened with terror as he tried to aim his weapon but Tyson was too quick for him and his jaws latched onto the man's wrist. Amit screamed in pain. He was wearing black leather gloves but they were more for show than protection and Tyson's teeth had ripped right through them. Tyson dropped to the ground, his jaws still clamped on the man's wrist. As soon as his paws hit the ground, he started doing what he was trained to do, backing up and shaking his head from side to side, throwing the man off balance and inflicting maximum damage. The Glock clattered to the ground.

Bird looked over at the sergeant. He was staring at Tyson in surprise, his mouth open. His carbine was pointed at the ground and his finger was flat against the slide. He began to raise the weapon and his thumb moved towards the selector switch.

Bird jumped to his feet.

The rear door opened and the third officer climbed out. She was pale skinned with blonde curls peeping from under her police baseball cap. Like the sergeant, she was holding an MCX.

Amit was still screaming, though Bird couldn't hear him. Amit tried to pull his arm away but that only seemed to intensify the pain, so he leant forwards and Tyson took the opportunity to pull him down to his knees, then kept pulling, the constant pressure keeping the cop from getting to his feet.

The sergeant raised his carbine to his shoulder and aimed at Tyson's flank.

Bird had taken two quick steps before the sergeant began to react. He swung the MCX around, his finger on the trigger, but he was slow and Bird reached him with his third step and used his left hand to push the gun away. The sergeant's finger tightened involuntarily and the gun went off. A round screeched off the pavement and buried itself in the tyre of a parked car.

The sergeant tried to swing his carbine around but Bird kept his hand on it. He smacked the sergeant's chin with his elbow and the man staggered back. Bird twisted the MCX from his grasp, then slammed the butt against the side of the sergeant's head. He crumpled to the ground. Bird kept a grip on the carbine and swung it into position to cover the female cop, who was now standing at the rear of the ARV. She had her finger on the trigger of her weapon but her mouth was open in shock and the barrel was pointing skywards. Bird shouldered his weapon. The sergeant had set the selector switch to semi, which meant the trigger fired single shots. Bird put a round into the rear tyre of the ARV, and another into the rear door. 'Drop your weapon!' he shouted.

The female cop froze. Bird knew that there was no way in hell that he was going to shoot a police officer, even one holding a loaded weapon. He just hoped that she wouldn't realize that.

'Drop your gun or the next round goes in your leg!'

The cop hesitated, then raised the gun above her head. 'Don't do anything stupid, we can sort this out,' she said.

'Put the gun on the ground, and kick it away,' said Bird.

The cop slowly put the gun on the tarmac and then kicked it away. It clattered into the gutter.

'You got handcuffs?'

The cop nodded.

'Handcuff yourself to the door handle.'

As the cop did as she was told, Bird looked over at Tyson, who was still dragging Amit along the ground and shaking his head from side to side. 'Leave!' Bird shouted and Tyson immediately released his grip on Amit's arm. Amit rolled over onto his back, sobbing, his injured arm pressed against his chest.

Tyson's ears pricked up and he looked over to the right. Then to the left. 'What can you hear, boy? Sirens?' Bird looked around, his mind racing. There was no way he was going to be able to talk his way out of this. And he didn't intend to get into a shooting match with armed cops. Despite all his training, the Met had virtually unlimited resources and it would only end one way. He looked over his shoulder. The patrol car was still parked at the entrance to the alley. The cops had stayed in the vehicle.

Tyson was looking up at him, ears erect, waiting for instructions. Bird nodded. He bent down and placed the carbine on the pavement. There was only one option. He nodded at Tyson. 'Time to run again,' he said.

CHAPTER 5

Ed Newfield slowed as the traffic lights ahead of him turned red and the ambulance came to a halt. They were in no rush, the body in the back was well dead and all they had to do was deliver it to St Pancras Mortuary.

The cause of death was clear enough; a gunshot to the man's chest. Shootings were still a relatively rare occurrence in London, especially when compared with stabbings, and the police had been out in force by the time Newfield and his paramedic partner had arrived on the scene. Jane Fleming was in her late twenties, a decade younger than Newfield, and about half his weight. They both had blue eyes, but that was the only thing they had in common. Fleming had tied her dyed-blonde hair back in a ponytail, Newfield's was thinning and combed over his freckled scalp. Newfield was a non-smoker but Fleming was a nicotine addict with yellowing teeth, and her hair and uniform reeked of smoke. Newfield was constantly having to remind her not to light up in the ambulance.

When they'd arrived at the scene, the alley had been cordoned off with police tape and two uniformed officers at either end were stopping anyone from walking through. Though at that time of the night, there weren't many pedestrians around.

They had parked in the road next to the alley and Newfield had watched as Fleming had carried out the examination of the body, and let her fill in the paperwork. She was still relatively new but handled herself well.

A police forensics team had arrived shortly after them, donned their white overalls and blue shoe covers and set about collecting swabs and taking photographs before a cigarette-smoking detective had told Newfield they could remove the body. The mortuary was less than a mile away; they'd be there in a couple of minutes. And dropping off the body wouldn't take much longer, unlike their trips to the borough's accident and emergency departments, where they might have to queue for hours before a patient could be admitted.

The light turned green and Newfield pressed down on the accelerator. He flinched as a black BMW X5 overtook him, engine roaring. 'Arsehole!' shouted Newfield.

'Probably drunk,' said Fleming.

'Yeah, well I'm not going to be in any rush to help him if he crashes. Fucking moron.'

They followed the BMW X5 across the junction. Then its brake lights went on and it stopped abruptly. Newfield stamped on the brake pedal and the ambulance screeched to a halt, stopping just a few inches from the SUV's rear bumper. 'You fucking idiot!' he shouted. 'What the fuck are you playing at?' He pounded on the horn. He looked in his rear-view mirror as a second BMW X5 pulled up behind him. 'What the hell is going on?'

The rear doors of the BMW in front of them opened and two men got out – big men in long coats. Newfield pounded on the horn again. One of the men, well over six feet tall with a jagged scar across his left cheek, walked over to Newfield's window and tapped on it. Newfield glared at the man then his eyes widened when he saw the gun the man had used to knock on the glass. 'Oh shit,' he said.

'What?' said Fleming. She looked over at the window and her jaw dropped when she saw the gun in the man's gloved hand.

The man tapped on the glass again, and Newfield wound the window down.

A second man appeared at Fleming's window. He was big too, with a shaved head and a square chin peppered with small scars.

He was also carrying a gun and he waved it at Fleming, then pointed for her to lower her window.

They heard a noise behind them and they both whirled around. A third man had pulled open the rear doors to the ambulance and climbed in.

'Don't look at him,' said the man outside Newfield's window. 'Look at me.'

Newfield turned his head. The barrel of the gun was just inches from his nose. His breath caught in his throat. He heard the ripping sound of the body bag being opened and he started to turn around but the man thrust the gun under his nose. 'Give me your wallet,' said the man.

'My what?'

'Your wallet.' The man pushed Newfield's head back with the gun. 'Now.'

'Okay, okay,' said Newfield. 'Sorry.' He pulled his wallet from his pocket and gave it to the man. The man opened it, took out Newfield's driving licence and tossed the wallet back. The man held the driving licence in front of Newfield's face. 'So, Edward Newfield, now I know where you live. If you give the police any sort of description of us, someone will pay you a visit. Are you married?'

The man had a heavy accent. Russian, maybe. Or one of those central or Eastern European countries that Newfield had read about in the papers. Nothing good ever came out of those countries, that much he knew. He nodded.

'Kids?'

'Two boys.'

'So, we'll rape your wife and your kids before we kill them,' growled the man. 'Then we'll beat you to within an inch of your life. You'll be crippled and you'll have to spend the rest of your life remembering what happened to your family.'

'I didn't see anything,' said Newfield. 'Not a thing.' A warm wetness spread around his groin and he realized that he'd soiled himself.

'Keep it that way,' said the man. He slipped the driving licence into his jacket pocket, then called out to the man in the back in a guttural language that Newfield didn't recognize.

The man in the back replied. He sounded like a dog, barking.

The man standing at the passenger side tapped his gun on the top of the Fleming's head. 'Licence,' he said.

Fleming fumbled in the top pocket of her shirt and pulled out her driving licence. The man took it from her and studied it. 'Miss Jane Fleming,' he said. 'So, no husband?'

'I'm engaged,' she whispered.

'I hope you have a long and happy life together,' said the man, in heavily accented English. He put the licence in his coat pocket. 'And the only way that's going to happen is if you forget everything you've seen.'

The man in the back stood up and said something. He was clearly unhappy.

The man next to Newfield barked back at him, and he climbed out and slammed the doors shut.

'You have a choice to make now, Edward,' said the man at Newfield's window. 'You and your partner can call the police. If you do that, you need to wait at least five minutes. And when the police do come, you don't give them a description of us or our vehicles. Do you understand?' The BMW X5 that had been behind them pulled out and drove down the road.

Newfield nodded fearfully.

'Or you can decide not to call the police. Just drive to wherever you were going and you and Jane can just pretend it never happened. Get on with your lives and this can just be an upsetting dream.' The man grinned, showing several gold teeth at the side of his mouth. 'It's your call, Edward. Yours and Jane's. I'll leave you to talk it through.'

The man turned and walked quickly back to the BMW, his long coat flapping behind him. The man who had taken Fleming's licence joined him and they climbed into the back of the vehicle. They slammed the doors and it sped off down the road.

CHAPTER 6

Bird ran along the pavement. He kept his parka hood up and his head down but he knew they'd have no problem tracking him on CCTV. The parka was distinctive enough but it was Tyson that would be the giveaway. He was running at Bird's side, matching his pace, ears back and tail out. There was a side road to their left. He slowed and turned. Tyson went with him.

Bird took a quick look over his shoulder to reassure himself that they weren't being followed. He was sure that the police would be flooding into the area – it would be all hands to the pump.

There was an intersection ahead of them and Bird went right. It took them onto a main road and he looked up and down but didn't see any police. A group of teenagers vaping on the other side of the road turned to look at him. Bird slowed. Running was a surefire way of drawing attention to himself.

Tyson matched his speed. There was a supermarket ahead of them, with a line of black waste skips to the side. Bird took another look around. There wasn't much traffic and definitely no police vehicles but he wasn't sure how long that would last. The first thing they'd do was to drive down all the roads in the vicinity of the shootings. The sooner he got off the street, the better.

He walked over to the skips. There were three of them, two had been pushed together and there was a gap of a couple of feet between them and the third. He pushed his way into the gap, then used his shoulder to move the middle skip away from the wall to make enough room for himself and Tyson. The supermarket was one of his regular haunts – they usually threw out food that was past its sell-by date in the early hours, and he was partial to their croissants. It was a good place to get meat for Tyson, who was especially fond of their pork sausages.

Bird squatted down with his back to the wall and took out his wallet. He used the light of his phone to read the card that Joel had given him. Across the top in capital letters was UNHOUSED OUTREACH PROGRAMME. Bird smiled thinly. Someone, somewhere, had decided that 'unhoused' was more acceptable than 'homeless'. Probably the same person who decided to switch 'disabled' with 'differently abled'. Underneath the heading was Joel's full name – Joel Kingsley – and a mobile phone number.

Bird put the card away and sent a text: **Hi Joel, it's Andy (and Tyson). Can we take you up on your offer of a lift?**

He stared at the screen for several seconds, then the reply arrived. **Sure, give me 10 minutes.**

Bird tapped out a second message. **We had to move.** Then he sent him a Google Earth screenshot that showed his position.

The reply came in less than a minute. **No problem. With you in 10.**

Bird placed his phone on the ground and pulled a bottle of water from his Bergen. He sloshed some into Tyson's plastic bowl, then took a drink.

Tyson lapped at his water, his tail wagging. Bird patted him on the back.

They needed to get out of the area. The police would probably be using a set of concentric circles for their search pattern, based on the fact that he and Tyson were on foot. For the first half hour or so they would concentrate their search within about half a mile of where he had last been seen. Then they would probably widen their search area to a mile. There was a chance that they would place roadblocks on the perimeter. If he wasn't found then they would widen their search area, out to two miles, maybe.

There were close to fifteen thousand people per square mile in London, but they knew exactly what they were looking for – a man with a Bergen and a dog. Bird wasn't prepared to abandon Tyson, and dumping the rucksack meant losing all his worldly possessions. He wasn't convinced that there'd be much benefit anyway.

A helicopter flashed overhead. It was gone before he had time to focus on it so he couldn't tell if it was a Met heli after him or a commuter flight. The Met heli would be fitted with infra-red cameras and his body heat would give him away, though the buildings either side of the alley offered him some protection.

The minutes ticked by. Cars drove by both ends of the alley. Several times Bird saw police cars, but they kept on going.

After ten minutes. Bird sent Joel another text message. **On your way?**

His phone vibrated almost immediately. **2 mins.**

It was followed by a second text. **North on Arlington Road.**

Bird picked up Tyson's bowl, shook it dry, and slid it into his Bergen along with the bottle of water. He stood up, shouldered the bag and pushed his way out from behind the skips. He took a look around and headed towards Arlington Road, keeping close to the wall. Tyson walked with him, his shoulder pressed against Bird's knee.

Bird looked south down the road. There was a white van heading towards them, then a motorcycle, then a line of saloon cars. He looked north and cursed when he saw a police car. He backed away and hid behind the skips again. His heart was racing and his palms were sweating, and it was only when the car drove by that he realized he had been holding his breath.

He exhaled and smiled ruefully at Tyson. 'Jumping at shadows,' he said. 'Sorry.'

He peered out between the skips. The police car was heading south. Two saloons, a Honda and a Volvo, were driving towards him. Neither slowed and both drove by. In the distance, a grey Prius switched on its hazard warning lights and slowed.

'That's him,' said Bird. He stepped out from the skips and jogged to the pavement. Tyson followed, sticking close. Bird waved at the Prius and the lights flashed. Bird looked left and right and jogged across the road to the passenger side. Joel wound the window down. 'Changed your mind, then?'

'Sorry, yeah. My bad.'

'Tyson's okay in the back?'

'Sure,' said Bird. He opened the rear passenger door. 'In,' he said. Tyson jumped into the back and Bird placed his Bergen next to him before closing the door.

'Everything okay?' asked Joel as Bird climbed into the front.

'I guess,' said Bird, pulling the door shut.

'You look stressed. Did something happen?'

'Not really.'

'I know how dangerous it can be on the streets at night,' said Joel. 'I've already spoken to a shelter in Islington and they have a spare bed ready for you. I mentioned Tyson and they said there's a place outside where he can be tied up. There are a few dog owners there.'

Bird grimaced. 'I just need a lift to Hampstead. I'll be fine there.'

'The C4WS shelter? I'm pretty sure they're full tonight.'

'Just the Heath, Joel. I'll be fine.'

'You're planning to sleep on the Heath? I'd advise against that.'

'I'll be fine.'

Joel nodded and pulled away from the kerb.

'This your car, Joel? Nice.'

Joel replied but Bird couldn't see his lips. 'Sorry, Joel, I have to lip-read, remember?'

Joel grinned. He turned his head slightly to the left. 'I don't want to take my eyes off the road, how's this?'

Bird twisted around in his seat and leant forwards. 'Yes, this'll work. But be careful.'

'Okay. I do ride-sharing in my spare time. Pays my way through uni.'

'Uber?'

'Some Uber, but Bolt pays better.' He grinned. 'And I can see you trying to change the subject, Andy. But if you don't want to tell me what's up, that's fine. I'm here to help, not pry. Your business is your business.'

'You're a star, Joel. Thank you.'

'So, where on the Heath?'

'Anywhere.'

'You've slept there before?'

Bird nodded. 'Now and again.'

Joel frowned as he looked in his rear-view mirror.

'What's up?' asked Bird, checking the side mirror. There was a grey BMW X5 behind them.

Joel was facing forwards again so Bird missed what the man had said.

'I didn't get that, sorry,' said Bird.

Joel turned to look at him. 'This guy is right up my arse. Has been for a minute or so. Arsehole.'

Bird could see two men in the BMW SUV. It wasn't a police vehicle. But Joel was right, they were close.

'Why do people drive like that?' said Joel. 'It's a twenty limit here anyway.'

'Just let him go by if he's in a hurry,' said Bird.

Joel slowed and moved over to the left. Almost immediately the BMW X5 accelerated and pulled out. It drew level with the Prius. Bird looked over. The front passenger was looking at them. Shaved head, crooked nose, hard eyes. The man's eyes flicked to the back seat of the Prius, where Tyson was sitting, staring out of the window. He said something to the driver but Bird wasn't able to read his lips. But from the look on the man's face, it didn't appear to be chit-chat.

'Turn off the road,' said Bird.

Joel looked at him. 'What?'

'Let's get off this road,' said Bird. 'Just hang a left.'

'What's going on, Andy?'

'Just make the turn,' said Bird.

The BMW accelerated away from them.

Bird looked at the side mirror again. There was another BMW X5 tucked in behind them. This one was green. It looked as if there were three men in the vehicle. Maybe four. 'Joel, please, turn off as soon as you can. Right or left, it doesn't matter.'

'There's nowhere to turn,' said Joel. 'What's going on, Andy?' He looked in the rear-view mirror. 'There's another one, behind us,' he said, his voice trembling. 'Who are they? What do they want? Are they cops?'

'No, they're not cops.'

'They're after you? What have you done, Andy? What's going on?'

Before Bird could reply, the brake lights of the vehicle in front of them went on. Joel braked hard, cursing out loud. The seat belt strained against Bird's shoulders and Tyson smacked against Joel's seat and fell to the floor.

Bird checked the side mirror. The BMW X5 behind them had also braked. The front passenger was on his phone.

The Prius came to a halt about six feet from the rear of the SUV. 'Joel, you need to run for it!' shouted Bird, as he grabbed the door handle.

Tyson had scrambled back onto his seat and was looking at Bird, waiting for instructions.

Joel pulled out his mobile phone. 'I'm calling the police!' he shouted.

'There's no time,' said Bird. He threw open the door and stepped out of the car. The front passenger door of the grey BMW X5 was opening. 'Run, Joel!' he shouted. 'Run.' He pulled the rear passenger door open and Tyson jumped out, tail wagging.

The doors of the green BMW were opening. Bird could now see that there were four men in the vehicle. He pointed at it. 'Attack!' he shouted.

Tyson charged towards the vehicle, his tail out straight behind him.

Joel had his phone to his ear. He was wasting his time, Bird knew – it would all be over one way or the other long before the police arrived at the scene. Bird pointed at him. 'Joel, for fuck's sake, run!'

Bird turned and ran towards the grey BMW. The passenger's left foot was already out. Bird kicked the door, smashing it against the man's leg, then grabbed it and banged it against the leg three times, hard. The man pushed against the door and Bird stepped back. The man was holding a gun in his right hand. A Glock. He aimed it at Bird's face but Bird slammed the door against the man's leg again. The gun went off but the shot went wide.

The driver was climbing out now. Bird couldn't see if he was holding a gun, but he had to assume that he was.

He pulled the door open, shuffled to the side and punched the passenger in the nose, feeling the cartilage practically explode as blood spurted down the man's chin. Bird grabbed the gun, twisted it out of the man's grasp and pulled the trigger twice, putting two rounds in the man's chest. He fell back into the car, a look of confusion on his face.

A round whizzed by Bird's face and clipped his ear. The pain was no worse than a bee sting but he felt the blood flow. He ducked down and a second round cracked through the air where his head had been.

Bird fired at the driver's chest. The man shuddered and his shirt turned bloody. Bird fired again and the driver fell back and slumped into the road.

Bird straightened up and looked back at the second BMW. Tyson had his jaws locked on to the leg of the front passenger and was dragging him out of the vehicle. The rear doors were open and the men at the back were climbing out, big men with shaved heads and black bomber jackets.

Joel opened his door and stepped out, looking left and right, his face drained of colour. 'Get away, Joel!' shouted Bird, but Joel stayed where he was, transfixed with fear.

The passenger nearest the pavement stepped away from the green SUV, pulling a pistol from inside his jacket. He aimed it at Tyson but before he could pull the trigger Bird put two rounds in his chest. The man fell back, his arms flailing, and the gun clattered on the pavement. Tyson continued to drag his quarry from the vehicle.

Bird looked back at Joel. 'Run, Joel!' he shouted.

Joel was frowning in confusion, trying to process what was happening around him. Bird was used to combat, so was Tyson, and they had both been trained to function under stress, but for a civilian, the ear-splitting crack of gunfire and the sight of blood often led to paralysis, literally rooting them to the spot. Most people had heard of the fight or flight response, but there was another reaction – freeze. That was generally what happened to civilians caught in a firefight. Joel had frozen, and that made him a sitting duck.

Bird ran around the front of the Prius. He grabbed Joel by the scruff of the neck. 'Come on!' he shouted.

The second rear passenger stepped away from the green X5, holding his weapon with both hands. It was an Uzi, Bird realized, or a MAC-10. With a bulbous suppressor. The standard Uzi fired at ten rounds a second, the MAC-10 at more than twice that rate, but at close range the difference was immaterial. The man's hair was receding and cut short, and as he turned his head Bird realized that the lower part of his left ear was missing.

Joel still wasn't moving. Bird aimed his Glock at the shooter but he was aiming one-handed and the moment he pulled the trigger he knew that he'd missed. The shot went high. He didn't want to let go of Joel but firing one-handed wasn't going to get the job done so he released his grip on the man's collar. He brought his left hand up to support his right but before he could take aim the machine pistol burst into life and a hail of bullets ripped through Joel, jerking him like a marionette. The windows of the Prius exploded.

'No!' screamed Bird.

The rounds kept coming and he had no choice but to dive onto the pavement and crawl behind the Prius for cover.

Joel fell against the car and slid to the ground.

Tyson was still playing tug of war with the front passenger's leg.

'Leave!' shouted Bird. 'Heel!'

Tyson responded immediately, releasing his grip on the man's leg and running back to Bird.

The machine pistol stopped firing. Bird's lack of hearing meant that he had no idea how many rounds had been fired. Ten, maybe. Twelve. Fifteen. He had no way of knowing for sure. The .45 ACP model of the MAC-10 generally came with thirty-round magazines, while the 9 mm magazine held thirty-two rounds. The original Uzi had a twenty-five round magazine but the thirty-two round magazine had later become standard. Bird didn't get a good look at the weapon, so there could be as few as five rounds left and possibly more than twenty. More than enough, either way, to make him keep his head down.

Tyson dropped down next to Bird. 'Sorry about this,' said Bird, patting Tyson on the back. He looked down the pavement towards the green BMW. The front passenger was lying on the pavement, the left leg of his jeans torn and bloody.

The driver's door opened and a booted foot stepped out. Bird lay on the tarmac, sighted on the boot and pulled the trigger. The round ricocheted off the ground. Bird tried to aim again but the boot disappeared and the door slammed shut.

Bird ran through his options. In a perfect world he'd be running against the direction of the vehicles, to make it harder for them to give chase. But three of the occupants of the green BMW were alive and at least one had a machine pistol. Running south wasn't an option.

The driver of the grey BMW was dead and his colleague wasn't far behind, so north was the better option, but as soon as he moved away from the Prius the guy with the machine pistol had an easy target. He had only seconds to decide what to do, because the men in the green SUV were going to get their act together, sooner rather than later.

He ejected the magazine of his Glock and did a quick count. He had fired nine rounds and there were eight left. He slotted the magazine back into place.

What pedestrians there had been on the pavement had run for their lives, but cars were still driving by, slowing as the drivers tried to see what was happening. Bird looked north. There was a side road about fifty feet ahead of the grey BMW. That appeared to be his only choice.

He nodded at Tyson. 'Stay close,' he said. He stood up and fired two quick shots in the direction of the green BMW. The guy with the machine pistol ducked. Bird fired again, more accurately this time, and the round screeched off the roof of the SUV just inches from where the man was hiding. Bird waited a second, fired again, then turned and ran. Tyson stuck to his heels.

Fifty feet wasn't far, not in the grand scheme of things, but it was one hell of a long way to run when there was a man aiming a machine pistol at your back. Bird tried to blot the gun out of his mind and concentrated on the pavement ahead of him. He had his head down and his arms were pumping. Tyson's run was considerably more graceful, and faster. Bird knew Tyson was having to hold himself back to keep pace. 'Run!' shouted Bird. If the firing started, he wanted Tyson out of the way.

Bird could have stopped and fired another shot but for all he knew the shooter already had his gun lined up. Better to stay low and run. He was halfway there. Twenty-five feet. Tyson was ahead of him now, running flat out. It was a beautiful sight, his powerful rhythmic strides propelling him forwards like a missile, his tail straight out like a rudder to keep his balance, his body low to minimize air resistance.

Bird began to zig-zag. It meant losing speed but made him a harder target. Tyson reached the side road. 'Left, left, left!' shouted

Bird. Tyson reacted immediately, turning on the spot and racing down the side street.

A window to Bird's left shattered and broken glass cascaded over the pavement. Rounds thwacked into the brickwork above the window, kicking up spurts of dust. He hadn't heard the shots and didn't know if the shooter was still firing but he kept low as he hurtled around the corner.

Tyson was about ten feet away, poetry in motion, his ears back and his tail out. 'Heel!' shouted Bird and Tyson slowed. Bird reached him in three paces and then Tyson stuck to his right knee, matching his speed.

There was no traffic on the side street, though there were cars moving either way along the main road ahead of them. There was an alley on the other side of the street and Bird checked both ways before rushing across the road. He stopped at the entrance and looked over his shoulder. There was no sign of either of the BMW X5s.

'Come on, boy,' he said, and headed into the alley. It was narrow, lined with brick walls dotted with wooden doors. By each door was an assortment of plastic rubbish bins. Bird continued to run. If the X5s gave chase he and Tyson would be sitting ducks. His chest was burning now and his knees were aching but he blotted out the pain and concentrated on the ground ahead of him. The alley was dark and the ground was uneven and the last thing he wanted was to trip and sprain an ankle. There definitely were times when four legs were better than two.

As he reached the midway point, Bird slowed and looked over his shoulder. His heart sank when he saw one of the X5s turning into the alley. It was too dark to tell if it was green or grey, not that the colour mattered.

Tyson was also looking over his shoulder. As they watched, the BMW switched its headlights on full beam. The glare wiped out Bird's night vision and he looked away, blinking. He grabbed at the nearest bin and toppled it over. The lid fell open and the contents spilled across the ground. Tyson stopped to watch him, his tail twitching from side to side. Bird grabbed another bin and threw it to the ground. And another.

The SUV continued to move towards them.

Bird pulled over two more bins, then ran down the alley to another group, which he also scattered on the ground.

The SUV was moving faster now. Bird threw two small recycling bins into the middle of the alley. The BMW X5 was a big vehicle – weighing close to three tonnes – and was capable of smashing through metal barriers. The bins were flimsy but Bird's hope was the plastic would jam the wheels.

He ran a few steps, toppled over two more large bins and half a dozen smaller ones.

The BMW hit the first group of bins. One of the large ones went under the bumper and then jammed. The car scraped it along the ground as it continued to move forwards.

Bird looked over at Tyson. 'Run,' he said, and started sprinting down the alley. Tyson stuck to his heels. The SUV's headlights threw their shadows against the sides of the alley.

Bird paused to pull over two more bins. The SUV had slowed and a second bin was now jammed under the bumper.

They ran out of the alley. Bird looked left and right. There was only one vehicle on the road, a black cab heading north, its light on. Bird jogged towards it, holding his hand up. Tyson stayed by his side. Bird wasn't sure what the rules were for black cabs picking up dogs, but the cab braked and came to a halt. The driver looked at him expectantly but Bird didn't say anything, he just pulled the door open and climbed in. Tyson joined him. 'Just drive, please,' said Bird.

CHAPTER 7

The driver was watching Bird in the rear-view mirror and Bird realized that he must have said something. He leant forwards and tapped on the glass partition. The driver twisted around in his seat, frowning. Bird flashed him a smile. 'Sorry, mate, I'm deaf. I can read lips but I need to be able to see your face.'

'Sorry, guv, didn't realize.' He began to speak slowly, emphasizing each word. 'I was asking where you want to go.'

It was a good question. 'The hell out of here,' was what he wanted to say, but he needed to be more specific. His brain raced, trying to come up with a destination. He needed somewhere close by, he needed to get off the streets as soon as possible. All he could think of was Billy O'Neill's flat, which was about a mile away. Billy was a former Army pal who had let him sleep in his garden shed for a few weeks before complaining neighbours had forced him out. It had been a few months since Bird had been in contact with Billy, but he was pretty sure that he'd help him out, at least for a day or two.

'Do you understand me?' said the driver again, enunciating each word. 'Where you go?'

Bird wanted to snap that he was deaf and not stupid, but there was nothing to be gained by antagonizing the man so he just smiled and gave him Billy's address.

The driver repeated the address syllable by syllable, then turned and drove off. Tyson had curled up at Bird's feet and he bent down and patted him on the back. A police car turned onto the main road ahead of them. Its blue lights were flashing and Tyson's ears pricked up so Bird guessed that the sirens were on. He settled back in his seat as he considered his options. He couldn't go to the police, not after he'd used the gun that he'd taken from the armed cop. He hadn't been aiming at the cop but he'd be facing a charge of attempted murder at the very least. Ten years behind bars, maybe longer. And they'd put Tyson down, no question.

Then there was the body in the alley. The first set of cops had seen him standing over the body and his prints would be on the gun. That was open and shut, no matter what he told them. They had heard the shot and Bird had been alone with the body when they arrived. That could be twenty years. Life, maybe.

Then there were the men in the BMW X5s. He'd killed in self-defence, there was no question about it, but that wouldn't make a difference and they would be determined to track him down. His Bergen was in the back of Joel's Prius, and if they were pros they would have grabbed it. There was enough personal stuff in the Bergen to identify Bird.

Just who the hell were these guys? Were they gangsters? Foreign spies? Or government-sanctioned killers? Whoever they were, Bird was between a rock and a hard place.

Murdering a man in a dark alley was one thing, but opening fire with a machine pistol in a busy street was a whole different ball game. They'd obviously come after Bird because he'd seen them kill the guy in the alley and didn't want him to identify them. The big question was would they now give up, or would they carry on looking for him? Bird took a quick look over his shoulder and his eyes widened when he saw a BMW X5 behind him. He slid down the seat, his heart racing. Were they following him? Had they seen him get into the black cab?

The taxi driver was slowing, getting ready to turn right. There were several cars coming towards him and he tapped the steering wheel as he waited.

The BMW moved to the left. Bird braced himself, though there wasn't much he could do if they opened fire – the rounds would rip through the black cab like a knife through butter.

The BMW drew level. Bird pressed himself back against the seat. If they did open fire his only option would be to try to get out the other side of the cab, but by then it would be too late.

He squinted to the left. The driver was a young blonde woman, early thirties, nodding as she spoke. There was another woman, a brunette, in the front passenger seat. Bird sighed with relief and the cab made the right turn as the SUV accelerated away.

The minutes ticked by. Bird didn't see any more police vehicles or BMW X5s but he remained tense. The taxi took a left turn and then a right. Bird recognized the street and sat up, peering out of the side window. There were terraces of white-painted houses running along both sides, cars parked nose to tail in the street. Billy's flat was in a building on the south side of the road, midway along the terrace.

The driver twisted around in his seat and said something, but Bird didn't catch it. 'Sorry, mate, I missed that,' he said.

The driver brought the cab to a stop and turned around. 'I said, is this okay, guv?' he said, slowly and clearly.

'Perfect, thanks,' said Bird. He reached into his pocket and pulled out a handful of change and counted out the coins. When he realized that he only had enough to cover the fare and a small tip, he poured all the coins into the cabbie's hand. 'Sorry,' he said.

'Money's money,' said the driver. 'Stay safe, yeah?'

'I'll do my best,' said Bird. 'Thank you.'

He climbed out and waited for Tyson to join him on the pavement before slamming the door. As the taxi drove away, Bird looked around. No pedestrians, no police vehicles, no BMW X5s. So far, so good.

He walked along to Billy's building. Billy's flat was in the basement, with its own entrance at the bottom of a narrow flight of concrete steps. There was a black wrought-iron gate at the top of the steps and Bird gingerly pushed it open. He took another look around and ushered Tyson down the steps, before pulling the gate closed.

There were black metal bars over the windows and a burglar alarm box fixed to the wall. It wasn't the roughest neighbourhood, but it was far from being a sleepy suburb.

Bird rang the bell. He left it thirty seconds before ringing again, then he rattled the letterbox. Tyson stared at the door with his ears up, and woofed quietly. 'Looks like he might not be in,' whispered Bird. He fished out his mobile and sent a text message to Billy's mobile number. **Are you there?** He waited a minute or so and when no reply was forthcoming he sent another. **BILLY????**

After another minute he sent another text message. **It's Andy. I'm outside your flat. I'm in a bit of a jam and I need your help.**

It was just before three o'clock in the morning and the fact that Billy wasn't answering suggested that he'd turned his phone off.

Tyson sat down and looked at him, waiting for instructions. Bird ran through his options. The police would ID him eventually, no question of that. The Army had his fingerprints and DNA on file. He didn't know if the police would have access to the Army's database, but he would have to assume that they did, which meant that sooner or later they would know who he was. He smiled grimly.

Bird squatted down next to Tyson. The cops wouldn't stop searching for him, not for a few hours at least. He wouldn't be hard to find, either, a homeless man with a big dog. His best bet was to lie low until the heat died down. He stared at his phone, willing it to show a message, but the screen stayed blank.

Billy was probably sleeping somewhere else that night. He had a girlfriend, Vicky, who worked in PR for an internet bank and had a place in Wapping, so maybe he was there. Vicky had never liked Bird, and she had disliked Tyson even more. Bird always suspected that it was she who wanted him and Tyson out of the garden shed and that Billy had only blamed the neighbours, but either way he knew that they had overstayed their welcome and he had handed over his key without protesting.

Tyson growled softly. 'I know, I know, we can't stay here all night,' whispered Bird. Anyone who walked by would see them if they looked down. And if a passer-by or a neighbour called the police, it would all be over. He frowned as he looked at the line of plastic boxes on the wall opposite the front door. There were six of them, each containing a gas meter. Billy usually left an emergency key under his box, had done ever since he had locked himself out and been forced to pay a locksmith a hundred and twenty quid to get back inside. Bird went over and groped under the bottom box on the left and grinned when he felt the key covered in duct tape. He ripped off the tape and kissed the key. 'Nice one,' he muttered to himself. He headed back to the door and unlocked it. Bird knew that the burglar alarm console would now be beeping, even though he couldn't hear it. He hurried inside, saying a silent prayer that Billy hadn't changed the code.

The code pad was on the wall facing him. He tapped in the four digits and breathed a sigh of relief when the console showed that the alarm was off. He ushered Tyson in then closed the door and slipped the bolt across. He didn't switch the light on. He knew the layout well enough to move around in darkness. He went through the sitting room, by the bathroom and bedroom on his left, and into the kitchen. He closed the door before switching on the light. The kitchen window looked out onto a walled garden, so no one could look in. At the end of the garden was the wooden shed that Bird and Tyson had called home for almost six weeks. There was a camp bed and an electric lantern and to be honest it hadn't been a bad place to stay. Bird had stayed in worse. Much worse.

He dropped his parka on a chair and went through to the bathroom. His ear was bloody but the bleeding seemed to have stopped. He opened the medicine cabinet, took out a cotton bud and a bottle of TCP, and dabbed at the wound. Once it was clean, he took an

Elastoplast from the cabinet and applied it. He looked down at the bath. It had been more than a week since he had showered, and much longer than that since he'd had a bath. Most days he was lucky to grab a wash in the toilets of a petrol station or a fast-food restaurant. Billy was already going to be spitting feathers that Bird was in his flat – having a bath wasn't going to make him any angrier. Bird turned the taps on and added a squirt of Radox Muscle Therapy Bath Soak.

While the bath was filling, he went back to the kitchen and opened the fridge. There was an opened pack of Richmond sausages on the top shelf. Bird took it out, put the sausages on a plate and placed it on the floor in front of Tyson. Tyson gulped them down as Bird checked out the rest of the contents of the fridge. There were several Marks & Spencer ready meals and packs of prepared salad, half a dozen cans of Guinness, a block of cheddar cheese and a jar of Hellman's mayonnaise. There was half a Hovis wholemeal loaf in the bread bin, so Bird made himself a cheese salad sandwich and popped open a Guinness. He had finished his meal and was halfway through the can by the time the bath was full.

Bird turned off the taps. He checked his phone. Still no reply from Billy. Billy ran a small security company, providing doormen to pubs and shops and security guards for building sites, and if he was short-handed, he would often work a shift himself. It wasn't unusual for him to be out all night.

Tyson's ears pricked up and he looked along the hall towards the front door. His tail was up and his ears were twitching, always a sign that he had heard something. Bird switched off the bathroom light, then tiptoed back to the kitchen and switched that light off too.

'Stay,' he said, and moved slowly towards the sitting room. The blinds were down so he couldn't see anything. He tiptoed over to the window and carefully separated two of the slats. There were two men outside, big men in long coats. One of them was close to the front door, his arms up as he worked on the lock. They might be the guys from the alley, but he couldn't be sure. There was a third man at the top of the steps. Bird let the slats fall back into place. There were two locks, both Banhams, which were difficult to pick.

Difficult, but not impossible. If they were professionals, it was just a matter of time.

Bird tiptoed over to the burglar alarm console and tapped in the four-digit number to set the system, then hurried back down the hallway. He headed back into the kitchen and pulled on his parka before unlocking the back door. He was about to leave but then grabbed the cheese from the fridge and stuffed it into his parka pocket. He took a knife from the knife block, wrapped the blade in a tea towel and put it in the inside pocket of the parka.

Tyson looked towards the front door. Maybe he had heard it open, or maybe the alarm console had beeped to announce that the system was set. Either way, Bird knew that he had to move quickly.

He headed outside and as soon as Tyson had followed him, he locked the door. He jogged towards the shed. The kitchen door was the only way into the garden. There were eight-feet high brick walls on either side and facing him was the rear wall of the house in the mews opposite. There were two windows set into the top of the mews house, but they were in darkness.

Bird looked left and right. There were six houses to the left, each with their own garden. There were ten to the right, so it was an easy call. He hurried over to the wall on his left and bent at the waist. 'Over,' he said.

Tyson didn't hesitate. He sprang forwards, jumped with his front legs extended and landed on Bird's back. Then he thrust himself up using his back legs to propel himself over the top of the wall.

Bird's jump was considerably less graceful. He jumped, grabbed the top of the wall and hauled himself over. He rolled over the top and dropped down onto a flower bed. Tyson stood watching him, and Bird would have sworn that the dog was grinning. 'How about you give me a leg up, next time?' whispered Bird. He stayed down in a crouch as he surveyed the rear of the house next door. Like Billy's building, the house had been converted into flats, with kitchen windows to the right and bedroom windows to the left. All the windows were dark.

Bird hurried across the grass to a flower bed next to the far wall and bent down. 'Over,' he said again, and Tyson needed no urging – he ran, jumped onto Bird's back and went over the wall in one smooth, fluid motion.

Bird followed, scraping his boots on the bricks as he hauled himself over. He fell heavily onto gravel, lost his balance and rolled over onto his back. Tyson licked his face, panting heavily. Bird could smell the sausages on Tyson's breath and he pushed him away. 'This isn't a bloody joke, Tyson,' said Bird. He got to his feet and wiped his hands on his parka.

The windows of this house were also in darkness, and Bird crossed the gravelled area as quietly as he could. As he reached the far wall, a light went on in the second-floor bedroom, casting shadows across the wall of the mews house bordering the garden. Bird looked up. There was someone in the window, looking down. The figure was in silhouette, but Bird was sure it was a man. The man put something to his ear. A phone. Bird cursed under his breath. He wasn't sure how quickly the police would generally react to a report of an intruder in a garden, but once they heard it was a man and a dog, they'd probably pull out all the stops. He ran over to the wall and bent down. 'Over,' he shouted.

CHAPTER 8

By the time they reached the last wall, Bird was out of breath and his arms and legs were aching. Tyson didn't seem to be having any problems, and was barely panting. Bird bent down and didn't even have to give the command before Tyson was up and over. Bird knew that there was a road on the other side of the pavement. He jumped up, hauled himself to the top and looked right and left. There were no cars or pedestrians. Tyson was looking up at him, wagging his tail, clearly enjoying himself. Bird kicked up his right leg and rolled over, pivoting in mid-air so that he landed on his feet. He let his knees take the strain and held his arms out to the side to maintain his balance, but he still fell back and hit the wall.

Tyson hurried over to offer his support. 'I'm okay,' said Bird. He patted Tyson on the head as he looked around. The heavies would have arrived on the road to his left and they must have at least one vehicle, so he had to go right, which was roughly south. He still wanted to head to Hampstead Heath, which was now to the west, because the Heath offered the best chance of concealment, but beggars couldn't be choosers. His pursuers hopefully wouldn't know which way he had gone. Would they have gone over the wall after him? And what about the burglar alarm? If it had gone off, they'd have been more likely to pile back into their vehicles and leave. Either way he had to move, and quickly.

'Heel,' he said, and started jogging down the pavement. There was still no traffic on the road so he ran across and turned into a side street. There were no pedestrians, so Bird ran at full pelt. He turned right, then left. Navigation had always been one of his strengths and he knew exactly where he was and where he was heading. The Hilldrop Estate was about a mile away to the south-west, and would offer him temporary refuge. It had been built by London County Council soon after the Second World War ended. The council had hoped that they were building homes for heroes, but over the decades the heroes had passed away and their places had been taken by drug dealers and families on benefits. There were a dozen or so four- and five-storey brick buildings at the junction of Brecknock Road and Carleton Road, with small yards at the front, and a children's playground in the middle of the estate. It wasn't exactly a no-go area for the police, but they mostly visited mob-handed in vans, with batons and Tasers at the ready. The drugs gangs that operated there had spotters monitoring who came and went, and strangers were easily spotted. A homeless guy with a dog could walk through the area with impunity, but heavies driving around in BMW X5s would attract attention.

The estate was just over a mile to the south-east of Hampstead Heath, so he could lie low there and make his way to the Heath when things had quietened down. He kept to the side roads wherever possible, ducking behind parked cars whenever he saw a vehicle approaching. He reached the estate without catching sight of a police car or a BMW X5.

Two youngsters with BMX bikes were sitting on a wall at the entrance to the estate. One of the boys was on his mobile. He could have been talking to his girlfriend or could be letting his gang know that they had a visitor, Bird had no way of knowing. But he did know that dawn was fast approaching and that was when the police tended to carry out their raids on the estate, so it made sense for the gangs to have watchers out.

Bird waved a hand in greeting. 'Have you got a ciggie?' he asked, playing the part of a homeless person down on his luck.

'Smoking's a killer,' said the lad who wasn't on his phone. 'Haven't you heard of cancer?'

'I'm trying to cut down,' said Bird.

'I can sell you puff or whizz, mandy or wonk. Whatever floats your boat.'

Bird knew that puff was cannabis and whizz was amphetamine, and was pretty sure that mandy was ecstasy, but he had never heard of wonk. Maybe he had misread the guy's lips. 'Wonk?' he repeated.

The boy nodded. 'Wonk. Special K. Kat. Ketamine.'

'Ah, the horse drug.'

'You want some?'

Bird shook his head.

The boy scowled at him. 'Then move on and stop wasting my time, bruv.'

Bird flashed him a thumbs up and headed into the estate with Tyson at his heels.

The sky ahead of him was streaked with red now. He walked towards the children's playground. There was a clump of trees close by and he sat down in the middle and stretched out his legs. Tyson curled up by his side, nose to tail. He took the packet of cheese from his pocket, broke off a piece and chewed on it as he considered his options. He was fairly sure that he had given the police and the X5s the slip. He doubted that they would find him on the Heath. There were almost eight hundred acres of hills, woodland and ponds, and it was next to the sprawling estate of stately Kenwood House. He and Tyson could drink from the ponds, and there were public toilets where Bird could wash himself. His razor was in his Bergen so he wouldn't be able to shave, and he'd be looking rough after a few days, but he could still keep himself clean.

He could go for weeks on minimum rations, but Tyson would need feeding. The Heath would only be a temporary refuge. At some point he was going to have to get out of London, but where could he go? He had been born in Sheffield and his parents still lived there, but they were getting on and it had been years since he had seen them. And if the cops did identify him, they'd probably put a watch on their house. He had a younger brother who lived in Doncaster, but they had lost touch and the last that Bird had heard was that he had a drugs problem and had been in and out of prison for burglary.

The only other place that Bird was familiar with was Hereford, the town that was five miles to the south-east of the SAS's Stirling Lines barracks at Credenhill. During his ten years with the Regiment, Bird had become familiar with most of the town's pubs and curry houses, but he had never been back since he and Tyson had been kicked out. Bird would have been ashamed to have been seen living rough in the town, and he didn't want to be constantly reminded of the life that he had lost.

His best bet would be to start again in a new city. Manchester, maybe. Birmingham. Or Glasgow. Somewhere he wasn't known. Somewhere that the cops wouldn't be looking for him. But with hardly any money and only his driving licence as ID, starting again was easier said than done.

He popped another chunk of cheese into his mouth, wrapped up the rest and put the pack into his pocket.

Headlights swept across the block ahead of him and a black BMW X5 drove onto the estate. It was followed by a second vehicle, another X5, green or grey or silver. So there were three cars pursuing him, at least. Bird cursed under his breath and took out the Glock. Tyson pricked his ears up.

The doors to the lead BMW opened and two men climbed out. Bomber jackets, jeans and baseball caps. They were holding guns. He couldn't make out faces – they were about a hundred yards away from Bird, on the other side of the children's playground. They were looking in his direction but Bird was fairly sure they couldn't see him. The clump of trees he was in was in total darkness.

Bird stroked Tyson's flank. There was no point in running, he would just draw attention to himself. A gunfight wouldn't end well, either, as he only had eight rounds in his magazine.

The doors to the second BMW opened and three men got out. Bird was pretty sure they had been in the second car from the shoot-out in Camden. The five men stood together. One of them pointed towards the trees where Bird was hiding. Bird frowned. There was no way that they could know where he was, surely?

Then two black Mercedes saloons arrived and came to a stop behind the BMWs. Eight young men piled out. Four had machetes that they held by their sides. Two were carrying what looked like Ingram machine pistols. Half a dozen men had appeared on the balconies of the block overlooking the vehicles. One was holding a shotgun, the rest were brandishing pistols. It looked as if the local drugs gang was defending its turf.

The men from the BMW X5s didn't pull out their guns – they had obviously realized that a gunfight would only end one way. They all kept their hands in plain view.

Two of the new arrivals walked over to the SUVs. They didn't seem to be armed but there was a lot of gesturing and pointing going on. Bird could imagine what was being said. The men from the SUVs raised their hands to show that they weren't a threat and they all slowly climbed back into the vehicles. After a few seconds, they drove off. The drug dealers watched them go until they had driven off the estate, then they got together into a huddle for a few minutes, obviously congratulating themselves.

The men disappeared from the balconies and after a few minutes the gang members got back into their cars and drove away. Job done.

Bird took out his phone and stared at it. It was the only way that the men in the X5s could have tracked him to the Hilldrop Estate. It also explained how they had managed to track him to Billy's flat so quickly. But how? If they had taken Joel's phone then they would have had Bird's number and seen the text messages, but it was a huge leap from having a number to tracking the location of the phone. Bird was fairly sure that only the phone companies could do that, and the police needed a warrant to get the information. How were the guys in the BMW X5s managing to do it?

Bird needed his phone, but not if it meant that the men with guns would stay on his trail.

But without his phone he was truly alone. He looked at Tyson and smiled. Not truly alone. He always had Tyson. He reached over and stroked the dog's neck again.

He sighed as he looked at the screen. If they had been able to track his GPS, did that mean they also had access to his messages and call records? That would mean that anyone he had been in touch with was also at risk. They had killed Joel without hesitation and had broken into Billy's flat without caring who was inside. Bird had no doubt that if Billy and his girlfriend had been home, they would have been killed. The phone was the only way they could have known that he was in the flat, which meant that he would have to dump it.

He scrolled through his messages, deleting them all.

Then he had a thought. WhatsApp was supposedly encrypted, so that only the sender and receiver could read messages on the app. Even if his pursuers had access to his texts and calls, they shouldn't be able to read his WhatsApp messages.

He opened the app and scrolled through his WhatsApp contacts. He stopped when he reached Ben Warren's details, listed under 'Sarge'. It had been almost a year since he had spoken with Warren, but he was the one person that Bird knew he could rely on. He tapped out a message. **Sarge, u there?**

It was coming up to six o'clock, which meant it would soon be dawn. Warren was an early riser, always had been, and Bird knew that it was his habit when he wasn't in action to run for an hour and exercise in the gym for another hour before breakfast.

Warren replied in less than a minute. **Hey, Deadman. What's up?**

I am in deep deep shit and need exfil. Exfil – exfiltration – was the military term for removing personnel from a hostile environment.

Where are you?

London.

I can be there in three hours.

Bird smiled thinly. No questions, no hesitation, no reservations. He was lucky to have Warren as a friend.

He continued to type. **Will wait for you at the Spaniards Inn car park near Hampstead Heath.**

Roger that, replied Warren.

I will be dumping this phone.

Understood. Stay safe.

Bird cleared all his WhatsApp conversations, then deleted his calls log and his contacts list. He deleted all the photographs on the phone, then pressed the button to restore it to factory settings. He considered destroying the SIM card and smashing the phone, but there was a way that he could use it to muddy the waters.

He stood up and looked around, then walked across the grass and past the children's playground. The two teenagers were still sitting on the wall and they looked over at him as he approached. Bird sniffed and made a point of wiping his nose with the back of his hand. 'Hey, what will you give me for this?' he said, holding out his phone, slurring his words.

The younger teenager took it and laughed. 'It's a fucking iPhone 8,' he said.

'It works.'

The teenager showed it to his companion and they both laughed. 'A fucking carrier pigeon'd be quicker,' said the older boy.

'It's a phone and it works,' said Bird. 'What can you give me for it?'

The older boy narrowed his eyes. 'What do you want?'

Bird rubbed his nose again. He didn't want anything, he just wanted rid of his phone but he had to play hard to get. 'Heroin.'

'Heroin?' The boy pulled a face as he looked at the phone, then he shrugged. 'Yeah, I'll give you two bumps but you're robbing me blind.'

'Three?' said Bird.

The boy held the phone out. 'Fuck off,' he said.

'Okay, okay, two bumps. Deal.' He wiped his nose again.

The boy took the phone back and nodded at his companion, who made a call on his mobile. Thirty seconds later a boy who couldn't have been more than ten years old appeared on another BMX. He held out a gloved hand and Bird took two small aluminium foil packages from him, each the size of a ten-pence piece. 'Thanks,' he said, but the boy had already pedalled off.

'Fuck off,' said the older boy, pocketing the phone.

Bird nodded and ambled away with Tyson at his heels. As he passed a drain he tossed in the two packages.

CHAPTER 9

It was just under three miles from the Hilldrop Estate to the Spaniards Inn. Bird kept to the side roads until he reached Gordon House Road. Dawn had broken by that time, and there was plenty of traffic. There was a railway bridge over the road to his left, and a block of flats to his right. Between them was the entrance to the Heath. He checked that there were no police cars or BMW X5s on the road before hurrying over.

There were several dog walkers and joggers around. The Heath was the perfect place for a man and his dog to blend in and no one paid Bird and Tyson any attention. The area at the south end of the Heath was called Parliament Hill – there was an outdoor swimming pool and a cricket ground, and beyond them a playground and paddling pool.

He kept to the right of Parliament Hill, one of the highest points in London, with views of most of the main tourist attractions including St Paul's Cathedral, the Houses of Parliament, the Gherkin and the Shard. He headed towards the Highgate Men's Bathing Pond, where a dozen hardy souls were already taking a dip in the freezing water, then cut west towards the B519 road which bisected the Heath. The B519 was known locally as Spaniards Road. Bird turned right and walked parallel to it, keeping to the undergrowth. Tyson was the perfect cover – anyone who did see him would just assume he was out walking his dog.

It was just after 8 a.m. when he reached the Spaniards Inn. The white-walled pub was a three-storey Grade-II listed building, built in 1585, with crossed swords painted above the entrance. Dick Turpin's father was a previous landlord, and the famous highwayman used to drink there while planning his raids. Keats and Dickens had also been regulars. But Bird didn't plan on going inside. His plan was to stay hidden until Warren arrived, which would be another couple of hours or so.

The pub was on the far side of the road. There was a covered bus stop nearby but Bird figured that his best bet would be to stay concealed in the undergrowth. The downside was that there was a fence running along the edge of the Heath, which blocked his view of the car park, but there was a break in the fence either side of the glass-sided bus shelter, so he managed to find a vantage point among the trees from where he could watch the entrance to the car park.

Credenhill was about 150 miles from London, and there were several road options, including the M40, the M4 and the A40. The routes varied in length but generally it took about three and a half hours to get from the SAS base to Central London. The Heath was to the north of the city and, true to his word, Warren arrived in a black Range Rover after a little over three hours.

He drove into the car park, away from the pub. There was another man in the front seat. When they climbed out, Bird realized it was Peter 'Tweedy' Harris. Harris lit a cigarette and blew smoke up at the sky as he looked around. He was wearing a black North Face fleece over a grey polo neck sweater, blue jeans and brown Army boots. Warren reached into the Range Rover and brought out a bottle of water. He unscrewed it and drank, then wiped his mouth with the back of his hand as he looked around. Warren was also in civilian gear, a black leather jacket over a white sweatshirt and black jeans. And, like Harris, the sergeant was wearing Altberg boots, though his were black.

Bird looked left and right, and once he was satisfied that the road was clear he made his way from his hiding place to a gap in the fence. He and Tyson jogged across the road and into the car park.

Warren and Harris saw him coming and immediately went into defensive mode, checking the area for potential threats.

'Good to see you, Deadman,' said Harris. He hugged Bird and patted him on the back. 'And good to see the land shark looking so well.'

Warren shook hands with Bird. 'You okay?' he said.

'I've been better,' said Bird. 'Can we get the hell out of Dodge?'

'No problem,' said Warren. 'Where do you want to go?'

'Out of London is all the plan I've got at the moment.'

Warren looked over at Harris. 'Why don't you drive so I can sit in the back with Andy? Let's head west. The way we came.'

'Sure,' said Harris. He climbed into the driver's seat. Warren, Bird and Tyson got into the back. Bird pointed at the boot and Tyson wriggled over the seats and made himself comfortable. 'How's he doing?' asked Warren.

'He's okay. Easily startled and loud noises still bother him.'

'We've all been there,' said Warren.

Harris put the car in gear and drove out of the car park.

'So, give me a sitrep,' said Warren, sitting side-on so that Bird could see his face. He listened without interrupting as Bird ran through everything that had happened, from seeing the man being shot in the alley up until the men in the BMWs had tracked him down to the Hilldrop Estate. They were driving through Windsor on the M4 by the time that Bird had finished.

'Fuck me,' said Warren. 'You've packed a lot into the past twelve hours. I can see why you needed an exfil.' He rubbed his chin. 'But why didn't you just tell the cops what had happened?'

'I tried, but they wouldn't listen,' said Bird. 'To be fair, I was standing over the dying guy, next to the gun that killed him.'

'Yeah, but you didn't pull the trigger.'

'No, but I took the gun off the shooter after he'd fired it.'

Warren nodded. 'So your prints were on the gun and you'd have picked up gunshot residue?'

'Exactly. I was up for talking it through with them but then they threatened to Taser Tyson and I couldn't let them do that. Tasers can kill dogs.'

'And you took out an armed response unit?'

'I didn't hurt them, Sarge. Just took their guns off them. But I shot out the tyres of their vehicle, so they could probably claim that I was shooting at them. Attempted murder. I'd be looking at twenty years.'

'Okay. That's not good. But you can identify the real killers. And the shoot-out you had with them shows that they're not figments of your imagination. How many did you shoot?'

'Three.'

'Dead?'

'Yeah.'

'How many in total?'

'Can't be sure. At least three vehicles, maybe more. At least eight men, almost certainly several more.'

'And who were they?'

'Dunno. Big guys. Heavies. Reasonably confident with firearms.'

'You don't think they were Secret Squirrels?'

Secret Squirrel. SAS shorthand for the intelligence services, MI5 and MI6.

'I really don't know. They had a confidence about them, that's for sure. They had no qualms about pulling out their guns in a public street. And I'm pretty sure they were tracking my phone.'

'You've dumped it?'

Bird nodded. 'Of course.'

Warren wrinkled his nose. 'What do you want to do? Once the cops ID you, it's only a matter of time. You can't run for ever.'

'I can try.'

'Can you, though? If it was just you, maybe. But Tyson is pretty distinctive.'

Bird sighed. The sergeant was right. He couldn't run for ever.

'Are you hungry?' asked Warren.

'Yeah.'

'Let's grab breakfast.' He leant towards Harris. 'Tweedy, find us a service station off the beaten path, somewhere with no CCTV.'

'Not a problem,' said Harris.

CHAPTER 10

Bird left Tyson in the Range Rover with the window cracked while he went into the cafe with Warren and Harris. Most of the vehicles in the car park were trucks. The cafe was half a mile south of the M4, next to a small garage in front of which was parked a tow truck. A large sign said that all repairs had to be paid for upfront, no exceptions.

No one paid them any attention when they pushed open the door to the cafe and went inside. There was a counter ahead of them and beyond it a kitchen where a stout woman wearing a chef's hat and whites was sweating over a grill. The menu was written in capital letters on a blackboard above the counter.

Most of the diners were eating alone, truckers reading newspapers or staring at their phone screens as they tucked into their food.

A man who looked well past retirement age smiled at them from behind a cash register, showing crooked yellow teeth. 'What can I get you gentlemen?' he asked.

'Three full Englishes,' said Warren.

'Eggs?'

'Sure.'

'I mean, how do you want your eggs?'

'Fried,' said Warren.

'Fried,' said Bird.

'Poached,' said Harris.

Warren looked over at Harris. 'Poached?'

'It's healthier.'

'You've got fried bacon, fried bread, black pudding and sausage, but you want the healthy option when it comes to the eggs?'

Harris shrugged. 'What can I say, I like poached.'

'White or brown?' asked the man.

'Eggs?' said Warren.

'Toast.'

Warren grinned. 'Got you. Whatever the healthy option is. And three teas.'

'And could I have half a dozen sausages to go, please?' said Bird.

'For the land shark?' said Harris.

'He missed breakfast,' said Bird. The men went over to a table by the window as the man relayed the order to the cook.

Warren and Harris sat together, facing Bird. 'This is one hell of a situation,' said Warren.

'Tell me about it,' said Bird.

'The one bright spot is that we're out of London, and now that you've dumped the phone, the bad guys hopefully don't know where you are. But we need to fix this, Andy.'

'I'm open to suggestions,' said Bird.

'I guess the big question is, who are the bad guys? If they're gangsters, then we can probably sit down with the cops and talk things through. You didn't hurt any cops, not seriously, and the bad guys were trying to kill you, so it was self-defence. Plus, you're a witness to the first killing.' He looked over at Harris. 'Tweedy, you're looking after the CTSFO team at the moment,' he said. 'Anyone there we could talk to?'

The CTSFOs – Counter-Terrorism Specialist Firearms Officers – were the most highly trained of the Metropolitan Police's 2,500 armed officers, and as part of their training they spent time with the SAS at the Credenhill base, honing their skills. Harris had been seconded to the CTSFO team, and had been responsible for putting them through their paces in the Killing House, the SAS's main training facility for hostage-rescue situations and close-quarter battle training. It was a two-storey building with rubber-coated walls to absorb rounds and extractor fans to clear out the choking fumes that came with repeated gunshots.

'I've got quite close to a couple of the guys,' said Harris. 'Do you want me to reach out to them?'

'Yeah, but softly-softly. See if they know anything about the guy who was killed. The way in, I guess, is to ask them about the shoot-out with the guys in the BMW X5s. But don't mention Deadman.' He looked over at Bird. 'Where did that happen? What road?'

Bird frowned as he thought back to where he and Joel had been when they had been attacked. 'Arlington Road,' he said.

'Right, so find out what you can about what happened in Arlington Road, then see if they know about the killing in the alley.' He looked at Bird again. 'Where was that?'

'Off Camden High Street.'

'What do I tell them?' asked Harris. 'I mean, the two I have in mind are good guys but at the end of the day they're cops. I start asking them about a shooting in London and they're going to wonder what's up.'

'Just say you had heard there was a shoot-out. Was it terrorism-related, were any of their guys involved – they're justifiable questions.'

The man at the counter appeared at their table with three mugs of strong tea and three plates of freshly buttered toast. 'Fry-ups are on the way,' he said, putting the tea and toast on the table.

'The big question is, what do you want to do while we're gathering intel,' said Warren. 'You need to maintain a low profile.'

'My plan was to stay on the Heath,' said Bird. 'I've lived rough there before. But after what's happened, I think I'm better off well out of London.'

'You lived rough on Hampstead Heath?'

'Just for a few days. I was between residences.'

'You were homeless?'

'I still am, Sarge. But it's no big deal.'

Warren shook his head in frustration. 'You should have told someone, Andy. You should have called me.'

'I'm fine.' He looked at Tyson. 'We're fine.'

'We need to get you sorted today and I don't see that Hampstead Heath is a sensible option. Look, you could lie low at Stirling Lines.'

Bird frowned. 'How would that work? The colonel's not going to allow it, is he?'

'I wasn't thinking of telling him, truth be told. Don't ask, don't tell. We can get you and Tyson in, no problem, and we've got so many guys on operations at the moment there's plenty of room.'

'What if someone sees me?'

'We'll keep you out of sight. But put you in fatigues, no one is going to give you a second look.'

'I don't want to get you in any trouble, Sarge.'

'Fuck that, Andy. Tweedy and I wouldn't be here if it wasn't for you. I mean, who the fuck throws themselves on a live grenade?'

'I tripped.'

Warren laughed and slapped the table. 'Course you did. Look, we'll do whatever it takes to keep you safe. If we get you into Stirling Lines, the bad guys won't be able to get to you. And the cops won't know where you are.' He grinned. 'Plus, you can get a shower and a change of clothes.'

Bird sniffed his armpit. 'A bit ripe?'

'A bit? What do you think, Tweedy?'

'Yeah. A bit.'

The man at the counter brought over their three plates and put them down in front of them. 'Anything else?'

'We're good,' said Warren. He waited until the man had gone back to the counter before speaking again. 'I don't see that there's a better alternative,' he said. 'You're a homeless guy with a dog and the whole of the Met will be looking for you. I know you were planning to lie low on the Heath, but that's easier said than done if every cop in town is looking for you. If they do ID you, they'll be all over your friends and family.'

Bird nodded. 'I hear you, Sarge.' He picked up his knife and fork and tucked into his breakfast. The other two men did the same.

'The men who killed the guy in the alley,' said Warren. 'What did they look like?'

'They were both big. Over six feet. They both had overcoats, I remember that. The first one I saw had slicked-back hair. The hair glistened, like he oiled it. The other guy had shorter hair. He had a dimple in the chin and close-set eyes, and I got the feeling that his nose had been broken several times. They both wore gloves.'

'And they both had guns?'

Bird shook his head. 'The second guy had the gun. A little Glock 42.'

'That's a girl's gun,' said Harris.

'It's the perfect concealed weapon,' said Warren. 'I've carried one a few times. It weighs less than a pound, six inches long.'

'Like I said, perfect for a girl's purse,' said Harris.

'Size isn't everything,' said Warren. 'But it suggests that the guys Andy saw were pros. What car were they driving?'

'I didn't see their vehicle. They ran away and the cops turned up.'

'And the next time you saw them was in Arlington Road?'

Bird nodded. 'I'm not a hundred per cent sure that it was them, but they were definitely on the same team. I was in an Uber and two BMW X5s boxed us in. Two guys in front, four guys behind. One of the X5s was green, the other was grey.'

'And what guns did these guys have?'

'Two of them had Glocks. I took one of them and used it against the rest of them. One of the others had an Uzi or a MAC-10. The rest I didn't see.'

'The Glock you had, where is it now?'

Bird patted his parka. 'Safe and sound,' he said.

'You'd better give it to me, Andy,' said Warren, holding out his hand. 'Getting you and Tyson onto the base might get me a slap on the wrist, but you bringing in an unregistered weapon is a whole different problem.'

Bird took out the pistol and passed it to Warren under the table. 'And of these guys, you took out three of them?'

'Yeah. Both guys from the lead car, although one was still breathing, just, last I saw. And one from the second car.'

'Did you get the impression they were pros?'

'I think so, yeah. They just bit off more than they could chew. But they knew what they were doing.'

'They were there to kill you, not take you prisoner?'

'They came out shooting.'

Warren nodded. 'So it was about silencing you because of what you'd seen?'

'I guess so.'

'See, if they were just hired muscle, they probably wouldn't care. There has to be a reason why they don't want to be identified.'

'Professional hitmen, sounds like,' said Harris.

'In multiple teams? Upwards of eight men?' said Warren. 'Pros generally work alone, maybe in pairs. But mob-handed like that?' He shrugged. 'There's something going on. Hopefully we'll know more when you've spoken to your CTSFOs.' He drank his tea. 'Seriously, Andy, you need to lie low in Stirling Lines until we get the lie of the land.'

Bird forced a smile. 'You've talked me into it,' he said.

They finished their breakfasts. Warren paid the bill and the man at the counter gave Bird the sausages wrapped up in aluminium foil. Tyson wolfed down the sausages as Warren drove them west, to Hereford.

CHAPTER 11

The SAS's A, B, D and G squadrons were based at Stirling Lines, along with the Special Reconnaissance Regiment and the 18 Signal Regiment, who provided communications and information systems support to the Regiment. Also on the base was Blue Thunder, aka 658 Squadron of the Army Air Corps, who used helicopters to support the SAS's domestic counterterrorism operations. The site had once been an RAF training school, but the SAS took it over in 1999. The 970-acre site was where the SAS did most of their training, and where they waited between operations. The full strength of the SAS was just shy of six hundred, but the Regiment was rarely at that level – it usually hovered around the five hundred mark. The base was at Credenhill, five miles north-west of Hereford.

A guard at the main entrance scrutinized Warren's ID while another guard ran a mirror underneath the vehicle.

The guard gave Warren back his ID and looked at Harris. 'Bloody, hell, Archie, don't you remember me?' said Harris.

'Rules is rules,' said the guard.

Harris gave him his ID card, and for the first time the guard looked in the back and saw Bird. His eyebrows shot up. 'Andy Bird. You're a sight for sore eyes.'

'Hi, Archie, long time no see.'

'Two years. At least. I never got the chance to say goodbye. You had that problem in Syria and then you were in hospital and then you were gone.'

'Yeah, the Regiment isn't great at leaving do's.'

'At least you beat the clock, that's something.'

'True,' said Bird. The names of SAS men who had died in combat were inscribed on plaques around the plinth of the regimental clock tower. Beating the clock meant surviving, and yes, Bird had survived. Just.

'Any ID will do, Andy. A veteran ID, or even a driving licence.'

'I have a driving licence,' said Bird, fishing it out of his wallet. He handed it over and the guard noted the details on his clipboard before giving it back. 'It's a pleasure seeing you again, Andy. A real pleasure.' He grinned at Tyson. 'You too, Tyson. Enjoy your stay.'

'Thanks, Archie,' said Bird.

Warren drove onto the base and parked by one of the barracks. 'Plenty of spare billets in here,' said Warren. 'There's only about a hundred guys on the base at the moment. Plus we're understaffed.'

'Can't get the help?'

Warren laughed. 'The Army's shrinking year by year, so every year the pool of potential recruits is getting smaller. The government has suggested that the Regiment lowers its standards but they're not having it. And it comes at a time when we've never been busier. We barely have enough to cover domestic terrorism never mind what's going on overseas. Anyway, grab a spare room, I'll go and fetch you some clothes and stuff.'

Bird and Tyson climbed out and Warren drove off. Bird found an empty room on the ground floor. The furniture was minimal, just a single bed, a wardrobe and a chest of drawers. Someone had left a plastic plate, bowl and mug on the chest of drawers, so Bird took the bowl along to a communal bathroom at the end of the corridor and filled it with water for Tyson. Tyson lapped it greedily.

Bird looked around the bathroom, recalling the day when he had first arrived at Stirling Lines as a fully badged SAS trooper. He had expected to spend his entire career with the Regiment, but the hand grenade had put paid to that. What was it they said,

God laughs when people make plans? He was probably pissing himself now.

Bird had no idea how this was going to play out. It was tough enough living on the streets, but being pursued by men with guns and cops wanting to arrest him took hardship to a whole new level.

Tyson finished drinking and looked at Bird expectantly. 'You hungry again? You and me both.'

He headed back to the bedroom. There was no bedding, just two Army-issue pillows. Bird kicked off his boots and lay down on the bed. Tyson jumped up and lay down next to him. Bird laughed. 'Mate, this is a single.'

Tyson snuggled next to him and Bird could feel the dog's warm breath against his neck.

'Fine,' said Bird, patting him. 'Just don't fart.'

CHAPTER 12

Bird was jolted awake by Tyson's frantic movements. He sat up. The dog was on the floor, hackles raised, spittle flying from his mouth as he barked at the doorway, where Warren was holding a stack of bedding and clothing in his arms.

'Tyson, easy, easy,' said Bird, sitting up. 'Friendly. Friendly.'

Tyson continued to bark. There was a crazed look in his eyes and Bird could see that the dog was preparing to launch himself at the sergeant. He stood up and stepped in front of Tyson. 'Tyson, down!' he shouted.

Tyson ignored him and continued to bark crazily.

Bird raised a hand and pushed the palm towards the dog, like a policeman stopping traffic. 'Down!' he shouted.

Tyson went quiet and dropped to the floor, his ears up, breathing heavily.

'Good boy,' said Bird, his voice softer. 'That's a good boy. Sit.'

Tyson obeyed. His ears were up and his tongue was lolling out of the side of his mouth.

'You okay, Sarge?' asked Bird.

'I'm okay, he just gave me a start. I've never been on the receiving end of that bark before. It's quite . . . intimidating.'

'Sorry. He shouldn't be doing that.' Bird patted his thigh. 'Heel,' he said.

Tyson hurried over and sat down in front of Bird, his head back, 'Good boy,' said Bird, patting the dog's head.

'What happened?' asked Warren, dropping the bedding and clothes onto the top of the chest of drawers. 'I opened the door and he just went crazy.'

'He gets like that if he's startled awake, especially if he's dreaming,' said Bird.

'PTSD?'

Bird nodded and rubbed Tyson's neck. 'He never used to be like this. But he changed after the grenade thing.' Bird grimaced. 'We both did. But he's getting better.'

'Tyson, I'm sorry I startled you,' said Warren. 'I hope we can still be friends.' He gestured at the bedding and clothing. 'Okay, so clean sheets and pillowcases. Underwear and socks and a set of fatigues. And a couple of towels. I should have some casual clothes for you this evening. There's a laundry bag there, too. Put your dirty clothes in there and I'll get them cleaned. I'll get your coat dry cleaned, too.'

'Thanks.'

Warren reached into his pocket and pulled out a British Airways toiletries kit. 'Got this a while back. Should have a toothbrush, toothpaste and a comb.' He reached into another pocket and pulled out a Samsung smartphone. 'Got you this, too. It's a pay-as-you-go SIM and there's about fifty quid on it.'

'You're a star, Sarge. Thanks.'

'Do you want to sleep some more?'

'I'm good. I'll freshen up and change.'

'Okay. I'll wait for you in the sergeants' mess. Take your time.' He grinned down at Tyson. 'You can come, but no barking, okay?'

Warren left and Bird shaved and showered, then changed into clean underwear and T-shirt before pulling on the fatigues. He pulled on his socks and boots, crammed his dirty clothes and coat into the laundry bag and placed it on the bed before heading over to the sergeants' mess, where Warren was sitting by the window nursing a mug of coffee.

'Thanks for this, Sarge,' said Bird, sitting opposite him. 'I left the laundry on my bed.'

'Not a problem, I'll get it sorted. You want a coffee? And they can rustle you up a bacon roll if you want one.'

'Coffee would be great,' said Bird. 'And a bacon roll would go down nicely.'

Warren went over to the bar and ordered a coffee from one of the civilian workers who ran the mess. As he got back to the table, Tweedy Harris appeared at the doorway. He headed over to the table but didn't sit down. 'I'm in the Close Quarter Battle House with the CTSFOs, and I had a quick word with one of them about the shootings in Arlington Road,' said Harris. 'His lot weren't involved because it wasn't considered terrorism related, but it's a weird one.'

'Weird in what way?' said Bird.

'The cops know there was a shooting – there were half a dozen 999 calls reporting it. And there was an Uber guy, dead in the street.'

'That was Joel,' said Bird. 'The guy driving the Uber.'

'Well, Joel was there, and so was his car,' said Harris. 'But that was it. No SUVs, no dead bad guys. Blood in the street, but that's all. They even picked up their cartridge cases.'

'Pros,' said Warren.

'Looks that way,' said Harris.

'What's happening investigation-wise?' asked Bird.

'They're pulling in all CCTV in the area,' said Harris. 'And appealing for witnesses.'

'What do they think happened?' asked Warren.

'My guy says that the early theory is that the Uber driver got caught up in the crossfire of a gang dispute.'

'No mention of Deadman and the dog?'

'Not so far.'

'And what about the guy in the alley?'

'He didn't know about that, but he's going to ask around and get back to me.'

Warren grimaced. 'So we're not much further on, are we? We know it wasn't gang-bangers. And to be honest, I don't understand why the cops don't realize that. Gang-bangers don't generally pick up their brass. Or carry away their dead. These guys are pros.' He looked at Bird. 'Was there much CCTV around?'

'It's London, there's CCTV everywhere,' said Bird. 'But we weren't near any traffic lights and I don't remember seeing any council CCTV cameras. I guess the cops will be appealing for dashcam footage at some point, and checking the shops in the area.'

'Most of the CCTV footage the cops release these days seems to be grainy and out of focus,' said Harris. 'If that's all they've got, they might never identify them.'

'What about you, Andy?' asked Warren. 'Would you recognize them?'

'Sure. I was up close and personal with the two in the alley. And I got a good look at the guy with the machine pistol who shot Joel. Ugly bugger, and a chunk of his left ear was missing.'

'Who is this Joel?' asked Harris.

'He was an outreach charity guy who was trying to help me,' said Bird. 'They killed him without a second thought.'

Warren nodded. 'Let's see what the cops come up with,' he said. 'In the meantime, best that you and Tyson stay here.'

'I've got to get back to the guys,' said Harris. 'I'll catch up with you later.'

The waiter brought a mug of coffee and two bacon rolls over to their table. The man grinned when he saw Bird. 'Andy?'

'Oli, how are you doing?'

'All the better for seeing you,' said the waiter. He was in his fifties, grey-haired with half-moon spectacles, wearing a white jacket over black trousers. 'How are you?'

'I'm good,' said Bird. 'What about Alfie?' He looked over at Warren. 'Oli's son was applying to join the Regiment.'

'He's in,' said Oli. 'Joined last year. He's with A Squadron. Out in Ukraine as we speak but obviously, I'm not supposed to know that. He'll be thrilled when I tell him I've seen you. He's so grateful for all the advice you gave him, especially about the jungle phase.'

The jungle phase of the SAS selection course came after the endurance test, and candidates had to spend at least six weeks in the jungles of either Belize, Brunei or Malaysia, surviving on Army rations while patrolling and training. It was where the recruits started to learn the basics of SAS soldiering, working in four-man teams on demolitions, survival techniques, reconnaissance, close-quarter battle fighting and contact drills. It was by far the toughest part of the selection process. The theory went that if you could be a good soldier in the jungle, you could be a good soldier anywhere. 'I'm glad I could help,' said Bird. 'But I always knew he would make it; he was very well thought of in the Paras. And he'll do well in the Regiment, I'm sure. Give him my best.'

'I will do,' said Oli. He nodded at Tyson. 'Would Tyson like some sausages?'

'He's had his breakfast, but thanks,' said Bird.

'We've got some nice lamb mince just come in,' said Oli. 'Organic. The chef's gonna do shepherd's pie but I'll keep some by for Tyson. Bring him around any time this evening and I'll look after him.' He winked at Bird as he walked away.

'You know everybody at Stirling Lines, don't you?' said Warren.

'It's having the dog that does it,' said Bird. 'They're great icebreakers.'

'Most people probably don't get the full-on attack experience like I got.'

'Yeah, sorry about that,' said Bird.

'Do you think he would have attacked me?'

Bird wrinkled his nose. 'I don't think so. He should only attack when he's given the attack command. But when he gets woken up unexpectedly, all bets are off. I think it depends what he was dreaming about.'

'Do you think he dreams about what happened?'

'Who knows? But sometimes when he's asleep I can see he's in distress. He's shaking and whining and he'll snarl. There's nothing I can do, because if I wake him up, he kicks off.'

'I never got the chance to ask you, but how are things?'

'In what way?'

'Well, you were sleeping rough, so things can't be going great.'

'It's temporary,' said Bird. 'It's tough to find a place that will allow Tyson and I'm not abandoning him.'

'You know the Regiment will help, if you reach out to them.'

'The Regiment threw me on the scrapheap, remember? And Tyson.'

'There are charities that can help, Andy. There's Help for Heroes, the Royal British Legion, and Who Dares Cares. All you have to do is ask.'

Bird shook his head. 'I don't want charity, Sarge. I'm not a basket case. I'm just going through a bad patch. Sleeping rough is no big thing, you know that. We've both been on ops where we lie hidden, pissing and shitting into plastic bags for days on end.'

Warren grinned. 'True that. But you had a house in Hereford, right?'

'Gave it up in the divorce. Gave it all up. It wasn't Sarah's fault; I'd become impossible to live with. I just walked away with the clothes on my back, pretty much.'

'And you can't get work?'

'My mate Billy gives me nightwatchman shifts from time to time. But he has to be careful – people don't like to find out that their security guard is as deaf as a post.'

'And the deaf thing, that's not going to get any better?'

Bird shrugged. 'They say not. There's a good chance those implant things would work, but I'd feel like a bloody cyborg. We'll see. At the moment I do okay reading lips. I can live with it.'

'And what about PTSD?'

'Not a problem.'

'Andy, you threw yourself on a live hand grenade. You must have assumed you were going to die.'

'Yeah, but I didn't.'

Warren grinned. 'You're a cool one.'

Bird shrugged again. 'In a way, the deafness is a blessing. If I wasn't deaf, I'd probably be jumping at every loud noise. That's one of Tyson's problems, though he's getting better. It really used to freak him out. He wasn't happy when the bad guys started shooting yesterday, but he didn't seem over-stressed. A year ago and he'd be a quivering jelly at the sound of gunfire.'

'He was in a bad way after what happened in Syria, wasn't he?'

'Yeah. I never realized dogs could get PTSD, but it's a thing. He used to freak out at loud bangs, but what really upset him was when things flew through the air towards him.'

'Flashback to the grenade?'

'Yeah, and some. A kid threw a ball at him once and he had a fit. On his back, legs in the air, thrashing around. Totally out of it.'

Tyson stood up and went over to stand in front of Bird, his tail wagging. 'He knows you're talking about him,' said Warren.

'He's a smart dog,' said Bird, patting him on the back. 'But you're getting better, boy. One day at a time, yeah?'

Tyson licked Bird's hand, then head-butted his knee.

Warren looked at his watch. 'Look, I've got to head off. I'm running a training course this afternoon over at Pontrilas. Aircraft hostage rescue.'

The Pontrilas Army Training Area was a training camp fifteen miles from Credenhill, and was where the SAS carried out major training exercises. On the site were three passenger jets which were used for hostage rescue practice, including a Boeing 747 that had once been flown by a Nigerian airline. There was also a full Tube train, the two-storey Killing House, a massive close-quarter battle compound and a huge indoor firing range.

'The colonel doesn't know you're here, so keep away from the admin block,' said Warren. 'You can hang out in your room, or use the gym. I'll be back before it gets dark.'

Bird finished his bacon roll. 'Thanks for this, Sarge.'

Warren shook his head. 'No need for thanks, Andy. I'm the one who's in debt. I owe you, end of.' He drained his coffee and stood up. 'Okay, catch you later. And don't worry, we'll fix this, I promise.'

CHAPTER 13

After he had finished his coffee, Bird took Tyson for a run in the grounds. Tyson had been trained not to chase balls or sticks because of the danger that he might grab an IED when in a conflict area, so exercising meant running alongside. These days Bird was lucky to manage a slow jog but Tyson joined in the game, running in circles around him, his tongue lolling out of the side of his mouth. Dogs usually barked when they were happy, but that had been trained out of Tyson when he was a puppy and now he only barked on command.

Their run took them over to the SAS kennels, where the Regiment kept its war dogs when they first arrived for duty. Each kennel had an exercise area, but once the dogs were fully trained, they spent all their time with their handler, eating, sleeping and training as a unit. Sarah was always complaining that he spent more time with Tyson than he did with her, and it was hard to argue with the truth. Bird had once explained to her that in combat his life would depend on the bond they had forged, but she hadn't taken that revelation well, so he never mentioned it again.

As they played, a handler wearing desert fatigues with a holstered pistol on his hip came around the corner of the kennel block. Bird recognized him immediately. It was Kevin Mackie, a Scot who had joined the SAS a couple of years before Bird. The dog was stuck to his heels. He was also a Belgian Malinois, but his colouring was much darker than Tyson's. As a pup he'd been called Blackie, but when he'd arrived at Stirling Lines a major insisted that the name was changed. Blackie became Boris and political correctness was satisfied, though the new name had sparked an embarrassing confrontation a year or so later when the then prime minister, Boris Johnson, visited the barracks.

Boris spotted Tyson. His ears pricked up, then his tail swished from side to side and he leapt forwards. Mackie opened his mouth to call him back and then he saw Bird and waved. 'Sight for sore eyes,' he said as he walked over. 'How the hell are you?'

The two men shook hands but Mackie turned it into a hug and slapped Bird on the back. As they broke apart, it was clear that Mackie had said something. Bird pointed at his right ear. 'Still deaf,' he said.

'Sorry, mate,' said Mackie. 'Just asking if this was a flying visit or if the top brass had seen the error of their ways.'

Boris and Tyson were greeting each other in the traditional canine fashion, standing nose to tail and sniffing each other's butts.

'The former,' said Bird. 'They'll never take me back. A deaf soldier's no use to anyone in combat. I'd have no idea where the shots are coming from.'

'Plenty of other jobs you could do.'

'Serving coffee in the officers' mess? No mate, I'm better off out of it.'

'So, how is Civvie Street?'

Bird shrugged. 'Not great, truth be told.'

Tyson ran off and Boris sprinted after him.

'Tyson looks in good form.'

'He's okay. But he's not the dog he was.'

'They said he had PTSD?'

Bird nodded. 'Yeah, definitely not good with loud bangs.'

'Who is?'

The two men laughed.

'Seriously, mate, if you need anything, just give me a call. I never got over how quick you went. One moment you were here, then you were out in Syria, and that was that.'

'I was in a few hospitals, they did a good job of putting me back together. But yeah, I never came back to Stirling Lines. I never really did get to say goodbye, but maybe it was better that way. At the time I was pretty pissed off at being shown the door.'

'You beat the clock, that's what counts. You both did. And you saved a lot of guys that day. You should have got a medal. You and Tyson.'

Bird scowled. 'Nah, I've never been for medals. You do the job because you do the job, it's never about the glory.'

The two dogs were playfighting now, gently biting each other and trying to push each other to the ground.

'You don't have a spare harness knocking around, do you?' asked Bird. 'I thought I might let Tyson wear one for old time's sake.'

'I've got one of Boris's old ones. Come on, let's have a look. They're about the same size.'

He whistled and Boris immediately stopped playing and ran over.

'Tyson!' shouted Bird, but Tyson was already running towards him. Tyson sat down in front of Bird, ears up, panting heavily, looking up at him.

'He's still got it,' said Mackie.

He took Bird around to the kennel block and in through the main door. There was a changing room beyond the door with lockers against one wall. A door led to a number of training rooms where the dogs could be put through their paces in different scenarios.

Bird smiled when he saw that his and Tyson's names were still on the door of his old locker. Mackie saw his reaction and patted him on the back. 'No one wanted to take your name down,' he said. 'There's been a few guys joined since you left, but none of them wanted to fill your shoes.'

'Bad luck?'

'No mate, out of respect for you and Tyson. Seriously, you're bloody legends.'

Bird opened his locker and smiled when he saw the photograph of Sarah stuck to the inside of the door. He'd taken it on one of their first holidays together, a week in Ibiza. That's where he had proposed to her, and where she had accepted. He pulled the photograph away from the door, and before he realized what he was doing he had put it to his mouth and kissed it. His cheeks reddened when he realized that Mackie had seen what he'd done and he slipped it inside the chest pocket of his fatigues. Mackie grinned but didn't say anything.

There was an old harness hanging at the back of the locker and Bird took it out. It was Tyson's old harness, made of Kevlar and canvas, with Velcro straps, steel D rings and a padded handle on the back. Unlike the state-of-the-art model that Tyson had been wearing on his last mission in Syria, the old harness didn't have its own power supply, USB slots or built-in cameras, GPS, microphones or speakers. Battery-powered cameras and microphones could be attached to the harness using the Velcro straps, but the quality was nowhere near as good as the kit on the new model.

Tyson sat at his feet, tail twitching from side to side.

'Look at him,' said Mackie. 'Raring to go.'

Bird knelt down, passed the harness over Tyson's head and fastened the straps under his belly and around his tail. 'Fits like a glove,' said Bird, standing up.

'Suits you, sir,' said Mackie. 'So, Andy, what are your plans?'

'Nothing fixed,' said Bird. 'Ben Warren said I can hang out at the base for a while.'

'Does the colonel know?'

'Not yet. So mum's the word.'

'Not a problem, I never saw you,' said Mackie. He frowned. 'Are you okay?'

'Sure. Why?'

'You look a bit tense.'

'I've had a rough few days,' said Bird. 'It's no biggie but the Sarge thought I could do with some R and R.'

'I thought you'd be on easy street, after what happened? You must have got compo, right? And a decent pension?'

'You know me, I've never been good with money. What about you? They keeping you busy?'

'Running us ragged, mate. The Regiment has got eight dogs now and I'm the only one here.'

'All overseas?'

'Mostly, yeah. Now anytime they want a door kicking in, they want a land shark to go in first. These new hi-tech rigs give all around sound and vision, they make room assaults so much safer. I tell you, once they find a way of attaching guns to the dogs, they'll do away with troopers altogether.'

'Nah, they'll always need a man with a gun to do the dirty deed,' said Bird.

'Yeah, you'd think that. But the guy who came out to tune up the new rigs says that they're looking to incorporate a weapon into the system, and that the plan is to link the tablet to AI. So the dog will go in and the AI will decide which targets to take out. The handler will press the button to fire the weapon, whatever it is, but the AI will be selecting the targets. It's a brave new world.'

Bird shook his head. 'It'll never happen.'

'I hope not, but I fear the worst,' said Mackie. He forced a smile. 'So, what are you going to do now? Boris and I are due in the CQB centre.'

'I thought I'd have a swim in the pool. Then maybe hit the gym. It's been a while since I've exercised.'

'Well, have fun. If you're around for a drink while you're here, let me know. But we're off the day after tomorrow.'

'Anywhere nice?'

'Definitely not nice. I'd tell you where, but then I'd have to kill you.' He laughed and patted Bird on the back. 'Seriously, mate, it's good to see you.'

CHAPTER 14

Bird was in the gym, lifting weights under Tyson's baleful stare. Bird grinned as he started his second set of double bicep curls, a ten-kilo dumbbell in each hand. 'It's okay for you, chasing rabbits and squirrels is all the exercise you need,' he said.

Tyson's tongue was sticking out of the side of his mouth and it looked as if he was laughing at Bird. Bird concentrated on his technique as he worked his biceps. He had been in the gym for the best part of an hour. He had given the swimming pool a miss when he realized that the entrance was visible from the admin block, so there was a chance that he'd be spotted by the colonel.

He was wearing the fatigues that Warren had given him, and his Army boots. During his time in the Regiment, Bird had almost never exercised in gym clothes or training shoes. Fitness was about being fit in the field – when you were in combat you didn't have time to change into gym gear. So, when he lifted weights he did it in street clothes or fatigues and when he ran, it was in Army boots and, more often than not, with a Bergen on his back.

As he finished the set, the gym doors opened and Warren headed towards him. He was wearing desert fatigues, had a holstered Glock on his hip and was carrying a black nylon holdall. 'Things are starting to move,' he said. 'Our MI5 liaison has been in touch. One of their spooks wants to talk to you.'

'Do they know who the bad guys are?'

'He didn't say, just that they need to talk to you ASAP. And they want a face-to-face.'

'Because?'

'I guess because they don't trust phones or Zoom or whatever the hi-tech equivalent of a face-to-face is these days.'

'And the meeting is with who? MI5 or MI6?'

'Our liaison didn't say, just that it's a spook.'

'So we're going to London?'

'Nope, the mountain is coming to Mohammed.' He looked at his watch, a stainless-steel Breitling. 'You've just got time to shower and change.' He handed him the holdall. 'I got you some casual clothes – there's a jacket in there and a couple of shirts that a guy who was RTU'd last year left behind.'

RTU'd – returned to unit – was what happened to troopers who failed to maintain the Regiment's standard.

Bird frowned. 'What do you mean, I've got time to shower and change? It's a three-and-a-half-hour drive from London.'

'They're using a heli,' said Warren. 'Looks like you're a priority. I figured it best they don't see you in fatigues, because that might look like you're here officially.'

'I hear you.'

Warren put the dumbbells back on their rack as Bird headed to the shower with his towel. Tyson followed at his heels. Tyson curled up on the floor as Bird quickly showered and pulled on clean underwear and socks, a blue long-sleeved denim shirt and blue jeans. There was a black bomber jacket with zip pockets that was a decent fit. He checked himself in the mirror. He doubted that it would be much use on the street when sleeping rough, but it was just the thing to wear to greet an intelligence officer.

He thrust the fatigues and towel into the holdall and zipped it up.

'Looking good,' said Warren as Bird headed back into the gym.

'Why was the guy RTU'd?' asked Bird.

'Wife trouble,' said Warren. 'He was on back-to-back missions in

Syria and Iraq for going on two years and she called time on his special forces career. The job or me, she said, and he chose her. She'd just fallen pregnant so he wanted more stability and figured he'd get that back in the Paras.'

'And why did he leave the clothes?'

Warren laughed. 'He'd lost weight. I kid you not, all that time out in the desert eating crap, he lost close to fifteen kilos. None of that stuff fitted him any more. So his loss, your gain.' He cocked his head on one side. 'I think I hear the heli. Leave the bag in a locker, you can pick it up later.'

Bird tossed the holdall in a wooden locker and he and Tyson followed Warren outside. 'Perfect timing,' said Warren, pointing at the helicopter, high in the sky off to the east.

They headed over to the helicopter landing area. It was a dark blue Eurocopter EC130, a civilian model with room for a pilot and six passengers. It did a slow circuit of the field, then came in to land. The skids touched the grass and the engine powered down. As the side door slid open, Bird saw that there were two passengers, a man and a woman. The woman climbed out first, and even though she kept her head down, Bird recognized her immediately and his face broke into a grin. 'Small bloody world,' he said.

Warren turned to look at him. 'What?'

'Don't you recognize her? The lovely "Emma" from MI6. The woman who briefed us at Incirlik.'

Warren shaded his eyes with the flat of his hand. 'Bloody hell. You're right.'

'That's a turn-up for the books. You think it's a coincidence?'

Warren snorted softly. 'No, mate, nothing is ever a coincidence with the spooks.'

The man followed her out. He was in his thirties, dark haired wearing a black raincoat over a blue suit. They both kept their heads down even though there was plenty of room under the still-whirling three-bladed rotor, and didn't straighten up until they were well clear of the helicopter.

The last time they had met, Emma had been wearing her dark brown hair pulled back in a ponytail, but now it was shorter and she had it loose. She had been wearing glasses then, but they were gone, and she had swapped her desert camouflage fatigues for jeans and a pale blue fleece. Bird smiled when he realized she was still wearing Timberland boots. They looked new, so they probably weren't the same ones she had been wearing in Turkey. Maybe she was loyal to the brand.

As Emma and the man walked across the grass, the helicopter's turbines died and the blades came to a halt.

Emma smiled, showing perfect teeth. 'Sergeant Warren, so glad to see you again,' she said, offering her hand. Warren shook. She was already smiling at Bird. 'And nice to see you again, Andy.' She shook his hand. She had a firm grip. Maybe too firm, thought Bird, as if she had something to prove. 'I'm so sorry about what happened to you in Syria. Nightmare. I wanted to visit you in hospital but I was pulled away on another job.' She frowned. 'I was told that you lost your hearing in the explosion.'

Bird nodded. 'Totally deaf in both ears, yes.'

Her frown deepened. 'But . . .' Realization dawned. 'Ah, you can read lips?'

'Pretty well, as it turns out.'

She released his hand and looked down at Tyson. 'And the amazing Tyson,' she said. 'Can I pat him?'

'Sure.'

Emma offered Tyson the back of her hand and he sniffed it and wagged his tail. 'Good boy,' she said, and patted him on the back. She straightened up, then gestured at the man behind her. 'This is Simon,' she said.

Simon shook hands with Warren and Bird. He looked pale, as if the colour had drained from his face. 'Could I have a drink of water?' he asked. 'I'm not feeling too good.'

'Let's go to the sergeants' mess,' said Warren. 'Are you okay?'

'I'm not good on helicopters, that's all.'

'Let's get you some water,' said Warren.

The mess was a short walk away. The dining room was empty, so Warren sat the new arrivals down at a table by the window and went in search of a member of staff.

Simon and Emma sat facing Bird. They were both smiling but Emma's eyes were ice hard, and then Simon winced and stared at the table, one hand on his stomach. He looked as if he was close to throwing up.

'So you're still a Secret Squirrel?' Bird said to Emma.

She smiled. 'Is that what you call us, really?'

'That's one of the polite versions,' said Bird. Tyson was sitting next to him and he reached down and patted him on the back of the neck. 'Are you both with Six?'

'Simon here is with GCHQ,' said Emma. 'I don't mean to sound patronizing, but do you know much about GCHQ?'

'You do sound patronizing, Emma,' said Bird. 'But fair play, other than that they're Secret Squirrels and they listen in to phone conversations, I probably don't know that much.'

'Okay,' she said. 'So, GCHQ – Government Communications Headquarters – supplies signals intelligence to the government. There are more than seven thousand men and women working for the organization, which is based in Cheltenham. There are two arms to GCHQ – the Composite Signals Organization, which gathers information and monitors email and phone, and the National Cyber Security Centre, whose mission is to keep the UK's communications secure.'

'Big Brother is watching,' said Bird.

'Big Brother is protecting its citizens,' said Emma. 'A lot of the missions that you guys are sent on, both in the UK and overseas, are a direct result of information gleaned by GCHQ.'

Bird nodded. He actually knew quite a bit about GCHQ, including the fact that there had been quite a kerfuffle in 2013 when Edward Snowden revealed that the agency collected all online data in the UK through the Tempora program. Basically, they see and store anything that passes through the country's fibre-optic cable networks;

every email, every internet search, every phone conversation, every text. GCHQ scoops up more metadata than the US's National Security Agency. Bird knew that Emma was right – having access to phone and email communication meant that the spooks were able to nip a lot of terrorist outrages in the bud, but it also meant an end to privacy. Everything that was done or said online was on a hard drive somewhere, ready to be scrutinized at the press of a button.

Warren returned with a bottle of water and a glass. He gave them to Simon and sat down next to Bird. 'Did I miss anything?' he asked.

'I was just bringing Andy up to speed on the work of GCHQ. That's who Simon works for.'

Simon poured water into his glass and drank some. The colour was starting to return to his cheeks. From where they were sitting they could see the helicopter through the window, but Simon was clearly making a conscious effort to avoid looking at it.

Oli the waiter came over. He was carrying a bowl of water, which he placed in front of Tyson. 'What can I get you?' he asked them. 'The chef's got a terrific shepherd's pie that I can definitely recommend. He uses real shepherds, I'm told.'

'We ate before we got on the chopper,' said Emma. 'But I'd love a coffee. Milk, no sugar.'

'Sir?' said the waiter, looking at Simon.

Simon shook his head and held up his glass. 'I'm fine with water.'

'Coffee, and I'll take the shepherd's pie,' said Warren.

'Me too,' said Bird.

'And I'll bring some of that mince for Tyson,' said the waiter. He headed back to the kitchen.

Bird and Warren sat back in their chairs. This wasn't a social meeting, the two spooks were there for a reason, so there was no need for chit-chat.

Emma smiled again, but there was little warmth in her eyes. 'So, the guy who died, the guy you tried to save, worked for GCHQ. That's why Simon is here, obviously.' She nodded at Simon, who forced a smile before taking another sip of water. 'Specifically, he worked for JTRIG. The Joint Threat Research Intelligence Group.' She said the last five words slowly and carefully, making sure that he could read her lips.

Bird shrugged. The name meant nothing to him.

'JTRIG is a dirty tricks unit of GCHQ,' Emma explained. 'They work through what they call "effects" operations, basically discrediting and disrupting enemies of the state by pretty much any means possible. They plant disinformation on the web, they use honey traps to expose enemy agents, they attack and destroy communication networks. As I said, dirty tricks.'

'I'd take issue with that, actually,' said Simon.

Emma grinned. 'Well of course you would, Simon, you work for them.'

'It's just that dirty tricks makes it sound as if we're doing something unlawful. That we're, I don't know, somehow shady.'

'So how would you describe what JTRIG does?' asked Bird.

Simon wrinkled his nose. 'I suppose I'd say that we monitor and influence internet communications, and covertly infiltrate online communities in order to sow dissension and disseminate false information.' He took another drink of water.

Bird grinned. 'Simon, mate, that sounds like dirty tricks to me.'

Emma reached inside her fleece and took out an envelope. She slid it across the table to Bird. He opened it and took out a photograph of a man in his thirties. Bird immediately recognized the thinning hair and the heavy jowls. He nodded. 'That's the guy they killed in the alley.'

'Sasha Brownlow,' said Emma. She took the photograph back and slid it into the envelope. 'He's been with JTRIG for the past five years. British father, Ukrainian mother. He had an appointment with an MI5 officer that morning. He was supposed to be meeting the officer at nine, in a coffee shop not far away from where he was murdered. Obviously, we assume the two events are connected.'

Bird frowned. 'I don't understand. You said JTRIG was part of GCHQ, but this Brownlow wanted to talk to MI5?'

'All we know is that he said there was something he needed to talk about. And he wanted to do it in person.'

'So whoever killed him didn't want him talking to MI5,' said Bird.

'That's what it looks like,' said Emma.

'So what did this Sasha do for JTRIG?'

'He was a hacker, basically,' said Simon. 'Had been since he was in his teens. For a few years he was a member of Anonymous, but it was when he was working off his own bat that he started to get into trouble. He started playing around with the Pentagon's computer system and came to the attention of the National Security Agency. The Americans were all for extraditing him but we stepped in and offered him our protection in return for him working for us.'

'In Cheltenham? That's where GCHQ is based, right?'

'No, a lot of the JTRIG people work from home or in locations away from Cheltenham,' said Simon.

'For plausible deniability?' said Bird.

Simon shifted uncomfortably in his seat. 'I wouldn't necessarily say that,' he said. 'It's more that most JTRIG employees don't respond well to the office environment. Especially a high-security environment like we have at Cheltenham. Sasha worked out of a flat in Camden.'

'Not far from where he was killed,' said Bird.

'Exactly.'

'So his killers must have known where he was working?'

'We'll get to that,' said Emma. 'Our priority right now is to work out who they are. We're obviously hoping that you can help us with that.'

'This JTRIG unit, who do they go up against?' asked Bird.

'Whoever we have to,' said Simon. 'The Russians, the Chinese, the Iranians. Some of our work is political but the National Crime Agency also works with us to attack various criminal groups.'

'The guys you saw, do you have any idea who they might have been?' asked Emma.

'They weren't Chinese, that's for sure. Or Iranians. They were big guys. Overcoats. Shiny shoes. Could have been Russians, I suppose.'

'You didn't hear them talk?' asked Simon.

'Andy's deaf, remember?' said Emma.

'Sorry, yes,' said Simon. 'It's just that talking to you, it's as if you're hearing everything.'

'Trust me, I'm not,' said Bird. 'But you guys are both easy to read. The guys in the alley, not so much. They hardly spoke but I didn't get the feeling that they were speaking Russian. They could have been cockneys for all I know.'

'When you lip-read, can you read different languages?' asked Simon.

'Some.'

'How many languages do you speak?'

'Fluently? Five.'

'Five?'

'I was a language specialist in the Regiment.'

'So which languages?'

'Arabic. Russian. Pashto. Kurdish.'

'That's four.'

Bird smiled. 'I was including English.'

'Of course. Yes.'

'And I can have a decent stab at French, German, Italian and Ukrainian. I know enough to make myself understood.'

'So you studied languages at university?' asked Emma.

'Nah, I left school at eighteen. Travelled for a couple of years and then joined the Paras. I could just pick up languages. Didn't have to study at all, the vocabulary just sticks. Then when I joined the Regiment, they sent me on courses for Arabic, Pashto and Kurdish. We use interpreters in those theatres but they can't always be relied on.'

'And Russian and Ukrainian?'

'I did some self-study when they said we were being sent to Ukraine.'

'You self-studied to fluency?'

'I got the basics. Like I said, vocabulary just sticks in my mind. Then I was in full immersion mode when I was in-country.' He shrugged. 'It's just something I can do. Though now that I'm deaf, it's not as useful as it was.'

'But you said you can lip-read other languages,' said Emma.

'It's a struggle. I have to assume that in the UK everyone is speaking English. If someone is speaking a different language then it takes me time to realize that.'

'The point I'm trying to make is that you've got skills that you should be using. I can see that being deaf would put an end to a military career, but the intelligence services could certainly make use of your language skills.'

'Is that what this is all about?' said Bird. 'You've come all the way to Hereford to offer me a job?'

Emma smiled. 'Would you be interested?'

Bird looked over at Warren, who was grinning. Like most members of the Regiment, they both had pretty low opinions of the intelligence agencies. Most were desk-bound warriors who didn't even know how to fire a gun if their life depended on it and who would spend their entire careers facing nothing more dangerous than a paper cut. 'I'd certainly give it some thought,' he said, and Warren snorted softly.

Emma looked over at Simon, who had slumped back in his chair. 'Simon, are you okay?'

'I don't feel good,' he said. His brow was bathed in sweat and a vein was pulsing in his forehead.

'Why don't I take you to see the doc?' said Warren. 'If it's motion sickness he can give you something to take for the journey back.'

Simon looked as if he was going to throw up at the thought of another helicopter flight. He nodded and got to his feet unsteadily. Warren helped him out of the mess.

'Is he always like this on helicopters?' asked Bird.

'I haven't flown with him before.'

'You're not a team?'

Emma shook her head. 'Not really.'

Bird leant towards her and lowered his voice. 'Can I ask you something?'

'Of course,' said Emma. 'I can't promise to give you an answer, but I'm open to questions.'

Bird smiled. The question on the tip of his tongue was whether or not Emma was her real name, but he figured she would lie if he asked her. Spooks never used their real names; it was in their DNA. 'The guy who died worked for GCHQ, and he was planning to talk to MI5, so why are you handling this? I'm assuming you haven't switched from Six to Five, because I'm told that rarely happens.'

'I'm still with Six. You're right, there tends not to be much movement back and forth between the agencies.'

'So the answer to my question?'

She smiled and he sensed that she was deciding whether to tell the truth or not. That was how the Secret Squirrels worked – everything they said or did went through the filter of what was best for their agency. 'It was felt that you might react better to a friendly face.'

He chuckled. 'Friendly?'

'Well, familiar. We have a history. And under the circumstances, it was felt that we needed to get you on-side right from the get-go.'

'Felt by who?'

'That's two questions, Andy.'

'I see this as basic intel sharing,' said Bird.

'I hear you. Let's just say that the powers that be want this to go as smoothly as possible and the key to that is to make you feel comfortable.' She smiled. 'So, tell me, is it working?'

'Do I feel comfortable? Not really.' He wrinkled his nose. 'By the powers that be, you presumably mean the bosses at MI6 and MI5.'

'That's right.'

'Sasha Brownlow died last night. How did your bosses know to pull you in so quickly?'

Her smile tightened. 'That's their job, isn't it? To stay on top of things.'

'I get that, but how did they connect Brownlow's death to me? The cops don't know, do they?'

'No, they don't.'

'So how do the powers that be know?'

'That's a good question.'

'I'm guessing it has something to do with the CTSFO that our guy spoke to.'

For the first time, Emma's smile appeared genuine. 'That would be a good guess.'

'Asking about the killing in Camden raised a red flag, did it?'

'When the query came from Stirling Lines, yes, very much so. It's all very well getting a CTSFO to make enquiries for you, but his ultimate loyalty has to be to his job. His boss called him back and of course he told his boss everything. Once we realized that you were involved, I got the call.' She shrugged. 'And here we are. So can I ask you something, Andy? Quid pro quo. As we're now sharing intelligence.'

'Sure.'

'When you saw the guy killed in the alley, you were sleeping rough, right?'

Bird nodded. 'Yeah.'

'I don't understand how that happens. You were injured in the line of duty, why weren't you looked after?'

'By the Regiment?'

'By the Regiment. By the Army. By the Ministry of Defence. I don't see how a hero ends up on the streets.'

'Plenty of former soldiers are on the streets, Emma. And a lot of them were special forces.'

'But why? You have a pension, right?'

'You have to do twenty years to get a pension. I was in just over ten.'

'But a disability pay-out?'

'I got that, sure. But it didn't last long, not when I got divorced.'

'You were married?'

Bird nodded. 'To a local girl. Sarah. It was hard enough being an SAS wife at the best of times, but after I was injured . . .' He shrugged. 'I was a nightmare to live with, I really was.'

'I'm sorry to hear that.'

'Yeah. I'm not proud of what happened. Early on, I'd wake up screaming most mornings, and I lashed out a couple of times. Not trying to hurt her, just thrashing around in my sleep. I moved into the spare room but that didn't really help. I was morose a lot of the time, in fact I spent more time with Tyson than I did with Sarah. Then I went into a downward spiral. I didn't want to be with anyone, I didn't want to talk to anyone. A few guys from the Regiment tried to get in touch but I pushed them away. Sarah decided she'd had enough and I moved out. A friend in London offered me some security work so I left Hereford.'

The waiter came over with a tray and three mugs of coffee. 'The shepherd's pies are ready,' he said as he put the mugs on the table.

'The guys should be back soon,' said Bird.

'I'll wait until they're here,' said the waiter, and he headed off.

'I still don't understand why you weren't offered support by the Army,' said Emma. She sipped her coffee.

'There's a lot of us,' said Bird. 'I was told that there are more than ninety thousand veterans getting compensation from the military. There were more than twenty-two thousand medically discharged during the Iraq and Afghanistan conflicts alone.' He shrugged. 'Some fall through the cracks, I guess.'

'I get the feeling there's more to it with you,' said Emma. 'You don't want to be helped. You want to stand on your own two feet.' She smiled down at Tyson. 'Four feet in your case.'

'I don't want charity, that's true,' said Bird.

Emma shook her head. 'After what you did to save your people out in Syria, it's not charity. You earned it.'

'It feels like charity,' said Bird. 'And this sleeping rough thing, it's temporary. I'll get through it.'

'I'll give you what help I can,' she said. He opened his mouth to protest but she cut him short by raising her hand. 'It's not charity, I think we can help each other.'

'Okay,' said Bird. 'Thank you.' He sipped his coffee. 'So you think that this Brownlow was murdered because of his work with GCHQ?'

Emma nodded. 'Simon was a bit touchy when I described what he does as dirty tricks, but JTRIG was set up in response to what the IRA was doing online, and they have to fight fire with fire.'

Bird frowned. 'Did you say IRA?'

Emma smiled. 'I did, but not the Provos. The Internet Research Agency, aka the Trolls from Olgino. Olgino is a suburb of St Petersburg, which is where the IRA is based. Well, I say IRA, these days they go by the name of Project Lakhta, but it's the same guys.' She sipped her coffee. 'The IRA was set up by Yevgeny Prigozhin, the guy who used to head up the Wagner Group before his plane exploded. It was set up in 2014 or thereabouts, in St Petersburg, basically as a troll farm to cause mischief in the US and Europe.

'Their first mission was to support Russia's activities in Ukraine, then they began supporting Trump in the 2016 elections. They had more than a thousand people working for them, setting up fake accounts on social-networking sites, newspaper sites, TikTok, Instagram. They were particularly active on the *Daily Mail* website, for instance, pushing Trump as the best option for US president, and talking down anyone who was critical of Putin. It's a huge operation. Their trolls watch American TV shows to get their phrasing right, and they use proxy servers to set up thousands of fake identities across all the social-media platforms.

'IRA was supposedly disbanded after Prigozhin died in 2023, following his failed military uprising against the Russian generals, but in fact the trolls were just moved around under the Project Lakhta umbrella. Their brief is still to disrupt the democratic processes in the West, incite civil unrest, and basically polarize communities, racially, politically and sexually. JTRIG was set up to counter the work of the Project Lakhta trolls. As I said, to fight fire with fire.'

'And that's what Sasha Brownlow was doing? Fighting fire with fire?'

'His aims were two-fold. To combat misinformation on Ukrainian news and social sites, and to spread disinformation on Russian sites.'

'So he'd be planting fake stories?'

'Basically, yes. Anything that might cast aspersions on Putin, or hurt morale re: the war in Ukraine, for instance. He and his colleagues had a wide-ranging brief.'

The main doors opened and Warren and Simon appeared. Simon was looking better than when he had left, and there was now some colour in his cheeks.

The waiter reappeared with two plates and a bowl on his tray. He put the shepherd's pies down in front of Bird and Warren, then placed a bowl of raw mince in front of Tyson. Tyson immediately started to eat.

Emma looked at the food on the table. Each plate had a generous helping of shepherd's pie, along with cabbage, carrots and peas. 'Actually, that does look good,' she said. She smiled at the waiter. 'Could I have some, please?'

'Of course,' he said. He looked at Simon. 'What about you, sir?'

Simon shook his head. 'Still fine with water.' As the waiter walked away, Simon took a sip and looked over at Emma. 'So did I miss much?'

'I was just bringing Andy up to speed on Sasha's role at GCHQ,' she said. 'Now you're back, I think he should run through what happened to him, from start to finish.' She flashed Bird a smile. 'And get tucked into your shepherd's pie. Don't worry about talking with your mouth full. We're good.'

CHAPTER 15

Bird went through everything that had happened as he ate his shepherd's pie. He had just got to the point where the men in the BMW X5s had killed Joel when the waiter reappeared with Emma's meal. Bird stopped talking until the waiter had put the plate down in front of her and gone back to the kitchen.

Simon and Emma said nothing as Bird described what happened at Billy's flat, and at the Hilldrop Estate. Emma ate with her fork and left her knife unused. Occasionally she would look over at Simon and nod, but most of the time she kept her eyes on Bird.

Warren finished his food first and sat back with his arms folded, listening as Bird continued to tell his story.

In all, Bird spoke for almost half an hour. He put in as much detail as he could remember about everything that had happened – he wasn't telling them a story, he was passing them intel, and every piece of information, no matter how small, could be important. Eventually he described arriving at Stirling Lines with Warren and Harris. 'And here I am,' he said. He still had half of his meal on the plate – he had done more talking than eating.

'So, as far as you being here goes, do you have official permission?'

'He doesn't,' said Warren. 'I brought him in and I'm responsible for him. I didn't run it by the colonel which might be an issue moving forwards. He'll obviously have seen your heli arrive.'

'I'll take care of that,' said Emma. 'My boss's boss will get someone at the MoD to make a call. That'll make Andy's stay here official and hopefully minimize any flak for you.'

'Much appreciated,' said Warren. 'But I think his nose is still going to be out of joint that I did it without his permission.'

'It'll be fine, I promise,' said Emma.

'You're making a lot of promises today,' said Warren.

'And I'll keep them,' said Emma. 'This is a matter of national security – MI5 needed help and you're a close friend of Andy's. We might have played fast and loose with the chain of command, but things were moving quickly and needs must. Once the colonel understands that, he'll be good.'

'There's one thing I don't understand,' said Bird. He grinned. 'Actually, there's a whole load of things that I don't understand, but there's one that's worrying me.'

'And what's that?' said Emma.

'I get that the CTSFO asking about Sasha's murder and the shoot-out in Arlington Road would raise a red flag with you. But you came to Stirling Lines to talk to me. That's what the MI5 liaison officer told the Sarge. So how did you know I was involved? How did you even know who I was?'

Simon looked across at Emma, and the two spooks held a look for a second or two. There was an almost imperceptible nod from Emma and Bird knew that she was the one who would do the explaining, so he sipped his coffee and looked at her over the top of his mug.

'We tracked your phone's GPS,' said Emma. 'At least a GCHQ team did. As soon as we knew that Sasha was dead, we did a search for all the phones in the area where he died. Later, after the shoot-out, we did a similar search for the phones in the vicinity of Arlington Road. Yours came up both times. And there were two other matches, too, so a couple of those involved in the shoot-out were also nearby when Sasha was killed. They were obviously using burner phones because they both went silent not long after the shoot-out. Your phone was on a contract in your own name and registered to an address here in Hereford. Then, when your friend Peter Harris starting pumping the CTSFO for intel, it wasn't hard to put two and two together.'

'You can do that, that quickly?'

'Of course,' said Simon. 'That's what we do. The police need warrants and it can take days to get the data they want from the phone companies, but so far as tracking is concerned, we just go ahead and do it.'

'It has to be that way, Andy – terrorism timelines are usually tight,' said Emma. 'Investigations have to be done in real time.'

Bird nodded. 'But here's the thing that really worries me. I get that *you* can track phones like that, but the guys who killed Brownlow, they were following me, so *they* must have been tracking my phone too. I was in the car and they ambushed me. Then I was lying low in a friend's flat and they tracked me there and nearly caught me. Then I tried hiding out on a council estate and they turned up mob-handed. It was only when I dumped my phone that I lost them.'

'You dumped the phone on the Hilldrop Estate?' said Simon.

'Yeah, gave it to a drug dealer. I hoped that would throw them off my trail. I think it worked.'

'It did,' said Emma.

'But you hear what I'm saying? They must have been tracking my phone, right? I get that GCHQ has that capability, but how could the bad guys have been doing that?'

'We're investigating that as we speak,' said Emma.

'They must have someone at GCHQ. That's the only way they could be tracking me in real time.' He stared at Simon. 'True?'

Simon shifted uncomfortably in his seat. 'It's one of the avenues we're exploring.'

'Maybe that would explain why Brownlow wanted to meet with MI5? Maybe he realized there was a traitor in GCHQ and the bad guys killed him to keep their source a secret.'

'That's certainly possible,' said Emma. 'We'll see where the investigation goes.'

'But you accept that there might be someone at GCHQ who is helping them?'

Emma held up a hand. 'I absolutely hear what you're saying, Andy. But conjecture is a dangerous thing. Let's wait until we have evidence before we draw conclusions. But before we go any further, there's something I need to tell you.'

Bird could see that she was serious, so he put down his fork. 'What?'

'Your friend, Billy O'Neill. I'm afraid he's dead.'

Bird's head swam. 'Dead?'

Emma nodded. 'I'm sorry, yes. He was tortured and killed in his flat. We think they were waiting for him and when he came back to his flat this morning . . .' She grimaced. 'I'm so sorry.'

Bird felt as if a steel band had tightened around his chest. 'Why would anyone . . .' He stopped as he realized he knew the answer to his own question. 'Me. They wanted to know about me. It's my fault.'

'You can't blame yourself.'

Bird gritted his teeth. 'I can. If I hadn't led them to Billy's flat he'd never have been on their radar. What about Vicky?'

'Vicky?'

'His girlfriend. I think he stayed with her last night.'

'She wasn't there.'

'What did they do to him?'

'I'd rather spare you the details, Andy, but it was bad.'

Bird cursed under his breath. 'Billy didn't know anything. I stayed with him for a while some time ago but I haven't spoken to him for a few weeks.' He frowned. 'How did you know about Billy?'

'We tracked your phone, remember. We could see where you went and how long you were there. We gained access to the flat this morning.'

Bird shook his head. 'The bastards. They don't care who they hurt, do they?'

'Clearly not.'

A cold hand gripped Bird's heart and he gasped. He stood up so quickly that his chair overturned and crashed behind him. Tyson sprang to his feet, snarling. Bird ignored the dog and stared at Emma, his eyes wide. 'We've got to go, now. If they knew about Billy they'll know about my wife. We have to warn her.'

'Your ex-wife,' said Emma. 'Sarah is fine. I swear. An MI5 officer and two armed police officers are at Sarah's house. They'll stay with her until this is resolved.'

Tyson continued to snarl so Bird bent down and patted him on the back. 'Easy boy. It's all good.'

Tyson stopped snarling. Bird stared at Emma. 'Why didn't you tell me as soon as you saw me?'

'Because I didn't want you flying off the handle,' she said. 'Please, sit down. Finish your food. Sarah is in no danger, you have my word.'

Bird picked up his chair and sat down slowly. Tyson lay down next to it. 'You should have told me straight away,' said Bird, sullenly. 'The moment you got here.'

'If I did, you might have overreacted,' said Emma. 'We needed to chat with you first, while you were calm.'

Bird looked over at Warren. 'And they wonder why we don't trust them,' he said.

'Never trust the Secret Squirrels,' muttered Warren under his breath. 'That's the golden rule.'

Emma ignored him and kept her attention focused on Bird. 'Andy, please don't say that. You can totally trust us. And Sarah is safe, you have my word on that.'

'I want to see her.'

'And we'll take you. But I've already had an update, she's absolutely fine and she's well protected.'

'But the fact that you're protecting her means that you think she's in danger.'

'After what happened to your friend Billy, yes, it's a possibility.'

Andy gritted his teeth. 'This is all my fault,' he said. 'I should have ditched my phone straight away.'

'You couldn't have known. And once they had your number they would have had your address here. Why is that? You're divorced, why is the phone company still using your old address?'

'I never got around to changing it,' said Bird. 'They don't send bills, it's all online. I think my bank account still uses the old address. Emma, do you really think they'll go to the house?'

Emma nodded. 'It's a possibility, yes. That's what we want to talk about.'

'We need to go, now,' said Bird, getting to his feet.

'Andy, she's fine. She's under our protection. We have time to talk.'

'Now!' repeated Bird, louder this time. Tyson picked up on the tone and growled menacingly.

'Okay, okay,' said Emma. 'There's no need to snap at me. Either of you.'

CHAPTER 16

Warren's black Range Rover pulled up outside what had once been Bird's home, a two-bedroom semi-detached house that backed onto a field where cows grazed around a towering electricity pylon. It had been almost three years since Bird had been at the house, and it was no longer his; he had signed it – and the mortgage – over to Sarah at the time of his divorce. There was a grey Prius in the driveway that he didn't recognize. There was a small patch of lawn at the front that had been neatly trimmed, a big change from when he had lived there, because he took care of the garden and his long absences meant it was often overgrown.

The house on the left belonged to an SAS trooper who had been with the Regiment for close to twenty-five years. His name was Barney Heyes, though everyone called him Fred, presumably through some tenuous *Flintstones* link. Heyes was in B Squadron's Mobility Troop, and his desert warfare skills meant that he had been out in the Middle East for most of the past two decades. Bird had overlapped with him a few times, and it was while they were out in Afghanistan that Heyes had told him that the house next door to his had become available. Bird and Sarah were about to tie the knot, so the timing was perfect. A broker had fixed them up with a mortgage, they'd furnished it by maxing out their credit cards, and all had been sweetness and light until Bird had thrown himself on the hand grenade out in Syria. He shuddered at the memory.

Emma put a hand on his shoulder. She was sitting in the back, behind Warren, and he turned to look at her. She flashed him a thumbs up. 'You okay?' Simon was sitting next to her. He seemed to have recovered from his bout of air sickness and the colour had returned to his cheeks.

Bird nodded. 'Good to go,' he said.

They climbed out. Heyes didn't appear to be at home. He spent his spare time working on an old MG sports car and whenever he was away he covered it with a tarpaulin held in place with ropes. The car was covered and the tarpaulin was dotted with leaves from a nearby beech tree.

Emma and Simon walked up to the front door. Emma rang the bell.

Bird and Warren waited by the Prius. 'Nice house,' said Warren. 'You bought it?'

'Mortgaged to the hilt,' said Bird. 'But it's Sarah's problem now.'

'Doubt I'll ever get married,' said Warren. 'It never seems to end well.'

'A few guys have managed to make it work,' said Bird. 'Kids seem to help. Providing the wife is okay bringing them up herself.'

'I've never wanted kids,' said Warren. 'I wouldn't wish my childhood on anyone.'

'Sarah and I said we'd wait a few years, until we were more settled.' He smiled ruefully. 'So much for that plan.'

Emma stepped back from the front door and looked up at the bedroom windows. She took a mobile phone from her fleece and put it to her ear.

'There's something wrong,' said Bird. He walked towards the house. Emma was frowning. She said something to Simon and he shrugged. Emma tapped out a number and put the phone back to her ear. It was clear from the look on her face that there was a problem. She looked up at the bedroom windows again.

'No one is answering?' said Bird.

Emma shook her head. She put the phone away.

'You left two firearms officers in there?' Bird asked.

Emma nodded. 'And one of our own officers. He's not answering. I tried one of the firearms officers and they aren't picking up either.'

'I'll break the door in,' said Warren, stepping forwards.

Emma took a small leather wallet from inside her fleece. She unzipped it to reveal a set of metal picks. 'No need, I've got this,' she said.

'Give me a second,' said Bird. He walked across the small lawn and bent down to move an apple-sized rock. Underneath was a Yale key in a small ziplock bag. He held it up. 'Sarah's always forgetting her keys.' Emma wrinkled her nose and put her picks away.

Bird headed for the front door and unlocked it. He pushed it open a fraction. 'Sarah? Are you there?'

'Andy, stay back please,' said Emma.

'Why, are you carrying? Because the last I heard, MI6 didn't carry firearms.'

Emma stepped away, realizing that he was right. If there were armed men inside, she wouldn't be able to do anything.

Bird clicked at Tyson. 'Heel,' he said. Tyson walked over and sat next to him, his ears up. Bird put a hand on the door. He looked down at Tyson. 'Search!' he said, and pushed the door open wide.

Tyson ran inside. He had been trained to run through the bottom floor of a house first so he ignored the stairs and hurried down the hall. Bird's jaw tightened when he saw the body on the stairs. It was a man, wearing a black bomber jacket, tight jeans and gleaming white Nikes. There was a Glock pistol on the stairs by his side. Bird couldn't tell what the man looked like because his face had imploded and there was blood and brain matter splattered across the wall. By the looks of it he hadn't even managed to get off a shot.

There was a doorway to the right. The sitting room, where he and Sarah had spent many an evening sitting on the low-slung IKEA sofa watching Netflix. Those evenings when he had been around, which truth be told were few and far between. Tyson went inside. If the room was clear, Tyson would reappear after a few seconds, but he stayed where he was. Bird followed him. There was another man dead on the sofa. He had been shot twice in the chest and there were large red splotches on his white polo shirt.

'Search!' said Bird, letting Tyson know he was to continue. Tyson turned on the spot and ran back to the hall. Bird followed him.

The next room down the hall was the dining room, but most of the time Sarah had used it for the scented candle business that she was always trying to get off the ground. Tyson did a quick circuit of the room and then headed back into the hall.

Warren was behind Bird now and they both followed Tyson down the hall to the kitchen. Bird's heart was in his mouth. He could smell the blood and the gunsmoke and he wasn't sure how he was going to react if he found Sarah dead in the kitchen. It was all his fault, there was no getting out of that – he had led the killers to Hereford, that was the only explanation for what had happened.

There was a man lying on the floor, his face a bloody mess, a pool of congealing blood around what was left of his skull. There was a gun on the floor. A Glock. Bird bent down and picked it up. It was a police issue Glock 17, with a magazine that held seventeen cartridges. He ejected the magazine. It was full. The man hadn't had time to fire it. He put the gun and the magazine on the counter by the sink.

There was another body on the floor by the back door, lying on its side. It was a man in his late twenties, his blond hair matted with blood. He was wearing a grey suit and brown brogues, clearly the MI5 officer.

Tyson bounded upstairs. They heard him moving room to room – padding, silence, a huff of breath, then claws on the landing again. He came back down and sat at Bird's heel. All clear.

There was no shattered glass, no sign that the shots had come from outside the house. Bird realized that he had been holding his breath and he sighed. At least Sarah wasn't there. 'What do you think?' Bird asked Warren.

'These two were either in here getting coffee or were pulled in by a distraction.' Warren turned and pointed to the front door, where Emma and Simon were now standing, looking up the stairs. 'Another guy, maybe two, come in through the front door. They take out the SFO on the stairs, then move to the kitchen. Bang bang, bang bang. One goes into the front room, shoots the guy on the sofa.'

'They were pros.'

'Hell yeah. Maybe they picked the lock. Came in with guns blazing. Probably suppressed. They made every shot count.'

Bird nodded. 'The guys who followed me to the flat in London picked the lock.'

'They know what they're doing.' Warren patted Bird on the back. 'I'm sorry about this.'

'It's a shitstorm, Sarge. I'm sorry I got you involved.'

Bird went back down the hall. Emma had closed the front door. Simon was continuing to stare at the dead firearms officer on the stairs. 'There's two dead in the kitchen, a CTSFO and a guy in a grey suit,' said Bird.

Emma's hand flew up to cover her mouth. 'Oh no. That's Justin. Oh my God.'

'There's another body in there,' said Bird, pointing at the front room. 'But no sign of my wife.' He forced a smile. 'Ex-wife. Sarah.' Tyson sat down next to Bird and he reached down and patted him on the neck.

Emma and Simon went into the sitting room. 'Stay,' Bird said to Tyson, and he followed them. Bird gestured at the body on the sofa. 'Is he one of yours?'

Emma shook her head. 'He was here when our team arrived,' she said. 'His name's Alex McBride, he said he was Sarah's partner.'

'Oh, yes, right. I knew she had a new guy but I didn't know his name.'

'He was living here. That's his car in the driveway.'

Bird nodded. He knew that Sarah had moved on but it always hurt to be reminded of the fact.

There was a phone on the coffee table with a yellow Post-it on it. 'WE WILL CALL' had been written on it in black capital letters. Bird picked the phone up.

'No, Andy!' said Emma. 'DNA. Fingerprints.'

Bird sneered at her. 'I'm fairly sure that the guys who did this would have known to wear gloves.' He took off the Post-it note and swiped the screen. 'It's not locked,' he said. 'It's obviously a burner, no calls made or received, and no texts.'

Emma held out her hand but Bird shook his head. 'No, I'm keeping this.'

Emma shook her head fiercely. She pointed at the phone and then at her own ear. 'They will be listening,' she mouthed. She held out her hand again and this time he gave the phone to her. It was a Samsung Galaxy. Emma looked at it then gave it to Simon. He snapped off the back cover and removed the battery, then refitted the cover. He took out his wallet, opened it, and fished out a metal paperclip. He straightened it out and used it to open the SIM card tray.

'Now they won't be able to call us,' said Bird.

'You're a civilian, Andy,' said Emma. 'You need to leave this to the professionals.'

Simon put the phone and battery onto the coffee table.

'How can you say that with a straight face after what happened to your people?' he said. He pointed at the phone. 'This is staying with me. And if they call, I'll be the one who talks to them.'

'Yes, but not on that phone. They'll have God knows what software in it to track you and eavesdrop. Look what happened last time they tracked you.'

Simon took a phone from his jacket. It was another Samsung. He used the paperclip to open the card tray and then slotted in the SIM card from the kidnappers' phone. 'We'll be tracking this one,' he said. 'And everything said on it, and every message it sends or receives, will be recorded in the cloud.' He gave it to Bird. He nodded at the phone on the table. 'I'll get our guys to check it out – the software and any hardware drivers they've installed might give us a clue as to who they are.'

Bird turned to glare at Emma. 'How could this happen?' he asked. 'You said they were professionals.'

Emma looked close to tears. 'They are,' she said. She grimaced and corrected herself. 'They were.'

'So why are they all dead and my wife is God knows where?'

'Andy—' said Warren.

'Don't "Andy" me, Sarge!' snapped Bird. 'They were supposed to be looking after Sarah. They were supposed to be protecting her. How could this happen?'

Warren raised his hands. It wasn't a question that he could answer.

Bird turned back to Emma. 'They can't have followed me here, so it must be one of your people who told them where Sarah was. That's the only explanation.'

Emma's eyes filled with tears and Bird suddenly felt like a bully. She might have been an MI6 officer but a colleague of hers had been murdered. Bird knew all too well what it felt like to lose a friend. He held up his hands. 'I'm sorry.'

Simon threw Bird a withering look and put his arm around her.

Warren tapped Bird on the arm and gestured at the door. Bird followed Warren out into the hall. 'What do you want to do?' asked Warren.

Bird held up the phone. 'I'll wait for them to call and see what they want. They've clearly taken Sarah for a reason.'

'But why? Because you can ID them? How does them kidnapping her stop you identifying them?'

'I guess they want a swap. Me for her.'

'But they have to know that you've already spoken to the cops. Kidnapping your ex-wife doesn't change that.'

Bird shrugged. 'None of this makes any sense. They killed the GCHQ guy in the alley and ran off. It could have just been a mugging gone wrong. But then they came back to kill me almost immediately. They could have just stayed away. What's the worst that could have happened? I barely got a look at them, right? Didn't see their car, didn't have any idea what they were up to. If I had spoken to the cops, what could I tell them? A vague description and that's it. But now, I've had a better look at them, I know they drive around in BMW X5s and it's obvious that they have a mole within GCHQ. There's clearly a bigger picture here, though I've no idea what it is. Yet.'

Emma came out of the living room. Her cheeks were flushed and her eyes were red but she seemed to have regained her composure. 'Andy, you need to let us handle this.'

'It's my wife they've got. This is down to me.'

'I understand how you feel, but you can't deal with this on your own.'

Bird gestured at Warren. 'I won't be on my own.'

'The Regiment can give him whatever help he needs,' said Warren.

'Absolutely, yes, you have a skill set that gives you an advantage if you're in a firefight. But this isn't going to be a shoot-out. This is a kidnapping, and resolving a kidnapping requires a different skill set. We need hostage negotiators, we need technical equipment, we need communications.'

'It's not rocket science, Emma,' said Bird. 'Someone will call and tell me what they want in exchange for Sarah. Whatever it is that they want, I'll give it to them.'

'And if that means they kill you?'

Bird smiled. 'I'm not an easy kill.'

'And they'll know that by now.' She put a hand on his elbow. 'I'm not saying that you shouldn't be involved, I'm just saying that a team effort is a better bet. For you and for Sarah.'

Bird held the phone up. 'Okay, but I talk to them.'

'I'd assume that they would want to talk to you. You're clearly the focus. But we need to be able to listen in.'

'And I decide what we do.'

'Of course. But I would like to at least offer you advice. Andy, I have a lot of resources that I can draw on, and I can do it with some degree of autonomy. You're former SAS, you can appreciate the advantages of autonomy. Let me help you.'

Bird looked at her for several seconds, then slowly nodded. 'Okay,' he said. He looked over at Warren. 'Yeah?' he said.

Warren flashed him a tight smile. 'Hell, yeah.'

Simon and Emma headed out.

'Do you trust them?' Bird asked Warren.

'About as far as I can throw them,' said Warren.

They left the house and followed Emma and Simon to the car.

CHAPTER 17

Emma was looking at the map of the UK on the wall. They were in a briefing room in the Regiment's admin block. There were a dozen plastic chairs and two large whiteboards dotted with diagrams drawn by the room's previous occupants. Simon was sitting at a table by the door, an open MacBook in front of him. Bird and Warren were either side of Emma. As soon as they had arrived at the camp, Emma had gone to speak to Colonel Brewerton in the admin block. Apparently, the colonel had already been contacted by the MoD and told her that the Regiment would be offering her whatever support she needed. She hadn't told Bird and Warren what sort of mood the colonel was in, but they doubted that he would be happy that they had lied to him and they were sure that at some point he would be having words with them to express that unhappiness.

Emma looked around to make sure that she had their attention. 'Just over two hours elapsed between my team arriving at the house and us finding them dead. I'm not a forensics expert, but it looked to me as if they had been dead for a while.'

Warren nodded. 'An hour, I'd say. The smell of gun smoke was strong but fading. And the blood had stopped spreading.' He looked at Bird. 'What do you think?'

'Between thirty minutes and an hour,' he said.

'So, if we say they'd been dead an hour when we found them, that means it's been nearly two since the killers left the house,' said Emma, glancing at her watch, a slim steel Cartier. 'Then they could be what, a hundred miles away? One twenty?' She tapped the map. 'So already they could be in Liverpool, Birmingham, Bristol. Hell, they could be nearly back in London.'

'You're not thinking of calling in the police, are you?' asked Bird.

'There's no point,' said Emma. 'We don't know what direction they're headed, or what vehicles they're using. We have to wait for them to call. The timing of the call is crucial, it'll tell us the maximum distance they can have travelled.'

'They're unlikely to be close by,' said Bird. 'They won't have had time to get anything fixed up.'

'Plenty of empty houses around, abandoned buildings and the like,' said Warren, looking at the map.

'Yeah, but this has to be out of their comfort zone,' said Bird.

'So you think they'll head back to London?'

Bird wrinkled his nose. 'It's a tough call. They're more likely to be comfortable in a familiar area, but on the other hand they're not going to want to be driving too far with Sarah on board. Swings and roundabouts.' He turned around to look at Simon. 'Can you do that GPS thing and track any phones that were at the house?'

'It's in hand,' said Simon. 'But these guys will almost certainly have turned their phones off now that they know we're after them.'

Bird turned back to Emma. 'The MI5 officer that was killed. What was his name? Justin?'

Emma nodded. 'Yes. Justin. He was the one who was supposed to meet Sasha at a coffee shop in Camden.'

'To talk about what?'

'Sasha wouldn't say. Just that it was important and they couldn't meet at Thames House. Justin said Sasha sounded scared, that he thought he was being watched. But he wouldn't tell Justin what was wrong, just that it was important. Very important. Justin pressed him but Sasha said that it was too dangerous to talk on the phone and he ended the call.'

'And what's happening with the house?' asked Bird.

'A clean-up crew is coming up from London to take care of things.'

'You can cover up four murders just like that, to make it look as if it never happened?'

'We don't want the press looking into it, do we? Okay, we can shut down journalists with a DSMA-Notice if we have to, but it's better not to raise a red flag in the first place.'

There was a stack of notepads, pens, pencils and markers, and a plastic box of metal paperclips on a table next to the map. 'What's a DSMA-Notice?' asked Bird. He picked up a couple of paperclips and began toying with them.

'A Defence and Security Media Advisory notice,' said Emma. 'Basically, an official request for editors not to publish or broadcast information for reasons of national security.'

'I thought that was a D-Notice?'

'It was, back in the day,' said Emma. 'From 1912 to 1993 it was a D-Notice, D for Defence, and then it was the DA-Notice – for Defence Advisory Notice – until 2015. Really, it's a rose by any other name – the DSMA-Notice does exactly what the old D-Notice did. But like I said, best that the info doesn't get out in the first place.'

'What about the families of the two CTSFOs?' said Bird. 'What are they going to be told?' He slipped the paperclips into his shirt pocket.

'Traffic accident, probably. But it's possible they might be told the truth about what happened – the decision will be taken at a much higher pay level than mine.'

'And what about the guy on the sofa? Sarah's partner? You're going to fake a car accident for him?'

'Possibly.'

'You can do that?' said Warren.

Emma nodded. 'We can. Either that or get it reported as a stroke or a heart attack.'

Warren shook his head contemptuously. 'Secret fucking Squirrel,' he said.

'It's a necessary evil, it has to be done,' said Emma. 'If the truth gets out then all eyes will be on GCHQ, and if it gets reported that there are security problems in the organization, then we lose credibility with our allies.'

'So to protect the reputation of His Majesty's Government, families are lied to about how their loved ones have died?' said Bird. 'That's sick.'

'I don't know about that, Andy,' said Warren. 'We've often held back the truth when our guys have failed to beat the clock. Sometimes it's best that parents don't know what was done to their son before he died. Better to tell a wife that her husband was blown up by an IED than telling them that he died in agony after being tortured for three days in the desert.' He shrugged. 'It's a tough call.'

'Nah, that's different,' said Bird. 'When the Regiment does it, it's to protect the families. This is about protecting the government.' He glared at Emma. 'What happens if Sarah gets killed? What will you tell everyone? That she had a heart attack?'

'Andy, I hear what you're saying, but—'

The phone began to vibrate in Bird's pocket and he pulled it out. He looked at Warren. 'You're going to have to do the talking,' he said. 'I won't be able to hear them. You'll have to pretend to be me.'

'I'll do it,' said Simon, holding out his hand.

'No offence,' said Bird. 'They'll know you're not me. The Sarge can do it.'

Emma nodded. 'He's right,' she said.

'Thanks a bunch,' said Simon. He sat back and folded his arms.

Bird nodded at Warren and accepted the call. He put it on speakerphone. 'Who is this?' he asked.

Bird couldn't hear the reply. He frowned at Emma. 'It's a computer-generated voice,' she mouthed. 'They say they have your ex-wife.'

'What do you want?' asked Warren.

Emma frowned, then mouthed at Bird again. 'Now they want the call to be taken off speakerphone.'

Emma nodded at Warren and he killed the speakerphone.

Warren continued to talk into the phone for a couple of minutes, mainly saying 'yes' and 'I understand'.

Eventually, the call ended. 'What did he say?' asked Bird.

'It's okay, we can listen to the conversation,' said Simon, taking the phone from Warren and tapping on the screen.

'Simon?' said Emma, gesturing at Bird.

'Oh, right, yes, sorry,' said Simon. 'I keep forgetting. Give me a minute. I'll get a transcript with the audio.'

He plugged the phone into his laptop and tapped on the keyboard.

'Basically, he wants Andy to drive out of the camp and head east,' said Warren.

'Okay, here we go,' said Simon. 'You'll hear the audio, but Andy can read a transliteration on screen.' He pressed a button on the keyboard and the speaker burst into life. Words began to appear on the screen and Bird moved closer to get a better look.

'If the police or the intelligence services are there, you must get rid of them,' said the computer-generated voice. 'If we see you with anyone else, your wife will die. Do you understand?'

'Yes.

'You have a car?'

'Yes.'

'Where are you now?'

'Hereford.'

'The SAS camp?'

'Yes.'

'Then get into the car and drive out of the camp. Head east on the A438. Once you have left the camp, we will text you with directions. Do you understand?'

'Yes, I understand.'

'Go now.'

'Okay. Yes.'

'You do exactly as we say, or your wife dies.'

'I understand.'

'Then understand this, it will not be an easy death. It will be long and painful and we will make sure that she knows that you are responsible.'

The call ended abruptly and Simon gave the phone back to Bird.

Bird straightened up. 'So he knows we're at Stirling Lines? I thought taking the battery out means they couldn't track us?'

'That's usually the case, yes.'

'So how the hell does he know where we are?'

'I can't answer that question, Andy. It could be they just put it together with Hereford.'

Bird put the phone away. 'I have to go.' He looked at Warren. 'Can I borrow your car, Sarge?'

'I'll come with you,' said Warren.

'They said I was to go alone. They'll be watching me.'

'They want to kill you, Andy,' said Emma.

'Yeah, well, that's easier said than done,' said Bird.

'We need to discuss this.'

'No, we don't. They told me to head east, and to go now.'

'We'll be following you.'

'If they see that you're following me, they'll kill Sarah.'

'We'll give you plenty of space. We can track the phone.'

'And then what? These guys are stone-cold killers.'

'We have a CTSFO team on standby.'

'They'd be related to the guys who died at the house?' said Bird scornfully. 'Fat lot of good they were.'

Emma's eyes hardened. 'There's no need for that, Andy.'

'There's every need. They were there to protect Sarah and they didn't do their job. If they had done their job, we wouldn't be having this conversation.'

'I'll come with you,' said Warren. 'I'll hide in the back.'

'I have to be alone,' said Bird. He looked down at Tyson. 'But Tyson can come with me. They didn't say anything about dogs.'

Warren looked at Emma. 'So I'll ride with you. The CTSFOs can follow behind.'

Emma held his look for a couple of seconds, then nodded. 'Okay.'

'But you stay well back,' said Bird.

'We will,' said Emma. 'That's what the tracker is for.'

She looked over at Simon and he nodded. 'It's through the GPS system so the range is unlimited.'

'Good to know,' said Bird.

CHAPTER 18

Warren gave Bird the key fob for the Range Rover. 'Please don't wreck her, I still have two years of payments to make before she's mine.'

'Kid gloves.'

'Just don't get shot at. Bullet holes are a bugger to patch up.'

Emma and Simon were standing by a vehicle from the SAS pool, a two-year-old white Audi A3 hatchback. Next to the Audi was a grey Toyota Land Cruiser. There were four men huddled in a group at the back of the Land Cruiser, all of them smoking. They were all wearing bomber jackets or leather jackets, jeans and boots. Bird would have recognized them as CTSFOs even if he didn't know who they were. They had hard eyes and a confident way of standing, legs apart and shoulders back, that came from the knowledge that they were carrying a concealed weapon. Emma went over to speak to them and they stomped out what was left of their cigarettes and climbed into their vehicle.

Emma walked back to the Range Rover and nodded at Bird. 'We'll hang well back and stay in contact with the CTSFOs,' she said. 'Just so you know, we'll be able to hear anything that's said within a few feet of the phone.'

'It's bugged?'

'Not bugged, it's just the way the phone is set up. It records all phone conversations, messages and internet activity on the cloud, it can be tracked in real time through its GPS, and it functions as a listening device.'

'Nice bit of kit for a Secret Squirrel,' said Warren.

'The point is, if Andy needs assistance, all he has to do is ask for it. We need to establish a code phrase, something that lets us know he needs us to move in.'

'How about "They're going to shoot me". Would that work?' said Bird.

'It has to be something that sounds innocuous but lets us know you're in trouble.'

'Like "Red skies at night, shepherd's delight", you mean?'

Emma chuckled. 'I'm guessing you haven't done much undercover work,' she said. 'Ideally you want a phrase that you would say as part of a conversation. Something that doesn't stick out. One of my favourites is "I've got better things to do with my time". You can say that at any point in a conversation.'

'Let's go with that,' said Bird.

'Excellent,' said Emma. 'Once we know where the meet is, we'll get as close as we can without showing out. If you need help, that's the phrase you use.'

Warren reached into his jacket and took out the Glock 17. He gave it to Bird. 'I took the liberty of filling the magazine,' he said.

'Better safe than sorry,' said Bird. He realized that Emma was staring at the gun. 'It's okay, it's just a tool of the trade.'

'You're a civilian, Andy.'

'On temporary secondment to the SAS,' said Warren. 'I'll vouch for him.'

Emma held up her hands. 'I didn't see anything,' she said.

Bird tucked the gun into his belt and opened the rear door of the Range Rover. He clicked his tongue to attract Tyson's attention. 'In,' he said.

Tyson jumped in and Bird closed the door. Bird looked over at Emma. 'What was that phrase again? "Time flies when you're having fun"?'

Emma opened her mouth to reply but he flashed her a grin. 'I'm only messing with you,' he said.

'Be careful, Andy. Seriously.'

'Careful's my middle name,' he said. 'Just remember, the object of this exercise is to free the hostage, Sarah. Keep the CTSFOs under wraps until she's safe.'

Emma nodded. 'Will do.'

Bird looked into her eyes. She was giving nothing away but he had the feeling that she was more interested in catching the bad guys than she was in rescuing Sarah. He would have bet good money that she'd be sending the armed cops in the first chance she got. He climbed into the car and drove to the exit. Archie was manning the gate and he grinned when he saw Bird at the wheel of the Range Rover. 'Not stolen the Sarge's ride, have you, Andy?' he said.

Bird jerked his thumb behind him. 'He's following in an Audi. And there's a Land Cruiser full of armed cops behind him.'

'You working again?'

'Just a training exercise.'

'Be good to have you back.'

'Thanks for that, Archie.' The barrier came up and Bird drove out, heading east along the A438. He kept his speed low and picked up the phone that Emma had given him. Keeping a careful eye on the road, he sent a text. **On A438 now.**

After a few seconds he received a reply. **Head for A40.**

Bird concentrated on the road. There was some traffic and he spotted a BMW X5 coming towards him, but there were two women in it and a child seat in the back. His eyes flicked to the rear-view mirror. The Audi was about a hundred yards behind him.

There was a nine-inch screen on the dashboard and he called up the satnav. The A40 ran west from Fishguard in Wales all the way to London. It passed close to Cheltenham, which was where GCHQ was based, so there was a chance that was the destination. He doubted that they would make him drive all the way to the capital, but it was an option.

Simon would have seen the messages, so Bird needed to lose his followers as quickly as possible. He reached over with his left hand, picked up the pay-as-you-go phone Warren had got him and placed it on his lap. He took a paperclip from his pocket and used his teeth to straighten it out, then pushed it into the small hole next to the SIM tray. The tray popped out, revealing his SIM card. He took the SIM card out and put it in the top pocket of his shirt, then checked his mirrors and speed.

He put his phone back onto the seat and picked up the phone that Simon had given him. He used the paperclip to eject the SIM card from that, then slotted it into the phone that Warren had given him. He checked his mirrors again. The Audi was about two hundred yards behind him now. He couldn't see the grey Land Cruiser.

He glanced at the satnav screen. The A438 was the quickest way to the A40, but he could use the A4172, a small road that went north–south, cutting through lots of small villages. Traffic would probably be lighter than on the A438, which meant he could put his foot down.

The GPS in the phone that Emma had given him would still be working, but any messages and calls would go through his own phone, so wouldn't be picked up by Simon.

He looked at the GPS again. The turn off for the A4172 was at a village called Trumpet, about fifteen miles from Stirling Lines.

He spent the next twenty minutes varying the speed of the Range Rover, getting his followers used to him being out of sight. He would accelerate, keep well ahead of them for a minute or so, then drop back. He knew they wouldn't be worried if they didn't have eyes on him because they would be relying on the tracker.

When he was a mile away from the turn off, he accelerated and picked up the GCHQ phone with his left hand. He used his thumb nail to prise off the back cover. It took almost a minute of fiddling to remove it, and the turn off was fast approaching. He took a quick look in his rear-view mirror. There was a slight bend in the road and the Audi was out of sight. He used his thumbnail to prise out the battery. It came out easily but slipped through his fingers and fell into the footwell. He tossed the phone onto the passenger seat and put both hands on the wheel. He wasn't sure how long it would take them to realize that the phone was no longer transmitting his position, but assumed that it would probably be just a matter of seconds.

There were traffic lights at the junction ahead of him, and they were on red. He kept accelerating. There was no traffic ahead of him and nothing on the A4172 so far as he could see. He went through the red light and pulled a hard right. A black and white timbered pub flashed by and then he was on the A4172 heading south. He kept accelerating hard. The road was narrow and there was no traffic. Hedges and fields whizzed by. The road was pretty much straight most of the time and on the few occasions he came across a car ahead of him he was able to speed by. He kept his speed above seventy for a couple of minutes, constantly checking his rear-view mirror. There was no sign of the Audi or the Land Cruiser.

He slowed down. It would take them some time to realize that he wasn't on the A438. The lack of a GPS signal would confuse them and they would probably drive faster, assuming that he was ahead of them. Every minute they drove along the A438, the further away they were. He doubted there was any way that they would find him. He took a deep breath. He was taking a risk, flying solo, but he didn't trust Emma. Four people had already died in Hereford on her watch and he wasn't prepared to risk adding Sarah to that list.

CHAPTER 19

'We have a problem,' said Simon, peering at his tablet. He was sitting behind Emma in the back of the Audi. Warren was driving. 'He's just gone dark.'

'Is it a malfunction?' asked Emma.

'Possibly. Or he could be somewhere where there's no signal.'

'He's on a main road, there are phone masts everywhere.'

'I don't know what to tell you.' He tapped on the tablet. 'He's gone.'

Emma looked across at Warren. 'He can't be far ahead of us, put your foot down,' she said.

'Roger that,' said Warren. The Audi accelerated smoothly.

'We saw him, what, three minutes ago? We're doing forty, even if he accelerated to seventy he can't be much more than a mile or so ahead of us.'

'You're obviously good at maths,' said Warren, still accelerating.

'Just catch him up, Sergeant Warren,' said Emma.

There was a truck ahead of them and Warren slowed. There were only two narrow lanes and there were double unbroken lines separating them. The road weaved left and right and overtaking the truck would be difficult.

'Sergeant, we need to get by,' said Emma.

'I hear you, but I can't see around the truck.'

'Sergeant, we don't have a working tracker, we need to keep eyes on Bird.'

Warren craned his neck to the side but he couldn't see what was ahead of the truck.

'Sergeant . . .'

Warren gritted his teeth. As usual, the Secret Squirrels were asking the impossible, without any consideration of the risks. He checked his rear-view mirror. The Land Cruiser was about a hundred yards behind them but the road was clear behind the CTSFOs. The truck wasn't doing much more than forty, which was a fair enough speed for the road conditions. But if Bird had accelerated then every second they stayed behind the truck increased the distance between them. Warren flicked on his indicator, flashed his lights to let the truck driver know that he was coming, then turned the steering wheel sharply as he accelerated. The Audi started to leap forwards but then Warren cursed as he saw a van heading towards them. He stamped on the brake and swung the Audi back behind the truck. The van's horn blared as it went by and Warren had a glimpse of an angry bald man with his mouth open, probably turning the air blue.

He waited a few seconds until the road appeared to be straight, and tried again, but this time he didn't flash his lights or indicate. The truck driver obviously knew what was happening and wasn't going to help by slowing down. Warren pulled over into the right-hand lane and immediately saw that it was clear. He stamped on the accelerator and the Audi roared past the truck. There were traffic lights ahead of them. They were green so Warren kept accelerating. He was about fifty yards from the lights when they began to change.

Emma pointed straight ahead but Warren had already made the decision to keep going and he kept his foot hard down on the accelerator. He went through the lights a second after they had turned red.

Emma looked over her shoulder. The Land Cruiser had stopped at the red lights. 'Twats,' she muttered under her breath.

There were several cars ahead of them but no sign of the Range Rover.

Simon was still tapping away impatiently on his tablet. Warren didn't know how reliable the technology was, but he was fairly sure that it wasn't a technical issue. Deadman had almost certainly found a way of disabling the tracker, and Warren understood why. The intelligence agencies couldn't be trusted; they always worked to their own agenda. They were clearly set on identifying and catching the men who had killed the GCHQ guy in London, which meant that rescuing Sarah would be a secondary objective. There was no way that Deadman would proceed on that basis, so cutting the link with his followers made perfect sense. He smiled to himself as the Audi hurtled along the road. They were almost certainly on a wild goose chase, but Emma and Simon didn't seem to be aware of that. It felt good to have one up on the Secret Squirrels.

CHAPTER 20

Bird's phone vibrated in his lap. He picked it up. It was an incoming call, number withheld. Bird gritted his teeth. He had to take the call, but he wouldn't be able to hear what was being said. He could explain his situation, but then they'd want to know how he'd managed to take the call when he was in the barracks. He accepted the call, put the phone to his mouth and spoke rapidly. 'I'm on the A4172, about three minutes away from the A40. I don't have hands-free and I don't want to be pulled over for using my phone. Text me where you want me to go next.' He ended the call.

He put the phone back in his lap. If they called back he'd be in trouble, but as the seconds ticked by he realized he might have got away with it. Eventually the phone vibrated to let him know he had received a message: **Take A40 to Churchdown.**

He looked over at the car's GPS screen. Churchdown was a village halfway between Gloucester and Cheltenham, not far from Gloucestershire Airport.

He checked his rear-view mirror again. No sign of the Audi or the Land Cruiser, and no BMW X5s.

He reached the A40 and followed it north around Gloucester. He was sure that Emma would be messaging him frantically, at least until she realized that he had deliberately given them the slip. She'd be furious, but Bird hadn't had a choice. The kidnappers had been clear, if he didn't go alone they'd kill Sarah. And everything they had done so far suggested they were more than capable of carrying out their threat. The big question was, what did they want? It clearly wasn't money, so why had they killed so many people and kidnapped Sarah? Was it just because they wanted him dead? Because he had seen their faces? Bird didn't have the best of memories but yes, he would recognize them if he saw them again and would probably have no problems spotting them in a police line-up. But what were they so afraid of? All he could do is give a description to the police – that didn't make it any more likely they would be caught. And there'd be CCTV footage, of them and their vehicles, surely that was more likely to lead to them being apprehended?

So was it something else? Had he seen something, or did they think he'd heard something? Something that they didn't want made public? Bird wracked his memory but nothing came to mind. They'd chased the GCHQ guy down the alley, and shot him. Bird had taken the gun from them but he had left it in the alley. Did they think he still had it? And why would that matter, because either way they must have realized that by now the police would have it.

His eyes flicked to his rear-view mirror. A grey BMW X5 had moved up behind him and was only a few yards away. There were two men in the front. Big men, but he couldn't make out their faces.

The SUV pulled out, accelerated, and moved alongside his Range Rover. The driver and passenger looked across at him. Both were wearing sunglasses. Bird only got a good look at the driver. His head was shaved and there was a thick scar across his cheek. The SUV drove alongside the Range Rover for a couple of seconds and then accelerated away.

Bird checked his rear-view mirror again. There was another BMW X5 behind him now. This one was black.

His phone vibrated and he reached for it. There was a message. **FOLLOW ME.**

The grey BMW X5 was about fifty yards ahead of him now. He matched its speed. The black SUV stuck to his tail. He could see two figures in the front but couldn't make out their faces.

UNDERDOGS

The grey SUV's indicator light started flashing, showing it was going to move to the left. Bird flicked his indicator on. The SUV slowed and Bird eased back on the accelerator. The black SUV was also indicating a left turn.

They left the main road in a tight convoy. Bird's eyes flicked across to the GPS. They were on the B4063 now, Cheltenham Road, red-roofed houses to the left, ploughed fields to the right.

They drove past an Esso petrol station and this time the grey SUV indicated right. Bird followed. They turned onto a two-lane road lined with brick-built semi-detached houses. The light was fading now and it was getting colder. They crossed a bridge over the A40, then after a few minutes took a left, and another left. They were driving slowly now so it looked as if they were approaching their destination.

They turned right down a narrow road lined with hedges, then the grey X5 came to a halt. The front passenger got out and pushed open a wooden gate. The SUV went through and Bird followed it. There was a gravelled area about the size of a badminton court in front of a double-fronted grey stone cottage with bow windows and a white door.

The grey BMW parked to the right of the front door. Bird parked on the left, facing the house. The black X5 drove slowly behind the Range Rover, blocking it in.

Bird stayed where he was, both hands on the steering wheel as the man closed the gate and went to stand next to the grey SUV. The driver climbed out. Both men were well over six feet tall, with wide shoulders. *The bigger they are the harder they fall* was the phrase that went through Bird's mind as he weighed them up, but he knew that it would take a lot to bring them down, the difficulty exacerbated by the fact that they had both taken Glocks out from under their coats.

The driver, the man with the scarred cheek, waved with his gun for Bird to get out of the car.

Bird put his hand on the door handle. 'Stay,' he said. Then again louder, just to be sure that Tyson got the message. 'Stay!'

He opened the door and climbed out.

'Put your hands above your head,' said the driver. He waved his gun for emphasis.

Bird did as he was told. He left the Range Rover door open behind him. He looked over his shoulder. The two men had climbed out of the other SUV. They were big men with shaved heads and black bomber jackets. Bird recognized them – they had been in the green BMW X5 in Arlington Road. One of them was the guy who had killed Joel with the machine pistol – Bird recognized the mutilated left ear immediately.

Bird turned to look at the driver of the first X5. 'I said don't look at them, look at me,' said the driver. 'Now put your hands behind your head and interlink your fingers.'

Bird did as the man said.

'Now down on your knees.'

Bird went down, left leg first, then right. The gravel bit into his knees.

One of the men behind him stepped forwards and began to roughly pat him down. When he'd finished, he grabbed Bird by the scruff of the neck and hauled him to his feet.

The driver had his Glock pointed at Bird's chest, the other man had his hands by his side. 'Where is my wife?' asked Bird.

'You'll see her later,' said the driver. 'Put your hands behind your back.'

'I want to see my wife.'

The man behind Bird slammed him on the side of the head. He might have said something, there was no way of knowing. Bird whirled around, his hands up defensively. The man was holding a heavy-duty zip tie. 'Turn around,' he growled. He was a big brute of a man with an ugly scar above his lip, a cleft palate that had been badly repaired from the look of it.

Bird's mind began to race. Four against one were tough odds at the best of times, but if he allowed them to bind his hands behind him, it would all be over. The man with the gun was the clearest threat, but would he shoot Bird in the back? If the aim had been to kill Bird, they wouldn't be bothering to tie his hands.

'Turn around!' shouted the man again. He snarled, showing yellowing teeth.

Bird did as he was told. The driver was still pointing his gun at Bird's chest and his finger was on the trigger. Bird took a step to the right. The gun followed him. He took another step. 'Stop moving!' shouted the driver.

The driver was in clear view of the Range Rover now. Everything depended on how quickly Tyson moved, and how the man with the gun reacted.

Bird looked over his shoulder. 'Put your hands behind your back!' shouted the man with the zip tie.

Bird raised his hands in the air. 'Okay, okay, I'll do what you say.'

'Do it now!' growled the man. 'Or I'll rip your fucking head off.'

Bird took a deep breath, his hands still in the air. 'Tyson!' he shouted at the top of his voice. 'Attack!'

The driver frowned in confusion. Bird looked over at the man with the zip tie, who also looked confused. Bird saw a flash of brown as Tyson jumped over the seats and scrambled through the open door. He hit the ground running. Bird pointed at the man with the gun. 'Attack!' he shouted.

Tyson headed towards the man like a guided missile. Strapped to the side of his Kevlar jacket was Bird's Glock 17, but Tyson was already running at full pelt, moving too quickly for Bird to grab the weapon.

The driver swung his gun around, but Tyson was a difficult target. Bird bent down, grabbed a handful of gravel, straightened up, and hurled the stones at the man's face. He was so focused on Tyson that the hail of gravel caught him by surprise and he stepped backwards, his gun pointing at the sky.

Tyson was in full attack mode as Bird ran towards the man. Tyson's eyes were fixed on the gun arm, his tail out, mouth half open, breathing through his nose. All four paws hit the gravel at the same time and he launched himself through the air, his jaws opening wide. The man tried to aim at him but he was too slow and the dog slammed into him. The man roared in pain or anger and fell back. Tyson went with him.

Bird bent down and ripped his Glock from the Velcro straps on Tyson's harness. He straightened up and assessed the situation, his mind working almost on autopilot. Overthinking could be deadly in a combat situation – it was best to rely on instinct. When faced with imminent death, the subconscious tended to make the right choices.

The second man from the grey X5 already had his gun out but his finger wasn't on the trigger yet. No matter, he was still a threat, so Bird put two rounds in his chest. The man staggered back, fell against the SUV, and slid to the ground.

Tyson was shaking his head from side to side and the driver's gun went off, the round hitting the grey SUV. Tyson flinched at the sound and released his grip on the man's arm. That would have never happened before the grenade incident – Tyson had been trained never to release his grip until Bird gave the command. Tyson backed away, whining, his ears down. The man grinned in triumph and swung his gun towards Bird. Bird shot him in the head. The man went still immediately, his face a crumpled red mess. Tyson crouched low to the ground, still unnerved by the gun going off so close to his head.

The man with the zip tie was fumbling in his jacket, presumably for a gun. Bird pointed at the man and shouted, 'Attack!' Tyson acted immediately, spinning around and charging at the man, whose eyes widened in terror. His gun had snagged on his jacket and Tyson reached him before he had managed to pull it out. Tyson jumped and clamped his jaws on the man's right arm.

The driver of the black SUV, the one with the missing lower ear, started to shout something but Bird didn't think it was English. The man had pulled a gun from an underarm holster. Bird pulled the trigger twice and both shots slammed into the man's chest. He fell back and his weapon tumbled onto the gravel.

Tyson hauled the other man to the ground. Bird walked over and pointed his gun at the man's face. 'Release!' he shouted.

Tyson released his grip on the man's arm and shuffled back. Bird kept the gun levelled just above the man's scarred lip. 'Don't move or I'll put a bullet in your head,' said Bird. 'Nod if you understand.'

The man nodded but he didn't seem the least bit scared and glared at Bird with undisguised hatred.

'My wife, is she in the house?' Bird asked.

The man shook his head.

'Is anyone in the house?'

The man shook his head again.

'Right, I need you to take your gun out using the thumb and one finger of your left hand.'

The man moved his hand towards his jacket.

'Slowly, very slowly,' said Bird. 'Your three friends are dead and I have absolutely no problem with you joining them.'

The man moved slowly, his eyes fixed on Bird's, slipping his hand inside his jacket and pulling out a Glock 19, similar to the one that Bird was holding but with fifteen rounds in the magazine. Bird took it from him. 'Roll over onto your front and put your hands around your neck, fingers interlinked.' Bird tucked the man's gun into his belt.

The man did as he was told. Bird stood up and looked around. He had no way of knowing if there were sirens heading his way, but Tyson's ears weren't twitching. He walked over to the gate, keeping his gun trained on the prostrate man. The road outside was clear. The nearest house was a hundred yards away and shots in the open air probably wouldn't carry too far.

He went back down the drive and looked up at the house. The man had said there was no one inside, which was probably true because anyone there would presumably have started shooting already. But if the house was empty, then he was no nearer finding Sarah.

Bird went over to the dead man sprawled next to the black SUV and picked up the machine pistol. It was a MAC-10, the .45 ACP model, with a thirty-round magazine.

Bird retrieved the other two weapons used by his attackers. They were Glocks, another Glock 19 and a Glock 30SF. The 30SF was a favourite of Bird's. It had a shorter grip, which suited him, but its main advantage was its calibre – it was chambered for the .45 ACP round, which gave it increased stopping power. Often in a firefight against multiple targets, there was no need to double-tap with it to neutralize a threat – one shot was enough. It came with a ten-round magazine and was about the same size as the Glock 19.

He kept a watchful eye on the man on the ground as he walked over to the Range Rover. He tossed the machine pistol and the Glocks onto the passenger seat. He kept the Glock 30SF with him, then locked the car. Tyson stayed next to the man on the ground, staring down at him as if daring him to move.

Bird went over to Tyson and looked down at the man. He kicked him in the side, then stepped back. 'Stand up!' he growled.

The man got to his feet. 'Can you hear sirens?' asked Bird.

The man frowned. 'What?'

'Sirens. Can you hear sirens? Are the police coming?'

The man shook his head. 'No.' His eyes were moving constantly, clearly looking around for anything that he could use as a weapon.

'Okay, then this is what I need you to do. You're going to carry your three colleagues to the SUVs, and put them inside. One wrong move and I'll put a round in your leg and that will make the job that much harder. Do you understand?'

'I understand.'

'The dog will be watching you, and he's a loose cannon. He might well decide to attack you off his own bat, so move slowly. No sudden movements.' He waved his Glock at the body by the grey SUV. 'Start with him.'

The man walked across the gravel, opened the rear door of the SUV and picked up the body. Bird moved to the side so that he could see into the back of the vehicle. He didn't want any surprises. The man threw the body over his shoulder, carried it to the car and tossed it into the back. The SUV's suspension bounced. The body probably weighed more than a hundred kilograms but the man made light work of it.

'Close the door,' said Bird.

The man slammed the door shut, then walked over towards the black SUV. Bird moved with him, and watched as the man opened the rear door. 'Back away!' shouted Bird. He had spotted something black and metallic and as the man backed away Bird saw that it was a pump action shotgun. 'Hands behind your neck, turn away from me and interlink your fingers!' shouted Bird. The man complied. Bird went over to the vehicle and took out the shotgun. It was a Remington 870 with a matte-black stock, 12-gauge with a shortened barrel and a four-shell magazine. Not a weapon you'd want to use over any real distance, but close up it would be deadly. And intimidating, which was usually the point of carrying a shotgun. A guy might look at a Glock and think about putting up a fight, but only an idiot would argue with a shotgun.

Bird backed away from the SUV, keeping the Glock aimed at the man. 'Right, turn around and put both bodies in the back,' he said. 'Tyson, heel!'

Tyson ran over to Bird and sat next to him, back straight and ears up.

They watched as the man picked up the bodies one by one and tossed them effortlessly into the back of the vehicle.

'Take off your coat and put that in,' said Bird.

The man removed his bomber jacket and laid it down on top of the bodies. He was wearing a brightly coloured Versace shirt, the long sleeves buttoned, a flurry of red, green, gold and white.

'Now your shoes. And socks.'

The man leant against the vehicle as he took off his shoes and socks and threw them on top of his bomber jacket.

'Now back away and get down on your knees,' said Bird.

The man did as he was told.

'Hands behind your head, fingers interlinked.'

Once the man was in position, Bird went over to the Range Rover, tossed in the shotgun, and slammed the door.

He pointed the Glock at the man. 'I'm going to ask you again, is there anyone in the house?'

'No. No one.'

'Because if there is, I will put a bullet in your spine. Probably two. We're going into the house, and if I so much as hear a mouse fart I will pull the trigger.'

'I don't know if there are mice inside, but there are no people. That I promise.'

Bird couldn't help but grin at the man's attempt at humour. Considering the fact that Bird had killed three of his companions and was pointing a loaded weapon at his face, the man was holding up surprisingly well. 'Get up,' he said.

The man got to his feet.

'Walk slowly to the door.'

The man headed towards the house, and Bird kept close enough to keep him covered with the Glock, but not so close that the man could turn and knock the weapon to the side. Ten to twelve feet was the sweet spot.

The man stopped in front of the door. His right hand moved towards his trouser pocket. 'Very, very slowly,' said Bird.

The man took out a set of keys and opened the front door.

'Wait!' said Bird. 'Step back!'

The man hesitated.

'Put your hands behind your head.'

The man did as he was told. Bird needed to make sure that the man didn't disappear inside the house and slam the door shut.

'Use your foot to push open the door. Slowly.'

Bird got closer to the man, keeping the gun aimed at the back of his head. 'Now move slowly into the hall.'

CHAPTER 21

Bird used a pair of large kitchen scissors to cut away the man's designer shirt. The man glared sullenly at him but didn't say anything. It had taken Bird the best part of twenty minutes to tie the man to the door, taking it step by step to make sure that he had no opportunity to put up a fight. By the time he had finished, the man was standing with his back to the sitting room door, both arms above his head, his right one smeared in blood where Tyson had bit him. There were wires running from his wrists over the top of the door, which were bound to the handle on the outside. Bird had found the wire in a kitchen cabinet, along with a roll of duct tape. Wires also led from the man's ankles, under the door and were again tied to the handle. Now the door was shut, and the man wasn't going anywhere. Tyson was sitting in front of a leather sofa, his nose on his paws, his ears up, as he watched what Bird was doing.

Bird had taken the scissors from a kitchen drawer, along with various knives, a corkscrew and a potato peeler, and had lined them up on a coffee table. Presentation was everything when it came to torture, or 'enhanced interrogation', as the Americans called it. Bird didn't intend to use the knives, but the man didn't know that.

Bird had been through the man's pockets. There were keys, a cigarette lighter, a red and white pack of Marlboro cigarettes, and a roll of money held together with an elastic band. No driving licence, no credit card, nothing that could be used to identify him. He was clearly a pro, and pros were hard to interrogate.

As he pulled away the last of the shirt material, Bird stood back and examined the tattoos that were all over the man's body. There were a lot of them, covering most of his chest and arms. There was a large spider on the man's left shoulder, a snarling tiger to the left of his stomach, and an equally aggressive leopard to the right. There were several skulls near his shoulders, teeth bared, and in the centre of the man's chest was an ornate Russian cathedral. To the left of the cathedral was a pretty young woman with long hair, a red rose against her cheek, and there was another rose on his left arm, covered in barbed wire entwined around a dagger.

'Nice tattoos,' said Bird in Russian.

The man's eyes widened but he didn't say anything. Bird undid the belt around the man's waist, then slid it out and tossed it onto the chair. He bent down and started cutting up the left trouser leg. He cut up through to the waist, then did the same on the right leg before pulling the material away and placing it on the chair. There was an eight-pointed star tattooed on each knee. On his right thigh was a hooded executioner, below it was a naked woman being burned at the stake, and on the shin was a horned devil writing in a book. On the left thigh was a penis wreathed in barbed wire, and a pig wearing a military uniform. There was a manacle tattooed around each ankle, and a bell on each foot.

All that was left now were the man's underpants, white baggy Y-fronts with yellow stains at the front. Bird wasn't happy at having to touch them, but he needed the man naked so he had no choice. He cut them at the sides and they fell to the floor. Bird held the scissors close to the man's shrivelled penis and snapped them open and shut. The man glared at him with pure hatred. 'Why have you been chasing me?' Bird asked in Russian.

'Trakhat svoyu mat,' spat the man. *Fuck your mother.*

Bird shrugged. 'My mother is dead. Has been for a while.' He pointed at the executioner tattoo with the scissors. 'Did you kill yours? Did you fuck her before you killed her? You look like the sort of man who would fuck his mother.'

That struck home and the man began to scream and curse as he struggled with his bonds. Bird took a step back and waited for the man to run out of steam. The wire was strong enough to hold him and the knots were secure. He wasn't going anywhere.

Eventually the man calmed down and glared sullenly at Bird, his jaw set tight, breathing through his nose.

'We are both professionals,' said Bird, still in Russian. He put the scissors on the table next to the knives. 'There is no need to trade insults. You have my wife and I want her back. We can still come to an arrangement. But you have to tell me what it is that you want.' He looked at Tyson, who was still lying down next to the sofa. 'Heel,' he said. Tyson immediately got up and sat down next to Bird, looking up at him, ears erect. 'Stand,' said Bird. Tyson stood. Bird reached down and grabbed the handle on Tyson's harness. 'Bark,' he said.

Tyson began to bark ferociously and the Russian jerked back against the door. Tyson tried to pull towards the man, but Bird held him back. He allowed Tyson to bark for a full thirty seconds before jerking the handle. 'Silence,' he said. Tyson immediately stopped barking.

'What is it you want from me?' said Bird. 'Did you want to kill me, is that what this is about?'

'Of course we want to kill you. I'll rip your prick off and shove it down your throat so that you choke in front of me, I'll—'

'Bark,' said Tyson, and Tyson began barking and snapping at the Russian. This time Bird took a step forwards so that Tyson was just a couple of feet away from the Russian's groin. The man flinched and turned his head away. 'Silence,' said Bird eventually, and Tyson fell silent.

'I told you, let's keep this civil, shall we?' said Bird, in Russian. 'Killing me isn't an option, but giving me back my wife is. So let's talk about that.'

The man stared at him sullenly but didn't reply.

'Is my wife alive? Or is she dead already?'

The Russian stared at him for several seconds. 'Zhivoy,' he said eventually. *Alive.*

Bird tried not to show how relieved he was. 'Where is she?'

'Trakhat svoyu mat!' The Russian spat at Bird but the phlegm fell short and peppered the floor.

'Bark,' said Bird, this time moving forwards so that Tyson's jaws were just inches from the man's groin.

The man's face was now bathed in sweat and a vein was pulsing in his neck. Bird wasn't surprised – Tyson in full flow was a terrifying sight. 'Silence,' he said and pulled him back. 'If you wanted to kill me, why didn't you do it outside? In the car?'

'You know why.'

'If I knew why, we wouldn't be having this conversation, would we? Why did you chase me across London? Why did you follow me to Hereford? I get that I saw you kill that guy in Camden, but so what? I don't know you from Adam.'

The Russian said something but Bird couldn't make out the words. 'Say that again,' he said.

'Brownlow gave you something, before he died.'

Bird shook his head. 'He didn't.'

'Well, he had it on him when he left the house. And it wasn't on him in the ambulance. It has to be with you.'

'What? What did he have?'

'An SD card.'

'A what?'

'An SD card. It stores information.'

'And what's on the SD card?'

'I don't know.'

Bird got Tyson barking again.

'I don't know!' screamed the man. 'Ya chertovski ne znayu!'

Ya chertovski ne znayu. *I don't fucking know.* Bird had the feeling that the man was telling the truth. He pulled Tyson away. 'So who do you work for?'

'Idi v zhopu.' *Kiss my arse.*

'I'll ask you one last time and then I'll let my dog sink his teeth into you,' said Bird, in Russian, sprinkled with a few choice obscenities.

'Fuck you!' shouted the man.

Bird pushed Tyson forwards, then pulled him back. 'Seize!' he shouted, and let go. Tyson rushed towards the man, his jaws open. The man screamed and twisted to the left as best as he could, trying to shield his privates. Tyson sank his teeth into the flesh above the man's left knee and began to shake his head. The man screamed and thrashed from side to side but Tyson held firm.

'Who do you work for?' shouted Bird. 'Na kogo vy rabotayete?'

The Russian continued to scream.

'Release!' shouted Bird.

Tyson immediately released his grip on the man's leg and stepped back. There were bite marks in the penis tattoo and blood was trickling down the man's knee.

'Good boy,' said Bird, pulling him back. Blood was splattering on the floor. The man was sobbing, his breath coming in short, frantic gasps.

'Next time he'll go for your balls,' said Bird. 'Is that what you want, to have your balls ripped off by a dog?'

'Idi v zhopu,' said the Russian, but his heart wasn't in it.

Bird shook Tyson's harness and let him move forwards. The man tried turning to the left, using his right thigh to shield his privates. Bird pulled Tyson to the side, giving him a clearer view. Tyson was barking and snapping, eager to get started. The man was screaming again, twisting and turning, trying to avoid Tyson's gnashing teeth. Bird moved forwards, Tyson's spittle peppering the man's skin. 'He's going to do it!'

'Fuck you!'

'You won't be fucking anyone, not after he's bitten off your cock. Now, who do you work for?' He stepped forwards and Tyson moved with him. His snapping teeth were just inches from the man's groin. The penis had shrivelled to the size of a cocktail sausage and his testes had almost vanished inside his body. Tyson was snarling with fury now and Bird was having trouble holding him back. Tyson's teeth scraped the man's testes and he shrieked. 'Okay, okay! Wagner, I work for Wagner. Now get that fucking dog off me!'

Bird pulled Tyson away. 'Silence!' shouted Bird and the dog immediately went quiet. He stopped pulling against Bird but Bird kept a tight grip on the harness handle.

'Wagner?' Bird repeated. 'You work for the Wagner Group?'

The Wagner Group was a state-funded Russian private security company, effectively a private army that carried out black ops for the president, Vladimir Putin. The group played a major role in Russia's invasion of Ukraine, and had supported regimes in Libya, Syria, Mali and the Central African Republic while allowing Putin to deny that Russian forces were involved. There were rumoured to be up to fifty thousand men working for the Wagner Group, many of them former convicts, and the group had been accused of war crimes including rape, torture and murder. It was possible that the man had been co-opted into the group – during the invasion of Ukraine, the ranks of Wagner and the Russian Army had been swelled by the addition of tens of thousands of criminals who were offered their freedom in exchange for their service.

The man nodded fearfully. 'I'm just hired muscle. It's a job. That's all.'

'Kidnapping my wife and threatening to kill her is just a job? Fuck you.' He jerked the harness handle. 'Seize!' he shouted and Tyson sprang forwards, jaws agape.

The man twisted to the side and screamed.

'Silence!' said Bird, and again Tyson went quiet. 'Where is she, my wife?' asked Bird.

The man shook his head. 'I don't know,' he panted.

'Bullshit.'

'No, no bullshit. My boss took her. He has her. I was sent to get the SD card.'

'And once you had that, what was going to happen?'

'I don't know.'

'Were you going to kill her or release her?'

'I don't know!' shouted the man.

'Your boss. What's his name?'

'Nikolay.'

Bird looked at Tyson. 'Sit!' he said firmly. Tyson obeyed immediately. Bird went over to the man's coat and took his phone from his jacket. It was a new iPhone with facial recognition. He took it over to the man and held the screen in front of his face until it was unlocked. Then he went through to Face ID and passcode. He switched off the Face ID. 'Passcode,' he said. 'Don't fuck me around or the dog bites you for real.'

The man gave him the six-digit passcode. Bird tapped it in and then reset it to his own code. He went through to the address book. It was all in Russian but Bird had no problem reading the names. There was no Nikolay.

'You lied,' said Bird, holding out the phone. 'I gave you a chance, and you lied.'

'No! He is there as Kolya. We call him Kolya.'

Bird checked the address book again. There was a Kolya, which was a common nickname for Russian men called Nikolay.

'You see? I am not lying.'

Bird slipped the phone into his jacket pocket and picked up the duct tape.

'So now you will let me go?' asked the man, but it was clear from the uncertainty in his voice that he knew it wasn't going to happen.

Bird didn't answer. He used his teeth to rip off a piece of duct tape, which he slapped across the man's mouth, then he used a longer piece on top of that, winding it twice around the man's head.

The man shook his head from side to side but Bird made short work of gagging him. Bird pointed a finger at the man's face. 'If you've lied to me, I'll be back and my dog will rip your balls off,' he said in Russian. 'Understand?'

The man nodded.

'Did you tell me the truth?'

The man nodded again, more enthusiastically this time.

CHAPTER 22

Bird walked over to his SUV with Tyson at his heels. He took out his phone and sent Warren a text message. **Video call now?**

Bird stared at the screen, willing the sergeant to reply, then smiled when Warren's name flashed up. He accepted the call and Warren's face filled the screen. Warren was clearly angry but he was speaking so quickly that Bird couldn't read his lips.

'Sarge, I need you to keep the phone pointed at your face and for you to speak slowly, that way I should be able to understand you.'

Warren's face filled the screen. 'You might have told me what you were planning to do,' he said.

'What I had to do, I had to do on my own.'

'Have you found Sarah?'

'I'm working on it. Look, where are you right now?'

'Sergeants' mess, catching up with some paperwork and getting a bite to eat.'

'Emma and Simon are still there?'

'Yeah, and she's not a happy bunny. She's convinced I was in on your little charade.'

'I'm going to ask them for a meet. If they ask you to go with them, give them some reason you can't.'

'Where are you?'

'Just outside Gloucester.'

'What the hell are you doing there?'

'It's a long story. I'll explain when I see you. Has my parka been cleaned yet?'

'Not yet. It's on my to-do list.'

'That's good, because I need you to check the pockets.'

'What am I looking for?'

'The Russians think that Brownlow gave me something. He didn't, but now I'm wondering if he put something in my pocket. He grabbed me just before he died, so it's possible.'

'Russians? They're Russians?'

'The one I've spoken to is. Wagner Group.'

'Shit. That's not good, Andy.'

'None of this is good, Sarge. What you're looking for is small, really small. An SD card.'

'That's it?'

'They can carry loads of data, photographs, videos. Could be all sorts on there. The tablet I used to use to track Tyson used micro SDs, could also be one of them.'

'And this dead guy slipped one into your coat?'

Bird shrugged. 'The Russian said they checked Brownlow's body and he didn't have it.'

Warren nodded. 'If I find it, what then?'

'I give them the SD card, they let Sarah go.'

'You trust them?'

'Whatever is on the card, they want it badly,' said Bird. 'But I'm not sure that I trust them. First, we need to see if we have it.'

'I'll go and check now,' said Warren.

Bird ended the call and dumped the Russian's Glock and all the other weapons he'd seized in one of the X5s, keeping only the Glock 17 Warren had given him and the Russian's phone. He drove down the road and spotted a large pub, with a car park next to it. The Old Elm Inn. He parked, climbed out, and used his phone to take a photograph of the pub's sign. He sent the photograph to Emma. She was a bright girl – he was sure she'd be able to join the dots.

He put his phone away and smiled down at Tyson. 'Why don't we have a bite to eat while we wait?' he said, and Tyson woofed in agreement.

CHAPTER 23

The door to the room that Andy Bird was using was closed, but Warren didn't bother knocking. The barracks building was pretty much empty and in silence. Most of the men who called the barracks home were on missions overseas, training or on leave.

Warren opened the door and immediately saw the filled laundry bag and went over to it. He undid the drawstring and pulled out Bird's parka. There were four pockets on the front: one on each side of the chest that closed with zips, and two at the bottom, left and right, with press studs. He unzipped the two chest pockets and turned them inside out, but there was no sign of an SD card.

He heard a noise behind him and turned around. Colonel Brewerton was standing in the doorway. He was in his early forties, with close-cropped chestnut hair flecked with grey, and was wearing four-colour woodland pattern fatigues with the sleeves rolled up to reveal some pretty impressive Para tattoos on his forearms. 'I thought that was you,' said the colonel. 'You planning on bunking with the enlisted men from now on?'

The colonel had a SIG Sauer on a holster on his waist and a Fairbairn–Sykes double-edged fighting knife strapped to his right thigh. He scrutinized Warren with unblinking brown eyes. Warren raised the parka. 'Deadman asked me to check his coat.'

'You're still calling him that?' He shook his head. 'I'm all for nicknames as a team-building exercise, but Deadman is a bit harsh, isn't it?'

'He was Birdman for years, but after the grenade thing . . .'

'It just seems unfair. I mean, you get called Bunny because your name's Warren and that's where rabbits live, fair enough, but he gets Deadman because he nearly bloody died. It's not really a laughing matter, is it?' He shook his head again. 'So why does he want you to check his coat? And where is he now?'

Warren's mind raced. He didn't want to lie to the colonel – that would only end badly – but he wasn't sure how much Emma had told him about what was happening. 'He went out,' said Warren. 'I'm not sure where he is now.'

'I was told that he was having to lie low here at Stirling Lines. National security.'

Warren nodded. 'That's pretty much it, yes.'

'You brought him onto the camp, right?'

'I did, boss. Yes.'

'And you didn't think to inform your commanding officer?'

'It was all kick, bollock, scramble, boss.'

'Middle of the night, was it?'

The colonel continued to stare at Warren with unblinking eyes. Warren could see that he already knew the answer to the question, so he shook his head. 'Breakfast time,' he said.

'So I was in my office?'

'Yes, boss. Sorry.'

The colonel closed the door, leant against it and folded his arms. 'I've been brought up to speed on what's happened, or at least as much as the Secret Squirrel woman is prepared to tell me. National security blah blah blah. So yes, we'll do whatever we can to keep Andy safe. And, yes, as his former sergeant you're probably in the best position to do that. But this is my Regiment and I will not have my men trying to run rings around me, no matter what the reason. Smuggling Bird into the barracks was treating me with contempt.'

'Boss . . .' Warren began but the colonel stopped him with a shake of the head.

'I get that you're loyal to your men, and I know you're in debt to Birdman after what happened out in Syria. But you brought Bird into Stirling Lines without telling me, and if anything had gone wrong, I'd be the one carrying the can. I am responsible for this base and everything that happens on it. You put me in a very precarious position.'

'I'm sorry, boss,' said Warren. 'I did it without thinking.'

'No, I'm pretty sure you knew exactly what you were doing. I just want to be sure that you don't do it again. Secret Squirrels can't be trusted, it's their nature. They'll tell you whatever they think is necessary to achieve their objectives. They love playing one hand off against the other. This Emma woman, you met her in Syria?'

'She briefed us on the operation to rescue the hostages in Albab. She said she was MI6.'

'She is with MI6, but I doubt that her name is Emma. She told me that Bird saw a GCHQ employee murdered and that the people who did it want to silence him. Those same people have kidnapped Bird's ex-wife and killed four people at her home here in Hereford. That's the point I was finally told what was happening.'

Warren nodded. 'That's pretty much it, yes.'

'This is a shitshow,' said the colonel.

'It is.'

'And I'm not sure if this Emma woman is capable of keeping a lid on it.'

'She's been talking about D-Notices or whatever they're called, using them to keep it out of the press. And they're cleaning up the crime scene and not calling in the cops.'

'Even though two cops died there?'

'Two cops and an MI5 officer. They don't want anyone to know.'

'And she said that she would handle the kidnapping?'

'She and the GCHQ guy with her. Simon. But Bird lost them.'

'He what?'

'The kidnappers phoned. They said they wanted Bird on his own. So he was driving and he gave Emma and Simon the slip.'

'And where were you while this was going on?'

'I was with the spooks. So when he lost them he lost me, too. Deadman was in my Range Rover.'

The colonel gritted his teeth and shook his head.

'Boss, I'm sorry. But Emma said you'd be okay about it, that someone from the MoD would be putting you in the picture.'

'No one likes being treated like a mushroom,' said the colonel, tersely. 'I was the last to know what was going on, how does that make me look?'

'Again, boss, I'm sorry. I made a mistake and if I could go back and do it differently, I would.'

'Were you armed?' Before Warren could answer, the colonel read the expression on his face. 'For fuck's sake, what were you playing at? You took a regimental weapon off base?'

'I never got out of the car, boss.'

'And if you had, and if you'd fired your weapon in anger, and if there had been a police investigation . . .'

Warren's first thought was to tell the colonel that that was a lot of ifs, but he decided that silence was the better option.

'The bottom line is, if you're acting as a lone wolf, there is nothing the Regiment can do to pull your nuts out of the fire.' The colonel sighed. 'Okay, I'm going to draw a line under this. We'll never talk about it. But if you ever, ever, pull a stunt like this again, your feet won't touch the ground and I'll have you RTU'd, are we clear?'

'Yes, boss. Crystal.' Being RTU'd – Returned to Unit – was just about the worst thing that could happen to an SAS soldier. In fact, the threat of being sent back to your original unit and all the embarrassment that went with that meant that most men would choose to resign from the Army instead.

'Right. So moving forwards, why are you going through Andy's coat?'

'The guy that he saw die in London, the GCHQ guy, Andy thinks he might have slipped something into his parka.'

'Something like what?'

'He said an SD card. A memory card. That might have been what the killers were looking for.'

'And have you found it?'

'Not so far.'

The colonel nodded. 'Okay, check it out.' The colonel moved to stand behind Warren as he methodically went through all the pockets of the parka, turning them inside out, one at a time. 'Nothing,' he said eventually.

'Now what?'

'I don't know. I'll give him the bad news. He said the bad guys would exchange Sarah for the card.'

'Sarah's his ex-wife?'

'Yeah. They killed her new boyfriend so she's obviously moved on, but he's going to do what he's going to do. You know what he's like. Loyalty is his middle name.'

'You say that like it's a bad thing,' said the colonel. 'Don't forget it's Andy's loyalty that means you didn't get blown to pieces in Syria.' He wrinkled his nose. 'How do you get in touch with him?'

Warren frowned. 'What do you mean?'

'Well, he's deaf, right? So the phone is out.'

'No, boss. He has his phone set to vibrate so he knows when he's getting a call or message. He's obviously fine with text or WhatsApp messages, and he can read lips, so FaceTime works too.'

'I'd never have thought of that,' said the colonel. 'I just assumed, you know, being deaf . . .'

'I often forget that he can't hear – his lip-reading skills are ace.'

'I'll tell you one thing I could never understand about his deafness – I went to see him when was in hospital here and the doctors said that they thought he would be a candidate for cochlear implants.'

'He mentioned them. What are they? Like a hearing aid?'

'No, they're a hi-tech thing. There's a microphone and a speech processor that sits behind the ear and then an implant with a receiver under the skin that connects directly to the auditory nerve. So even people who are totally deaf like Andy can hear, after a fashion. But he said he wasn't interested.'

Warren nodded. 'He said he'd feel like a cyborg or a robot or something.'

The colonel shrugged. 'Plus, the doctors say that the implants don't recreate hearing. The nerve is stimulated and the brain has to recognize the signals as sound. Andy said he just wanted to get on with his life.'

'Yeah, well, that didn't really work out for him. He was homeless, living rough in Camden when he saw the murder.'

'That shouldn't happen. There are charities that look after servicemen who fall on hard times.'

'He doesn't want charity,' said Warren. 'He's definite about that.'

'He's a bloody hero,' said the colonel. 'It's not charity, the country owes him a debt.'

'Yeah, well, he doesn't see it that way.' He looked at his watch. 'I'm going to tell him that the SD card isn't here.'

'Go ahead,' said the colonel.

Warren wasn't thrilled at the idea of the colonel listening in but he didn't have a choice. He sent Bird a text message. **Okay to FaceTime?**

The reply came within seconds. **Yes.**

Warren looked at the colonel. 'He can talk.'

'I want a word with him,' said the colonel.

'Roger that,' said Warren. He video-called Bird. Bird was outside with blue skies and wisps of cloud behind him. Warren moved the phone closer so that Bird could focus on his mouth. 'There's no SD card in your coat,' he said. 'I checked twice.'

'Shit.'

'Colonel Brewerton wants to talk to you.'

Warren saw the look of annoyance flash across Bird's face, but then he forced a smile. 'Sure.'

'I'll hand you over.'

Warren gave the phone to the colonel. 'You need to hold it close to your face and keep your mouth in view,' he said.

The colonel moved the phone closer to his face. 'I see that you've been winning friends and influencing people, Bird,' he said, speaking slowly and clearly.

'I'm sorry, boss,' said Bird. 'Mea culpa. And please don't blame the Sarge. I begged him for help.'

'Sergeant Warren and I have already had a conversation, and I'll tell you what I told him. I'm not happy about the way you used the base as a refuge. You've built up a hell of a lot of goodwill at Stirling Lines after what you did in Syria and you'd be well advised not to piss it away. You should have come to me straight away, Andy. Strings would have been pulled.'

'I'm sorry, boss. Really sorry.'

'As I said to Sergeant Warren, we'll draw a line under everything that has happened, but moving forwards there has to be total transparency. No more lies, no more subterfuge.'

'Understood.'

The colonel frowned. 'Where are you?'

'A pub outside Cheltenham, waiting for Emma from MI6 to pick me up.'

'This Emma from MI6 says that the guys who have taken your ex-wife are Russians.'

'Yes, boss. Wagner Group.'

'Wagner Group? Are you sure?'

'Got it from the horse's mouth, boss.'

'What does that mean?'

'I interrogated one of their people. Best you don't ask for specifics, boss.'

The colonel nodded. 'Well, if Wagner are carrying out operations on British soil, that makes it terrorism-related. I'm going to temporarily second Sergeant Warren to the CRW Wing.'

The Counter-Revolutionary Warfare Wing was a specialized unit within the SAS that dealt with counterterrorism. The unit was responsible for training whichever squadron was on counterterrorism rotation, and trained troopers in VIP close-protection techniques.

'I'll make sure that he and anyone who is assisting him gets the required authorization to carry concealed weapons,' continued the colonel. 'Just be careful.'

'I will do, boss.'

'And is Tyson with you?'

Bird moved the phone to show that the dog was lying at his feet.

'Give him my best,' said the colonel, but then he realized that Bird couldn't see his face. He waited until Bird's face was filling the screen again before repeating what he said.

Bird grinned. 'I will do, boss.'

The colonel gave the phone back to Warren. 'Swing by my office when we're done and we'll do the paperwork.'

'Thanks, boss.'

Warren waited until the colonel had left the room and closed the door before holding the phone in front of his face. 'Okay, he's gone.'

'I thought he'd be angrier than that.'

'The colonel's a straight arrow, and expects everyone else to be the same. In hindsight, it was a mistake not to tell him right away.'

'But if he'd turned us down, then what?'

'We should have trusted him, Birdman. The colonel is SAS through and through.'

At any one time there were more than two dozen officers within the SAS. Each of the four squadrons – A, B, D and G – were headed by an OC, an Officer Commanding, usually an army major. The second in command of each squadron was a captain. Each squadron was divided into four specialized sixteen-man troops – Air, Boat, Mobility and Mountain – and each troop was led by a captain. Most captains spent between two and three years in the Regiment before heading back to their unit, but because of the limited promotion prospects within special forces, few of them returned. Colonel Brewerton was one of the exceptions – he had served as a captain and as a major, and two years earlier had been promoted to colonel. He was well liked by the SAS troopers, but more importantly he had their respect. Most officers were disparagingly referred to as 'Ruperts', but Warren had never heard the term applied to Colonel Brewerton.

'I hear you, Sarge.' Bird chuckled. 'Actually, I don't, obviously, but I get what you mean. So we have to be upfront with him from now on?'

'He's made that clear,' said Warren. 'What's done is done, but if we lie to him again, I'll be RTU'd.'

'I'm sorry, Sarge.'

'It was my call, Birdman. No need to apologize. But from here on in, we have to keep him up to speed.' He held up the parka so that Bird could see it. 'There's definitely not an SD card in your coat.'

'Shit.'

'What do you want to do?'

'Can you get your hands on another card? Like I said, the tablet I used to use with Tyson had a card. There's bound to be more there at Stirling Lines. I just need something to get me through the door.'

'What door?'

'The door to wherever they've got Sarah.'

CHAPTER 24

Bird sat at a trestle table in the garden in front of the Old Elm, nursing a mug of coffee. Tyson lay at his feet, a bowl of water by his nose. Bird had eaten fish and chips and Tyson had wolfed down four large pork sausages.

It was a warm evening, and Bird had taken off his jacket and placed it on the seat next to him, making sure that the Glock 17 was well hidden.

There were only two other people outside the pub – an elderly couple with a chocolate-coloured cocker spaniel who sat in silence, side by side, reading newspapers. He had the *Telegraph* and the woman, presumably his wife, was reading *The Guardian*.

From where he was sitting, Bird had a clear view of the road that ran in front of the pub. There was a zebra crossing in front of the pub, and a small car park to the right. He checked his watch. It had been just over an hour since he had called Emma, so she should be arriving at any moment. As he looked up, he saw a white Vauxhall Corsa heading towards him. As it slowed, he saw that Emma was driving and Simon was in the front passenger seat. There was no one in the back.

Emma indicated, even though there was no other traffic on the road, and turned into the car park. She switched off the engine and they climbed out. They stood together at the back of the car, talking. Bird sipped his coffee and smiled down at Tyson. 'They're working out who's gonna be good cop, and who's gonna be bad cop.'

Tyson pricked up his ears and his tail twitched.

Emma and Simon started walking towards him and it was clear from the look on Emma's face that she was playing bad cop. He smiled up at her as she reached his table. 'Can I buy you a drink?' he said. 'And I can recommend the fish and chips. Large cod fillet, battered to order in dairy-free beer batter, served with homemade chips, peas, tartare sauce and salad. Best fish and chips I've had in years, I can tell you.'

'What the hell do you think you're playing at?' she hissed.

He shrugged. 'Just washing down my meal with one of the tastiest cups of coffee I've had in a while,' he said.

'You're lucky I didn't have you arrested,' she said. 'One phone call is all that it would take.'

'Well, we both know that's not going to happen, don't we? One phone call to the *New York Times* and your GCHQ fiasco is going to be in the public domain. I doubt that the Yanks would give a toss about your DNA Notice or whatever you call it.'

'DSMA,' said Simon, and Emma threw him a withering look.

'Where the hell did you go?' said Emma.

'Why don't you grab a coffee or maybe a nice crisp Chardonnay and we can sit here and talk like adults,' said Bird. 'If you'd prefer, you can stand there and play the angry school ma'am but you have to know that it's not going to work with me. Sticks and stones and all that. To be honest, after you've had a live hand grenade explode underneath you, words really can't hurt you.'

Emma glared at him and grunted in frustration, but Bird could see that she knew he was right. She looked over at Simon. 'Cappuccino,' she said. Simon nodded and headed into the pub. Emma sat down opposite Bird and interlinked her fingers. 'Seriously, Andy, what you did was not cool.'

'My wife's life is at stake here, Emma. Cool or not cool, I'll do whatever it takes to save her.' She opened her mouth to speak and he raised a warning finger. 'And if you even think of saying that she's my ex-wife, I will set Tyson on you.'

'I wasn't going to say that,' she said. 'Why would I? Of course you're going to do whatever is necessary to protect Sarah. But we're on the same side here.'

'Are we?' Bird grimaced and shook his head. 'You see, it seems to me that your primary aim is to ensure nothing damages the relations you – the intelligence agencies – have with the Americans and the rest of the so-called good guys. If you don't keep a lid on what's happened, the Yanks will regard you as untrustworthy and stop sharing intelligence with you.' She opened her mouth to reply but Bird silenced her with a wave of his hand. 'I don't know too much Secret Squirrel stuff, but I do know something about the Five Eyes.'

The Five Eyes was an intelligence alliance between the United States, the UK, Canada, Australia and New Zealand. During the 1960s, the five countries had shared intel through the Echelon network – mainly to monitor goings on in the former Soviet Union, but Five Eyes had expanded the system to monitor all communications worldwide.

'Five Eyes is based on trust,' said Bird. 'And if the other four members stop trusting the UK, it could well become the Four Eyes. Or they could replace the UK with the Germans. The Germans would love to be in the Five Eyes, right?'

'This is all hypothetical,' said Emma. 'And way above our pay grade.'

Bird smiled thinly. 'I don't have a pay grade,' he said. 'I don't get paid, remember?'

'I've already told you, that can be remedied,' said Emma. 'You have skills that the intelligence services can make use of. They *should* be making use of them. But first they need to trust you, and what you did today doesn't inspire trust, does it?'

'I will always put friends and family first,' said Bird.

'Above King and Country?'

Bird laughed. 'Of course. What have King or Country ever done for me? Here's a question for you, Emma: how many former servicemen are living rough across the UK? Men and women who have risked their lives to defend King and Country and are now being left to fend for themselves.'

'I don't know,' she said quietly.

'Well, it's a lot. Hundreds, maybe thousands, including my good self. So no, I have zero allegiance to King and Country. But I'll do whatever I have to do to save Sarah. If that means treading on your pretty little toes, that's tough.'

'It's not about treading on my toes,' said Emma. 'It's about maintaining national security.'

Simon returned with two coffees. He put one mug in front of Emma and sat down next to her. 'So, what did I miss?' he asked.

'Nothing much,' said Bird. 'I was just explaining to Emma that rescuing Sarah is my priority at the moment. I've discovered that the Wagner Group is behind all these killings. The main guy is called Nikolay, also known as Kolya.'

Emma frowned. 'How exactly did you come by this information?'

'That's not important,' said Bird. 'These guys are trouble. The Wagner Group are mean sons of bitches.'

'How do you know that they're involved?' asked Emma.

'You seem more interested in how I got the intel than about the intel itself.'

'Where did you go, Andy?'

'I went looking for Sarah. I didn't find her but I spoke to one of the guys who took her. He doesn't know where she is, but this Nikolay does. In fact, there's every chance that Nikolay is with her, so if we find him, we find her.'

'And this guy you *spoke* to, he told you he worked for the Wagner Group?'

'He did.'

'He just volunteered the information?'

'We had a chat. Me, him and Tyson.' Bird grinned. 'Tyson can be persuasive. But I need you to identify this Nikolay character for me.'

'What do you know about the Wagner Group?'

'Just that they're Putin's freelance stormtroopers. He uses them when he wants to keep bad stuff at arm's length. But to be honest they're a busted flush these days, especially after Yevgeny Prigozhin launched a mutiny against Putin and then died in a very iffy plane crash that was almost certainly Putin taking care of business.'

'But the group is still active in Syria and Mali,' said Emma. 'Did you know that?'

Bird nodded. 'There are units that used to be part of Wagner Group that are still active, but the group was Prigozhin's personal fiefdom from the start. Putin always denied that Russia had anything to do with Wagner's activities in Africa, for instance. But he also admitted that Wagner was fully funded by the Russian state to the tune of a billion dollars a year. Basically, Putin wanted to have his cake and eat it. But the mutiny put paid to that. As soon as Prigozhin was dead, Putin insisted that every member of Wagner swore an "oath of allegiance" to the Russian state and now the units tend to report to your Russian military intelligence counterparts at the Federal Intelligence Service, which in turn reports directly to Putin. He has more control over the Wagner people now, but he's no longer able to claim plausible deniability.'

'Did the guy you spoke to say that he's working for Putin or the FIS?' asked Emma.

'I didn't ask him. But after Prigozhin died, I know a lot of his people went freelance. They still use the Wagner name, but that doesn't mean they are officially sanctioned. It's messy.'

Emma sipped her coffee. 'So you're saying that the guy you spoke to was quite happy to tell you that he works for the Wagner Group?'

Bird grinned. 'I wouldn't say that he was happy, no.'

'And where is he now, this guy?'

Bird flashed her a tight smile. 'That's not really important, is it?'

'Well, if he was one of the men who killed Sasha, then it is.'

'He wasn't. No question.'

'What about the shoot-out in Arlington Road? Was he there?'

'I don't think so.'

'You don't think so?'

'It was a bit hectic, and dark. I didn't see all their faces.'

Emma sipped her coffee again. 'What is it that they want, Andy?'

'I guess they want me. They'll exchange me for Sarah.'

Bird had already made the decision not to tell them about the SD card. If the information on the card was important to national security, then there was every chance that Emma would simply refuse to use it as a bargaining chip. She had made it crystal clear where her priorities lay, and Sarah wasn't even on her radar. He also wasn't going to tell them about the phone he'd taken from the Russian. That was one ace he planned on keeping up his sleeve.

Emma frowned. 'But they had you. You spoke to this guy, this Wagner Group guy, so why didn't they release Sarah?'

'They were trying to fuck me over. They wanted me to go with them but I said I wasn't having it.'

'You said "they". So there was more than one?'

'That's not the point, Emma. They didn't have Sarah. This Nikolay does. He's the one you need to worry about.'

'I think I'll be the judge of what I should be worried about, Andy.'

'What you need to worry about is how they knew where Sarah was,' said Bird. 'You tracked her down through my phone, but how could the Russians do that? The house is in her name now, and she had a new man in her life. But they had no trouble finding her and killing her minders. I don't see how Russians, even Wagner Group Russians, could find her that quickly. They must have had help. And by help, I mean someone within the Security Services. MI5 or MI6 or GCHQ.'

'We're looking into that, Andy. We're as keen as you to know if there's a traitor on our side.'

'Yeah, well, I wish I had more faith in you guys,' said Bird. 'Based on past experience, I won't be holding my breath. And when you do find out where Nikolay is, you need to tell me.'

'With a view to you doing what?'

'With a view to me setting Sarah free, obviously.'

'Single-handed?'

'Me and Tyson. Maybe a few old friends from Stirling Lines.'

Emma shook her head. 'That can't be your call, Andy.'

'I'm not getting the cops involved. You saw what happened at the house. They're not up to fighting these people. The CTSFOs are good, but they're still cops and generally cops find any excuse not to pull the trigger. And when you're up against animals like the Wagner Group, that approach only ends one way. The colonel has already said we can use SAS guys if needed.'

Emma wrinkled her nose. 'Okay, I accept that. We can use the SAS. That could well work to our advantage.' She looked over at Simon. 'That works, right?'

'I don't see why not.'

'What about checking on the Wagner Group?' said Bird. 'Presumably you have files at MI6.'

'Lots of them,' said Emma. 'We should go to GCHQ – it's only ten minutes away. We can get a feed from London and I can start running photographs by you.'

'Let's do it,' said Bird. 'You lead the way and I'll follow you.'

CHAPTER 25

Emma parked her Vauxhall in an outdoor car park. It was huge and cars stretched for as far as the eye could see, hundreds upon hundreds of vehicles still there even into the evening. Bird pulled up next to her in the Range Rover. 'There's something I should tell you,' he said as he climbed out.

'I'm all ears.'

'I'm still carrying.'

'Carrying?'

'The Glock that the Sarge gave me. I just thought it might be an issue if we're going inside GCHQ.'

Emma muttered under her breath and held out her hand. Bird pulled the gun from his jacket and gave it to her. She put it into the Corsa's glovebox and slammed it shut.

Simon gestured at the building across the road. 'Welcome to the Doughnut,' he said. Ahead of them was an imposing four-storey glass and steel circular building the size of Wembley Stadium, ringed by razor wire-topped fences. CCTV cameras on poles covered the areas both sides of the fence. It looked as if a massive flying saucer had been set down in the middle of a prison.

'The Doughnut?' repeated Bird. Tyson jumped out of the back of the car and stood next to him, ears up.

'The Doughnut. That's the nickname of this building. It was designed in a doughnut shape around a large garden. It was finished in 2003, cost over a billion quid, covers a hundred and seventy-six-acre site, with five and a half thousand people now working here.'

'All listening in to phone conversations and reading emails,' said Bird. 'Big Brother.'

Simon gave Bird an unamused smile and started walking to the entrance, which was set into the fence.

'Andy, if it wasn't for the work they do here there would be a lot more terror atrocities committed in the UK and around the world,' said Emma as she walked with Bird and Tyson. 'GCHQ's signals intelligence has saved hundreds of lives. Thousands maybe. When the police or the SAS go in with guns drawn, it makes the national news. Almost all of GCHQ's work stays below the radar. They nip plots in the bud.'

'By spying on everybody,' said Bird. 'By doing away with privacy.'

Simon turned around to look at him. 'It's not like that, Andy. We're not listening in to every conversation, we don't have the manpower to do that. But we store calls and emails and have the facility to go through them looking for keywords. We spy on the bad guys, and we're damn good at it.'

Bird shrugged. 'I'm not convinced. I don't like the idea that if I tell a mate that my party bombed someone here will listen into the conversation.'

'They won't. But if you were to tell a mate that you had a gun and were planning to shoot the prime minister then yes, that call might well be listened to.'

'Do you intercept a lot of calls like that?'

'From people threatening to kill the PM? A lot. More often emails or social media posts, though. Either way, there are a lot of nutters out there and they need to be monitored.'

They reached the entrance, where Simon showed his ID to a uniformed security guard and explained who Emma and Bird were. 'I'll need to see IDs,' said the guard gruffly.

Emma handed over hers. 'I only have a driving licence,' said Bird, taking it from his wallet.

'That'll do,' said the guard. He was barely out of his teens and his uniform seemed to be too big for him. He was growing a moustache in an attempt to make himself look older but it was straggly at best and, if anything, it made him look younger.

Bird passed his driving licence to the guard, who looked down at Tyson and wrinkled his nose. 'The dog can't come in,' he said.

'He's an emotional support dog,' said Bird. 'If he's not with me, I might kick off.'

The guard frowned. 'What?' he said.

'It's okay,' Simon said to the guard. 'I'll vouch for the dog. He's part of an ongoing investigation.'

The guard's frown deepened and he scratched his chin. 'I'll need to talk to my manager.'

'Best do that,' said Simon. 'Because we really do need this dog inside.'

The guard nodded and walked away.

'So why did they build it in the shape of a doughnut?' asked Bird.

'They say it's to cut down on the possibility of eavesdropping,' said Simon.

'Seriously?'

'That's what they say. Having the offices overlooking open space means that any sound is dispersed. If there was no garden, spy satellites would find it easier to listen in.'

'Is that even possible?' said Bird. 'Eavesdropping from outer space?'

Simon grinned. 'You'd be amazed at what we can do these days,' he said. 'And anything we can do, the Chinese and the Russians can do, too.'

The guard returned. 'The dog can be admitted, but I'll need to see ID.'

'Oh, that's ridiculous,' snapped Emma. 'Tyson is a dog.'

'No, that's okay,' said Bird, taking out his wallet. 'I still have his Army ID.'

'Are you serious?' said Simon. He took the photo ID card from Bird and frowned as he studied it. 'Wait, Tyson is a non-commissioned officer? So he outranks you?'

Bird grinned. 'It was done to wind the handlers up,' he said. 'In the States, military working dogs are always one rank higher than their handlers, supposedly to prevent handlers from abusing or mistreating them. One of our officers was embedded with the Navy SEALs and when he came back he thought it'd be funny to institute the practice with the Regiment. All our dogs were promoted.'

'So you have to salute your dog?' Emma asked.

Bird shook his head. 'Special forces don't salute,' he said.

Simon showed the card to Emma and she laughed. 'That is perfect,' she said.

Simon gave the card to the man, who scribbled down the details on his clipboard before handing both cards back to Bird and pressing a button to open the gate. They walked through. The guard grinned and flashed Tyson a sarcastic salute.

Simon took them into the main building. 'Basically, we have two circular buildings, one inside the other, with a total floor area of one and a half million square feet,' he said. 'In between the two buildings is what we call the Street, which is how we move from one part of the building to another. It's covered in glass so that it's usable in all weathers.' He grimaced. 'I'm starting to sound like a tour guide,' he said. 'Let's grab a coffee in the restaurant. It's going to take time to get up and running. We're fixing up a feed from MI6 and we'll need to talk to Sasha's boss. He's in a meeting for the next half an hour.'

'I thought you were Sasha's boss?'

'No, I worked with him at JTRIG, but I was never his boss. His boss is a guy called Graeme Carmichael. He'll be along later.'

'But you know Sasha, right?'

'Knew him, yes. I'd met him a few times in person but mostly we spoke online. So we'll eat, yeah?'

'Sure,' said Bird, though truth be told, food was the last thing on his mind. He couldn't stop thinking about Sarah and what she must be going through. She must have been in a state of absolute panic and to make it worse they had probably told her that he was the reason for her abduction. That would make no sense to her, obviously. She had wanted him out of her life for good, she'd made that perfectly clear. Had she seen them kill the CTSFOs and the MI6 guy? And what about her partner, the guy shot on the sofa? Had she seen him die? Sarah was the type who had to watch horror movies through her fingers, and she'd never, ever asked Andy for war stories. His job was his job and she never wanted him to bring it home. If they were in a pub with other members of the Regiment and someone started talking about a combat situation, Sarah would make an excuse and leave. So he could only imagine the state she was in now, taken prisoner by a group of Russian thugs. His heart was racing and he clenched his fists. They would pay for what they'd done. He'd make sure of that. They'd pay with their lives. He took a deep breath. He'd get his revenge, but it was going to take time. He needed to get all his ducks in a row before he could start blasting away at them. He forced a smile. 'Let's get some caffeine. I have a feeling it's going to be a long night.'

Simon took them along to a huge open-plan restaurant. Bird's jaw dropped as he looked around. 'This is huge.'

'Seats six hundred,' said Simon. 'They don't want us wandering around outside during breaks so they are geared up for serving food for everyone. Plus there are shops, a gym, a chapel – everything you need.'

'It's a prison, mate,' said Bird. 'From the outside, it even looks like a prison.'

Simon got the coffees while Emma and Bird found a free table by the window overlooking the garden. Simon also bought a dozen chicken nuggets for Tyson. He put the plate under the table and Tyson ducked under and started eating.

Simon sat down opposite Bird and gestured at the garden. 'That's big enough to contain the Royal Albert Hall,' he said.

'Why would they want to move it from London?' asked Bird.

'No, I mean it would . . .' Simon stopped and shook his head when he realized that Bird was pulling his leg. 'Yeah, right, got it. Anyway, below the garden are banks of supercomputers that do all the number-crunching and data storage. There's a memorial there, too, to GCHQ employees who died in the line of duty.'

'Are you serious?' said Bird.

'We lost five guys in Afghanistan,' said Simon. 'It's not all desk work.' He saw the look of scorn that flashed across Bird's face and he held up his hands. 'Okay, yes, fair enough, most of it is, yes.'

'Let's not forget that Sasha lost his life,' said Emma.

Bird nodded. 'Fair point,' he said.

'No one is comparing it to what you do, Andy,' said Emma.

'Did,' said Bird. 'Past tense.'

'Oh, I think that the events of the past twenty-four hours demonstrate that you still have what it takes,' said Emma.

Bird's phone rang. It was Warren making a video call. Bird got up from the table and walked away from Emma and Simon to take the call. He found an empty table with no one within earshot and sat down.

'Okay, I've managed to snaffle an SD card,' Warren said. 'What do you want me to do with it?'

'Can you bring it here?'

'Where's here?'

'I'm at GCHQ. Cheltenham.'

'Secret Squirrel Central,' said Warren. 'Sure. Colonel Brewerton gave me carte blanche, pretty much, remember? And I can use a few of the guys. We'll drive over. I'll need to pull them and the kit together, and brief the colonel, so we'll be a few hours. How are things going there?'

'Ticking over. They're going to run pictures of Wagner Group guys past me to see if I can recognize anyone. Look, Sarge, I'm getting a bad feeling about the way it's going here. They seem more interested in tracking down the Wagner guys than rescuing Sarah. I need you to take the initiative.'

'Okay. In what way?'

'Once you get to Cheltenham, can you call the kidnappers? Their boss is a guy called Nikolay. I'll text you his number. You can pretend to be me and say that you've got the SD card. He's spoken to you before and he doesn't know what I look like – there's no reason for him not to believe you.'

'Okay, but then what?'

'Get proof of life, then arrange a handover.'

'After what happened last time, he'll be wary.'

'He won't know for sure what happened last time, will he? None of the guys he sent are in a position to tell him. He'll assume from the radio silence that there was a problem, but he won't know for sure.'

'And if he asks?'

'Then tell him that the men he sent had no intention of releasing Sarah so they deserved what they got. Tell him if he is serious about making an exchange, he can have the SD card but we need to get Sarah back in one piece. They obviously really want it, and if that's the case then they have an incentive to release her.'

'What if they realize we don't have the real SD card?'

'They'll have to check it, right? And we'll only hand it over when we've seen that they are ready to exchange Sarah.'

'It's a risk, Andy. One hell of a risk.'

'It's our best chance, Sarge.'

'I hear you, Andy. Let me give him a call and see where we stand.'

'Let me know, yeah.'

Warren nodded. 'Of course.'

'You'll need to come tooled up.'

'You've still got the Glock I gave you?'

'Sadly not. The lovely Emma confiscated it.'

'Any requests?'

'Any Glock'll be fine –' Bird thought back to the cottage – 'but a 30SF would be great if you have one.'

'A 30SF it is. I'll bring a few flashbangs, comms and night-vision gear. The works.'

'Thanks, Sarge. I owe you.'

'No mate, I owe you.'

Bird ended the call. He sent Warren a text with Nikolay's phone number and went back to join Emma and Simon. 'Everything okay?' asked Emma.

'I've applied for Universal Credit,' lied Bird. 'They're making me jump through all sorts of hoops.'

'You think they'd be more helpful in your case,' said Emma. 'I mean, you were injured in the line of duty.'

'The mission was classified and will be for the next fifty years, so I can't talk about it.'

'If you think I can help, let me know,' said Emma.

'I will,' said Bird. He didn't enjoy lying to Emma, but she was a Secret Squirrel and he knew that not everything she told him was the truth. What goes around, comes around.

CHAPTER 26

After they had finished their coffees, Simon took them along the Street to a lift, up to the top floor, then down a grey-carpeted corridor to a door labelled OPERATIONS ROOM 4176. Simon pushed it open. There were windows along one wall but they were covered with grey blinds. There were two groups of three tables, pushed together to form triangles, and each table had a high-backed executive chair, a keyboard and three monitors. There was a low sofa against a wall, facing the windows. 'We need an operations room?' said Bird.

'It's not that, it's that most of the workspaces are open-plan and having visitors makes life difficult,' said Simon. 'They'd rather you were here, out of the way.'

'Because I'm not to be trusted, obviously,' said Bird.

Bird saw Simon open his mouth to protest so he grinned and held up his hand. 'I'm joking,' he said. He dropped down onto one of the chairs and stretched out his legs. Tyson went under one of the tables and lay down, his eyes open and ears up. 'I've enjoyed the tour and the coffee hit the spot, but the clock is ticking and I'm no closer to getting my wife back.' It was Emma's turn to open her mouth, and again Bird held up a hand. 'Ex-wife.'

'I'm still waiting for my people to send through all they have on Wagner Group employees who might be active in the UK,' said Emma. Her mobile buzzed and she took it out of her pocket and looked at the screen. 'Speak of the devil,' she said. She put the phone to her ear and walked away, standing with her back to them as she had a brief whispered conversation.

When she had finished, she sat down at the table next to Bird. 'We're up and running,' she said, tapping on her keyboard. A picture appeared on her middle screen and she scooted her chair over to the left so that Bird could get a better look.

'Our people have used CCTV footage to identify the three men you shot and killed in Camden,' she said.

'The two usually go together,' said Bird.

Emma frowned. 'I'm sorry?'

'When I shoot someone, generally they die,' said Bird. 'That's how we're trained. There's no shoot-to-wound nonsense. But sorry, I didn't mean to interrupt.' He gave her a disarming smile.

'Right,' she said. 'So the three men you killed were all members of Wagner Group.' She tapped on her keyboard and three head and shoulder shots filled the screen. Bird recognized all three. The one on the left was the passenger in the grey SUV, the one whose gun Bird had grabbed and used. The one on the right was the driver, who Bird had shot in the chest. The photograph in the middle was the rear passenger of the green SUV.

'All three joined Wagner a year into the Russian invasion of Ukraine,' said Emma. 'At that point, Yevgeny Prigozhin was visiting most of the prisons in Russia offering pardons to anyone who signed up for six months. It didn't matter what offences they had committed – all three of these men were serving sentences for murder, and the guy in the middle was also a serial rapist who had raped and strangled four women.'

'But the six months will have long passed,' said Bird.

'They were encouraged to stay longer than the six months,' said Emma. 'They were paid three times what a regular Russian soldier earned. They were also offered certain perks. Raping Ukrainian women was encouraged, as was looting. Not surprisingly, a lot decided to stay on.'

'And these three just waltzed into the UK?' said Bird.

'They almost certainly flew in on a private jet owned by a Kremlin-friendly oligarch,' said Emma. 'These days, Border Force check fewer than ten per cent of private jets arriving in this country. MI5 and MI6 have pointed out the dangers of this policy several times but nothing changes. Border Force says that the vast majority of the arrivals are regular travellers and that they simply don't have the manpower to check each and every flight.'

'They seem to have enough people to meet all the dinghies crossing the English Channel every day,' said Bird.

'Yes, well don't get me started on that,' said Emma. 'At Six it's not so much of an issue, but Five's surveillance workload has risen ten-fold since the dinghy business boomed. So anyway, we have identified these three, what I'd like you to do now is to look at photographs of Wagner Group personnel who fit a similar profile.'

'Sure, but I'm not a great one for remembering faces.'

'Let's see how you get on,' said Emma.

'What about guys called Nikolay? Or Koyla?'

Emma nodded. 'It's a common name, and a common nickname. Plus, you probably haven't seen him yet, right?'

'Not that I know of, but he might have been one of the two guys who killed Sasha.'

'Good point,' she said. 'Okay, let me call up the Nikolays and Koylas first.' She bent over the keyboard and tapped on it for several minutes before moving her chair away from the desk and pushing the mouse towards him. 'There are thirty-seven possible matches,' she said. 'Just click to move on to the next picture.'

Bird nodded and clicked the mouse. A single photograph flashed up. It was a head and shoulders shot of a man in his thirties, shaven headed with thin lips and a wide nose who was glaring at the lens as if he was about to rip the heart out of the cameraman. Bird shook his head. 'No,' he said.

He clicked the mouse and another picture appeared. This one

was a photograph of a man in fatigues, holding a Kalashnikov and standing over the bodies of three Arabs. Bird shook his head again. 'No.' He clicked again, and again. He had just clicked for a tenth time when the door opened and a man in his forties appeared, wearing a dark blue suit, starched white shirt and a pale blue tie with black dots on it. His black hair was swept back, showing a prominent widow's peak and his eyes focused on Simon. 'Ah, Simon, so this is the right room.'

'We've only just got here,' said Simon. He gestured at Emma who had already got to her feet. 'Emma you've already met. And this is Andy Bird.'

The man held out his hand as Bird stood up. 'Graeme Carmichael,' he said. 'I was Sasha's manager.' He had the look of a farmer, with broken blood vessels across his cheeks and deep lines around his eyes, as if he spent a lot of time squinting. 'This is a nightmare. I still can't believe that he's dead.'

Bird shook the man's hand. It was big, like a shovel, but there was no strength in his grip and the flesh had the feel of cold chicken. 'Andy Bird,' he said.

Carmichael frowned. 'Simon said you were deaf.'

'I am.'

'So do you have hearing aids or something?'

'I read lips.'

Carmichael's eyebrows went up. 'And you do it bloody well, clearly. I'd never have known.'

'I'm fine so long as you're looking right at me.'

'I'll try to remember that,' he said. He had slowed down his speech and was clearly trying to enunciate more clearly for Bird's benefit.

Carmichael sat down at the table to the left of Bird and adjusted his shirt cuffs. He was wearing cufflinks that seemed to be crossed golf clubs. He smiled at Emma. 'Have you made any progress?'

'We're still gathering intel,' she said.

'If there's anything you need, anything we can do, just ask.'

'Thank you,' she said.

Carmichael looked over at Bird. 'So, you're in the SAS?'

'I used to be.'

Carmichael frowned and looked across at Emma. 'So he's a civilian?'

'Yes, but still governed by the Official Secrets Act,' she said.

'Even so, I'm surprised that you've involved a civilian in your investigation. In fact, I still don't fully understand why MI6 is taking the lead on this. I didn't think that murder investigation fell within your remit.'

'Andy was a witness to Sasha's murder,' said Emma. 'The only witness. He was then hunted and almost killed by the men who murdered Sasha. So it makes a lot of sense for Andy to be involved. I've worked with Andy before, so it made sense for me to run the investigation.'

'But I was told that Sasha was due to meet with someone at MI5 before he was killed. Why aren't they running the investigation?'

'They're very much involved,' said Emma. 'Because of the sensitive nature of Sasha's work, MI5 moved quickly to take the investigation from the police. Then when they found out that Andy was a witness, they checked his background with the SAS and my name came up as a previous contact. They figured that a friendly face might come in useful, so I was co-opted to the investigation.'

'So you were taken on because you're a pretty face?'

Emma smiled without warmth. 'A friendly face, is what I said.'

Carmichael held up his hands in surrender. 'My apologies,' he said. 'This is a very unique situation, obviously, and it's taking some getting used to.'

'It is a very unusual situation, yes,' said Emma. 'I'm effectively acting as senior investigating officer. Prior to joining MI6 I was an inspector with the Metropolitan Police, where I was SIO on several major investigations, including two murders, so I know the drill.'

'I really wasn't asking for your CV,' said Carmichael. 'I'm sure that you're more than capable. So, the police aren't involved in the investigation?'

'We're holding off calling them in,' said Emma. 'I'm sure the last thing you want is plod knocking on your doors. And we're trying to keep this below the radar as much as possible.'

Carmichael shrugged. 'That hasn't happened with the shootings in Camden, obviously. That's all over the news.'

'There were a lot of witnesses,' said Emma. 'But luckily no phone video. It's been put down as a gang turf war, drugs-related.'

'And the kidnapping of Mr Bird's wife – ex-wife – has not been made public?'

'Definitely not,' said Emma.

'So the plan is what, wait until the kidnappers get in touch and negotiate?'

'We're hoping to identify the men responsible and then get a location,' said Emma. 'But if they do get in touch, all well and good.'

'Then send in SCO19?'

'I have an SAS counterterrorism team I can use,' said Bird.

'Really?' said Carmichael. 'This has been agreed by the SAS?'

Bird nodded. 'The guys who kidnapped my wife are pros and aren't afraid of shooting police officers.'

Carmichael nodded. 'And you don't know what it is that the kidnappers want?'

Bird frowned. 'What do you mean?'

'Well, from the sound of it, they went to a lot of trouble to kidnap your ex-wife.'

'If by trouble you mean slaughtering four innocent people, then yes, they did.' Bird was already taking a dislike to the man. He reminded him of many of the officers who were assigned to the SAS for short periods just to get the Regiment on their CV. They were usually university-educated, from good families, and more often than not were a bloody liability in combat.

'What I mean is that this wasn't random. Presumably this isn't about money, is it? I doubt that the SAS pays much better than the regular Army. Forty thousand?'

'Thereabouts,' said Bird. 'But I'm not employed at the moment so money isn't an issue.'

Carmichael's eyes sparkled. 'That's exactly my point. They went to a lot of trouble to kidnap her but it can't be about money, can it? Because there isn't any. So they must want something else. So what is it, do you think? What do they want?'

Bird held the man's look as his mind raced. He knew exactly what the kidnappers wanted; an SD card that they assumed Sasha had given him. But Bird didn't have the SD card and didn't know where it was. What he did know was that he didn't trust Carmichael, not one bit. There was something off about the man, he just seemed over-eager, flashing insincere smiles and doing lots of head nodding as if trying to get Bird to agree with him. 'I'm not sure,' he said eventually. 'Maybe they are worried that I can identify the men that killed Sasha.'

'So you think they want to swap you for your ex-wife and then, what? Kill you?'

'That's all I could think of. As you said, it can't be about money, can it?'

'Did Sasha say anything to you, before he died?'

'I was at the side of the alley when they chased him and shot him. I intervened and they ran off. By the time I got to him, it was all over, pretty much.'

Carmichael nodded slowly. 'So he didn't say anything to you? Not a thing?'

'He was in a lot of pain. He'd just been shot. I think he might have said "eighty", but that wouldn't make any sense.'

'Eighty? Eighty what?'

'Just eighty. I might have misread his lips. Like I said, he was in a lot of pain.'

Carmichael sat back in his chair and looked over at Emma. 'None of this gets us anywhere, does it?'

'What about Sasha?' asked Bird. 'Why would anyone want to kill him?'

'That doesn't make any sense either,' said Carmichael. 'We tend to remain faceless here at GCHQ, so it rarely becomes personal.'

'Presumably it's tied in with the fact that he asked for a meeting with MI5,' said Bird.

Carmichael frowned and looked over at Simon. 'You told him that?'

'I did,' said Emma, before Simon could reply.

'I didn't realize that information would be released outside the intelligence agencies.'

'Andy was with the SAS, he's got security clearance.'

Carmichael looked back at Bird. '*Was* with, past tense,' he said. 'You said you're not currently employed, correct?'

Bird smiled coldly. 'I'm in between jobs at the moment, yes,' he said. 'So, why was Sasha so keen to meet with MI5?'

'I really couldn't tell you,' said Carmichael.

'Can't or won't? Is this about my security clearance?'

'I'm sorry, I wasn't being evasive. It's because I genuinely don't know,' said Carmichael. 'Sasha ploughed his own furrow, as they say. He was a valued member of our team, but he was rarely here at Cheltenham. Most of his work could be done from home. In fact, in his line of work, we encourage working from home.'

'It gives you plausible deniability, you mean?'

Carmichael waved away the suggestion. 'No, not at all. He's on staff.' He grimaced and corrected himself. 'He was on staff. But the sort of work he did involved solo projects, working alone.'

'Dirty tricks, right?'

Carmichael gave Simon a withering look. Simon looked startled and Carmichael turned his gaze back to Bird. 'I don't know who's been telling you that, but everything we do at JTRIG is legal and above board, as is everything we do at GCHQ. There is nothing in the least bit dirty about what we do.'

'No offence meant,' said Bird, who was actually enjoying the discomfort he'd caused the man. 'But the sort of work you do, discrediting and disrupting enemies, well, you presumably wouldn't want it known that it was being done here.'

'That's not really an issue,' said Carmichael. 'You've heard of VPNs, presumably.'

'VPNs?' repeated Bird.

Carmichael smiled patronizingly. 'Virtual private network,' he said. 'Basically, a VPN sets up a digital connection between your computer and a remote server owned by a VPN provider, which then encrypts your personal data, masks your IP address so you can't be tracked or traced, and lets you avoid firewalls and the like.'

'So everything you do is untraceable?'

'Not untraceable, no. But it wouldn't be obvious that it was originating here. That's not why Sasha worked from home, though. Most JTRIG staffers don't come into the office – most of their work is computer-based and doesn't require the use of our databases.'

'So Sasha would use his own computer at home? In Camden?'

Carmichael frowned. 'How do you know that . . .' He tailed off and glared at Simon again. 'I think you and I need a conversation about security,' he said.

'Sir, I was told to brief Mr Bird on the—'

Carmichael waved his hand to silence Simon. 'We'll discuss it later,' he said dismissively, before turning back to Bird. 'To answer your question, yes, Sasha would have had a computer at home, probably several. He would carry out his assignments and check in, usually via email but occasionally on encrypted Zoom or Teams calls. The nature of his work meant that he wasn't bound by nine to five, in fact he'd often be online late at night and early mornings.'

'And why do you think Sasha was killed?'

Carmichael frowned. 'What concern is that of yours?'

Bird resisted the urge to snap at the man. Was he deliberately being obtuse? 'Because the kidnapping of my ex-wife is obviously connected to his death.'

'Well, yes, that's clear enough. But only because you were a witness to the killing. That's clearly why you were targeted, because of what you saw. But as to why Sasha was killed, I'd say that was irrelevant.'

'Really? Even though we know it was members of the Wagner Group that killed him? It wasn't a random mugging, it was an assassination.'

'But again, does that matter? And I thought it *was* a robbery. A mugging.'

'Who told you that?' asked Bird.

Carmichael frowned. 'And what is this about Wagner Group?' He looked over at Emma. 'The Wagner Group? The Russians are involved in this?'

'You didn't know?' said Bird.

'I was told that Sasha had been killed in an alley. Shot. No one told me anything about the Wagner Group being involved.' He looked over at Emma again. 'Why am I only just hearing this?'

'We've only just received that information,' said Emma. 'Literally in the past few hours. We've had confirmation that the three men killed in London were working for Wagner Group. We've been running photographs of Wagner operatives past Andy in the hope that he'll be able to recognize more of them.'

Carmichael's eyes narrowed. 'Am I being deliberately kept out of the loop here?'

'Absolutely not,' said Emma.

'So explain to me how MI6 knows that Wagner Group is involved in this, and I don't.'

Emma looked at Bird and he realized that she was expecting him to provide the explanation, and that was a problem. A big problem. The reason he knew who was behind the killings and Sarah's kidnapping was because he had tortured one of the Russians, and that Russian was still tied up in the house in Churchdown. Emma might well be allowed to carry out hard interrogations, but Bird wasn't, and if the police were to get involved Bird would almost certainly be facing charges. He looked at Carmichael and smiled. 'I just realized that they were Russian, which means that they would either be Russian mafia, Russian mercenaries – which meant probably Wagner Group – or the GRU.'

Emma was frowning now because what he was telling Carmichael didn't match with what he had told her, but she didn't say anything.

Carmichael was also frowning. 'But you're deaf. And while it's clear that you are a very capable lip-reader, how does that equate to you knowing that he was Russian?'

'One of them cursed in Russian after they killed Sasha.'

'You speak Russian?'

'Svobodno govoryu po-russki, umeyu chitat i pisat.'

Carmichael nodded. 'I can see that you're fluent,' he said. 'And your accent is good. Very good.'

'Thank you.'

'How many languages do you speak?'

'Five. Including English.'

'And you can lip-read in all five?'

'Yes, pretty much.'

'Arabic?'

'Naema, kama anani ujid allughat alearabia.'

Carmichael nodded again. 'When this is over, we should talk. You could be a real asset to GCHQ.'

'I'm not sure that I'd want to work as a Secret Squirrel. Plus, I'm told that Tyson wouldn't be welcome.'

'Tyson? Who's Tyson?'

Bird pointed under the table. Carmichael frowned and bent down to see what he was pointing at. He saw the dog, swore, pushed himself back and stood up so quickly that his chair tipped over and crashed against the floor. Tyson was up on his feet, ears back, snarling and baring his teeth. Carmichael was still swearing as he backed away, his hands up defensively. Tyson moved towards him, then went into a crouch as he prepared to launch himself through the air. Carmichael shrieked in terror.

CHAPTER 27

'Good boy, Tyson,' said Bird. He was holding a Tesco carrier bag that Emma had found for him and he was waiting for the dog to do his business under a bush in the garden at the centre of the Doughnut. She'd suggested that Bird take Tyson outside after he had managed to grab the dog's harness and pull him away from Carmichael.

Carmichael had been visibly shaken by the incident, even though Tyson hadn't come close to biting him. He kept shaking his head as Bird had tried to explain what the dog had been through, how he had ended up with PTSD and how he didn't react well to loud noises. Tyson appeared to be equally disturbed by what had happened and kept looking over at Carmichael and baring his teeth. Eventually Carmichael had left the operations room, muttering darkly under his breath. No one mentioned that he appeared to have wet himself.

'Is he often like that?' asked Emma, as she watched Tyson sniff around the bush.

'Only when he's caught off guard,' said Bird. 'If there's a loud noise or he gets woken up abruptly.' He forced a smile. 'That's one of the few good things about being deaf – loud noises don't affect me. But I can lash out if you wake me up unexpectedly.'

'I'll bear that in mind,' she said, and then smiled. 'Not that the occasion is ever going to arise, obviously.'

Bird chuckled. She hadn't mentioned the disparity between what he had told her about his intel on Wagner Group and what he had said to Carmichael. It had obviously registered with her, he'd seen it on her face, so he figured she was waiting to see if he would raise it. He was perfectly capable of playing her at her own game, but it was something that needed to be discussed, and sooner rather than later. 'So,' he said. 'About what I told Carmichael.'

'Yes?' she said, and smiled as if she had no idea what he was referring to.

'I'm going to be honest with you, I don't trust the man. I don't think he has my best interests at heart.'

'Well to be fair, Andy, he doesn't know who you are. And your dog did try to kill him.'

'That's a bit of an exaggeration,' said Bird. 'Tyson never actually bit him.'

'Only because you grabbed his harness.'

'Okay, fine. But he did startle Tyson.'

'I think Tyson startled him.' She grinned. 'Sorry, we're getting off subject. You were saying that you don't trust one of GCHQ's most senior employees.'

'I'm sure he's passed all the security vetting and I'm sure he's not a closet Communist, but you saw the way he reacted to the suggestion that GCHQ employees use dirty tricks.'

'Simon is the same, as you know. No one at GCHQ sees what they're doing as breaking any rules.'

'That's exactly my point. They seem to be sticklers for following the rules, which means if he finds out what I did to the Wagner Group guy to get the intel on Nikolay, I could be in big trouble. He's likely to go to the cops, right?'

'I don't know him well enough to make that call, Andy.'

'Well, I know the type. I've had to deal with more than my fair share of Ruperts like him in my time.'

'Ruperts?'

'It's what we call officers. Some of them are fine, but some of them are just like Carmichael, walking around as if they have a stick up their arse. Guys like him are more interested in furthering their own career than they are in getting the job done. So if he finds out what I did, he'll see it as his duty to tell the authorities, which means it's game over for me.'

'What exactly did you do, Andy? You never went into specifics.'

Bird wrinkled his nose. 'Here's the thing, Emma. Can I trust you?'

'Of course you can. What a thing to say.' She put a hand over her heart. 'I'm hurt, Andy. Truly hurt.'

For a second or two, Bird thought she was serious, but then he realized that she was joking.

'Of course, you're a Secret Squirrel, you couldn't tell the truth if your life depended on it.'

'That's harsh, Andy.'

'Tell me this, then. Is your name really Emma?'

She wrinkled her nose. 'That's not a fair question.'

'Yes, it is. You know my name.' He gestured at the dog, who was now squatting under the bush, his nose up in the air as he strained to evacuate his bowels. 'And you know Tyson.'

'But we're told to never use our own names when we're working. It's protocol.'

'I'll take that as a no, then. See, how can I trust someone who won't even tell me her real name?'

'I could have dropped you in it with Carmichael,' she said.

'You could have, yes, but I got the feeling that you're not a fan.'

'He's a prig.'

'Yeah, a fucking prick.'

Emma laughed. She moved her face closer to his and enunciated slowly. 'I said prig. Not prick.'

Bird grinned. 'So my lip-reading isn't perfect.'

Tyson finished doing his business, so Bird bagged it and dropped it into a waste bin. There were quite a few people walking around the garden – it was clearly the favoured place for quiet conversations, even at this late hour.

'I don't know if I can trust you, Emma, or whatever your name is, but it's clear that like most Secret Squirrels you're not averse to bending the rules. You had no problem covering up the killings in Hereford, did you?'

'The end justifies the means.'

'Exactly,' said Bird. 'Which is the position I was in. I needed to get the intel from the Wagner Group guy and there was only one way of doing that.'

'Is he dead, Andy?' she asked quietly.

'He wasn't when I left him,' said Andy. 'He was tied naked to a door and bleeding from a few wounds, so I can't be sure that he's still alive. But I couldn't tell Carmichael that, could I? My feet wouldn't touch the ground. And Tyson would be in big trouble.'

'Why would Tyson be in trouble?'

'I sort of used him to intimidate the Wagner guy.'

'Intimidate? You mean you set Tyson on him?'

Bird grimaced. 'Yeah, I guess I did. But you see why I can't tell Carmichael what happened. If it gets out that Tyson bit the guy, he could well get put down.'

'You can't leave the guy tied to a door, Andy. Not if he's bleeding.'

'He was probably one of the team who killed the cops and your guy in Hereford.'

'Then he needs to be arrested and charged with that. Andy, if the guy dies, you could be up on a murder charge.'

'Can't you make him disappear, like you did with the bodies in Hereford?'

'He's not dead, Andy. At least I hope he isn't. Look, you need to tell me where he is. I'll get him collected and we can see what he needs in the way of medical treatment. Then we can see if we can turn him.'

'Turn him?'

'He's already told you about this Nikolay, right? Wagner Group won't like that one bit. They are ruthless when it comes to punishing transgressions, and your guy will know that. We might be able to offer him a way out. And if he comes on side, there'll be no repercussions for what you and Tyson did. It's a win-win.'

Bird nodded thoughtfully. 'Okay,' he said eventually. 'But it's a bit more complicated than one guy tied to a door.'

'You've told me this much, Andy. You might as well tell me everything.'

Bird grimaced. 'This guy, the guy I interrogated. He wasn't the only one at the house.'

'Okay.'

'There were four of them, in two BMW X5s. They intercepted me en route and escorted me to this house. They were claiming that my wife would be there, but she wasn't. I figured they were going to kill me, so I got my defence in first.'

Emma frowned. 'You did what?'

'I did what I had to do to defend myself.'

'Spit it out, Andy.'

'I killed three of them. Their bodies are in two SUVs outside the house. Along with their weapons. One of those is a Glock 30SF, which I handled more extensively. The Glock in your glovebox is the SAS one Warren gave me, though, and was also fired at the cottage.'

Emma closed her eyes and shook her head.

'They started shooting first, Emma. It was self-defence.'

'I'm sure it was,' she said. 'But you're not making this easy for me.'

'If you can cover up the deaths of CTSFOs, I'm sure you can bury three Wagner thugs.' He grinned. 'No pun intended.'

Emma nodded and sighed. 'In for a penny, I suppose. I'll need the address.'

Bird's eyes narrowed. 'Can I really trust you, Emma?'

She nodded. 'You can. And my name is Ashleigh.'

CHAPTER 28

Bird sat down in front of the three monitors and Tyson curled up under the table and put his head on his paws. They had stopped off for coffees on the way back from the garden and Bird sipped his as he clicked on the mouse to call up the next photograph. He had checked out all the Nikolay and Kolya possibilities but drawn a blank, and was now working his way through the rest of the photographs. 'How many pictures did you get?' he asked Emma, who was sitting at the table next to him.

'There's about two thousand,' she said.

'Are you serious? Why so many?'

'We've had a data dump from Europol, and from intelligence agencies across Europe. Brexit has made cooperation more taxing, but often we can talk to someone we know personally within each agency. The Ukrainians have been helpful, obviously, though they do tend to kill any Wagner Group fighters that they come across. More than two hundred photographs are from our own database – our agents are always gathering intel on the group. But they aren't all definitely in Wagner Group. We've included Russian criminals that have left the country and Russians who served time in British and European prisons. And I've thrown in Russian spies from the Federal Security Service, the Foreign Intelligence Service and of course the GRU, who we know have worked in Europe before.'

Bird nodded. The GRU was the Main Directorate of the General Staff of the Armed Forces of the Russian Federation, which ran the country's military intelligence service and ran its own special forces units. Unlike the Federal Security Service and the Foreign Intelligence Service, which reported directly to the Russian President, the GRU was controlled by the Minister of Defence.

'The German intelligence agency also gave me a data dump of former Spetsnaz soldiers,' Emma continued. 'The willingness of these men to kill and their methods suggests that at least some of them might have a special forces background.'

Spetsnaz was a catch-all term for the special forces units across the former Soviet Union, though originally it was reserved for the GRU's special operations unit. Unlike the SAS, which only admitted the very best of the best, any thug with a Kalashnikov could end up in a Spetsnaz unit.

Bird studied the photograph on the screen. The face looking back at him was a hard bastard, no question of that. A thick brow, menacing hooded eyes, a snub nose that looked too small for the face, and thin, bloodless lips. He looked like a killer, but he wasn't one of the men that Bird had crossed paths with, so he clicked the mouse and studied the next photograph.

Emma looked at her watch. She had phoned her boss and requested a clean-up crew to visit the house in Churchdown, where they were to collect three dead bodies and hopefully one live one, but she had been told that it might take several hours. Apparently, it was a busy day for body disposal.

Bird had clicked on about a hundred more photographs without seeing anyone that he recognized when his mobile buzzed. He took it out of his pocket and studied the screen. It was from Warren: **We're in the Cheltenham Travelodge. On the A40. About a mile from you.**

Salubrious? wrote Bird.

Warren sent him a smiley face, followed by, **It's not bad. How's it going?**

I'll call you. Walls have ears.

Bird put his phone back into his pocket.

'Everything okay?' asked Emma.

'Sergeant Warren and his lads are close by,' said Bird. 'We'll have a better idea of where we stand when we get a location on the Nikolay phone.' He stood up. 'I just need the bathroom,' he said.

'Down the corridor, first left and it's on the right. It's unisex.'

'Good to know,' said Bird. He stood up and bent down so that he could see Tyson. 'Stay!' he said.

Tyson's ears pricked up but he kept his nose on his paws.

Bird left the room and walked along to the bathroom. It was indeed unisex and designed for single-person usage, so there was no danger of being overheard. He locked the door and sat down before video-calling Warren.

'Please don't tell me you're having a dump,' laughed the sergeant.

'I just wanted somewhere quiet,' said Bird.

'It's GCHQ, every room will be bugged,' said Warren. 'Every breath you take, every move you make.'

'I think even GCHQ would baulk at bugging a toilet,' said Bird. 'So, are you okay?'

'All good,' said Warren. 'I've got Tweedy, Shotgun and Tommo with me and the boss has echoed expenses. There are no minibars in the rooms but Tweedy has brought a very nice bottle of Scotch and Tommo has a case of beer. The boss gave us the okay to take any gear we want so we're all sorted.'

'Are you still okay to phone this Nikolay character and get the ball rolling?'

'If that's how you want to play it, sure. But let me run something by you. You know Nikolay's phone number and you're sitting there at GCHQ. Can't they run a track on the number?'

'They can, but then I'd be in their hands and I'm not sure I can trust them. I've told them that they can use your guys but I get the feeling they'd rather stick with the cops, even after what happened in Hereford. And even if we get a location, we don't know if Sarah is there or what state she's in. If you phone them, at least you can insist on proof of life. If we get a location, we'll have to go in guns blazing and these guys are pros. Shock and awe won't cut it, they'll fight to the last man.'

'Okay, it's your call, obviously. Let me brief the guys and then I'll start the ball rolling. Stay safe, mate. And try to get a bit of kip – you'll need it.'

Warren ended the call and Bird put his phone back in his pocket. He went back to the operations room via the canteen to pick up coffees and muffins, which were well received by Simon and Emma on his return.

He sat down at his table, reached out for the mouse again and clicked it. The face of a man in his fifties filled the screen. The head was shaved and there was a small scar across the man's chin. Bird frowned and scratched his own chin. It might have been one of the men at the Hilldrop Estate, but they had been wearing baseball caps so it was hard to be sure. Bird really wasn't great at remembering faces, but after a few seconds he decided that it wasn't the guy and he clicked the mouse.

The next three pictures were of men he was sure he hadn't seen, before the fourth made him sit up straight and almost gasp. It was the man who had shot Joel. He waved Emma over and pointed at the screen. 'He's the one who killed the civilian in Camden.'

'You're sure?'

Bird nodded. 'Yeah. I'm sure.' He pointed at the man's mutilated left ear. 'I recognize that,' he said. 'And the hairline. It's him. He's one of the guys I . . .' He left the sentence unfinished.

'Killed?'

'He was going to kill me, no question.'

'So you got your defence in first?'

'That's why I'm here. One second later and I'd be the dead one. He had a MAC-10, so he wasn't messing around.'

'And where is he now?'

'In one of the X5s.'

Emma pulled up a chair, sat down and tapped on the keyboard. After a few seconds a PDF appeared on screen. They both peered at it. 'Leonid Utkin,' said Emma. 'Served five years in a penal colony in southern Russia on drugs and assault charges. Killed two prisoners during his first year and was given two life sentences. Was released early to join Wagner Group in 2023. Served in Ukraine. Says here he had a K designation, whatever that means. No record of him having entered the UK.'

'He was cannon fodder,' said Bird. 'Wagner Group officers stayed well away from the zero line, which is what they call the front. They usually sit in bunkers and give their orders over the radio. The professional mercenaries – more often than not former Spetsnaz soldiers – are given an "A" designation and are usually held in reserve until the Ukrainians have been weakened. The guys like Utkin, who were recruited from prisons, get a "K" designation and are often used to draw fire. They're sent in waves, every twenty minutes or so, and most of them just get mowed down by machine-gun fire. But it uses up ammunition and gives the "A" guys time to identify the firing positions.'

Emma pulled a face. 'Why would they do that? They must know they'll be going to certain death.'

'Sometimes they give them amphetamines to get them hyped up, but they also know that if they take so much as one step back they'll be shot by their own officers. I'm not sure they all realize that when they sign up, but once they are on the front line, there's no going back.' He forced a smile. 'No pun intended.'

'I'm not sure you know what a pun is,' said Emma. She tapped on the keyboard again, then pushed her chair away and waved for him to continue. He clicked the mouse and sipped his coffee. He didn't recognize anyone in the next hundred or so photographs, but then his eyes widened when he saw the face of the man he'd tortured in the house in Churchdown. There was a name and date of birth along the bottom of the picture. Victor Zolotov. He was only five years older than Bird, which was a surprise because Bird had assumed he was in his fifties.

'I've got another,' said Bird, and he moved to the side so that she could get to the screen. 'He's another criminal.'

'How do you know?' asked Emma as she pulled the chair over to sit next to him.

'He's covered in tattoos.'

'How—?' began Emma but then she realized what he meant. 'He's the man you questioned?'

Bird nodded. 'Questioned, interrogated, tortured. All of the above. He has a large spider on his left shoulder, climbing down, which in the world of the Russian mafia is the mark of a thief, but the fact that it was crawling down meant that he had given up stealing.'

'How would you know that?'

'We did a course on it before we went to Mali a few years back. Wagner Group were causing havoc there and a lot of them were former prisoners. Get to know your enemy, they said. This guy had his whole life spelt out in tattoos. There's a tiger and a leopard on his stomach, both signs that he has a hatred of authority. There are several skulls near his shoulders which is another symbol of standing up to authority, and they were almost certainly done when he was behind bars. On his chest is an ornate Russian cathedral, with three domes. Each dome represents a prison sentence, so Zolotov has been in prison three times. To the left of the cathedral he has a young woman with long hair and a red rose against her cheek, which shows that he has been initiated into the Thieves in Law. You know about them?'

Emma shook her head.

'They're a loose Russian criminal fraternity similar to the mafia. They originally formed as a way of controlling the criminal underworld inside prison camps, but they're now active around the world. That tattoo is his calling card.'

Emma tapped on the keyboard to call up Zolotov's record and she read through it as Bird continued.

'On his left arm is another rose, covered in barbed wire on a dagger, and that's symbolic of a criminal who had been imprisoned before he was eighteen. So he's almost certainly not former military, but a Russian mafia thug.'

Emma nodded. 'Bang on,' she said. 'Three times in prison, twice for assault and finally for murder. Released early to join the Wagner Group.'

'He has an eight-pointed star tattooed on each knee, a sign that he was a high-ranking member of the Thieves in Law, basically signifying that he would get on his knees for no man. On his right thigh is a hooded executioner, which shows that he had killed a family member. He has a manacle tattooed around each ankle with a bell tattoo on each foot, which means that he had served prison sentences of more than five years, and the bells mean that they had been served in full.'

'That is amazing,' said Emma. 'Why would they do that?'

'It's their thing,' said Bird. 'And these guys are proud of what they do, they're not ashamed. That's why I had no qualms about setting Tyson on him. The tattoos told me what a nasty piece of work he was.'

Emma read through the file. 'Yeah, nasty piece of work is putting it mildly,' she said. 'He was in Ukraine for a while, and in Africa, but there are three outstanding murder warrants in Venezuela.'

'Venezuela?'

Emma nodded. 'It says here that he arrived in Caracas in January 2019 to provide security for President Nicolás Maduro. They flew into Cuba on chartered aircraft from Russia, then from there they flew on regular commercial flights, which is where they were picked up by the Americans, which is how come we have this intel. The Americans didn't interfere and at the time the story was that they were there to protect Russian business interests. But shortly afterwards three students who were vocal opponents of the regime were found buried in a forest, arms zip-tied behind them, shot through the back of the head. The cops found CCTV footage of Zolotov and other Wagner Group heavies throwing the students into the back of a van the week before the bodies were found, but by then all the Russians involved had left the country.'

'So he's got form for murder for hire?' said Bird. 'That's good to know.'

'It might give us some leverage over him,' said Emma.

'What, you mean get him to help you? These guys are hired killers.'

'It depends what he knows.'

'Emma, these people have been murdering civilians in cold blood. For no good reason. And he might well have killed your colleague in Sarah's house.'

Emma held up her hands. 'It was just a thought.'

'Yeah, well, it's a shit thought. No matter what information he has, Zolotov deserves to spend the rest of his life behind bars. They all do.'

'You're right. Of course, you're right.'

Bird looked into her eyes but found it impossible to tell if she was being truthful or not. That was to be expected, she was an MI6 officer and they lied for a living. A Secret Squirrel was not to be trusted. Ever. He picked up his coffee and sipped it. If he was to be sure of getting Sarah back safely, he was going to have to put his faith in Warren and the SAS team.

CHAPTER 29

Warren looked around the room. He had the undivided attention of the three men with him as he explained what Bird had asked him to do. Peter 'Tweedy' Harris had opened one of the windows and was standing next to it smoking a cigarette. It was a no-smoking room but Harris had a forty-a-day habit that had to be fed. Sitting on a chair by the desk was Al Gatrell and sprawled in the room's single armchair was Ryan 'Tommo' Thompson. There were no twin rooms in the hotel and none with connecting doors, so Warren had booked four rooms next to each other on the top floor, initially for one night but with the understanding that their stay might be extended.

They had carried kitbags into the hotel and left them in Tommo's room, with a 'Do Not Disturb' sign on the handle. Cheltenham was a low-crime city, but they didn't want to tempt fate by leaving their gear in the Range Rover. The SUV had the dubious honour of being the most stolen vehicle in the UK, with up to 2 per cent of some models being taken by thieves. 'So, I'll make the call and we'll see how it plays out,' said Warren. He tapped out Nikolay's number and sat down on the king-sized bed. He put the call on speakerphone. It was answered on the third ring by a burst of Russian followed by a pause.

'You'll need to speak English,' said Warren.

'Who the fuck is this?'

'You know who the fuck this is. Is that Nikolay?'

'Fuck you.'

'Yeah, well, fuck you too. We can trade insults all night long, or we can talk about exchanging the SD card I have for the hostage you have.'

'You have it? You have the card?'

'I do.'

'Where was it?'

'The man you killed slipped it into my coat pocket without me knowing.'

'Have you looked at it?'

'Of course I've looked at it. How else would I have found it?'

Nikolay said something in Russian, presumably cursing. 'I meant have you looked at the contents of the SD card.'

'I don't care what's on the bloody thing, I just want Sarah back.'

'Where are you?'

'Where are *you*?' snapped Warren.

'I am the one with the hostage. So I am the one in control here.'

'Yeah, and I'm the one with the SD card that you seem quite happy to kill for. I'm going to need proof of life. Let me talk to her.'

'That's not going to happen.'

'Then send me a picture. With a newspaper.'

'I don't have a newspaper. Where do you think I am, a fucking library?'

'Then send me a video. Have her say the date.'

'First, you send me a picture of the SD card. Then I will send you the video.' The line went dead.

Warren retrieved the SD card and took a picture of it, then sent it to Nikolay's number. He sat looking at the screen for the best part of five minutes, wondering if the Russian was just toying with him. Finally, his phone vibrated to let him know that he had received a message. It was a short video. He pressed the screen to start it. Sarah was dishevelled and tears were running down her cheeks. Her eyes were wide and staring and her voice was trembling as she spoke her name and the day's date. When she had finished, someone held up her left hand. It was smeared with blood and her little finger had been sliced off just above the lower knuckle. She stared at the screen and began to scream and then the video ended.

'That Russian is one nasty piece of work,' said Harris. He blew a plume of smoke through the open window.

'He'll get what's coming to him,' said Warren.

CHAPTER 30

The door opened and Emma brought in a tray with coffees, sandwiches and a bowl of water. Simon hurried over to help her. 'How's it going?' she asked as she put a mug of coffee down in front of Bird.

'Slowly,' he said. 'I've done more than three hundred, but as I said, I'm really not great with faces. And most of these file pictures are just head and shoulder shots. Most of these guys I saw at a distance. The ones I got close to are mainly . . .'

'Dead?' she finished for him.

Bird tried not to grin but failed miserably. 'They started it, miss,' he said.

This time it was Emma who couldn't stop herself from grinning. Before she could say anything her phone rang and she turned away from Bird to take the call. Bird suspected that she was wary of him reading her lips. The call went on for a couple of minutes, then she stood by the window staring at her phone screen. She flicked at her screen several times and he realized she was looking at something, photographs or videos, and it was clear from the way that her eyes hardened that she wasn't happy with what she saw.

Eventually, Emma put the phone away and walked over to Bird. He pushed his chair away from the table and looked up at her, knowing that it wasn't going to be good news.

'So, the clean-up team has been to the house in Churchdown, and removed four bodies,' she said.

Bird frowned. 'Four? You mean three bodies and Zolotov?'

'Zolotov is dead, Andy.'

'He was fine when I left him. Well, not fine, obviously. But he was very much alive.'

'Somebody slashed his throat. With a kitchen knife.'

Bird shook his head. 'That isn't possible.'

She took out her phone, tapped on the screen and held it out.

Zolotov's head was down and his chest was covered in blood. 'He wasn't like that when I left, I swear.'

Emma swiped on the screen and showed him another picture, this one of a bloody knife on the floor. Bird recognized it immediately – it was one of the knives he had taken from the kitchen. 'This appears to be the murder weapon,' she said. 'It's being tested for DNA and prints as we speak.'

'And they'll find my DNA and prints all over it, and the rest of the knives that I took through from the kitchen. But I didn't use any of them on him. I didn't have to. I had Tyson.'

Emma stared at him for several seconds, then she nodded. 'Okay, let's say that I believe you. If you didn't kill Zolotov, who did? And what would they have to gain by his death?'

Bird shook his head. He couldn't answer either question.

CHAPTER 31

Warren thought long and hard about where they should carry out the exchange. It had to be somewhere where there were people, or at least CCTV, so that the Russians would think twice about firing their weapons. Except, of course, they hadn't thought twice about shooting in public in London.

He decided that they might as well try to arrange it close to the hotel, as it was familiar territory and right next to the A40 in case they needed to beat a hasty retreat. He and Ryan Thompson did a walk-around and quickly found the perfect location, literally on the hotel's doorstep.

'What do you think?' Warren asked Thompson.

Thompson looked back at the hotel in the distance, the lights in the lobby shining brightly, but most of the rooms above now in darkness. He nodded. 'Yeah, this will work.'

'I'll call him now,' said Warren and took out his phone. The call wasn't answered and eventually it went through to voicemail. Warren spoke slowly and clearly. 'If you want your SD card back, answer the phone next time I call.'

He looked around. There were several CCTV cameras covering the area, but further away there was a section of the car park that looked devoid of cameras. 'I want to do the meet in daylight, but if we park over there, we won't be caught on film,' said Warren. 'But so long as they don't get too close, everything *they* do will be on record.'

'Do you think they'll give up Sarah?' asked Thompson.

'I hope so,' said Warren. 'But if they don't, we'll take her from them. We're not leaving here without her.'

His phone rang and he looked at the screen. It was Nikolay returning his call. Warren let it ring for several seconds before answering. He didn't give the Russian the chance to speak. 'Right, this is what's going to happen if you want the SD card. There's a KFC just off the A40, close to the Travelodge. There are half a dozen parking spaces there. You can pull up at one end, the end nearest the restaurant. We'll be at the other. You let Sarah walk towards us, one of us will bring you the SD card. Then if everyone is happy, we walk back to our cars.'

'If you try anything, the woman will die.'

'No one wants that, Nikolay. You want your card, we want Sarah. Then we can all get on with our lives.'

'I am serious. You try anything, anything at all, and the woman dies.'

'I think we all understand the rules, Nikolay. We'll see you there at six a.m., on the dot.' He ended the call and looked over at Thompson. 'That should do the trick, right?'

'Is Kentucky Fried Chicken a restaurant?' asked Thompson.

Warren frowned. 'What do you mean?'

'Well, is McDonald's a restaurant? Is Pizza Hut?'

'They serve food. That makes them restaurants.'

'Yeah, but they don't have waiters or waitresses, do they? And there's no service charge. And no knives and forks. No plates. So I don't think they're restaurants.'

'So what do you think they are?'

Thompson shrugged. 'I don't know, Sarge. That's why I was asking.'

'But whatever we call it, this'll work, won't it?'

Thompson turned back to look at the hotel. 'Yeah,' he said. 'It'll be fine.'

CHAPTER 32

Bird, Simon and Emma had taken turns grabbing some sleep on the sofa. The two spooks were clearly exhausted, and Bird's time in the Army had conditioned him to be able to get at least some shuteye even in times of high stress. He was just relieved his brief nap hadn't been interrupted by nightmares. His phone vibrated. It was a message from Warren. **Handover is on for 6 a.m. Come to the Travelodge now.**

He put his phone away and looked over at Emma, who was fast asleep on the sofa. Should he tell her, or not? The downside of telling her was that she might well interfere and then it could all go belly-up. But if he didn't tell her and it all went wrong anyway, then she might well withdraw her protection, at which point Bird would be well and truly screwed. She was already having second thoughts about him because of Zolotov's death, if he lied again there'd be nothing to stop her throwing him to the wolves. But Bird's priority was to rescue Sarah, and Sergeant Warren and his Counter-Revolutionary Warfare team were in the best position to do that. He stretched and yawned, and turned to Simon, who was studying one of his monitors through bleary eyes. 'Think I'll take a walk, stretch my legs and rest my eyes,' he said. 'You don't have another plastic bag for Tyson, do you?'

'I'm afraid not.'

Bird stood up. 'I'll see if I can get one from the canteen.'

'I'll come with you,' said Simon.

'Nah, it's okay,' said Bird. 'I need to use the bathroom as well.'

'Hopefully not into a carrier bag,' said Simon.

Bird laughed. 'That's okay, I'm house trained.' He bent down to look at Tyson, who was curled up underneath the table. 'Come on, Tyson. Walkies.'

Tyson's tail started to wag and he walked over to the door.

'I won't be long,' said Bird. 'Do you want anything from the canteen?'

'Water would be good,' said Simon. 'Maybe another sandwich. Cheese salad if they have it.'

Bird opened the door and headed out with Tyson at his heels. He started walking towards the canteen, but then took the corridor to the exit. Getting out of GCHQ was a lot easier than getting in – all he had to do was to press a button to open a turnstile. After a few steps a door opened automatically and he and Tyson were outside.

It was a half-mile walk to the Travelodge, and they were in reception in less than ten minutes. He sent Warren a text on the way and the sergeant was waiting for him when they arrived. 'How's life in the Doughnut?' Warren asked.

'Still looking at photographs,' said Bird. 'Sarge, the Wagner Group guy I interrogated in the Churchdown house is dead. Killed with a knife I touched, so my prints will be all over it.'

'That's not good.'

'It's shit,' said Bird. 'Emma believes me but there's no evidence that he was alive when I left the house, so if the cops ever get involved I'll be in big trouble.'

'And you being here isn't exactly going to build trust, is it?'

'I need to be here, Sarge. It's my fault Sarah got involved, the least I can do is get her back safely.'

Warren grimaced. 'Yeah, about that. There's something you need to know, Andy. The bastards cut off one of her fingers.'

'No way!'

'I'm sorry. I asked for a video of proof of life and that's what they sent me.'

'Show me.'

'That's not a good idea.'

'Show me!' said Bird, louder this time. Tyson flinched at the sound and Bird patted him. 'Sorry, boy,' he said. 'I didn't mean to startle you.'

'Okay, okay,' said Warren. He reached into his jacket pocket, took out his phone and played the video for him.

Bird watched in horror, shaking his head. 'I'm going to kill them, one by one,' he said.

'That's a given, Andy,' said Warren. 'But let's get her back first.' He looked at his watch. 'Right, let's go upstairs and get you kitted out.' He gestured at Tyson. 'Is he coming with us?'

'He's on my team,' said Bird.

'He should come upstairs for the briefing then,' said Warren.

They went up in the lift to Warren's room. Peter Harris, Al Gatrell and Ryan Thompson were there and they all greeted Bird. 'We're going to get Sarah back,' said Thompson. 'And we'll teach these Russian bastards a lesson.'

The rest of the team nodded in agreement.

CHAPTER 33

Bird and Warren decided to sit in the back of the Range Rover with Tyson on the floor between them. Harris was driving and Gatrell was in the front passenger seat. Bird and Warren had Glocks in underarm holsters. Harris had his gun in the door storage compartment and Gatrell's was in the glove compartment.

Warren looked over at Bird. 'You okay?'

Bird nodded. 'Sure.'

'We take this nice and slowly,' said Warren. 'They'll get what they deserve but our first priority is to get Sarah back.'

'I hear you, Sarge. I'm good.'

'Okay,' said Warren. 'Let's do this.' He patted Harris on the shoulder. Harris put the car in gear. He drove slowly out of the Travelodge car park and took them along the road that curved around the back of the KFC outlet. Two BMW X5s were parked in the two bays closest to them. One was black and one was grey. There were no other cars there this early in the morning.

There were two men in the black SUV and four men and a woman in the grey vehicle. Bird could see that it was Sarah, sitting in the back with a heavy either side.

They drove by the two BMWs and reversed into the bay at the far end.

Warren grinned. 'That should have caught them by surprise – they were probably expecting us to come in from the A40. If they have any reinforcements, that's where they'll be.'

Harris parked but left the engine running. Warren and Bird climbed out. Tyson stuck close to Bird, his ears up as he sniffed the air. 'You okay?' asked Warren.

'Sarge, I'm fine,' said Bird.

'And you're okay to let me take the lead?'

'Sure, Sarge. Go for it.'

They took a few steps away from the Range Rover, moving so that Harris and Gatrell wouldn't be in the line of any fire.

The two men in the black SUV climbed out. Bird recognized them immediately, as much by their clothing as anything – baseball caps, bomber jackets and jeans. They were two of the men who had been at the Hilldrop Estate. They moved to stand about twenty feet apart, either side of their car, hands free at their sides. Their jackets were open, they'd be able to pull out their guns in less than a second.

Tyson stood up, his hackles raised, knowing that the men weren't friendlies. Bird reached down and patted him on the neck.

The rear door of the grey SUV opened and a man in a long overcoat got out. 'That's the guy who shot Sasha in the alley,' said Bird.

'You sure?'

'Yeah, I recognize the broad jaw, the dimple in the chin and the close-set eyes. But the clincher is that plaster across his nose. I'm responsible for that.'

'Good one,' said Warren.

The man bent down and pulled Sarah from the car. She was wearing a blue denim shirt and white jeans that were spotted with blood. She was holding her left hand, which was wrapped in a bloodstained towel. She was unsteady on her feet and as she raised her head Bird realized she was blindfolded.

Another man got out of the other side of the car and walked around to Sarah. He moved behind her and removed the blindfold. Bird recognized him, too – it was the second man from the Camden alley, more than six feet tall, burly with a square jaw and slicked-back hair.

The drivers of the SUVs stayed where they were.

Sarah blinked as she looked around. She gasped when she spotted Bird. 'Andy, you've got to help me!' she shouted, but she was cut short by the man next to her slapping her on the back of the head and telling her to keep quiet.

The Russian with slicked-back hair walked towards Bird and Warren. His long overcoat was open. The two heavies in baseball caps moved to stand either side of him, but kept their distance.

'You have the card?' asked the Russian in heavily accented English.

'I do,' said Warren, reaching into his jacket pocket. The Russian's hand moved inside his coat, his jaw tightening, but Warren took out the small plastic case containing the SD card and held it up. 'Now you let Sarah join us and I'll give it to you.'

The Russian pointed at Bird. 'Why am I talking to you? He is the one who had the card.'

'My friend is deaf,' said Warren.

'Deaf?' repeated the Russian.

Warren jabbed a finger at his ear. 'Deaf. He can't hear.'

The Russian turned around and spoke to the man with the plastered nose, who was holding Sarah. He shrugged and replied in Russian.

'Do you want this or not?' asked Warren.

The guy with the slicked-back hair turned and held out a gloved hand. 'Give it to me.'

'Let the woman go first. We get her, you get this.' Warren held up the SD card.

The Russian reached into his pocket and Warren and Bird both went for their guns but then he held up his hand. 'I am not taking out a weapon,' he said. 'I need to check the card. You can relax.' His hand went back inside his coat and reappeared holding an iPhone. There was a card reader attached to the bottom of the phone. Bird stared at it. That wasn't good news at all. The reader would allow the Russian to see exactly what was on the card. Bird turned to look at Warren and it was clear from the look on the sergeant's face that he had come to the same conclusion. 'Give me the card,' said the Russian. 'If you try anything, the woman dies.'

'Hey, we don't want anyone to get hurt today,' said Warren. He held out the SD card and took a few steps forwards.

'Stop!' said the Russian with slicked-back hair. 'Place it on the ground and then go back to your friend. The deaf one.'

Warren did as he was told. He bent down slowly, placed the card on the ground, and went to stand next to Bird. The Russian looked over at them. 'Fold your arms,' he barked.

Bird and Warren did as they were told.

The Russian walked forwards cautiously, then bent down and tried to pick up the card. His glove made it difficult so he took it off, shoved it in his pocket, and picked up the card with his bare hand. He used his teeth to pry open the plastic case, which he then spat on the ground. He slid the card into the reader and tapped on the phone's screen.

'If this all turns to shit, you take him, and I'll go for the guy holding Sarah,' whispered Bird.

Warren said something back but his head was to the side and Bird missed it. He was about to ask Warren to repeat himself when the Russian looked up from the phone. He was snarling and clearly not happy. He transferred the phone to his left hand and pulled out his gun with his right. A Glock. He pointed it at Warren. 'Do you think we're stupid?' he said. 'Did you think we wouldn't check?'

Warren shrugged. 'We figured it was worth a try.'

'So the woman dies, that's what you want? You are idiots.'

Warren smiled and slowly unfolded his arms. He pointed his right hand at the guy with slicked-back hair, folding his third and little finger into his palm, forming a gun with his thumb as the hammer. 'Last chance,' he said quietly.

The Russian laughed. 'Are you serious?' he asked. 'You think this is a game?' He turned around to look at the guy with the plaster on his nose. The other man laughed, replied in Russian, then spat on the ground. He pulled a MAC-10 from inside his coat and aimed it at Sarah's chest. Sarah began to sob.

'Fine,' said Warren. 'Don't say I didn't warn you.'

He faked firing the imaginary gun as he pointed it at the Russian's face. 'Bang!' he said.

The Russian's oily head exploded and blood and brain matter splattered across the tarmac. The body slumped to the ground and the man with the MAC-10 stared at it in horror. 'How the fuck did you do that?' he said, his close-set eyes on the body.

Warren shrugged. He pointed his two fingers at the man. 'Bang!' he said again.

The man opened his mouth but before he could say anything a round smacked into his back and blew him apart. The legs gave way and the body crumpled to the ground.

'Sarah, run!' shouted Bird.

Sarah stumbled forwards and then began to run towards him, tears streaming down her face, her eyes wide with fear.

The two Russians in baseball caps were fumbling for their weapons.

CHAPTER 34

Thompson took a slow breath, released half of it, and sighted on the chest of the man with the baseball cap who had been standing on Sarah's left. Thompson was a big fan of the Gepárd GM6 Lynx semi-automatic rifle, and had been ever since he had been given the opportunity to use it. The Ministry of Defence had ordered 150 of the guns and distributed them among the SAS, SBS, and the Special Reconnaissance Regiment and they had been used to good effect across the Arab World. It had a range of just over a mile, but Thompson's targets were only a couple of hundred yards away in the KFC car park and clearly visible from the hotel bedroom window. He had watched the Russians get out of their SUVs and walk towards Warren's Range Rover. He had seen the Russian take the SD card from Warren and seen his reaction when he realized the card wasn't the one they wanted. Warren had given the signal to shoot and Thompson had had all the time in the world to put a round in the back of the man's head.

The Lynx weighed just twenty-three pounds and was less than four feet long, but it packed a punch that could bring down a helicopter or stop an armoured car in its tracks. The snipers that used it often referred to it as the Howitzer, partly because on firing, the barrel retracted like an artillery gun into the body of the rifle, to absorb the enormous recoil.

It was a semi-automatic so when one shot was fired, the next was immediately ready to go. The action meant an experienced sniper could empty the five-round magazine in less than three seconds. Thompson was in no rush, though. The Russians clearly had no idea what was going on.

Thompson had aimed at a second Russian, squeezed the trigger and sent a round into the back of his target, right between the shoulder blades. The round went straight through, blowing a fist-sized hole in the ribs and ricocheting off the ground. The man crumpled like a deflated balloon.

Sarah started to run, her arms flailing, and had covered about ten feet when Thompson squeezed the trigger on the man to her left.

Three shots fired, two left in the magazine. Thompson had two more filled magazines on the windowsill, ready to go. More than enough.

The man on Sarah's right had his gun out but it was pointing up in the air as he looked around to see where the rounds were coming from.

Warren had drawn his own weapon and was bringing it to bear on him. Thompson beat him to it, planting a round between the man's shoulder blades.

Sarah was just a few feet from Bird now.

The drivers of the two BMW X5s were climbing out of their vehicles. Warren turned towards them, his Glock at the ready. Thompson smiled to himself. There was no need to steal the Sarge's thunder, but just to be on the safe side he aimed at the chest of the driver of the black SUV.

CHAPTER 35

Bird stepped forwards and put his arms around Sarah. She collapsed against him, sobbing. 'It's okay, you're safe now,' he said, and hugged her.

Warren took a step towards the Russian SUVs as Harris and Gatrell climbed out of the Range Rover, guns drawn. Both Russian drivers had exited their vehicles and pulled handguns from their jackets. One fell without firing a shot, another victim of Thompson's sniping skills, and Warren double-tapped the second driver.

'Come on, we need to get out of here,' Bird said, guiding Sarah towards their Range Rover. Harris helped put her into the back seat and climbed back behind the wheel.

Bird looked at Harris. 'Any sirens?' he asked.

'I don't hear any.'

Bird looked around. They were far enough away from the KFC outlet that no one there would have seen what had happened, but any staff inside on an early shift would probably have heard the shots and if they did, they'd be calling 999.

Bird climbed into the back of the Range Rover and put his arm around Sarah. She was still sobbing. Warren jogged back to the car and squeezed in the back, a tight fit with three adults and a Malinois. Gatrell climbed into the front passenger seat and Harris put the car into gear. Within minutes they were on the A40, heading west to Hereford.

Cheltenham General Hospital had an A&E department but Sarah's mutilated finger wasn't life-threatening and the medics at Stirling Lines would be able to deal with it away from public scrutiny.

Warren took a pack of paracetamol from his jacket and passed it to Bird. 'Give her a couple of these, they'll take the edge off.' He opened the glove compartment, took out a bottle of water, and gave it to Bird.

Bird gave two tablets to Sarah and she popped them into her mouth. He handed her the bottle and she drank deeply. 'We'll take you to Hereford and you'll be looked after there.'

'What's happening, Andy? What did they want?'

'I'm not sure,' he said. 'I'm just so sorry that you got dragged into this.'

'They shot Alex. Is he okay?'

Bird didn't answer immediately and she realized from the look on his face what had happened. She burst into tears.

'I'm so sorry, Sarah,' he said.

'This is all your fault,' she said between sobs. 'I thought I was rid of you for good and now look what you've done.' She shuddered. 'They cut off my finger,' she sobbed.

'I'm sorry,' he said, but he knew that saying he was sorry didn't change anything. She was right. He had brought all of this on her, it was all down to him. And no matter what he said or what he did, that would never change.

Warren took his phone out of his pocket and put it to his ear. He spoke for several minutes, then put the phone away and twisted around in his seat. 'Emma's not happy, obviously,' he said. 'I told her she was going to need a clean-up crew behind KFC and she seemed to think we might have overreacted.'

'We rescued Sarah, that's all that matters.'

'No arguments here,' said Warren. 'But Emma seems to think that six bodies is a bit excessive.'

'We did what we had to do,' said Bird.

'I explained that. But she felt that we should have told her in advance that we'd be using a sniper.'

'Because obviously she would have given us the green light, wouldn't she?'

'She's just covering her arse,' said Warren. 'But she's not happy that we're heading back to Hereford.'

'We don't have a choice – if we take her to A&E they'll inform the police. Besides, we can protect her in Hereford.'

'Why do I need protection?' asked Sarah. 'Isn't it over?'

'We need to get the men behind this,' said Bird.

'Because they . . . might come after me again . . . is that what you're saying?' She said between sobs.

'I just want to make sure that you're safe,' said Bird.

'It's a bit late for that, isn't it?' She held up her bloody left hand. 'They chopped off my finger!' she shouted. 'They chopped off my sodding finger!'

Bird opened his mouth to reply but realized that there was nothing he could do that would make her any less angry or afraid, so he just shook his head. He nodded at Warren. 'Call Emma back and give her Nikolay's mobile phone number. She'll want to know how we got it – just tell her that it's the number we used to contact Nikolay about the handover. Keep it vague. Don't mention the phone I took from Churchdown. She can get the people at GCHQ to track the number, hopefully. Tell her that once they have a location, they should call you. These guys are more than a match for the cops, even the CTSFOs.'

Warren nodded. 'Will do.'

'Oh, and tell her that Nikolay isn't one of the dead guys. If she wants to know how I know, you can tell her that I recognized all of the six we killed – I'd seen them before in London. None of them are the boss, I'm sure of it. So he's still out there. And he'll still be wanting his SD card.'

'But I don't tell her about the SD card, right?'

'I'm keeping that card close to my chest,' said Bird. 'No pun intended.'

'You know, I think that one day you're going to be a Secret Squirrel yourself,' said Warren. 'You've got the moves.'

'It's never gonna happen,' said Bird.

Warren grinned. 'Never say never.'

CHAPTER 36

Emma's phone rang and she picked it up. It was Warren. As she took the call, Graeme Carmichael walked into the room. Carmichael sat down on the sofa and crossed his legs carefully. 'Sorry, I need to take this,' Emma said, and hurried out into the corridor.

She took the call. 'Now what?' she said. 'Are you calling to report more dead bodies?'

'Just passing on a message from Andy,' said Waller. 'We have a phone number for Nikolay and he suggests you get GCHQ to work their magic and come up with a location.'

'Let me speak to him.'

'He's a bit tied up at the moment. Not literally, but you know what I mean. He says he's sure that Nikolay isn't one of the dead guys so we need to find out where he is.'

Emma felt her grip tighten on her phone and she forced herself to relax. 'Sergeant Warren, tell Andy I'm going to need to talk to him about this at some point,' she said. 'This is not how things are done.'

'I absolutely hear you and understand you,' said Warren. 'But trust me, these are exceptional times. I'll text you the phone number.'

Emma opened her mouth to reply but the line was already dead. 'Arrogant bastard,' she hissed as she put her phone back in her pocket.

She went back into the office where Carmichael was still on the sofa. 'Is there something wrong?' he asked.

'These SAS guys, there's too much testosterone buzzing around them. That might be necessary when they're in combat, but in the real world it's a pain in the arse.' Her phone buzzed and she looked at the screen. It was the text message from Warren.

'If this is about the six bodies they left in the street just a few hundred yards from here, I feel your pain.'

'We got lucky on that,' said Emma. 'No civilians actually saw what happened, we're in the process of pulling what little CCTV there was in the area, and the police have been squared away. No, the problem is that Andy Bird has only just given me a phone number for Nikolay, the leader of this Wagner team. He must have had it for a while, but he clearly waited until he got his wife out of danger before he handed it over.'

'Ex-wife,' said Carmichael.

'Exactly. Ex-wife. If he'd given us this number earlier, we could probably have the whole team under wraps by now. It's the mobile number that Nikolay is using – almost certainly a burner, but it's the number that the SAS used to arrange the handover.'

'Let me have the number and I'll expedite tracking now,' said Carmichael.

Emma read out the number and Carmichael scribbled it into a notebook. 'Did he tell you what happened there?'

'Just that they were picking up Sarah and then the Russians started shooting. But according to our guys on the scene, none of the Russians actually fired their weapons and most of them were shot in the back.'

'What?'

'They had a sniper, in the Travelodge. Now, there's no doubt that the Russians had guns, and they've proved that they're more than happy to use them, but even so, the SAS seemed to have been playing fast and loose with the rules of engagement.'

'I hope this doesn't turn into another Gibraltar,' said Carmichael. 'So, once we have a location, what then? We send in armed police? CTSO19?'

'They want to handle it themselves. They're taking Sarah back to Hereford so they'll only be an hour away. What alternative do we have? Gloucestershire Police? I mean, they have armed units but I'm not sure they'd be capable of taking on these Russians. That leaves us with the Met, and they're two and a half hours away. So the SAS are closer.'

Carmichael nodded and tapped his notepad. 'Let's get a location for the phone first, then we can decide who to call in.'

CHAPTER 37

Bird had offered to put Sarah up in a hotel, but she had insisted on going home. Bird was partly relieved because he didn't have the money to pay a hotel bill. He had phoned Emma while Sarah was being treated in the SAS's medical centre. A doctor there had done what he could to repair the damage to her hand and given her antibiotics and a strong painkiller, but his options were limited because the Russians had thrown away the finger once they had snipped it off with pruning shears. Emma had confirmed that a cleaning crew had removed all evidence of the killings, including the bodies. Even so, Bird's heart was in his mouth when she unlocked the front door and stepped into the hallway.

'Let me go first,' said Warren. He had driven them to the house, along with Harris. Three other SAS troopers had followed in a Honda CR-V from the regimental carpool, which was parked outside.

'No,' said Sarah firmly. 'This is my house, I'm not living in fear.' She walked down the hallway and into the living room. She folded her arms and stood staring at the sofa. Warren and Bird came up behind her. The sofa was where her boyfriend died, but there was no sign of that now, no bloodstains, no bullet damage, nothing to indicate that a man had lost his life there.

Bird put his hand on her shoulder and was about to say sorry, but she flinched and stepped away from him. He raised his hands and tried to smile apologetically but it came out like a snarl and he realized he was only making things worse. Warren realized what was happening and guided Bird to the side. 'Are you sure you want to stay here, Sarah?' he asked.

She nodded without looking at him.

'We can find a place for you in the barracks, if you'd rather.'

'This is my home,' she said. She turned to look at him. 'Why, do you think I'm not safe here?'

'You're safe, I promise. There are three of my best guys outside and they're not going anywhere.'

'You can't protect me for ever.'

'We'll have them soon, Sarah, don't worry,' said Warren. 'Wheels are in motion.' He smiled. 'Don't suppose you could rustle up tea for the guys, could you?' he asked.

'Sure. Of course.' She took a last long look at the sofa and then headed off to the kitchen.

'That's a bit harsh, considering she can only use the one hand,' said Bird.

'She needs to stay busy or she's going to brood,' said Warren.

'Do you think she'll be okay here, Sarge?'

'They won't get near her even if they try,' said Warren. 'But why would they try? It didn't work out so well for them last time – they'd be crazy to even think about trying it again.'

'So you think they'll just give up? Walk away?'

'I think they've invested too much to walk away at this point,' said Warren. 'How many men have they lost? Twelve? Thirteen? I've lost count. But if they were the walking away kind, they would have walked away already. Whatever is on that SD card means a lot to them.'

'To them, or to whoever is paying their wages,' said Bird.

'True. But no matter why or who, I don't see them giving up. But it'll be you they'll be after, which is why we need to stay on the offensive. Keep them on the back foot.' Warren's phone rang and he walked away to answer. He spent a couple of minutes talking and then put the phone away. 'They've got a location on Nikolay's phone,' he said.

'That was quick,' said Bird.

'Looks like Carmichael expedited it as he promised,' said Warren. 'Emma is going to send me the address. It's a farm outside Cheltenham. We'll get kitted out and head out ASAP.'

'Who can we take?'

'Tommo and Tweedy are on standby, but Shotgun is heading Syria way. I'll ask the colonel who else we can take from CRW Wing. We can call en route.'

They went through to the kitchen where Sarah was standing by the kettle. 'We've got to go, we've got a lead on the bad guys,' Warren told her. 'The three men outside will be looking after you, and like I said, they're my best guys. But you have my number and Andy's, if you have any worries, any worries at all, you call me. And if at any point you want to stay at Stirling Lines, that offer is still open.'

Sarah forced a smile. 'Thanks, Ben. I appreciate everything you've done.' She looked over at Bird, who had remained in the doorway. 'I'm sorry I snapped at you before, Andy.'

'That's okay.'

'I'm in a bit of a state, but that's no excuse for what I said.'

'We're good,' said Bird. He had to fight the urge to walk over and give her a hug, sensing it was the last thing she wanted, so he just raised his hand in acknowledgment of her apology.

'Right, I'll let the three guys outside introduce themselves, me and Andy and Tweedy need to get our skates on,' said Warren.

Bird followed Warren down the hall to the front door, where Harris was waiting. Warren tossed him the car keys. 'You'll need to drive, Tweedy, I've got some calls to make.'

Bird called Tyson and the dog hurried out of the living room, tail wagging. They left the house but left the front door open. Harris stood at the garden gate, eyes scanning the surrounding area, and Bird and Tyson stayed by the porch until Harris gave them the all-clear. Warren went over to the CR-V and spoke to the three troopers as Bird and Tyson got into the back of the Range Rover.

Harris got into the driver's seat. Warren finished briefing the troopers and two of them went into the house to be with Sarah. Warren was already on his phone as he climbed into the front passenger seat and he was still talking when they arrived at Stirling Lines. Archie was on the early gatehouse shift again, but he still made them all show ID before admitting them.

Warren finished his calls and twisted around in his seat so that Bird could see his face. 'Right, we're all good to go. Colonel Brewerton has given us the green light and assigned three more guys from CRW Wing in addition to Tommo and Tweedy. We can take whatever we want from the armoury. I'll send you a text with a link to the location, you can check it out on Google Maps. It's a farm that's been put up for auction. The guy that was running it died a few months ago and it's been stuck in probate, so it's supposed to be empty.'

Bird tapped the location into Google Maps as they drove slowly through the garrison. It was called Willow Farm and was about ten miles north of Churchdown. The satellite map showed a small farmhouse, two large barns and a silo, and a line of brick buildings with a paved yard in front of them. The nearest neighbour was another farm, about half a mile away. The farm couldn't be seen from the nearest main road and Google didn't provide a walk through for the narrow track that led from the road to the farm. It appeared to be the only way that a vehicle could approach, which wasn't good news.

They arrived at the armoury and piled out of the Range Rover. Ryan Thompson was standing by a grey Land Rover Defender. The rear door was open and two troopers wearing desert camouflage fatigues were loading kitbags into the back.

Thompson waved over at Warren. 'I've got HKs, a selection of Glocks and my Lynx rifle. I've snaffled some comms in case we need it, flashbangs and some grenades. Full body armour and helmets.'

'Sounds good, Tommo,' said Warren. 'Did you get us a drone?'

'I got us two, just to be on the safe side. And Dusty has just been on a drone course, so he's keen to show us what he can do.'

The two troopers finished loading the gear into the Defender and slammed the door shut. Tyson flinched at the sound then began to bark at the two men. 'Friendly,' said Bird, but Tyson continued to bark.

Both troopers were clearly used to dealing with dogs – they stood their ground and raised their hands to show that they weren't a threat.

'Tyson, friendly!' Bird shouted and this time the dog stopped barking. 'Sit!' said Bird firmly and Tyson obeyed, albeit reluctantly.

Both men lowered their hands. 'These guys joined after you left,' said Warren by way of introduction. 'Jimmy Rhodes and Ross Black, AKA Dusty and Cilla.'

Bird nodded at the two troopers. Black was the taller of the two, his tanned skin and unkempt beard signs that he had recently returned from somewhere hot, sunny and life-threatening. Rhodes had curly black hair and a decent-sized moustache. He began signing with his hands but Bird cut him off. 'I can't sign, mate, sorry.'

Rhodes frowned. 'The Sarge said you were deaf?'

'Yeah, I am, but I never learnt to sign. I read lips. How come you can sign?'

'My mum's deaf,' said Rhodes. 'And she was always crap at lip-reading so it was easier to sign.'

'We'll get Dusty close enough to do an overhead recce with the drone before we decide what to do,' said Warren. 'It's a good job that Queenie isn't with us because he'd be wanting us to parachute in.'

'It looks like there's only one track in, so we'll probably need to go on foot across the fields,' said Bird.

'Let's see what the drone shows us,' said Warren.

A third trooper walked out of the armoury carrying two large kitbags. 'Body armour and helmets,' he said.

Warren gestured at his Range Rover. 'Put them in the back of mine,' he said. 'Andy, this is Rick Parker. We call him Nosey.' Parker's nose was of normal size, but he did have large eyebrows that almost met over it, and hair that was so black and glistening that it looked as if it had been dyed.

'Pleasure,' said Parker, nodding at Bird.

Bird nodded back. Parker loaded the bags into the back of the Range Rover. 'Right, Birdman. Tommo and Tweedy with me, you guys take the Defender. We'll RV about half a mile from the farm; there's a business park we can use. I'll lead the way. Should take us just over an hour. Any questions?' He was faced with shaking heads. 'Right, let's do it.'

CHAPTER 38

The SAS team reached the business park in a little more than an hour, but as they approached the entrance Warren's phone buzzed. He answered it, and after a short conversation he twisted around in his seat. 'Change of plan,' he said. 'Dusty has just pointed out that the business park is adjacent to Gloucestershire Airport, and if we launch the drone anywhere near it we'll have the police all over us. So, Dusty is going to find us an alternate. We'll follow his lead.' Harris slowed and after a few seconds the Defender overtook them.

They followed the Defender for the best part of ten minutes, then it indicated left and turned off the main road and onto a track that ran between two fields filled with lines of potato plants. Once the road was out of sight behind them, the Defender came to a halt and Harris pulled up behind it.

They all climbed out and looked around. They could hear the faint buzz of traffic from the road, but there was no one around and no buildings within sight. Rhodes opened the rear of the Defender and unzipped one of the kitbags. He took out a large drone, almost two feet across, and placed it on the roof of the vehicle, then opened a black case to take out a controller the size of a paperback book. He slotted his mobile phone into the controller, tapped on the screen to call up an App, then flicked a switch on the side of the drone. He stood away from the Defender and placed his thumbs on two joysticks. 'Chocks away,' he said, and the propellors began to whirr.

The drone moved smoothly up into the air. Rhodes took it up two hundred feet and checked the video feed on his phone.

Bird looked over Rhodes' shoulder. He could see both cars and then he saw himself. It was a surreal experience, seeing himself from above. He looked up. 'Say cheese,' said Rhodes, and he pressed a button to take a picture. The quality was excellent – it was possible to make out facial features even from that height. 'And off we go,' said Rhodes, pressing one of the joysticks. The drone headed west. They watched the screen as the drone passed over fields and hedges.

'There's the farm,' said Rhodes. 'I'll take her up another hundred feet.' His thumbs worked the joysticks and the drone rose. The farm was at the far right of the screen but Rhodes adjusted the camera and centred it on the buildings.

Warren was standing on the other side of Rhodes, peering at the screen. 'I don't see any vehicles,' he said. The car-parking area in front of the brick buildings was empty and there were no vehicles outside the farmhouse. 'Can you look into the barns.'

'I'll have to go lower,' said Rhodes. 'Let me do a flyover first.' He took the drone over the buildings and then did a slow circuit. All the men peered at the screen. There were no vehicles or farm equipment to be seen. And no lookouts, which they would have expected to see if the Wagner Group were in residence.

'Place looks deserted,' said Warren.

'Maybe they pulled out after we rescued Sarah,' said Bird.

Warren patted Rhodes on the shoulder. 'Let's make sure,' he said.

Rhodes nodded and took the drone lower. Bird felt a sudden wave of nausea as the ground seemed to jump up at him and he looked away, blinking. Tyson looked up, sensing his discomfort. He wagged his tail and pushed his head against Bird's knee. Bird bent down and patted Tyson's neck. He looked back at the screen. Rhodes had taken the drone down to just a few feet above the paved area and flew it in front of the brick buildings. 'I don't see anybody, Sarge. No people and no vehicles.'

'We need to be sure,' said Warren. 'We'll drive up, but Tommo can provide us covering fire in case it's a trap.'

Thompson nodded. 'Works for me.'

Rhodes packed his drone away and they climbed back into their vehicles. They reversed back along the track until they reached a point where they could turn around, then Harris led the way in the Range Rover. They reached the main road and drove towards the farm.

There was no signpost to indicate the name of the road they were looking for, but Harris was using the car's GPS and it gave him plenty of warning to make the turn. There was an estate agent's sign with details of the forthcoming auction of Willow Farm planted next to the hedge.

As the farm came into view, Harris pulled over. The Defender drew up behind him and Thompson climbed out. He opened the rear of the Defender and took out a green metal gun case. He gave the Range Rover a wave then climbed over a fence and began walking quickly across the grass.

They waited by the side of the track until Warren received a text from Thompson. **Good to go.** He showed the screen to Harris. Harris nodded and drove forwards. The Defender followed.

The track was rutted with car tracks. It was clear that it had been well used, but there was no way of knowing how fresh the tracks were. They reached a five-bar gate, which was open, though there was a heavy chain and a large padlock hanging from it. The chain appeared to have been severed.

Harris accelerated and headed towards the farm. The Defender held back. The farm was almost certainly deserted but it was standard procedure to leave plenty of space between vehicles when there was any risk of attack.

Bird peered out of the side window as they approached the farm buildings. There was still no sign of life. 'Sarge, why not send me and Tyson ahead first? Just to be on the safe side.'

Warren twisted around in his seat. 'You sure?'

'Better safe than sorry.'

Warren nodded and gestured for Harris to stop. Bird and Tyson climbed out. Warren wound down his window. 'First sign of trouble, run like the wind,' he said.

'I'll be fine,' said Bird.

'I was talking to the land shark,' said Warren. He pulled a Glock 30SF from his underarm holster and passed it to Bird. He grinned. 'Break a leg.'

Bird laughed and took the gun, then started jogging along the track to the farm. Tyson stuck to Bird's side, ears back and tail straight out behind him. Bird kept his gun close to his thigh, his finger off the trigger. His eyes scanned the area, looking for any sign of movement. As he got closer he began to zig-zag. If there was a sniper in the farmhouse, he might as well try to make it difficult for him. Tyson followed his movements. It was something they had practised for hours at Stirling Lines.

As they got closer to the main building, he saw that all the windows were closed, which meant a sniper was extremely unlikely. He slowed and Tyson immediately matched his pace. Bird looked over at the nearest barn. There were two large metal doors, which were fully open, and he could see that the barn was empty. He walked over to the line of brick buildings. There were metal shutters over the windows and all the doors were closed.

He signalled to the Range Rover, and Warren and Harris quickly joined him. 'They've gone,' said the sergeant.

'Because they know we don't have the SD card?' said Bird. 'Or because they knew we were coming?'

'We took down six of them, Birdman. If they've any sense they'll run off back to Russia.'

'One thing about the Wagner Group, Sarge, they never retreat.'

'We should give the house a going over, just to be on the safe side,' said Warren. He headed towards the front door. 'Wait!' said Bird. 'Let Tyson do his thing first.'

'They've gone, Birdman. If they were ever here in the first place.'

'Yeah, but they might have left something behind.'

Warren nodded thoughtfully. 'Okay, go ahead.'

Bird patted the side of his leg. 'Heel,' he said. Tyson hurried over and sat down next to him, pressing against his leg, his head up and his tongue protruding from the side of his mouth. 'Good boy,' said Bird. He pointed at the front door. 'Check,' he said.

Tyson rushed over to the front door, stopped a few feet from it, then approached it cautiously, tail wagging and ears up. He began sniffing, initially concentrating on the doorstep but then moving up to the door jambs. Then he stopped suddenly and backed away. He lay down with his head on his paws, growling softly.

'That's a hit,' said Bird. 'He smells something.'

'What, an IED?' asked Warren.

'Some sort of explosive, but his nose is also sensitive enough to smell the smoke from a fired gun. Whatever he smells, we'd be better off finding another way in.'

'Let's try the back,' said Warren. He led the way around the building to the kitchen door. He and Bird peered in through the window. There was a large Aga stove and a pine table piled high with pizza boxes and fast-food containers.

Bird called Tyson to heel, then pointed at the kitchen door. 'Check,' he said. Again, Tyson hurried over and sniffed the floor and the door, but this time he sat down, his tail twitching from side to side.

'That's the all-clear,' explained Bird.

Harris tried the handle but the door was locked. Two hard kicks splintered the wood and a third had it crashing open. Bird had his Glock at the ready and he stepped into the kitchen with Tyson sticking to his heels.

The three troopers from the Defender had all joined them, and they followed Bird inside. Harris pulled his gun from its holster and he and Warren followed the team inside.

Bird moved slowly down the hall to the front door. 'Heel,' he said, and Tyson tucked in close. He saw the booby trap immediately. A thin wire, possibly fishing line, stretched across the door. One end was pinned to the door jamb, the other was connected to a cardboard box standing on a chair to the right of the door.

'Stay,' said Bird and Tyson immediately sat. 'Stay back, guys,' Bird said. He looked over his shoulder to check that they had heard him.

'Birdman, don't even think about being a hero,' said Warren. 'You're not even on the payroll.' He walked up to Bird and stood next to him.

'It's nothing complicated, Sarge.'

'Yeah, maybe not, but you've already used up your nine lives.'

'That's cats, Sarge.'

'Stand down, Andy, this is my pay grade.'

Bird nodded reluctantly and went back to stand with Tyson. 'You really all should leave the hall, just in case,' said Warren, as he approached the cardboard box. Nobody moved. 'Good to see that I still carry authority,' said Warren. He peered into the box for several seconds, then reached inside with both hands. 'Looks like C4,' he said. 'Commercial detonator and a Duracell battery, pulling the wire closes the circuit and Bob's your uncle. Anyone got a pair of scissors?'

Ross Black stepped forwards, taking a Swiss Army knife from his pocket. He pulled out a small pair of scissors. 'Any good, Sarge?'

'Perfect,' said Warren. He took them and went over to study the line stretched across the door. 'Looks simple enough, all I have to do is cut the line.'

'Sarge, you're sure about this?' asked Rhodes.

'Demolitions isn't my speciality,' said Warren. 'But I don't see anything untoward. It's a simple enough circuit. And the line isn't under any pressure, is it? If it was, then cutting it might be a problem. But as it is, I think it's a simple matter of cutting the line.' He grinned. 'Now you've got me worried.'

'I'm sure it'll be fine,' said Rhodes.

Warren reached out with the scissors and snipped the line. Bird realized that he was holding his breath and he sighed with relief when the line parted and nothing happened. 'Nice one, Sarge,' he said.

'The bomb is still live,' said Sarge. 'We'll need to get an EOD team out.'

'Sarge, I'm demolitions trained,' said Black. 'I can make it safe.'

Warren handed him back the Swiss Army knife. 'You didn't say anything earlier, Cilla. Slipped your mind, did it?'

Black grinned. 'You seemed to be having fun with it.' He went over to the box and looked inside. 'Yeah, this won't take long.'

'Okay, the place is obviously deserted but give it the once-over,' Warren said to the team. 'See if we can work out when they bailed, and keep an eye out for more booby traps.'

Harris, Rhodes and Parker headed upstairs. Bird and Warren went back to the kitchen. Tyson ran ahead of them, tail twitching. He began sniffing at something next to the table by the window. Bird bent down and picked it up. It was a Samsung Galaxy phone that had clearly been stamped on several times.

'Please tell me that they left the SIM card in,' said Warren.

Bird shook his head. 'No, and they took the battery out.'

'So they knew the phone was being tracked.'

'I'd say so.'

Tyson was still excited by something under the table so Bird knelt down to get a better look. There were another three busted phones there.

Warren opened the fridge. There was milk, cheese and packs of sliced meat inside. He checked the labels. 'All well within their use-by dates,' he said. There was a rubbish bin by the door and Bird lifted the lid and looked inside. He found half a sliced loaf, which still seemed fresh. Underneath the loaf was a plastic supermarket carrier bag. He pulled it out and opened it. Inside he found a receipt. He held it up to show Warren. 'It's from early this morning,' he said.

There were several dirty mugs in the sink. Bird went over to touch the kettle with the back of his hand. It wasn't hot to the touch but it wasn't cold. 'I don't think they've been gone long,' he said.

Harris, Rhodes and Parker came down the stairs. 'They've cleared out,' said Harris.

'Okay, let's call it a day,' said Warren. 'Dusty, can you and Nosey take the Defender and pick up Tommo? Take Cilla with you, and assuming the IED has been made safe you can take it back to Stirling Lines to dispose of. Tweedy, are you okay to go with them?'

'Sure thing, Sarge, what about you?'

Warren looked over at Bird. 'I think we need to have a chat with the puzzle masters,' he said.

CHAPTER 39

Warren drove Bird to GCHQ. Tyson sat on the back seat, panting all the way. They had to wait in reception for fifteen minutes before Emma collected them.

'We can get coffees, but we need to talk where there's a computer. There's something I need to show you.'

'That sounds ominous,' said Bird.

Emma flashed him a cold smile but didn't say anything. She took them along to the canteen and bought three coffees.

'Any chance of a few sandwiches?' asked Warren. 'I'm a bit peckish. Missed the buffet breakfast at the Travelodge – early checkout.'

Emma sighed and bought three plastic-wrapped sandwiches.

'And maybe a banana?' said Warren. 'One of my five a day.'

Emma paid for the food and they headed down a grey corridor to an office with two workstations and a small sofa. She waved them to the sofa and leant against one of the desks. Bird and Warren sat together, Tyson curled up nose to tail at Bird's feet.

'I'm assuming you don't have good news for me,' Emma said, sipping her coffee.

'The phone was there but the Russians had gone,' said Warren. 'And not long gone by the look of it.' He ripped the plastic from a ham and cheese sandwich and bit into it.

'They were tipped off,' said Bird. 'Had to have been.'

'Why do you say that?' said Emma. She took another sip of coffee.

'Look at the timing,' said Bird. 'The morning that we start tracing the phone is the morning that they pack up and leave. That can't be a coincidence. And they knew to take the batteries out of the phones and to smash them.'

'In our business, coincidences happen all the time,' said Emma. 'You can't make a case based on coincidences, Andy, you need evidence to back it up,' she said.

'They left the front door booby-trapped, with an IED,' said Bird. 'So they knew we were on to them.'

'After you killed six of their team they might well have decided to call it a day,' said Emma. She flashed him another cold smile. 'Except they haven't got what they want, have they, Andy?'

Bird frowned. 'What do you mean?'

Emma stared at him with unblinking eyes for several seconds, then turned around and tapped on a keyboard. Bird and Warren stood up and moved either side of her to look at the monitor on the desk. A CCTV video was playing and it took Bird a couple of seconds to realize that it was footage taken from outside the KFC car park. He glanced at Warren, whose jaw was clenched in frustration – the sergeant must have missed a camera when he did his recce last night. The Range Rover was at the edge of the screen. Bird and Warren were in the middle with the Russian who had examined the SD card. At the far right of the screen was Sarah with the Russian heavy at her side. They were flanked by the two heavies wearing baseball caps. Emma let the video play for almost half a minute, then she tapped on a key to freeze the picture. The resolution wasn't good enough to see what the Russian was doing but Bird knew exactly what he was looking at.

'So, what did you give him, Sergeant Warren?' asked Emma.

Warren sighed and looked over at Bird. Bird nodded. There was no point in lying, not now they had Sarah safe and sound.

'It was an SD card,' said Warren.

'And what exactly was on this SD card?'

'A couple of videos.'

'What sort of videos?' asked Emma.

'Training videos, mainly.'

Emma tilted her head on one side. 'And why were you giving training videos to Wagner Group assassins?'

Warren shrugged but didn't answer.

'And judging from their reaction, training videos wasn't what they expected, am I right?' pressed Emma.

Again, Warren didn't reply, so Emma looked at Bird. 'Perhaps you'd care to enlighten me, Andy.'

'We needed to get my ex-wife back, and they would only exchange her for an SD card that they thought Sasha Brownlow gave me before he died.'

'But Sasha didn't give you an SD card?'

'Definitely not, no. So we gave them any old SD card, and when it kicked off we did what we had to do.' He shrugged. 'We got our defence in first.' Bird shrugged again. 'Anyway, we got Sarah back, so all's well that ends well.'

'If by "ends well" you mean six dead bodies less than a mile from here, then I think we have a different definition of what "ends well" means. And it hasn't actually ended, has it? They want the SD card and they still haven't got it. So presumably they will keep trying to retrieve it.' Emma sighed in frustration. 'So, what could be on the real SD card that the Russians would want so badly?'

'Presumably Sasha came across something during the course of his work that he felt he should share with MI5—' began Bird.

'We have no idea why Sasha wanted a meet with MI5,' interjected Emma. 'We just suspect it's why he was killed.'

Bird grimaced. 'But I think whatever he wanted to share was on an SD card,' he said.

Emma frowned. 'What aren't you telling me, Andy?'

'Okay, I'll tell you. Just don't get upset.'

Emma gritted her teeth. 'I'll do my best. Just tell me what the hell you've done.'

'It's no biggie, Emma, really. The Russian I interrogated told me about the SD card. But I know that Sasha didn't give it to me so—'

'So you kept that information to yourself? You've known about it all this time?'

'If I'd told you, you'd have told Simon and he'd have told Carmichael. And frankly, I'm not sure who I can trust at the moment.'

'Are you saying you don't trust me?'

'You're a Secret Squirrel,' said Warren as he peeled his banana. 'Truth is never a constant with you people.'

Emma glared at him. 'When I want your opinion, Sergeant Warren, I'll be sure to ask for it, but until then I'd rather you kept your observations to yourself.'

Warren shrugged and chewed on his banana.

'You should have told me, Andy.'

Bird shook his head. 'They had kidnapped Sarah. She was all I cared about just then. If you had known about the SD card you'd hardly have allowed me to hand it over, would you?'

'You didn't have the card, so it's irrelevant. But what isn't irrelevant is that you went behind my back.'

'And I apologize for that. But needs must. As far as what is actually on the SD card they want, have you checked Sasha's computers? That's what you guys are good at, right?'

Emma ignored the jibe. 'MI5 sent people into his flat not long after his body was identified. His computers had gone. Along with the contents of his desk and any notebooks that he might have had. But for all we know, it was Sasha himself who removed his computers. Maybe he was leaving.'

'Leaving?'

'Leaving the country or GCHQ, I don't know. I do know that there were no signs of a break-in.'

'What about CCTV video of Sasha leaving with his computers?' asked Bird.

'What are you getting at?' said Emma.

'Well, if the computers were there and now they're not, there must be video of them leaving the apartment. With the Russians or with Sasha. Either way, there should be video of them being removed – there's CCTV all over Camden, private and publicly owned.'

'Well, there isn't any footage,' said Emma testily. 'Or at least I was told there wasn't.'

'But there should be,' said Bird. 'And if there isn't, well that raises questions, doesn't it?'

'This isn't about Sasha Brownlow's computers, though, is it?' said Emma. 'If the Russians had his computers then they wouldn't need to kill him, would they? And from what you've said, it's this SD card that they want, not the computers.'

'Maybe the SD card is in his flat somewhere. Did you search for it?'

'Why would they search for a bloody SD card?' snapped Emma. 'I've only just been told about it. But the flat would have been comprehensively searched, by professionals.'

'Yes, but they weren't looking for an SD card, were they? I'd like to have a look myself.'

'You'd be wasting your time,' said Emma. 'They were professionals.'

'They might have been professionals, but they didn't have Tyson.' Tyson growled when he heard his name and Bird patted him on the neck. 'And nobody at MI5 mentioned that Sasha might be handing over an SD card?'

Emma shook her head. 'No.'

'Is it possible they knew about it but decided not to tell you?'

Emma wrinkled her nose. 'I suppose so.'

'What did they tell you?'

'That Sasha Brownlow had arranged a meeting with an MI5 officer and that he was killed before he could attend the meeting.'

'And who told you this?'

'My boss at MI6. Why?'

'Okay, after your boss had told you that Sasha had been murdered, did you then talk to someone at MI5?'

'Yes. I was briefed by the officer who Justin worked for. As I told you before, Justin was due to meet Sasha face-to-face, away from Thames House, but he never turned up.'

'And you were brought in because you were a friendly face, that's what you said.'

'That's what I was told. You and I had a history, albeit a brief one, and it was decided that I should be the one to go to Stirling Lines with Simon from GCHQ. By then we knew that you had seen Sasha killed, and that the people responsible were after you.'

'So all you know is what your boss and the MI5 officer told you?'

'That's about right, yes. Is that a problem?'

'And the MI5 officer didn't mention an SD card?'

'No. Andy, where are you going with this?'

Bird sighed. 'I'm not sure. There's just something not right about this. You didn't know about the SD card, but the Russians did. They went to the trouble of kidnapping my wife – my ex-wife – to force me to hand it over. How can that be?'

'I don't know.'

'Well, I think we need to know, Emma. The SD card is clearly the key to this, whatever *this* is.' He took a deep breath and sighed. 'We need to talk to this MI5 officer.'

Emma opened her mouth to argue, but then shrugged. 'Maybe you're right,' she said. 'I'll see what I can do.'

'Before we go to Sasha's flat. Okay?'

'Andy, I said I'll see what I can do. MI5 isn't at my beck and call. And I'm sure the MI5 officer won't want to talk to the SAS.'

Warren grinned. 'I'll try not to take that personally,' he said. 'I've got work to do back at Stirling Lines anyway,' said Warren. He sipped his coffee and grimaced. 'And the coffee's better there.'

Emma nodded at Bird. 'Fine, I'll arrange a meeting before we head off to Sasha's flat. But please don't give him a hard time. Not everybody appreciates your sense of humour.'

Bird smiled brightly. 'I'll be on my best behaviour,' he said. 'And I'll make sure Tyson doesn't take a piece out of his leg.'

CHAPTER 40

Emma found a place to park in the street a short walk from where she had arranged to meet the MI5 officer. She had to use an app to pay for parking and it took several attempts before it would accept her payment, by which time she was muttering darkly under her breath and her cheeks were flushed. They were in Camden, not far from the canal and a few hundred yards from the alley where Sasha had been murdered.

'I've just had a thought,' said Bird as Emma put away her phone.

'Well, I hope it's not lonely in there, rattling around on its own.'

Bird grinned. 'Now who's the one with the non-appreciated sense of humour?'

Emma started walking towards the canal. Bird and Tyson fell into step with her. Tyson was wagging his tail, happy to be out in the open air. 'So, what's the thought?' Emma asked.

'Maybe Sasha did have the SD card when he went into the alley, but he could have dropped it in the struggle,' said Bird. 'It's tiny, right, easy to miss?'

'Well, yes, except SOCO would have gone over the crime scene with a fine-tooth comb and they didn't find anything. Just the gun, with your fingerprints on it. If Sasha had dropped the card in the alley, they would have found it.'

They reached the canal and walked alongside it. There were several bars and cafes overlooking the water, busy with people having late lunches and early drinks.

'This guy we're going to meet, what's his story?' asked Bird.

'His name is Ralph, he's been with Five for almost ten years. I don't know much about him, truth be told. We tend not to share personal information.'

'Where did you meet him, when he briefed you?'

'Why, are you worried he's not genuine?'

'I don't trust anybody any more.'

'Look, I'll be honest with you, Andy . . .' She stopped herself when she saw the look of disbelief on his face. 'Seriously. I'm telling you the absolute truth. Ralph might well not be his real name. But he briefed me in Thames House and his boss was there. And his boss is a face you'll recognize from the media. Ralph is a genuine MI5 officer, you have my word.'

'Okay, so if you are serious about telling me the absolute truth, Ashleigh isn't your real name, is it?'

Emma sighed mournfully. 'Please don't do this, Andy.'

'Absolute truth, is what you just said. So I'll ask you again – is Ashleigh your real name?'

She sighed again. 'No,' she said eventually. 'My real name—'

Bird held up his hand to stop her. 'No, it's okay,' he said. 'We can stick with Emma.'

They reached a cafe and Emma nodded at a man sitting at a table overlooking the canal, with a coffee and a muffin in front of him. 'That's him,' she said.

To be fair, he did look like a Ralph – he was tall and trim with jet-black hair and steel-framed spectacles. His dark blue suit looked made-to-measure and his crisp white shirt gleamed in the afternoon sunlight. He stood up and flashed Emma a beaming smile, and air-kissed her on both cheeks. 'So good to see you again,' he said, as if they were a couple of old mates who were getting together for a catch-up. He flashed Bird another beaming smile. Ralph had either been born with perfect teeth or had spent a small fortune on dental work. 'And you must be Andy,' he said. 'Who Dares, Wins, right?'

He shook hands with Bird. His eyes widened for a second and the smile froze when he saw Tyson, but almost instantly the smile was back. 'What a splendid dog. What is he, a Belgian Malinois?'

'He is,' said Bird.

'They are magnificent dogs,' he said. 'Our family always had golden retrievers, as thick as shit and only ever think about their stomachs.' He waved at the chairs. 'Why don't you guys sit and I'll arrange some coffees. Unless you want something else?'

'Coffee is fine,' said Emma. 'Latte for me.'

'Just black coffee for me,' said Bird.

'Anything to eat?'

'I'm good,' said Emma.

'A sandwich,' said Bird.

'What sort?'

'Cheese, chicken, tuna, whatever's going. Maybe some chips if they have some.'

Ralph grinned. 'Your wish is my command.' He headed off to the counter.

Emma and Bird sat down. Tyson curled up next to Bird's chair. 'Well, he seems nice,' said Bird.

'I can never work out if you are being sarcastic or not,' said Emma.

'No, I'm serious. Well educated, good family, golden retrievers, what's not to like? He's what I'd imagine the archetypal spook to be. Probably recruited at Oxford or Cambridge when a tutor had a quiet word with him in a quadrangle.'

Emma laughed. 'It's not like that any more,' she said.

'Yeah? What university did you go to?'

'Durham.'

'And did somebody whisper in your ear?'

She laughed again. 'They certainly did not. I applied through their website, like everybody else – and I didn't join straight from uni. I was a copper, remember?'

Ralph returned. 'Something funny?' he asked.

'Andy thinks all spooks are still recruited from Oxbridge.'

'I think he's probably right,' said Ralph as he dropped down onto his chair. 'Helps to keep out the riff-raff.' He smiled. 'I'm joking, obviously. Coffees are on the way. Along with a tuna sandwich and chips. I'm assuming you meant British chips and not the American version. Why don't they just call them crisps like we do?' He adjusted the creases of his trousers and smiled at Emma. 'So, to what do I owe the pleasure?'

'Andy wanted a chat. Just so you know, the guys who killed Sasha also kidnapped Andy's ex-wife.'

Ralph's jaw dropped. 'What? Are you serious?'

'It's been a busy couple of days,' said Emma. 'Positively frantic. The killers appear to be members of Wagner Group. They kidnapped Andy's ex-wife but we managed to get her back.'

'We?' said Bird, grinning.

She flashed him a cold smile. 'Fine. You and your SAS mates got her back.'

'Well, this just gets curiouser and curiouser,' said Ralph.

'Your man Justin had a meeting scheduled with Sasha, right?' said Bird.

'I didn't know his name was Sasha at the time,' said Ralph. 'Just that he worked for GCHQ and he needed to talk to somebody from Five.'

'And he called you direct?'

'No, I don't know who he called in the first instance. In fact, I am fairly sure that the initial contact came through email. The email was passed to my boss and he told me to make contact. I actually suspected we were dealing with a timewaster, so I passed it on to Justin. Justin emailed back and forth and arranged to meet.'

'So you never actually spoke to Sasha?'

'No, but Justin did. Sasha wouldn't give any details over the phone. It was all cloak and dagger. Justin thought he might be a fantasist, but Sasha gave him some details that made him think that he might possibly be a genuine GCHQ employee.'

'And why did Sasha want to make contact?'

'He said he had information about GCHQ. He wouldn't give Justin specifics and insisted on a face-to-face.'

'And you don't know what this information was or what form it was in?' asked Bird.

Ralph frowned. 'What do you mean?'

'Did he mention an SD card?'

'Why do you ask that?'

Bird's eyes narrowed. 'Is that a yes?'

'I'm not sure that you are cleared for operational matters,' said Ralph.

'So that's definitely a yes,' said Bird. He gestured at Emma. 'What about Emma? She has security clearance, obviously.'

'Well, yes, but that information was need to know.'

Emma's lips tightened. 'So you're saying that I didn't need to know?'

'At that stage, all we knew was that Brownlow was dead and that a former SAS trooper had witnessed the killing. We had the ID of the trooper . . .' He smiled at Bird. 'Your good self, and my boss decided that a familiar face . . .' He nodded at Emma. 'That would be you, should be sent in to liaise with said former SAS trooper.'

'And you didn't think to tell me that perhaps the killers might have been after the SD card?' asked Emma.

'When you were called in, we didn't know who had killed Sasha. It could have been a random mugging.'

'No, by that stage the bastards had been chasing me all over London, so they were clearly after something,' said Bird.

Emma nodded in agreement. 'He's right, Ralph. You should have told me.'

Ralph shrugged carelessly. 'What can I say, other than to repeat that it was need to know?'

'Did someone tell you not to give me the information?' asked Emma.

'I think my boss made some crack about loose lips sinking ships, meaning that I wasn't to say too much. I think he took the view that if a GCHQ employee wanted to speak to MI5 then something was amiss and no one could be trusted.'

Bird looked across at Emma. 'There you go,' he said.

'Yes,' she said. 'That's strange.'

'What's strange?' asked Ralph.

'Right from the start, the Wagner Group guys were looking for the SD card,' said Emma. 'They searched Sasha after they killed him, they kidnapped Andy's ex-wife to pressure him into handing over the card – which he didn't have. And when he did eventually give them an SD card, as a way of rescuing his ex-wife, the first thing they did was to check the contents.'

'And they realized straight away that it wasn't what they were looking for,' said Bird. 'So the big question is, how did they know? How did they know that Sasha had an SD card filled with intel? Emma didn't know, the only people who did know were you and Justin and presumably your boss. You did tell your boss, I suppose? About the SD card?'

Ralph frowned and rubbed his chin. 'Actually, I don't think I did. Justin told me that he had arranged a meeting with Sasha, and that Sasha had intel for him. Justin asked Sasha if it was paperwork and Sasha said he had files on an SD card. He said he'd give Justin the card after they'd met. But I didn't tell my boss that. I said that Sasha was claiming to have intel for us, and after he was killed my boss was adamant that us knowing what the meeting was about should be kept within Five – sorry, Emma. But I'd never mentioned the card to my boss in our earlier briefings. Justin wanted to see what he actually got from Sasha before we promised anything specific.'

'Which means that only *three* people knew about the card – you,

Justin and Sasha,' said Emma. 'So that being the case, as Andy asked, how did the Wagner Group thugs know about it?'

Ralph put up his hands. 'I don't like the turn this conversation is taking,' he said. 'I'm starting to feel that I'm being accused of something here.' He stopped speaking when he saw a waitress heading their way with a tray, flashed her a smile and then began talking about football, as if in mid-flow on the subject. The waitress put their coffees on the table, gave Bird his sandwich and chips, and placed a bowl of water in front of Tyson. Tyson got to his feet and began to lap furiously. Ralph thanked the waitress and continued to ramble on about football until she was out of earshot. 'So are you accusing me of something here, Emma?' he said eventually.

'Of course not,' said Emma, giving him a dismissive wave. 'I'm just trying to get an understanding of what's going on. You said that only you, Justin and Sasha knew that he was planning to give you the intel on a card.'

'And that's true. I didn't tell anyone else. So, if the Wagner Group did find out, it's not down to me.'

'So do you think that Sasha told them?' said Bird. 'Because that wouldn't make any sense at all.'

'Of course I'm not suggesting that Sasha told anyone,' said Ralph tersely. 'That would be ridiculous. But I am telling you unequivocally that the Wagner Group people didn't find out from me.'

'They're very tech savvy – they were able to track my mobile right across London, and once they knew about me, they were very quickly onto my ex-wife.'

Ralph frowned. 'That's not generally something private contractors can do,' he said. 'Not without a lot of help.'

'Secret Squirrel sort of help?' said Bird.

'I don't see that there's any other way that they could have that sort of technical ability,' said Ralph. 'What about you, Emma? What do you think?'

'Somebody must have told the Russians about the SD card, and about Sasha, and presumably the same somebody helped them track Andy. I don't see that anyone at Six could be involved, I was assigned purely as a friendly face and my boss only knew what your boss told him. And that sort of GPS tracking is more MI5 territory.'

Ralph smiled ruefully. 'You really are determined to dump this on me, aren't you?'

'There's always GCHQ,' said Bird. 'It would be easy enough for them to spy on one of their own.'

'Exactly!' said Ralph. 'And if the information Sasha had was damaging to GCHQ, they'd have a vested interest in keeping a lid on it.'

'You think that GCHQ is in league with Wagner Group? That they conspired to have one of their own people murdered?'

'I think that's more likely than someone at Five tipping them off,' said Ralph.

'And Sasha didn't give Justin any indication what the intel was that he was so keen to give you?' said Bird.

Ralph shook his head. 'Just that it was important and that we needed to see it.'

'And it was clearly something that Sasha couldn't share with his own boss,' said Bird.

'That's the inference, yes.'

Bird looked over at Emma. 'As unlikely as it sounds, maybe GCHQ, or someone at GCHQ, has been using Wagner Group freelancers to do their dirty work. That does sound more likely than Ralph here being a double agent.'

Ralph smiled sarcastically. 'Thank you so much for the vote of confidence,' he said.

'You're welcome,' said Bird. 'Look, it seems to me that the key to this is the missing SD card. Sasha didn't have it on him, and despite what the Wagner Group guys think, I don't have it, so maybe it's at Sasha's home.' He looked at Emma. 'I know you said the place had been searched and that they found nothing, but maybe they just missed it. Maybe it was too well hidden.'

'It was one of our search teams,' said Ralph. 'And these guys are professionals. Some of them are former house thieves and cat burglars.'

'See now, I've never understood why anyone would go to all that trouble to steal a cat,' said Bird.

Ralph opened his mouth to protest but stopped when he realized Bird was pulling his leg. He looked over at Emma. 'Is he always like this?'

'I'm afraid so,' said Emma.

'I would have thought you'd be taking this more seriously,' Ralph said to Bird.

'Oh, trust me, I can be as serious as a heart attack when I need to be,' said Bird. 'But right now I've got a decent cup of coffee and a very tasty tuna sandwich and chips, so I'm as happy as Larry.' He took a bite of his sandwich and moaned contentedly. Tyson looked up and Bird broke off a piece of sandwich and tossed it to him. Tyson snapped at it and swallowed without chewing. 'The thing is, the team that went in would only have been looking for computers. No one had told them to search for an SD card.' His eyes hardened as he stared at Ralph. 'And that's down to you.'

Ralph held up his hands. 'I wasn't told that the flat was being searched until after the event.'

Emma nodded. 'It's true. My boss liaised with Ralph's boss regarding the search. And Ralph's boss didn't know the intel was on an SD card.'

'Water under the bridge,' said Bird. 'We need to work out how to move forwards.' He looked over at Ralph. 'So, you've arranged access to Sasha's house, right?' he said.

'It's a flat. Not far from here. I had a text just before you got here saying our man will be there in a couple of hours. He's on another job at Canary Wharf. But I'm not sure what you expect to find – as I said, our guys are very thorough.'

'Tyson is pretty good at sniffing things out, him being a dog and all.'

'He can sniff out an SD card?'

Bird shrugged. 'He can tell when something isn't right,' he said. 'He's trained to find explosives and weapons, and we did some training on electrical equipment that included work on phones and SIM cards. He's a smart dog.'

'He sounds it,' said Ralph.

'I think you should come with me when we have a look around Sasha's place.'

'Oh, I intend to,' said Ralph.

'I'll come, too,' said Emma.

'Actually, I think you should go back to Cheltenham,' said Bird.

'Why, exactly?'

Bird grinned. 'Because if I'm right, there's something you'll need to do for me.'

CHAPTER 41

Emma left for Cheltenham as soon as she had finished her coffee. Bird and Ralph drank a couple more coffees at the cafe and Bird ordered a second sandwich and chips. Ralph laughed. 'So the Army really does march on its stomach,' he said.

'Ex-Army,' Bird responded. 'Two things a soldier will never turn down – the chance of food and the opportunity for sleep.'

'And sex?'

'Sorry, Ralph, you're not my type. But thanks for the offer, very flattering.'

Ralph began to protest and then he laughed. 'You are terrible, Andy. You get me every time.'

'Do I, Ralph? Or do you fake it?'

'Now, that's a terrible thing to say, Andy. I'm a genuine person, trust me.'

'You're an MI5 spook, and in my experience Secret Squirrels are never to be trusted. You know how to tell when a spook is lying?'

Ralph grinned. 'When his lips are moving. That's an old one. But I hear what you're saying and I can't really disagree with you. A large part of my job is winning people over and getting them to trust me.'

'By lying to them?'

'If necessary, yes. If it's for the greater good.'

'How do you live with yourself? Lying all the time?'

Ralph laughed. 'Andy, I could ask you the same question. Not about lying, but the stuff you'll have done when you were with the SAS. And over the past few days, too. How many men have you killed? Emma tells me there were six in that car park alone.'

'They deserved what they got.'

Ralph held up his hands. 'And I'm not disagreeing with you. The point I'm making is that we all do unpleasant things from time to time, but we can live with ourselves because we know that if we didn't do those unpleasant things the world would be in a worse state than it is.' He grimaced. 'Do you mind if we change the subject? I'm not a great one for introspection.'

'Football?'

'Oh yes,' said Ralph. 'Now you're pressing my buttons.'

They chatted about football, and rugby, and several other ball sports, for the best part of two hours, then Ralph took a short call on his mobile. 'Right, we're off and running,' he said, putting his phone away. 'My car's nearby but parking is a pain in the arse around here so we can walk.' He paid the bill, put the receipt in his wallet, and led Bird away from the canal. Tyson stayed close to Bird's right leg, tail wagging, clearly happy to be on the move.

They walked through Camden to a street of terraced houses, many of them painted in pastel colours. There were cars parked on both sides of the road and Ralph gestured at a white Transit van with the name and details of a locksmith on the side. 'That's our man,' he said.

'That's a bit obvious, isn't it?' said Bird as they walked up to it.

'Hiding in plain sight,' said Ralph. 'Guy gets out of a van like that and starts fiddling with a door lock, nobody gives him a second look.'

The breaking and entering expert was a cheerful plump man in his fifties wearing a flat cap and a long sheepskin jacket that gave him the look of an East End market trader. He was carrying a black and yellow Stanley toolbox. 'Forgot something, did you?' he asked cheerily.

'Sorry, Ron,' said Ralph. 'We just need a look around, you can push off after you've let us in, I'll lock up when we leave.'

'No problem,' said Ron. He went up to the front door, placed the toolbox on the step and took out an electric pick gun. He inserted it into the lock and within thirty seconds he had the door open. He led them inside into a hallway. There was another locked door leading to the ground-floor flat and a flight of stairs to the top-floor flat.

Ron started work on the ground-floor door and again had it open in less than thirty seconds. 'There you go,' he said, putting his pick gun back into the toolbox. 'You've got my number, give me a call if you need me again.'

'Will do, Ron, thanks,' said Ralph. As the locksmith let himself out of the building, Ralph took Bird inside the flat and closed the door. It was minimalist in the extreme: stripped pine floors, sterile white blinds and very little in the way of furniture. In the sitting room there was a black plastic sofa, a square black coffee table – on which there were half a dozen empty pizza boxes and a dozen empty cans of Diet Coke – and a large desk with a high-backed executive chair. 'That's presumably where Sasha worked,' said Ralph. 'You can see the plugs and wiring on the floor, whoever it was just ripped the computers out.'

'Yeah, I wondered if Sasha might have taken his computers himself. But if he did, obviously he would have taken his power cords, wouldn't he?'

Ralph nodded. 'I don't see a problem with that logic.'

There was a three-drawer black metal filing cabinet next to the desk. All the drawers were empty.

Tyson sat next to the sofa.

'You seriously think he can sniff out an SD card?' asked Ralph.

'We can certainly try,' said Bird. He went through to the kitchen. It was tiny, with a gas hob that looked as if it had never been used, and a fridge which contained nothing but more cans of Diet Coke. He opened the cupboards and saw only crockery and kitchenware. There were no cans of food, no boxes of cereal, in fact there was no food at all. 'What does this guy eat?' asked Bird.

'Takeaways,' said Ralph. 'He used Deliveroo and Uber Eats several times a day.'

The bedroom contained a single bed and a black wardrobe. Bird opened the wardrobe. Most of the clothing was black.

'This is how a lot of these computer nerds live,' said Ralph. 'Their whole life is online.'

Bird went back into the sitting room and looked around. There was a smoke detector in the ceiling. 'Did your guys check that?' asked Bird.

'For what?'

'A bug. A camera. Ralph, mate, if only you, Justin and Sasha knew about the SD card, maybe the Russians were doing their own spook stuff.'

'They were spying on him, you mean?'

'Just a thought,' said Bird.

Ralph pulled the chair away from the desk and placed it under the smoke detector. Bird held the chair steady while Ralph climbed up and unscrewed the cover of the detector. Ralph whistled softly. He reached into the detector, ripped something out, then stepped down off the chair. 'Looks like you were right,' he said, holding out his hand. There was a small stainless-steel disc the size of a pound coin with two wires running from it. In the centre of the disc was a small glass blob. 'Sound and vision,' said Ralph. 'And this is state of the art.'

'Government kit?'

Ralph nodded. 'I would say so.'

'So MI5, or GCHQ?'

'Well, I'd need to get our tech boys on the case to be sure. It could be Chinese or Russian. Or the Israelis. They're all big on tech stuff.'

'I'd bet good money this is GCHQ kit.'

'You think they were spying on their own man?'

'I think someone in GCHQ was, yes.'

Bird's phone buzzed and he took it out. There was a text message from Emma. **Heading into his office now. One minute.** Bird smiled and put the phone away.

'Good news?' asked Ralph.

'My wife,' lied Bird. 'Ex-wife. She's just checking in.'

'Is she okay?'

'It could have been a lot worse,' said Bird. 'She's as strong as a horse, though. Stronger than me a lot of the time. If women could join the SAS, she'd walk Selection. Look, I need to make a quick call, okay?'

Ralph frowned. 'You're deaf, how do you make a phone call?'

'FaceTime.'

'Of course,' said Ralph. 'Lip-reading. I would never have thought of that.'

Bird went through to the bedroom and closed the door before calling Emma. She answered almost immediately. 'How's it going, Andy?' she asked, holding the phone so that he could see her lips close up.

'We found it,' he said.

'Seriously?'

'Well, Tyson did the heavy lifting. It was hidden behind an electric socket in the bedroom. I'm not surprised the search team missed it. What do you want me to do with it? Ralph says we should take it to Thames House.'

Emma turned her face away and said something. Because he had a side view, he couldn't read what she was saying. Then she looked back at the camera again and smiled. 'Mr Carmichael says you should bring it here, to GCHQ. Sasha is – was – a GCHQ employee, so strictly speaking the SD card is GCHQ property. Plus, they have experts who can analyse whatever's on the card.'

'Will do,' said Bird. 'I'll get Ralph to arrange transport.'

'Are you sure that's a good idea?'

'I think he's keen to make himself useful.'

'Okay, I'll see you when I see you. Mr Carmichael will have his experts ready to examine the SD card. Well done, Andy.'

CHAPTER 42

'I didn't expect to be working as your chauffeur today,' said Ralph. They were in Ralph's Peugeot, heading west on the M40, coming up to Reading.

He had half turned to talk to Bird and Bird missed half the words but he got the gist. 'Yeah, sorry about that, but they wanted me back at GCHQ ASAP.'

Bird had no qualms about lying to Ralph. Ralph was a Secret Squirrel and Secret Squirrels only told the truth when it suited them. Bird was fairly sure he knew who had betrayed him to the Wagner Group killers, but there was still an outside chance that someone with MI5 was the bad apple and until he knew for sure it was safer to keep Ralph in the dark.

The traffic was light, the evening rush hour not quite underway, and Ralph stuck to the middle lane. He looked across at Bird. 'You okay if I put the radio on? I hate driving in silence and I can't talk to you without taking my eyes off the road.'

'Go for it,' said Bird. Tyson was behind them, sprawled across the back seat.

Ralph turned to look at Bird again. 'Any preference?' He realized what he'd said and laughed. 'Sorry, stupid question.' He selected a radio station, turned up the volume and began tapping on the steering wheel in time to whatever he was listening to.

Bird checked the side mirror. There was a Mini Cooper behind them. Ralph was still in the middle lane and the Mini passed them on their left, the female driver giving Bird a dirty look as she went by. For a man who was employed by the Security Service, Ralph didn't seem to take much interest in counter-surveillance and rarely glanced in his mirrors.

Bird checked the side mirror again. There was a white BMW SUV behind them now, in the left lane and matching their speed.

Bird's phone vibrated and he took it out of his pocket. It was from Warren. **BRACE BRACE BRACE** and a smiley face.

A second BMW SUV, this one black, had moved over to the outside lane.

Bird tapped the dashboard. 'Ralph, mate, can you move over to the left.'

Ralph looked at him, frowning. 'What?'

'Just get in the left-hand lane, it'll make our lives easier.'

Ralph looked at his rear-view mirror and shrugged. 'Sure, whatever. I always feel safer in the middle lane.'

Ralph flicked his indicator on and moved over to the left lane. He checked his mirror again. Bird had his eyes fixed on the black SUV, which had moved into the middle lane. The white BMW moved in behind it and the two cars accelerated. Bird could now see a third SUV, this one a grey Honda CR-V. It was in the inside lane. Behind it was a white Transit van.

Bird's heart was starting to pound now and he took slow, deep breaths. He wasn't carrying a gun so he was going to be a bystander to whatever happened next.

The black BMW went by. Bird looked to the right. He only got a good look at the passenger. He was a big man wearing a baseball cap, staring straight ahead, his jaw tight.

The black SUV moved into the lane in front of them without indicating. Its brake lights didn't go on but the vehicle began to slow. The white SUV drew level with the Peugeot. At the same time the Honda CR-V came up behind them, boxing them in. In the side mirror, Bird could see there were two men in the vehicle.

Ralph had finally realized that there was something wrong, and he was looking around frantically.

There were three men in the white SUV. The front passenger and the rear passenger were both holding guns. Glocks. Ralph cursed. The front passenger gestured for them to pull over, and then pointed his gun at Ralph.

'It's okay,' said Bird. 'The cavalry is on the way.'

'Cavalry? What the hell are you talking about?'

The black SUV's brake lights came on and Ralph had to stamp on his own brakes to avoid a collision. The white SUV slowed to keep level with them. The windows came down and the man in the front passenger seat began screaming at them to stop.

Bird looked in the side mirror but all he could see was the Honda. He twisted around in his seat. Two white Transit vans were coming up behind them in the outside lane.

Ralph turned to look at Bird. 'What the fuck's happening?'

Bird patted him on the leg. 'Just go with the flow, Ralph,' he said. 'It'll all be over soon.'

The lead Transit van pulled up alongside the white BMW. Bird recognized the driver. It was Jimmy 'Dusty' Rhodes. The side door opened revealing Warren and Harris, both cradling HK carbines.

The second Transit van drew level with the Honda. Again, the side door opened to reveal two men with guns – Ross 'Cilla' Black and Ryan 'Tommo' Thompson. There were three men in the Honda and the front passenger was holding a machine pistol.

The rear passenger in the white SUV moved over to the right and began shooting at the Transit but he only managed to get off one shot, which shattered the SUV's window, before Warren returned fire with a rapid double tap that blew the shooter away.

The black SUV accelerated but Harris shot out its tyres and the car began to weave from side to side before spinning off the motorway. The white SUV picked up speed but the Transit matched it and both vehicles pulled away. Harris fired at the vehicle's front tyre and it blew apart. The BMW's driver lost control, and the SUV flipped onto its side and rolled off onto the verge.

Bird twisted around in his seat. The occupants of the CR-V were shooting at the second Transit van. Bird realized that Rick 'Nosey' Parker was at the wheel. Parker braked and the shots from the CR-V went wide. Parker accelerated again and Black and Thompson raked the car with rounds. A cloud of steam erupted from under the bonnet. The three men in the car continued to fire at the Transit. Most of their shots missed, but Black was hit in the chest and Bird cursed under his breath. But Black continued to fire, and Bird realized that the SAS men were all wearing body armour.

Bullets raked the Honda, and the front and rear passengers jerked as if they were being electrocuted. The driver's head exploded in a shower of red and the car span off the motorway, turning around twice before coming to a halt.

'Pull over, Ralph,' said Bird.

Ralph did as he was told. His hands were trembling on the wheel and his mouth was open. Bird tried not to smile. Ralph clearly wasn't used to being around live ammunition.

The two Transit vans pulled up behind their car and the SAS men piled out.

Ralph blinked at Bird. 'What just happened?'

'We took out the bad guys.'

'Why? Why did they attack us?'

'They thought we had the SD card. They were trying to get it before we delivered it to GCHQ.'

Ralph frowned in confusion. 'But we didn't have the card. We never had the card. Tyson didn't even look for a bloody card.'

'That's right.'

'Andy, what the hell's going on?' He gestured at the SAS team by the white vans. 'And who are these guys?'

'SAS,' said Bird. 'The cavalry.'

'They just happened to be passing?' He shook his head. 'Of course not. You planned this, didn't you? It was a set-up? You knew that the Russians would be after us?'

'I had a good idea, yes.'

'How?'

Bird grinned and tapped the side of his nose. 'Need to know,' he said.

Warren jogged over to them. Bird told Tyson to stay and climbed out. 'Nice job, Sarge,' he said.

Warren grinned. 'We try to please.' He bent down to look at Ralph, who was still shaking, and grinned. 'I thought you MI5 guys were all stirred but not shaken,' he said.

'James Bond was MI6, and he liked his Martinis shaken not stirred,' said Ralph. 'It would have been nice to have been given some notice.'

Warren grinned. 'Need to know,' he said. 'We've called in the cops, so there'll be an ARV here shortly. We're in Thames Valley policing area so they'll be the first responders, but I'm sure you guys can do what you normally do and take it in-house.'

Ralph nodded. 'I'm on it.'

'I'm going to take Andy and Tyson to GCHQ – obviously there's a lot to discuss after what happened,' said Warren.

Ralph nodded. 'Okay, okay.' He took out his phone and tapped on the screen with a shaking hand.

Bird closed the front passenger door and opened the rear to allow Tyson out. Tyson immediately started sniffing at the grass verge and then ran over to the CR-V and cocked his leg against it.

Bird and Warren walked over CR-V too. All the CR-V's windows were smashed and the three occupants were clearly dead.

Tyson stopped urinating and looked back down the motorway, ears and tail up.

'Sirens,' said Warren. 'There's an ambulance on the way, too.'

The white BMW was fifty feet away, lying on its side. Bird walked over and looked through the rear window. The passenger in the back was dead, with two wet red patches in his chest. The driver and the front passenger were unconscious, but didn't appear to have life-threatening injuries. 'Looks like they'll finally get people to question,' said Bird.

Black and Rhodes were running towards the black SUV. Two men were climbing out, brandishing guns. Both SAS men shot twice and the Russians went down. Black and Rhodes rushed up and kicked their guns away but there was no need – the two Russians were clearly dead.

The traffic had slowed to a crawl and the occupants of the cars on the motorway were staring at the carnage in horror, but no one stopped. Black and Rhodes pulled out baseball hats with POLICE on them. They started waving at the cars to keep moving.

Bird and Warren went over to the bodies by the black BMW. Tyson sniffed at one of the bodies.

'That's Nikolay,' said Bird.

'How do you know?' asked Warren.

'He's one of the men in the photographs that Emma showed me in GCHQ. My memory hasn't been great since what happened in Syria, but it's definitely him.' He knelt down and went through the man's pockets. He found two mobile phones and showed them to Warren. 'These should tell us everything we need to know,' he said.

He stood up. A Thames Valley armed response vehicle had arrived. Ralph hurried over to them and began to explain the situation. An ambulance pulled up, its lights flashing. Two paramedics piled out and looked around, wondering where they should start. Ralph pointed over at the white SUV.

'Looks like Ralph has everything in hand,' said Warren.

'You reckon he wet himself?' said Bird.

Warren laughed. 'Probably held it in – wouldn't want to ruin that nice suit.'

'You're ready to drive over to GCHQ?'

Warren nodded. 'Oh yes,' he said. 'I'm looking forward to this.'

CHAPTER 43

A GCHQ employee was waiting for them in the reception area with ID badges. He introduced himself with only his first name – Greig. He was in his mid-twenties with hair that was already thinning and his pale blue eyes blinked at them behind square-framed spectacles. He had a badge for Tyson, which he clipped to the dog's collar. 'I've been asked to confirm that you're not carrying guns,' he said.

'No guns,' said Warren with a grin. 'But I've got a hand grenade. Does that count?'

Greig's eyebrows shot up but he smiled when he realized that Warren was joking. 'Right, fine,' he said.

'Seriously, we left everything in the car,' said Bird. 'Where is Emma?'

'She's in Mr Carmichael's office,' said Greig. 'I was told to meet you and escort you there. Follow me, please.'

Greig took them up to Carmichael's office, he knocked and they heard Carmichael's voice asking him to come in. Carmichael was sitting behind his desk and his jaw dropped when he saw them walk into the office. Emma and Simon were sitting at the desk too, and Emma stood up and hurried over to them. 'How did it go?' she asked.

'What's going on?' asked Carmichael, but he was ignored. Carmichael looked over at Simon, but Simon averted his eyes.

Greig left, closing the door behind him.

'Exactly as planned,' said Bird. 'The Sarge and his team carried out the operation perfectly.'

Warren threw Emma a mock salute. 'All part of the service,' he said.

'What is happening here?' asked Carmichael, louder this time. He was still sitting at his desk but had pushed his chair back, as if trying to put more distance between them.

Bird turned to look at him. 'Nikolay is dead,' said Bird. 'Along with six more of his stooges.'

'Dead?' repeated Carmichael.

'Very,' said Bird.

'What about the SD card?'

'There is no card. We couldn't find it.'

'But you said . . .' Carmichael didn't finish the sentence. The colour had drained from his face.

Bird took out the two phones he had taken from Nikolay. He handed them to Simon. 'These should show who tipped the Russians off, but I think we already know the answer to that question.'

'Yes, we've had Mr Carmichael under observation ever since you phoned from Sasha's flat,' said Emma. 'We saw him tracking your mobile phone and passing on your details to Nikolay. Presumably to one of those phones.'

'You can all get out of my office, now!' hissed Carmichael.

'We're not going anywhere,' said Bird. He grinned. 'Funny old world, isn't it? We've got the SAS here, and MI6, and we're at GCHQ, but nobody has the power of arrest. For that we'll need a common or garden police officer.'

'Arrest for what?' said Carmichael.

'For conspiracy to murder, at the very least,' said Emma. 'You found out that Sasha was about to talk to MI5 and you gave his details to the Russians. Then you helped the Russians track Andy.'

'I would love to see you prove that in a court of law,' said Carmichael.

'Oh, I'm sure you covered your tracks,' said Emma. 'But you must have used a GCHQ phone or a burner to call Nikolay today. Whatever, you were being watched via internal CCTV, so we'll be able to see when you were using a phone and match your calls to calls received by Nikolay. You and I were the only people who knew that Andy was coming back here, and I sure as hell didn't share that information with anybody.'

Carmichael stood up. 'I've had enough of this,' he said. He walked around his desk and headed towards the door.

'Bark!' said Bird.

Tyson jumped to his feet and began barking ferociously at Carmichael. He stepped back, holding his hands in front of his face. 'Keep that bloody dog away from me!' he shouted.

'Get back behind your desk,' said Bird. 'You're not going anywhere.'

Carmichael hesitated, but then Tyson took a step towards him, barking even louder. Carmichael scuttled behind his desk and sat down. He put his head in his hands and moaned.

'Silence!' shouted Bird and Tyson stopped barking. 'Good boy.'

CHAPTER 44

Bird, Warren and Emma went to the canteen. Simon had taken Nikolay's phones to get them checked. The police had arrived and taken Carmichael into custody, but there had been some confusion as to what he should be arrested for. The two detectives eventually settled on arresting him for making a disclosure deemed to be damaging under the Official Secrets Act 1989. But before he could be taken away, the director of GCHQ had appeared. After speaking to Emma, he had spent half an hour on the phone before announcing that Carmichael was to be taken to Thames House for questioning by MI5 investigators.

Transport then became an issue, with the two detectives claiming that, as Gloucester Constabulary officers, they weren't allowed to take prisoners to London. Warren had offered but the director clearly wasn't happy at the SAS being involved. Emma had said she would arrange for armed officers from the Met to transport Carmichael, and that had required more phone calls. In all, they had to spend an uncomfortable three hours in Carmichael's office before the Met cops arrived. Carmichael was again arrested and cautioned, and the officers insisted on handcuffing him before leading him out.

'The thing is, we're a little light on evidence,' said Emma, as they sat at a table at the far end of the canteen. 'We know he tipped off the Russians about Andy coming back from London, but that's what, conspiracy to attempted robbery? Conspiracy to attempted murder? Or is it just a breach of the Data Protection Act?'

'He sent a Russian hit squad to kill me, Emma,' said Bird. Tyson was sitting under his chair, his head on his paws.

'But we don't know why, do we? And I doubt that Carmichael is going to roll over and confess. If he just keeps his mouth shut, he might well wriggle out of it.'

'You seriously think he might get off?'

'We don't have a motive.'

'Maybe they paid him,' said Bird. 'It's as simple as that.'

'I'm sure that they'll put his finances under the microscope,' said Emma. 'But it doesn't seem likely, does it? To throw away his career and his life for money? There has to be more to it than that.'

'I'll get the coffees,' said Warren. He headed over to the counter.

'I just wish we knew what information Sasha had,' said Emma.

'Whatever it was, it must have been proof that Carmichael was bad,' said Bird. 'And that was obviously why he wanted to speak to MI5 rather than someone within GCHQ.'

'That makes sense,' said Emma. 'But how do we prove that? His computers have gone and if there was an SD card we don't know where it is now. It's a pity that Nikolay is dead – he could have answered a lot of questions.'

'I'm sure Tyson would have been happy to help.'

'I didn't mean we'd torture him, Andy. That's not what we do. But we could have offered him a deal.' She sighed. 'At least we've got the two guys who weren't killed.'

'I wouldn't expect them to say much,' said Bird. 'They're sure to know what happened to the guy I questioned. If they talk, they die.'

'We'll see,' said Emma, 'but I fear that you're probably right.'

Warren returned with a tray of coffees, several packs of sandwiches and an empty plate with a few crumbs on it.

'What was on the plate?' asked Bird.

'A sausage roll. I got it for Tyson.' He placed a coffee in front of him.

Bird frowned. 'What happened to it?'

Warren looked shamefaced. 'I ate it. Sorry.' He looked down at the dog. 'Sorry, Tyson. It's been a long day and it looked so good. I'll get you another one.' He handed Emma her coffee and put the sandwiches on the table.

'You ate it?' said Bird.

'Yeah, sorry. I'll get another one.'

Bird frowned. 'Say it again,' he said. 'Say you ate it.'

'What?'

'Just say that again. Word for word.'

'I ate it,' said Warren, saying each word slowly.

'Faster.'

'What?'

'Faster. Please, Sarge. Humour me.'

Warren sighed. 'I ate it.'

Bird groaned. 'Oh no,' he said.

'What's wrong?' said Warren.

'When Sasha died, he was trying to speak to me. I could barely read his lips because blood was pouring out of his mouth. I thought he was saying "eighty". He said it twice before he died. At least that's what I thought he was saying.'

'And?'

'He wasn't saying "eighty". He was saying "I ate it". He was talking about the SD card. He didn't give it to me, he swallowed it.'

Warren's jaw dropped. 'So it's what, in his stomach? Then it's fucked. The acid in the stomach would have attacked it, right?'

'Not if it was in one of those little plastic cases, maybe.'

Warren grimaced. 'That's pretty disgusting, Andy.'

'I can't argue with that. But if it's in his stomach, it's retrievable.'

'By cutting him open?'

'That's what happens in a post-mortem anyway, right?' He looked over at Emma. 'Where is Sasha's body?'

CHAPTER 45

Early the next morning, Emma drove Bird and Warren to the Westminster Public Mortuary in Horseferry Road, not far from Lambeth Bridge. The body had been moved from St Pancras Mortuary the previous day. The mortuary was the biggest in the country and could process more than a hundred dead bodies at a time, but they were only interested in one – Sasha Brownlow.

They left Tyson in the car with the windows cracked and had to wait in reception for fifteen minutes before a middle-aged doctor wearing green scrubs and a surgical cap emerged through a set of double doors, a mask loose around his neck. He introduced himself as Dr Sanjay Mukherjee and said that he would be carrying out the post-mortem.

'We'd be grateful if you could pay particular attention to the contents of his stomach,' said Emma. 'We think he might have swallowed something of interest.'

'Well, he's been in here for more than forty-eight hours so anything in his stomach will probably be well digested by now. What specifically do you think he swallowed?'

'An SD card,' said Emma.

'The stomach acid will have dissolved any metal in the . . .' the doctor began, then he stopped himself. 'Ah, yes, they come in those little snap-shut plastic cases, don't they? Yes, you might be lucky, but the sooner we get started the better. Do you want to watch?'

'That would be great, yes, thank you,' said Emma.

'We'll use the Iain West Forensic Suite,' said Dr Mukherjee. 'You can watch over CCTV, so you don't have to put up with the smell.'

He took them through the double doors and along a corridor, then showed them to a small office which had three CCTV monitors on a table, in front of which were half a dozen high-backed chairs. There was a window which looked onto a tiled room with three stainless-steel dissection tables and a line of six large refrigerators against one wall. He waved them to the chairs. 'As soon as the body is delivered, I'll start. Normally there is a procedure to be followed but in view of the urgency I'll make a preliminary incision and then whip out the stomach.'

'That would be great, thank you,' said Emma.

They sat down as Dr Mukherjee left the room.

'So, how have you been since I last saw you at Incirlik?' Emma asked Warren.

'Ducking and diving,' said Warren.

'Ducking and diving anywhere in particular? Other than killing Wagner Group thugs here in the UK, obviously.'

Warren laughed. 'I could tell you, Emma, but then I'd have to kill you.'

Emma chuckled. 'I'm pretty sure that my security clearance is higher than yours,' she said.

'It's not a competition,' said Warren.

'It sounds like it is,' said Emma.

Their conversation stopped when two orderlies in green scrubs wheeled a trolley into the examination room. They removed a pale blue sheet to reveal the body of Sasha Brownlow. Together, they lifted it off the trolley and onto the metal table closest to the window.

Dr Mukherjee appeared, the surgical mask now covering his mouth and nose. He had a microphone clipped to the top pocket of his scrubs. He walked over to the window, nodded at them, and pointed at the microphone. 'Hopefully you can hear me over this,' he said.

There was a speaker on the wall above the window. Warren nodded and Emma gave him a thumbs up.

Dr Mukherjee went back to the body and used a stainless-steel hose hanging from the ceiling to wash it. When he had finished, he replaced the hose and examined the bullet wound in the centre of the man's chest. Warren relayed the doctor's observations to Bird. *'Cause of death almost certainly the shot to the chest, which from the position suggests that the bullet penetrated the heart. I'll examine the heart later.'*

Mukherjee moved around and turned the body onto its side so he could examine the back. Again, Warren relayed the doctor's observations to Bird. *'No exit wound, so I am guessing that the bullet is still in there. I don't know if that will help your case.'*

He eased the body back down and went over to a tray of stainless-steel surgical instruments. He picked up a large scalpel and made a Y-shaped incision in the trunk, with the arms of the Y extending from each shoulder and meeting at the breastbone. From there he took the base of the Y down to the pubic bone, taking care to run around the navel. It was a deep cut and clearly required a lot of effort. When he had finished, he used the scalpel to peel away the skin, muscle and soft tissue. He pulled a large flap of skin up and over the face, revealing the rib cage.

The doctor spoke and again Warren repeated the information to Bird. *'At this point, I would usually crack the chest and remove the heart and lungs, but obviously you want me to cut to the chase. I would now say that there is no doubt that gunshot was the cause of the death – the heart is in pieces. Died of a broken heart, literally.'* The doctor pulled the flaps of skin apart to reveal the abdominal organs. *'Again, usually I would remove the adrenal glands and the kidneys and the liver, followed by the spleen and the intestines. But in this case, I shall go straight to the stomach.'*

He put the bloody scalpel back on the tray and picked up a pair of scissors. He reached his gloved hand into the body and cut the stomach free. Warren grinned. 'He says we're lucky not having to smell this, he suspects that Brownlow had a curry as his last meal.'

The doctor placed the stomach in a steel bowl and carried it over to a sink where he washed it clean. He left the bowl in the sink and went to retrieve a small scalpel from the tray, then he used it to slice open the organ. Warren grinned at Bird as he listened to what the doctor was saying over the speaker. 'He says the smell is really bad. Ripe, he says.'

The doctor ran the stomach under the tap once more, then reached for something. 'Bingo!' said Warren. The doctor turned around to hold up a small plastic case, not much bigger than a ten-pence coin.

Emma sighed with relief. 'Finally, we get to see what this is all about,' she said.

CHAPTER 46

Emma drove Warren and Bird to Thames House, the MI5 building in Millbank that overlooked the river. Thames House was a Portland stone neoclassical building decorated with sculptures and coats of arms with Latin mottos. The coats of arms represented the City of Westminster, the City of London and the Port of London Authority, all previous occupants of the building. MI5's crest flew from a flagpole on the roof. At the bottom of the crest was their Latin motto – *Regnum Defende*. Defend the Realm.

Ralph was waiting for them in reception. He seemed in a much better state than when Bird had last seen him at the side of the M40.

He had to sign them in and they were given badges to wear. He actually had a badge for Tyson, which he clipped to his collar before taking them up in a lift to the third floor. He led them along to the offices of technical support, where Emma gave the SD card to a young man wearing a Hugo Boss suit and gilt-framed spectacles. Ralph introduced him as Amar. His office was lined with shelves filled with electrical equipment and there were three computer monitors and two laptops on his oversized desk. Tyson ducked under the desk, did two complete turns and then lay down.

Amar slotted the card into a reader connected to a laptop. He sat down at his desk and tapped on a keyboard for several minutes, occasionally leaning forwards so that his face was only a few inches from his screen.

'Is it encrypted?' asked Emma.

'No, it's not that, it's just that there are so many files here. Dozens. It's going to take some time to look through everything.'

'Are any of the files named Carmichael?' asked Emma.

Amar nodded. 'Several.'

'Have a look at those first.'

Amar nodded and tapped away on his keyboard. 'It's a money trail,' he said. 'Bank accounts in the Cayman Islands and Gibraltar that Carmichael has access to.'

'Where was the money coming from?' asked Ralph.

Amar peered at the screen. 'It moves around a lot, but Russia seems to be the origin.'

'So Carmichael was being paid off?' asked Warren. 'It *was* about money rather than ideology?'

'It looks like it,' said Amar. 'There's close to a million US dollars hidden away.'

Warren frowned. 'So Carmichael was on the take and Sasha found out?'

'I'd say so,' said Amar.

'But why would Sasha be looking at Carmichael in the first place?' said Bird. 'He worked from home, he barely knew him, right?'

'Let me have a look,' said Amar. 'There's a lot of Russia-related files. And Ukraine files.' He clicked on his mouse and leant towards his centre screen.

'We need to know why the Wagner Group were involved,' said Warren. 'It can't have been that Carmichael was paying them to protect him. It makes more sense that whoever was running the Wagner Group was also paying Carmichael. Carmichael was the hired hand. They were paying him for intel, obviously. And using Wagner Group to get their dirty work done.'

'Okay, so there's a lot of very good intel here about how the Russians were mounting cyberattacks on Ukraine,' said Amar. 'But then everyone knows that, pretty much.' He looked up at Ralph. 'Not sure why he'd want to give you this – it's not exactly public knowledge but it's not top secret.' He clicked the mouse again a few times. 'Ah, again there's a money trail. Money going from Russia to various offshore accounts owned by high-ranking Ukrainian politicians and army officers. All good stuff, but again, I don't see why a GCHQ analyst would want to pass it on to MI5. It's the sort of intel that would routinely be given to the Security Service anyway.' He clicked on the mouse a few times, and then smiled. 'Ah, now that's interesting,' he said.

'What's that?' said Ralph.

'Your guy had been hacking into various Russian databases. Government databases. Including some SVR networks. He's obviously very talented. A maestro.' Amar rubbed his chin. 'He penetrated the Russian databases and found intel that could only have come from GCHQ. Intel that GCHQ had obtained about Russian cyberattacks on Ukraine somehow found its way onto Russian computers.'

'So, Sasha found data that Carmichael sold to the Russians?' said Bird.

Amar clicked on his mouse again. 'That's what it looks like. Your man found the GCHQ intel, then went looking for the source. He nailed the source and then followed the money. Or maybe he followed the money to find the source. I'll need time to decide whether the chicken or the egg came first.' He sat back in his chair. 'This is good work. And he's identified a whole load of bank accounts linked to Wagner Group, some of them here in the UK. If our financial guys move quickly, they could hoover up millions. I'd like to meet this guy and shake his hand.'

'I'm afraid that ship has sailed, Amar,' said Ralph.

'Something bad happened to him?'

'I'm afraid so,' said Ralph.

'I can see why. This is very damaging for GCHQ. And for this guy Carmichael. If this ever gets out, it'd trash GCHQ's reputation.'

'It won't get out,' said Emma. 'Not now. We'll be able to keep a lid on it.'

'You won't be able to keep a lid on it if Carmichael appears in court, will you?' said Bird.

'There are trials behind locked doors with the press barred from reporting. It happens.'

'It needs to go to court, one way or another,' said Bird. 'A lot of people died because of Carmichael. He needs to be punished.'

'He will be,' said Emma.

'You're sure that he won't be offered a deal? Information in exchange for a reduced sentence, or even his freedom?'

Emma shook her head. 'That won't happen, Andy. You have my word.'

Bird looked into her eyes. He had no way of knowing if she was being truthful or not. 'He killed my friends and he hurt my wife,' he said quietly. 'My ex-wife. If he walks, he dies. You have my word on that.'

Emma smiled thinly. 'I believe you,' she said.

Warren put his hand on Bird's shoulder. 'We've got this covered, Birdman,' he said.